the TIME COLLECTOR
TIME WEAVER
HEART of COGS

JACINTA MAREE

RAGNAROK
PUBLICATIONS

CRESTVIEW HILLS, KENTUCKY

TIME WEAVER: HEART OF COGS
Ragnarok Publications | www.ragnarokpub.com
Editor In Chief: Tim Marquitz | Publisher: J.M. Martin

Published by Ragnarok Publications, LLC
206 College Park Drive, Ste. 1
Crestview Hills, KY 41017

ISBN-13: 9781941987872
Worldwide Rights
Created in the United States of America

Editor: Gwendolyn Nix
Cover Illustration: Cris Ortega
Graphic Design Coordinator: Shawn T. King

To mum and dad,
Even without magic, you help make my
wishes come true.

CHAPTER
ONE

I have a clock for a heart...

And the man who put it there tried to take it out.

Living life with a bronze ticker has taught me one valuable lesson. Time is precious. I realize this a little too late now that I face my death. The very thing that was put into my chest to save me is destined to be my undoing. To have time will save the lives of many. To buy time, I must be sacrificed. I must die for him, for everyone, to be free.

H E'S HERE FOR you again, Elizabeth."
Tightness gripped her, reeling Elizabeth backwards. As with each visit, the clock in her head started its count down. *Don't let it be today. Please, not today.* With a gulp, she peered out the window where, from their second-story drop, she could see Arthur Beaumontt step out of his car. Anxiety bubbled. *Oh, please, not today.* Arthur Beaumontt lurked around the corridors of her school just as often as her nightmares. It became so frequent she didn't know which one was the reality. At this moment, it didn't matter. He was here.

Elizabeth feigned a laugh. "Impossible. He can't be here for me. My bidding isn't until next week."

The girl gave her a one-shouldered shrug. "Looks like you'll be getting that rope necklace sooner than you thought." She turned and walked off with the rest of the girls in tow.

Elizabeth pulled back from the window in fear of Arthur looking up and spotting her, plagued by the thought of her hanging, neck cracked, from the ceiling. Belonging to the Academy of underprivileged ladies had saved her from the streets and brothels, but had perhaps also delivered her to a far worse evil. An evil called Arthur Beaumontt.

"What are you doing standing about?" A shrill voice came up from behind. One of the teachers swiped Elizabeth across the back of the head. Elizabeth fumbled with her mop and bucket. "Get back to work."

"Sorry, mistress." Sweat teased Elizabeth's hair, sleeking white loose strands to the curve of her neck. The clock kept ticking down, always aware that her life could change at any devastating moment. She hoisted the bucket higher and fleeted down the hall. In a week, she would turn eighteen, and as school policies dictated, she would be sold to one of the noble houses. A personal maid, a thing, a piece of property, to a wealthy household.

Being trained for a life of servitude swelled her ankles, burnt her fingers, and pulled her muscles to exhaustion. But she would never complain as the alternative was a reality best ignored. The Beaumontts were the power among the nobles, and it was seen as improper to buy anything the Beaumontts wanted. So, if Arthur wanted her, he was going to get her. End of story.

Elizabeth disappeared down the corridors with her fellow students, becoming a single blotch of pale blue among the sea of identical dresses. From behind, a hand spun her around. She should've known it was him the moment he touched her. His hot hands were always sweaty.

"Why is it every time I see you, you seem to only get uglier?" A smirk curdled his mouth. Arthur Beaumontt, a boy dressed in his father's wealth, chuckled without any hint of joy. He always said such things. Called her ugly. Worthless. Unwanted. Behind her back, she could hear the hallways emptying, the rest of the girls sheltering behind closed doors.

In her surprise, Elizabeth's voice trembled. "You're not allowed up here, this area is off limits."

"Don't be stupid." He waved his hand to shut her up. "Those rules don't apply to me."

She locked her jaw down, dropping her face of expression. "Very well. I have chores. Excuse me."

As she turned to leave, Arthur snatched her arm, swinging her back around and shoved her against the wall. He leant closer in a manner he thought was exciting, pressing his chest against her shoulder and barricading her between his two arms.

"I won't be long. They won't even notice you're missing. Still looks like no one has even bothered to try and match my bid. Who knew you were going to be so cheap."

Forget the chiming, her world felt as though it was imploding. The school halls felt as narrow as his grip, as close as his lingering breath. It took everything in her control not to jump out the window. "A lot can happen in seven days."

His eyebrow arched. "It'll be the shortest week of your life." He inched in closer and Elizabeth clenched the bucket to her chest. He grinned at her trembling grip. "When you're with me, you'll forget all about your pathetic life in this poor excuse of an institution."

"Mr. Beaumontt?" His driver's voice called from down the hall. "Sir? You're required back at the manor."

Arthur's voice growled, "Can't you see I'm busy?" Irritated, he pushed off the wall and smacked the bucket out of Elizabeth's hands. It hit the ground with a rattle, emptying soapy spuds across his shoes. "Argh! You clumsy bitch." He slapped her. "I'm going to send the cleaners bill to the academy. Make sure you work double to pay for it." He tore the broom from her and threw it across the hall. "Fetch, you dog."

She didn't move toward it. She didn't dare.

"Sir?" The driver called again.

Arthur stared her down. She didn't meet his gaze. Eventually, he stepped forward and whispered, "I'll break you soon enough." And left. Elizabeth waited for the sound of his shoes to disappear before slumping into the spilled water. A timid body stepped out from behind the corner, feeling it now safe to reveal herself.

"Elli? Oh my God, are you okay?" The girl knelt down and checked Elizabeth's stinging cheek.

"I'm okay, Sara." She pulled Sara's hand away. "I think I was just a bit overwhelmed."

Using her apron, Sara soaked up the dirty water and wringed it back into the bucket. She lingered before speaking, "What are you going to do?"

"I won't let him purchase me," Elizabeth said with more confidence then she felt.

"You won't have a choice."

"I still have time. Doctor Wicker could be coming back any day now. He'll buy me. I know for sure." Her fingers stiffened, and as she glanced down she noticed they were trembling. She clasped her hands together, but the sinking feeling remained.

Sara turned her head away, trying to hide her concern. Or her doubt. She then dug into her pocket, fetching out a small vial no larger than her thumb. "If the doctor doesn't make it back, then take this." Elizabeth recognized it immediately. Not two months ago, Susan Wand drank something similar when sold to a brothel. Her body flailed beneath the poison, liquefying her insides until she vomited up red. It was not a pretty death, nor a fast one. Sara had not seen what Elizabeth saw, or she may not have offered the drink so easily.

Elizabeth shielded the vial and ushered it back. "No, I can't. I'll never do that to my mother."

"Death is a far kinder option than life with Arthur Beaumontt. If he buys you, you'll be dead either way. You can choose to end it on your terms. Please, just keep it for when he comes for you." She pushed the vial back before standing up. She offered her arm out. "No more of this grim business, let's go eat."

Elizabeth grinned weakly, accepting the extended arm.

The Academy was a large brown building, dotted with open blue window panels and a large chrome chimney opening and snapping shut like a boiled kettle cap. But, among the vast, growing population overfilling the city, the academy was no larger than a pin head on a map. Heavy pollution darkened the skies over the industrial area, an area known as the Pitts. Vulgar folk stuck together in gangs, the fumes sunken into the cobble bricks, shadowing the streets with thick smoke and grime. Beneath the Pitts the sewerage collected, the churning of the pipes right beneath the cracked roads kept a steady hum through the night. In the summer the smell was horrendous. During the day, the streets were filled with beggars, pubs, the homeless and small gatherings of thieves. Small dwellings were smashed together on stumpy stilts, barely an inch off the ground and away from the slushing of sewage pools below the concrete roads. During storms, the drains would overflow and all the residents would sandbag their front doors in fear of leakage.

A few stretches away from the Pitts were the docks. Among the docks, large ships pressed up against the wooden piers while the overhead long necked cranes, churning and clicking in their awkward movements, hauled pallets off ships. The smell of salt and fish scented the air, dirtying clothes and sticking to skin like sweat. The sea level moved in breaths, but when the tide was too low, the larger boats extended large chrome legs that untucked themselves from the bottom of the boat's belly. The thick, chicken shape stilts extended down to the ocean floor, standing the boats up and keeping them level with the boardwalk.

With sweet rolls in hand, Elizabeth and Sara planted themselves down at the docks, legs swinging effortlessly over the piers. Loud, rolling drums from the overhead airship caught Elizabeth's attention, followed by the ripple of excitement heading up the streets. Elizabeth, licking her fingers clean, glanced over her shoulder and up toward the Golden City. The updraft pulled the large balloons away from her, turning them into specks.

"What's all that about?" Sara also twisted around, tearing the bun in half.

Air balloons as fat as houses rained confetti below. Faint music from trumpets and amplified piano rose among the chatter. The larger towers of the inner capital were choppy and clustered together, becoming spikes planes had to dodge around carefully. As the parading air balloon disappeared, she heard the soft announcement of the doctor's return. *The doctor.* Hope slapped Elizabeth fast. She dropped her bun as she scrambled to stand.

"What? Elizabeth? Where are you going?"

"Sara, he's back! He's back!" She kicked off into a run, leaving Sara no choice but to follow.

Both girls leapt onto the tailgate of the passing tram following the direct tracks toward the main Capital. The only way to breathe from the over-packed tram was to stick their heads out of the side windows.

"How do you know it's him?" Sara bent over the bar, trying to catch her breath.

"The colors." Elizabeth reached out and opened her palm, catching the raining confetti "They are dark blue. That's the color of the Wickers."

Doctor Wicker, like most of the noble families, had a color as well as a symbol to represent his family history. His family name was the feather-tailed quill often pairing dark blue and pearl white together.

In the golden city, where the descendants of nobles lived behind giant golden gates, there were no fishy smells or men sleeping on the streets doused in beer and vomit; up there, it was perfect. It was called the Divin Cadeau. The Divine Gift.

Elizabeth tilted her head back, swarmed by an old warm rush while looking upon the golden gates. It was filled with incredible mansions, most housing their own stables and pitches, where prestigious stores boasted rare jewels, the most desirable gowns, and finest cuisines. The best of everything was up there.

The tram followed the throat of the main roads into the golden estate, where on either side of the highway were large statutes of legendary war heroes and leaders holding national flags held above their heads. The giants were washed in gold, their shadows casting long silhouettes over the rest of the settling city. Only in the roughest of winds did the large flags move.

"We can't stay for long." Sara tapped her on the shoulder. "Twenty minutes, then we have to leave."

Elizabeth's face glowed as she smiled, obviously not listening. "You know, the first time I met Doctor Wicker was almost fifteen years ago, on the day the soldiers returned from war."

"Yes, you've told me many times before." Sara laughed.

Elizabeth closed her hand into a fist, gently pressing the confetti in her palm. "Last time they celebrated, it was red paper they dropped from the skies."

There had been red triangle flags too, flapping like loose tongues along ribbon wire that were tied from posts to balconies all around the city walls. The red flags were beautiful as they waved from above, a vibrant dash of color bold enough to wash away the ugliness from the polluted waters below. When they fell from their strings, they littered the floor like puddles of blood.

Elizabeth and her family had stood in line against the side of the road, held back by wooden barriers. The elite fleet paraded up the center parting, where the nobles and returning heroes sat at the back of their open vehicles and waved to the people with large but tired smiles. Her father, Michael, hoisted three year-old Elizabeth up and sat her on his shoulders where she could see out across the crowds and up the hill to the peak where Governor Beaumontt and his family lived. Her older sister and brother were tall enough to fight for their own space among the bystanders, and her mother, Ana, kept her arm hooked in Michael's grip.

Driving in from behind the governor's coach were the second highest nobles; the Wellingtons, who were the treasury; the Keller's, honored ambassadors; and thirdly, Doctor Wicker, a highly proclaimed doctor and highest ranked man in his entire profession. His clientele limited only to the rich and famous. His youth only made his title more impressive. His luxury lifestyle and cold politeness pinned him as the most sought after bachelor in the entire state. Elizabeth could have sworn she even caught her mother's eyebrow perk when the doctor drove past, subtly waving like the rest of them.

"He saved my life, you know. If he hadn't been there fifteen years ago, I would've died on the pavement," Elizabeth exhaled. The memory was foggy, disjointed with time, but all she knew for sure was that Doctor Wicker had rescued her the first time her heart gave out.

From that part of her life, all she could remember was the strangulation of her tightening chest. The pain had soon made her quiet as it tore through her body and washed her in blue. The surrounding adults formed a circle of surprised gasps as she went rigid. When the blurs all mixed together, she wasn't sure who scooped her up, but he was strong and smelt of cigar smoke. He waved something underneath her nose that let out a strong stench of eucalyptus oil. The scent immediately calmed her. Next thing she knew, she was looking up at the dark shadow of Doctor Wicker as he pressed a cold stethoscope against her skin.

Sara jabbed her with her elbow, jolting Elizabeth out of her reminiscing. "We're here. Let's hurry."

With the rest of the crowd, they climbed off the tram and rushed to the growing mob lining the roadside. Against the barriers, Elizabeth and Sara pressed forward, disoriented by the crowds cheering behind. Unlike the parade fifteen years ago, none of the elite waved to the people from their vehicles. Not even Doctor Wicker stretched his hand outside the tinted window. He drove past without so much as a glance, his distinct automobile keeping at a fast and constant pace.

"He's there," Elizabeth whispered, just as the large clock ticked over, signalling twelve long gongs. Lunch hour was over.

"Come on, Elizabeth, you can see him after." Sara pulled on her arm. Elizabeth ducked under the bar and ran out onto the road. She got two steps in when an arm yanked her back, pushing her back against the gate.

"Stay behind the lines!" The guard held her against the barrier. Despite it, she kept smiling, noticing the car press on the brake lights and linger for a moment. Though it was hard to tell, she could see Doctor Wicker's shadow shift as he looked at her over his shoulder from the back seat.

CHAPTER
TWO

MOTHER? MOTHER, I'M home." Elizabeth arrived to her quiet home after the sun had set. A gentle warmth moved in from the back, and as she did every night, she slipped out of her shoes and unbuckled her petticoat, hanging it on the hook by the door. She hadn't stopped smiling since the parade. Even as she got back to the school—panting hard and late from lunch—she didn't let her face drop. She turned to lock the door when she heard muffled voices coming from down the hall. With her hand still on the knob, she twisted back at the noise. Only she and her mother lived in their one-level flat and that muffle belonged to a man. Elizabeth held her breath.

"Mother? Are you there?" she called just as the voices stopped. The lights were off except for a gentle flicker of orange casting shadows across the hallway. She edged along the walls toward the lounge room, where a man's silhouette stood in front of the lit fireplace, admiring a family picture.

"Sir Beaumontt?" Elizabeth stopped as Harold Beaumontt, the governor to the country and father to Arthur, glanced over his shoulder.

"Ah, Miss Blackmore, how nice to see you."

She curtsied anxiously. "I didn't know we were expecting company."

"My intention was meant to be a quick visit, seems time has gotten away from me." He stepped up to her and tucked one hand into his pocket, clinking the chains of a pocket watch. The shadows painted black strokes across his face, shielding his expression. "How have your studies been treating you? I'm aware you'll be eighteen in a week."

Elizabeth's chest squeezed. *Is he here about my bidding?* Harold Beaumontt was the only gentle person in the entire Beaumontt family. He had three sons, the youngest, Arthur, was a known bully and thug to most of the girls at the academy. Then there was Jeremy who remained away at war followed by Timothy, the eldest and next in line to take his father's place. Elizabeth never liked the governor's wife, Lady Claudia, or the way she would loom her shadow over others. Her head was always tilted, no doubt trying to catch whispers of gossip.

"Yes, sir." Elizabeth curtsied again.

"Arthur has brought it to my attention of his interests. Rest assured you would be welcomed into our household." Elizabeth didn't speak. Couldn't speak. Harold cleared his throat and stepped around the lounge chair separating them. "I should warn you, his intentions are not—"

"Elizabeth?" Ana stepped out from the hallway with what appeared to be a long black coat folded over her arm. A soft waft of lavender followed her in. "Darling, I was just about to escort Governor Beaumontt out."

Harold stepped back, acting as though he hadn't said anything beyond hello and moved back toward the entrance, "Oh, yes, my coat. Thank you. Well, thank you Ms. Blackmore for your time. I hope I haven't been too much of an inconvenience."

"Never, Sir. It was my pleasure. And please, call me Ana."

"My lady Ana." Romantic sparks electrified the air. Uncertainty filled Elizabeth, but she clenched her teeth together to bite back her outburst. Stares lingered. Smiles pinched their flustered cheeks red. Elizabeth felt her own blood boil, but for very different reasons. When Ana returned from leading Harold out, her guilty smile lengthened.

"Mother?" Elizabeth crossed her arms, unsure what expression she should wear.

"It's not what you think, Elizabeth." Ana held her hand up before easing herself into the chair facing the fire pit. She had her fingertips to her forehead, as if trying to massage out a building headache. Her shoulders slouched with exhaustion.

"If it is or if it isn't, you can't go around with married men. People will talk."

"He was looking for someone who can make good pies. It was strictly a business proposition."

"And this conversation had to happen so late?" Anger gripped her tone.

"We had…ahem…" Ana cleared her throat as she turned herself around, picking up the cup of tea that had long gone cold. "We got caught up chatting."

"You might be a single woman, but he is not a single man. If Lady Claudia hears her husband is spending his afternoons with you, I fear what wrath she could unleash." Elizabeth walked over and knelt by her mother's knees, resting both her hands on the armrest. She let the anger subside as a new thought popped into mind. "I understand you get lonely, but Governor Beaumontt is not the right choice. Doctor Wicker, on the other hand, is an excellent suitor. He just arrived back in town and—"

Ana's smile dropped for a moment before she turned her face away. "You should go see him, dear. It's been far too long."

"You should accompany me. I know he thinks fondly of you."

"Tsk!" Ana snorted. "He didn't think much of me when Michael had us thrown to the streets. Even after knowing all of that, knowing of your heart condition, never did he seek us out."

Elizabeth gently bit her lip. Defeated by her mother's words, she dropped her hands from the armrest. Sometimes, she thought it would be easier to accept Arthur as her new master, to take his cruelty silently and collect the money to buy a place out of the Pitts. The shaming on her mother had been difficult. Elizabeth was only eight when they were tossed to the streets, but she had grown accustomed to their struggles. Ana took the heavier toll; guilt a vicious rat gnawing her away. It had rained so hard that day; the roads had been swallowed under the rippling black water and the storm clouds darkened the sky into night. Michael was just a shadow in the doorway, arm pointing out, shouting until his voice cracked.

Neighbors watched with nervous interest as Ana scrambled up and tried to cover eight-year-old Elizabeth from the cold. Her two other children, Sam and Penelope, had watched from the kitchen window crying. Their small frames just dark outlines, only their fists visible as they hammered against the glass. Gossip was faster than any train or airship; news and talk scared Ana into hiding. All she could afford was the hut down in the Pitts. She had fought against it, but the only way to stop starvation was to sell Elizabeth into the Academy. A decision that continued to haunt her.

Elizabeth lowered her voice. "Arthur Beaumontt came again this morning to the academy. He's already put in his bid. In a week's time, I will be sold to him. I will get money and send it back; you don't need to seduce his father…"

Ana leaned forward, cupping her daughter's face. "I won't allow that. I'm not seducing the governor. I have no feelings for the man."

Mildly relieved, Elizabeth shook her head. "Doctor Wicker is the only man left who can save me."

"Do not look to men. They are not our saviors." Ana scooted off the chair, crouching down eye-to-eye with Elizabeth. She eased her finger under Elizabeth's chin, gently tilting her head back as tears swelled. "My beautiful daughter, words cannot express how sorry I am that this has happened. I wish I could make everything right again."

"Wishes aren't real, mother." Elizabeth whispered, and gently pushed her mother's hand off.

Ana exhaled. "You're becoming more and more like him, such a beautiful face. I'm sure he'll be so happy to see you're doing so well. You should go see him tomorrow."

The connection between the Doctor and Elizabeth was obvious. Similar to him, she had sickly blonde locks; the tint so pale, it was as if someone had dumped white ash on her head. She was washed with a pale complexion and long clumsy limbs, completing the sickly attire. The final straw was the frail heart condition inherited through the Wicker bloodline. A child bore out of a love affair did not extend the same titles, so although Elizabeth was of Wicker blood, she was not welcomed as a noble woman.

Doctor Wicker had no other children and never had a wife, so it had confused Elizabeth when he didn't extend marriage to her mother. *Perhaps he never wanted a family?* She considered. *Perhaps she wasn't the child he wanted; boys were always much more sought after than girls.* Despite being a constant presence when she was younger, he had disappeared for six years, and today was his first appearance since then. Timing couldn't be any more crucial. If she wanted to be spared a life with Arthur Beaumontt, then Doctor Wicker was her only hope.

CHAPTER

THREE

LATER THAN USUAL, Elizabeth made her way home from the academy the following day, tucking her chin into her chest as her teeth chattered, trying to work the heat back into her body. The days were hot, but the nights were always chillingly cold. The frost would nip her fingers blue and spread ice all across the windshields and windows. Just as she reached out to grab onto the front door, the door was pulled inside, revealing Harold and her mother giggling behind it. Elizabeth stepped backwards as they both halted. Harold corrected his collar before nodding over his shoulder.

"Thank you for your time, Lady Ana." He smiled with a tip of his hat.

"You're always welcome here, Governor Beaumontt." Ana curtsied and took a step backwards, allowing enough space for Harold to squeeze past.

"Miss Blackmore," he greeted Elizabeth as they crossed paths. Elizabeth greeted back and moved inside. She shot Ana a sharp look, one only given with serious scolding. Ana simply shook her head. She closed the door and turned to walk toward the kitchen.

"Not now, Elizabeth."

"Didn't you listen to anything I said?" Elizabeth growled, stomping out of her shoes and wrenching her coat free. "Why was he here, again? Don't tell me he wants to talk more about *pies?*" She followed Ana into the kitchen as she returned to cooking a stew.

Ana threw her hands up in frustration. "What do you want me to do, Elizabeth? I can't very well just shoo the governor out of my house."

"This is only going to get you into more trouble. Even if it is innocent, rumors will spread and Lady Claudia is not a kind woman. If she thinks you're having an affair—"

"Let them speak." Ana turned to the window, "Their meaningless words can't hurt me."

"No! Stop it! This isn't just about you anymore." Elizabeth buried her face into her hands, trying to muffle her frustration. No doubt neighbors watched their doorstep. No doubt Lady Claudia had ears in the Pitts. Elizabeth's watched the shadows, remembering how fast it tore her world down before. There were always signs of a storm coming. The stares. The gossip. The mistakes of her mother. She grabbed her chest, feeling her panic unleash. "If something were to happen, what am I meant to do?" There remained pieces that were never put back together, not completely. Her mother moved as an incomplete puzzle. One big hole through her chest.

Ana stopped and looked over at the crack of Elizabeth's voice. "Elizabeth, no, darling, no." She pulled her daughter into her arms, cupping her cheeks. Elizabeth weakly tried to steer her face away, embarrassed by her tears. "I'm not going to let that happen again, I promise. We'll be okay. Nothing bad will happen, sweetheart."

Ana pressed her forehead against her daughter's before kissing her tenderly on the cheek. "I didn't want to say anything just in case, but it really is business we're discussing. It turns out the governor loves my dessert pies so much he's going to help me open my own store. It'll be in Rosefire, somewhere nice where I can make more money and buy at least half of your wage. You wouldn't have to be a live-in servant after all."

"What?" Elizabeth turned her face up; her cheeks reddened and skimmed with tears. "Is he really going to help you open your own shop?"

Ana nodded, biting into her smile. "See, your mother knows what she's doing," she mocked playfully as Elizabeth snorted, dabbing her eyes with her fingertips. Her cruel and sudden accusation to her mother's morals pulled at her heart.

"I'm sorry…I shouldn't have—"

"It's okay. There's nothing to apologize over. Harold is kind, but there's nothing more between us."

Elizabeth scooted over and took a seat as Ana returned to the pot. "I haven't given up on Doctor Wicker. I'll try again tomorrow to speak to him, explain exactly what is happening. I'm sure he'll bid for me."

Ana turned her face over her shoulder, cocking a sly smile. "There's no doubt in my mind. Any man would want to call you his own, but out of them all, Doctor Wicker will provide the best future for you."

DURING THE NIGHT, Elizabeth found herself shivering. The cold was so bad it stirred her awake and turned her toes blue. The heavy shadows distorted her room; taking her a moment to adjust her eyes as she rolled herself out of bed and eased her bare feet to the ground. She then took the torch from her bedside and turned it on. Something else stirred within her. A sense, a tingling that didn't match the quietness of the house.

Elizabeth poured herself a cup of water from the kitchen and toasted her toes next to the dying embers in the fire pit. The carpet itched the exposed skin on her feet, making them tingle. She settled into her mother's reclined chair, shutting her eyes briefly. She jerked upward, unaware she had fallen asleep. As she made her way back to her room, she heard a subtly creak in the floorboards. Elizabeth slowed and took a step back. Holding the light forwards, she rounded the corner to where her mother's room was. The hall was long and empty. Darkness concealed most of it. Until something shifted in the shadows. Just out of sight, an outline of a body stepped up to her mother's door.

"Who's there?" Elizabeth called out. The door creaked open, throwing moonlight across the man's tall physique. She couldn't see much beyond a straight nose and glint of blond hair. The man unsheathed a dagger and stepped into Ana's room. Panic threw Elizabeth forward, making her drop her glass, shattering it across the ground.

"No! Wait! Don't!" She ran down the hall only to find the man was gone and the room remained undisturbed. *Wait, a dream?* She spun around, utterly confused. Rattled, she climbed onto her mother's bed and shook her. "Mother, wake up."

She didn't respond. A fast, cold nip pinched her finger tips where she brushed them against her mother's cheek. Elizabeth shook her harder. Ana's body flopped. Her body rolled limply, her face relaxed in her slumber.

"Mother?" She then pressed two fingers against the pulse in her mother's neck. When she couldn't feel anything, Elizabeth pressed her ear to her chest, hoping to feel her breathing. Silence. Unnatural silence, a silence only present in the vacancy of life. Elizabeth propped her mother's head up between the smooth of her palms. Color faded from her cheeks. She checked for stab wounds and bloodstains, but there was nothing. Her cold body was the only give away that a human laid in her hands. Impossible. It was impossible.

"No! Please wake up!"

Elizabeth shouted and shook her, no longer gentle. It got harder to breathe. Harder to think.

"Wake up! Mother?"

"Mother!"

"Mother!"

Impossible. It was impossible. It had to be.

CHAPTER
FOUR

ELIZABETH'S CHIN FELT sewn to her chest. Her neck weakened, unable to lift her head. Her body folded over, cradling herself as she huddled in the corner. *How is this possible? Am I going crazy? How did this happen?* She kept pulling on her memory like a reel of film, revisiting the exact moment the man stepped out of the shadows. She remembered his hand reaching the door knob. She remembered the door glided open at his push. She remembered the blade. She could still see his profile cradled against the moonlight. Yet it didn't make sense. Was she not fast enough? Where did he go? How did it happen?

Her mother's body had been taken away long ago, but she could still see how the sheets fell against her form, leaving a soft imprint on the bed. Elizabeth crunched her fingers through the bulk of her hair, trying to dig up answers. The doctors proclaimed a stroke took her mother's life, but that's not what she saw. Ana was murdered. How they did it and left no marks on the body, she couldn't understand. It had been hours since the funeral, maybe even a whole day, and Elizabeth still couldn't find the strength to lift herself up. Ana's friends came to mourn her and help pay for her burial. They looked at Elizabeth with deep remorse, patted her on the shoulder, and passed on their condolences, but it was wasted breath. Elizabeth was alone now. No amounts of *I'm sorry* were going to help her.

WITH THE PASSING week, Elizabeth's shattered world only grew darker. Time never stopped even when her reason to live collapsed, turning familiar rooms into unrecognizable spaces, mocking her with her mother's fading presence. And tomorrow, she was going to be sold. The realization came to her during the blood sunrise. Red warmed the streets, peeling back the ice as time felt both fleeting and unbearably slow. Lack of sleep left her delirious. Everywhere she looked, she saw Ana. Even with all the pictures turned down, the furniture moved to create a lounge that wasn't hers, a kitchen that wasn't theirs, but she was still there, in every creak of a floorboard and the catch of her reflection. Ana was there. Haunting her.

Elizabeth cried so hard the tears felt heaved up from the pit of her stomach. When the sadness hollowed her out, Elizabeth felt like she could not get lower. With nothing left, she ran out into the streets in her sleeping attire and bare feet. Letters piled up outside her door, formal inquests about her absence from the academy. She looked like a ghost amongst the dew; blue veins tattooed her pale skin as white hair unbundled from its messy bun. She reached Doctor Wicker's house and stormed right up to the intercom by the barred gates. She took the handle and brought it to her lips. As the receiver end was picked up and the sound of someone's breath tickled against her ear, Elizabeth felt her chest tighten.

"I need to speak to Doctor William Wicker immediately. Tell him it's Elizabeth Blackmore. I don't care if I have to wait all day, I must speak with him." Her tone didn't shift despite her knees shaking. The intercom's heavy breathing continued. Elizabeth stepped around to see the house through the bars of the gate. There were two cars parked there—William's and another she couldn't recognize. All the lights were off and the curtains were drawn.

"This is an emergency—"

"It's me."

She froze. His voice rang with familiarity, bringing forth a collage of memories. She remembered him walking into her room, big hands combing back her white bangs. He greeted her with a hot tea, a lemon wedged on the side, her favorite. She remembered the first time she disobeyed his instructions against playing tag with the rest of the children, and how he scooped her up when she fell down, unable to collect a breath. She even remembered the moment he confronted Ana; his face soft as he whispered, 'Is she mine?'

She slumped against the post. "Doctor Wicker?" He didn't reply, but she could still hear him breathing. "My mother…"

"I know. I'm so sorry, Miss Blackmore." His voice dropped with genuine remorse. Elizabeth waited for him to keep speaking, for him to say something, *anything* that would give her reason to hope. She folded her lips in to stop herself from shattering. Her eyes rolled upwards, blinking furiously to stop the tears.

She eventually whispered, "I need your help."

He gently sighed, "I truly am sorry," before hanging up. Numbness took her first, taking her strength as her fingers fumbled with the phone, causing her to drop it. The mouthpiece dangled by the end of the cord as a man hangs from a noose. The world became quiet. Her mind snapped in two, her thoughts running into the ground. *That was it*, she thought. *Game over.*

LUKEWARM WATER FILLED the bathtub. She sat at the bottom of the drum, water rising past her ribs and pulling the fabric of her dress against the side. In her nimble fingers, she cradled the vial of cyanide. She had popped open the lid but couldn't bring the tiny bottle to her lips. If she killed herself, her mother's murderer would get away without justice. Even though she feared life with the Beaumontt's, the rage inside her wouldn't let her budge. Even if it meant bending to the whims of Arthur Beaumontt, she will find the fiend who killed her mother and she would end him. Yet, she did not rise from the water. She did not drop the poison. She studied it. Memorizing it. Imagining the acidic doze tearing up her insides, spewing up red. Imagined dying. Imagined meeting her mother again.

A loud bang jolted Elizabeth out of her daze. The water had long gone cold. She edged the tap off with her toes, but the water had already overspilled the edge on to the floor. Her wrinkled skin felt frozen as she turned her head toward the front door. The banging continued. Urgently. Wanting her attention. She looked at her numbed, emptied hands. *No vial?* Below her grip, the broken vial sprawled out across the floor in shards. Poison bubbled and washed away with the tub water. The person knocked three more times before silence followed. Soon, all that was left was the sharp drip of a leaking pipe. Elizabeth eased herself down until the water crept up to her chin and pressed against her ear drums. The dripping echoed in the body of the water. Loud, but distant. Without taking a breath, she slipped under the surface.

Tiny air bubbles escaped her nostrils and lips. It was heavenly tranquil with a low hum rippling across the water from edge to edge. It could be coming from the churning pipes underneath her or the traffic right outside her window. Her vision was hazy through the water and clouded by strands of white hair floating in suspended space. As if preparing for sleep, she felt her eyes get heavier and her vision begin to shift. She closed her eyes. Her body softened. Her chest deflated, pushing more bubbles to the surface.

When she opened them again, a shadow stepped over and drove a hand down, hoisting her up. As she rose, water spraying everywhere, she inhaled a long and frightened gasp.

"What are you doing?" Sara leant over the bath edge, running her hands over Elizabeth's face, trying to clear the hair away. Elizabeth coughed and choked on the inhaled water.

"Sara?" she spluttered. Sara jumped up to grab a towel. "What are you doing here?"

"I've been so worried. I haven't heard anything from you in days." She helped ease Elizabeth to a stand before she hugged the towel around Elizabeth's body, helping her climb out of her drenched gown. Elizabeth wasn't sure if Sara hadn't noticed the broken bottle or elected to ignore the disturbing thought her friend could have already drunken the deathly dose. She ducked in and out in moments, returning to the bathroom with a dry clean outfit.

"I don't want to get dressed."

"You can't sit there in the nude." Elizabeth turned her face away as Sara stepped around her, bringing out a brush. She started to comb through Elizabeth's hair, yanking at her scalp as the bristles got caught in the knots. There was more knocking on the door. Sara called out over her shoulder, "We're coming."

"Who's that?" Elizabeth clenched her towel closer to her body.

"Mr. Beaumontt is waiting." Sara tucked a loose strand behind Elizabeth's ear. "You've been purchased."

Elizabeth didn't remember getting dressed, only Sara's rough hands as she forced Elizabeth into a long skirt and cream blouse. And as she passed the front window, she caught sight of Harold Beaumontt standing by the front threshold with his car parked on the curb. She jerked her head away as Sara took her to the lounge. Sara invited Harold in while Elizabeth waited on the couch in front of the fireplace.

"Thank you for helping me, Miss Coven." Harold Beaumontt nodded toward Sara as she curtsied in reply. She glanced wearily over at Elizabeth, who hadn't turned her gaze away from the ash pile.

"Miss Blackmore, let me just say how truly sorry I am for your loss. Your mother was such a beautiful and wonderful woman. I know how much she meant to you, and how much you meant to her. Ana truly was loved."

Elizabeth took a deep breath. Hearing him say her name curled her hands into fists. *Stay calm, you can do this. You can do this.* He stepped around to face her and tugged his hand out of his pocket, pulling out his pocket watch.

Elizabeth rolled her gaze upwards, her face tightening into a scowl. "Are you here about the bidding?" Even her voice strained with loathing.

"Yes, actually." He tucked his watch back in. "And quite the bidding war it was, very spectacular. Arthur placed his last bid just this morning for a price that was far out of reason. I would have to sell half my staff just to pay his debt. I came here to withdraw the bid, but your head mistress has informed me it was unnecessary."

"Wait, unnecessary?"

Harold glanced down at her, eyes unfamiliarly gentle for a Beaumontt and a soft tilt of a smile. "Someone had already outmatched the bid. Doctor Wicker, if my information is correct."

Elizabeth bolted upright. "He did?"

"Ah, Sir William."

She spun around as Doctor William Wicker stepped out from around the corner, his soft but full gray hair combed back into a stiff, ashy flame. He looked older, but in a good way, as wine ages with grace and value. Though he seemed tired, William kept his posture straight and his blue eyes calm.

"Governor Beaumontt," he greeted with a nod. Harold chuckled and clapped him on the back.

"None of this Governor business. I just wanted to ensure that our young Miss Blackmore is holding up okay."

Her eyes shot up to meet William's, and though she could hear them talking, the connections weren't being made in her head. She glanced over at Sara for confirmation that this wasn't a dream. Sara's eyes were just as large, her cheeks pinched pink in happiness. She gave her a brisk nod, biting back her laughter.

"Thank you for your concern, Governor Beaumontt, and please pass on my apology to your son, Arthur. I understand the news will be upsetting for him."

Harold cleared his throat with a cough. "It'll do that boy some good to hear *no* once in a while."

William gently reached out to take Elizabeth's elbow. "If you don't mind, Miss Elizabeth, we should get going. I'll have my men return for your things."

Elizabeth almost couldn't stand. He called her by her name. It was incredibly personal, incredibly foreign. But this whole thing felt unreal. She must be dead. It was the only possible solution. She was dead, and this was her version of heaven. But then, where was Ana?

As William helped her stand, her knees wobbled and her head felt stuffed with stones. She felt too heavy to be a spirit. Too angry to be in heaven. She looked up at William, unsure of her own feelings. *Why didn't he tell me earlier? Why wait until the last minute?* She jerked her head away from his gaze in fear he'd read her inner turmoil and change his mind. She didn't even look at Sara or turn to grab her more personal things. She went straight out to the car, sick that she had been within two seconds of killing herself. If he had said something sooner and not led her to believe she was deserted, the notion of suicide would never had crossed her mind. And for that, Elizabeth's knuckles curled, she blamed him.

CHAPTER
FIVE

ITTING IN THE car, Elizabeth couldn't break her looping thoughts. *When am I going to wake up? When am I going to get to the front door and find Arthur standing there, slapping bundles of money against his palm as if he had won the lottery? How can this be happening?*

They drove out of the disease-infested Pitts, along the blue sea caressing the docks, up through Rosefire and past the line of golden statues, through the large emporium gates and into the high society of the Golden City. It had gotten its nickname from the synthetic golden trees plotted throughout the streets.

"Miss Elizabeth?"

She jerked her head upwards. From the large, iron black gates the Wicker mansion was separated by fresh, cut grass and a lone water fountain in the middle of the circular drive way. Yards of garden beds distanced Doctor Wicker's estate from his neighbors. Though every mansion was impressive in structure, Doctor Wicker's stood out as the largest. At the threshold of William's manor waited the butler. Elizabeth accepted William's hand as he helped her out of the car and took her inside. She took a breath. The air was clearer and lighter, even the sun felt warmer on her cheeks. In the Pitts, the sunlight couldn't reach the ground through the bulk of the over-packed houses.

"This is Mr. Harry Smith. He has been with us for the past few decades." He took her through the main foyer as Elizabeth felt her head tilt back. She had been to his clinic many times, but never to his actual house. The ceiling arched upwards like a dome, mimicking a church's gracious rounded halls.

"I apologize. I don't have the time to give you a grand tour, so feel free to wander. But please keep in mind that only my personal quarters are off limits. If you need me, you can find me in the east library; though it's preferred that you don't disturb me unless it's an emergency. We dine over in the west wing; Harry will collect you when it's time. Until then, Harry, can you please show Miss Elizabeth to her room?"

He turned to leave as Elizabeth reached out. "Wait? What about my duties? You haven't given me any orders." He looked confused. "You bought me, remember? I am a maid, not a guest."

"Oh, right." He signalled to Harry as he pulled out a scrolled parchment and a pen. "Sign here."

Reluctantly, Elizabeth picked up the pen. "What is it?"

"Legal documents." He urged her to be quick as she signed her name at the bottom. As soon as her pen lifted, William took the scroll away. "Tomorrow morning we'll start you off with your studies."

"Studies?"

"Harry will tutor you from eight until one, and then you will continue on your own with private study." William continued speaking over his shoulder. "We'll have weekly tests, to ensure you are understanding all the material properly. All standard procedures."

She ran to catch up with him. "Wait, what studies?"

"For your future, of course."

"My future?"

"Unless you intend to remain a servant for the rest of your life…" William glanced at Harry, "which is fine, but I thought you would like the chance to broaden your horizon. It's a big world out there, and we need bright minds to illuminate it."

HARRY TOOK ELIZABETH up the curved staircase to the next story, and then down the hall where her room was positioned next to a large portrait of a white-haired woman dressed in jewels and an elegant gown. She was surprised to see William displaying pictures of his family, be it thanks to his cold and detached reputation out in the public, she had suspected he had no living relatives left. Similar to William, the woman wore the family crest on her clothing, and her white hair was pulled back into curls, sitting underneath a large brimmed hat. She was also stunningly beautiful.

Harry stepped to the side, allowing Elizabeth space to walk in front of him. When she opened the door, she was welcomed by a large, exquisite room with a king-size, four-poster bed attached to the roof like a chandelier, dangling inches off the carpeted floor. The motorized bed posts would lower the bed closer to the ground for her to climb on, before bringing it back up off the ground so it could rock gently during the night. There were four fat cushioned chairs sitting around a table with a motorised chess game set up by the windows. In the back corner were two large cupboards and at least three floor-to-ceiling windows, all with separate curtains tied back by velvet rope.

"This can't be right. Is this for me?" Elizabeth turned back to find Harry had left.

She walked to the dresser where a collection of lace collars and bracelets were sorted across the desk. In the center, made of a pearl wax, was the symbol of the Wicker crest, the feather-tail quill. She picked one up and measured it against herself. They were slightly too small so she put it back down. She headed outside and started to roam the hallways, lightly touching the golden framework of the portraits lining the walls.

Only one-sixth of the Wicker family members carried the white hair gene. She was quick to notice that unlike their brunette and blonde siblings, the white-haired Wickers didn't have children, or even a spouse. In every picture, they stood alone and serious. It was through their siblings' marriages that the white gene sprouted out like weeds among flowers. The only picture of William was when he was sixteen years old standing next to his younger sister. He was very handsome with a small, cocked smile, dressed in dark brown hunting gear with his arm resting on the chairs arm rest. This was what she had wanted, yet Elizabeth couldn't shake the anger that swirled from her stomach.

"Is something the matter, young miss?" Harry was at the bottom of the stairs looking up. His black attire was kept impossibly wrinkle free; the exact opposite to the aged lines worn into his face. The white collar was pinched right under his chin, so that every time he gulped his Adam's apple got wedged. Elizabeth huffed and crossed her arms.

"Something doesn't feel right."

"You are welcome to take a nap if you feel unwell."

"That's not it."

"I can send up some warm tea?"

"No, thank you. I just—"

"I'll get the bath running. You must be exhausted."

"Just stop!" She felt herself shout and push off the railing to face Harry directly. He flinched at her outburst as Elizabeth covered her mouth. "I'm sorry. I didn't mean to shout, but right now, all I want is to speak to Doctor Wicker."

Harry's constant dry lips trembled at her request. "I'm sorry, miss. He's working."

"This is important." She lowered her hands. "Please?"

HARRY TOOK HER to the front door leading into the east library, but didn't follow her in. The library was no doubt the largest part of the house, aside, of course, from the main foyer. William placed himself in one of the corners, a low, oil-burning lamp illuminating the disarray of heavy text books across the desk. He was nose deep in the pages and didn't glance up at her approach, his hand cupping his chin as the other flipped through pages feverishly.

Elizabeth approached. She had so many burning questions, but there was one in particular she felt boiling away inside of her. "Why didn't you come back for us?"

He tilted back, surprised, before snapping the book closed and taking his glasses off. "Miss Elizabeth, I didn't hear you come in." He pushed back his chair and walked over. He cupped her cheeks, tilting her chin up. "I've been meaning to check your heart. Have you been keeping up with your medications?"

There he goes again, always the doctor, nothing more. If they didn't share such facial similarities, she could have accepted that all she ever could be. She had parts of Ana in her, in how her cheeks curved softly, the crisp, blue eyes and her lips puffed out with natural pink squeezed into them. Her ashy-blonde locks were still slightly damp from her bath, curling around her face in limp twists. Though their hair was naturally very light, their eyebrows were dark and full with a dominant arch. She jerked her chin out of his palms, repeating herself, "Why didn't you come back for us?"

Did she even have a right to be mad? Even though he was her biological father, it had been Michael who kicked her out onto the streets. William had always extended a helping hand, but he acted as a doctor treats a patient. Not a father to a child.

William put both hands in his pockets, his dark brown vest and matching tie curved against his lean body. "I had to find someone first."

"May I ask who?"

"It's not important," he dismissed her and turned away, which only breathed more fuel onto Elizabeth's spitfire rage.

She stepped around the table to follow him. "It must've been important if you abandoned us for them. Was it a second family? A lover? A job or a chance to make more money?"

"You really don't think highly of me?"

"I thought the world of you, but that world chipped away every year you didn't come back for us. You didn't help us even though we had nothing. All those cold nights, all those missed meals because we couldn't... I know you didn't ask for me, but—" She clenched her teeth together making her jaw ache. She didn't dare say. She didn't dare call herself *his child*. "My mother is dead."

"You think that's my fault?" he asked calmly.

"You can take some of the blame," she snapped. "If we had some protection, then maybe he never would've gotten into our house. She would still be here with me."

"Hang on," William turned back. "Ana died of a stroke." Elizabeth bit her tongue and lowered her head. "Right?" he urged.

"That's what the reports say." She spoke under her breath.

He sighed. "We'll discuss this later. You should get dressed for supper. Put something warm on before you catch a cold." He returned to his chair, picking up his glasses and sitting them at the edge of his nose. Elizabeth lingered for a moment, feeling the all-too-real touch of being alone in the world.

"You still haven't given me any orders." She calmed her tone and wiped her hands down her dress, pushing out the creases. '

"You're not a servant in my house," he said, his voice directed toward the books.

"I'm not a guest either."

"You are my daughter."

A nerve snapped inside her. The word *daughter* coming out of his mouth felt like a cruel joke. She couldn't stop herself. The words flew out. "Don't start treating me like family." A pain twitched in her chest.

She took a step back, resisting the urge to cup where the ache surged.

William perked his head up, his expression unreadable. "Then I order you to put a coat on and meet me downstairs for supper."

CHAPTER
SIX

SHE HAD PUT on a thick coat over her dress and waited patiently in the dining area. William greeted her as the clock ticked over to eight and a loud ping sounded. Harry followed him in carrying a silver tray. Elizabeth bolted upwards to help him when William ordered her to stop.

"It's fine. Sit down."

She reluctantly took her seat. As dinner was served, Elizabeth found herself without an appetite. Instead, she pushed her food around the plate glumly.

"Is it not to your liking?" William, pausing mid-bite, glanced upwards. Their utensils hitting the plates were the only chatter through the eerily quiet hall. Even Harry made sure not to gulp too loudly.

"The food is fine. It's just I just don't feel hungry."

"What's the matter? I thought you wanted this?" he spoke again, his tone always annoyingly calm.

"My being here doesn't change the fact my mother is gone." She meant to whisper but her words carried across the table.

He hesitated briefly. "Would you rather be with Arthur Beaumontt?"

The mere mention of Arthur Beaumontt gave Elizabeth the chills. His cruel smirk flashed and his last words crawled over her. Now she definitely lost her appetite. "No, no of course not. I just feel like…" She slumped a little more in her chair, searching the rafters for an answer. "I feel like I shouldn't be anywhere."

William eased his fork down and picked up his napkin, dabbing it lightly at the corners of his mouth. "I don't quite understand."

She sighed, but how could he? A man living in such a big house for so many years alone. No wife. No close family. Part of her doubted he even had any friends.

"I know this is tough for you. Money can't bring your mother back, but I know she would be happy knowing you're in safe hands. That reminds me…" He dug his hand into his pocket and pulled out a locket. It was oval shaped with gold plating and a white pearl face. There was a picture of a faint silver outline in the center of the watch face of their family crest. "This is for you."

He reached over and placed it in front of her plate. Elizabeth looked down at it, then back at William, and then back at the locket unsure what to say.

"The center plating is made of precious gold. I had a little left over from a project, well, anyway, happy birthday."

She gently reached over and picked it up. The locket was sealed shut with a tiny hook; the whole size of it was no larger than two thumbs held side by side. The metal was cool to the touch and very smooth. On the perimeter of the pearl face were the workings of brown, gold, and silver cogs. Whatever pent-up misery she hung onto seemed to dissolve through her fingertips. She even cracked a smile, which she hadn't been able to do since her mother's passing.

"Thank you," she whispered and brought the locket to her chest. At the front door there were three quick taps. Harry dashed around to answer it. There was a moment of hushed conversation before Harry returned, coughing gently to get William's attention.

"Sir, he is here."

William immediately pushed back his chair and slipped into his coat. "Please excuse me, Miss Elizabeth." He briefly nodded before turning to the door. Elizabeth craned her neck from her seat to see who he was talking to, but the door swung shut just as a shadow passed by.

AFTER HER MEAL, Elizabeth retired to her new chambers. The silence felt unnatural. She couldn't sleep without the bustle of traffic crossing her window or the churning sewage pipes. The loneliness crept up on her as Elizabeth peered out across the vast space of her room. The walls were too far away and the roof was too high, making Elizabeth squirm under the sheets. Even with all of her belongings in the vacant space, the room still felt like a void.

She turned over and pressed her head into the smooth cloth of the pillow. In the silence her thoughts became shouts, throwing questions that she didn't know the answers too. How much did she really know about Doctor Wicker? Not that long ago, Doctor Wicker was nothing more than a pair of barred gates. Elizabeth flipped over for the fifth time. Her reality was living in a house with an unfamiliar man, though he was a favorable choice compared to Arthur, the fact still stood that he was practically a stranger. He even invited mystery guests into his house without so much as an introduction. Elizabeth drew her lips in with unease. Maybe there were answers to his secrets she didn't want to know.

Despite her night's sleep, Elizabeth woke up as though she hadn't slept for weeks. She squeezed her headache behind her eyes before rolling over and sitting up. Even in the daylight, her new bedroom seemed too large. On eight o'clock, Harry came by her door and set out work for her to tackle. Today's topic: mathematics. She sat in the music room, a textbook propped open and a blank piece of paper set in front. It took her longer than she'd hoped to understand the equations.

Despite her embarrassment, Harry never once made her feel inferior. The grip of a pen felt strange in her hand. She wasn't meant for writing and problem solving, she was meant for cleaning. Outside the window, she noticed an unfamiliar car parked in the courtyard.

"Harry, who does that vehicle belong to?"

Harry twisted around in his chair. "Ah, that belongs to your father's guest."

Father? Elizabeth paused on the word. Referring to William as her father felt unnerving and misplaced to her ears. She tried to clear her throat, but the uncomfortable pinch in her voice was still there. "Is he here now?"

"I do believe so."

"Can I meet him?"

Harry blinked back at her slowly. "I don't believe that is wise."

"Is there a reason why?" she said, but Harry turned back with nothing else to say. His silence fueled her curiosity. *Well…isn't that just suspicious.* Elizabeth settled back into her chair, her eyes turning back to the paper whereas her mind remained stuck somewhere else. "Harry…do you believe it will be okay for me to visit a friend?"

"I can arrange the driver for you. Which household?"

"She's actually at the academy."

Harry nodded. "I will collect your pieces then, Miss."

"My what?"

Harry indicated with his head for her to follow as they made their way back to her room. He motioned to her drawer once more to where the lace collar cuffs and bands were lined along the dresser.

"I can't wear them." She flinched back. To wear the Wicker crest in public was as much as an insult as if she paraded around mocking the Queen. The symbols of the noble households were the birth-rights of all the descendants. If Elizabeth wore the Wicker crest, she feared she'd be stoned to death the moment she stepped outside. "I can't go out in them."

"You don't like them?" She jolted as William stepped around the corner.

"I, well, it's not that I don't like them. It's just, you know, it's not appropriate." Flustered, Elizabeth stumbled over her words.

"Not appropriate?" William stepped around her and walked to the dresser, picking up a few pairs to bring them back. He held them out on a flat palm. She followed his gaze down before delicately picking one up. It was of matching royal blue and black lace, framed around the crest that mimicked a blooming rose. William cleared his throat. "I had them made a while ago. I didn't know if you would like the colors."

"You made them a while ago?"

"Yes, for when I came to collect you," he said.

As she felt the sting of his words surge through her, Elizabeth clenched her jaw and ground her teeth. "You don't have to force yourself to accept me. I am your servant! That is why I am here. That is it. You definitely don't have to go around showing everyone I'm your love-affair daughter." She shoved the band back into his palm.

"Are you ashamed of me?"

Elizabeth scoffed as if he had just made a distasteful joke. "Aren't you ashamed of *me*? I mean, look at me." She spun. "I'm not exactly a noble woman."

A small smile curled William's face as it reached his eyes, "You're a Wicker; you have nobility in your blood."

As fast as the anger spiked, her chest deflated, letting the hot air rush out of her. She exhaled her words as though exhausted. "If you had all the intentions of welcoming me into the family, why do it now? Why did you wait so long? We needed you…"

"You must understand the situation I was in."

Unable to help herself, she scoffed. "I do understand. We were imposing on your bachelor lifestyle."

William sighed and pinched at the collar near his throat. "Miss Elizabeth, there are certain traits and genes within the Wicker family, especially those carrying mine…our…appearance, that makes childbearing an impossible feat. All my life, I believed I would never father children, and thus when you were born, it was difficult for me to hope you could be from my blood. I approached the situation poorly. In my youth, I couldn't accept it, but now I wished I had acted differently. For that, I am incredibly sorry."

Elizabeth eased back, gently touching her stomach pained by the thought she too could be infertile or William could not be her father. "So I am not—"

"There are no doubts in my mind that you are of Wicker blood. Your heart condition, your white hair, your face…when I finally came to accept the miracle of *you*, I knew there was something of dire importance I needed to attend to first."

"Like your guest?" Elizabeth pointed out. William stopped, but didn't turn his gaze to her.

"Exactly. But, who he is, is none of your concern. You are not to approach him. Do you understand?"

Elizabeth shifted over onto her other foot. "You make him sound like he is part of the underground mafia."

Obviously missing her joke, William only shook his head. "Don't fret about it. Just please, stay away from him. Promise me you will?"

He reached out and grabbed her shoulder, forcing her to look up at him. Elizabeth felt guilt pinch at her knowing it was a promise she couldn't keep. "I promise."

SOME NIGHTS THE mysterious car was parked outside, some nights it wasn't. Every time this guest moved about the house, he was hushed through closed doors and under the veil of shadow. Elizabeth almost tore her hair out with the yearning to see who this man was. She just wanted to catch his face. This man was the reason William stayed away for so long. He was the reason they were never a family, why Ana and herself suffered for years. She needed to know why.

One night, she accidentally caught him.

It was past midnight and Elizabeth woke to a scratchy throat and a terrible nightmare. She had been back in her old house, back in the hallway where the sinister man stepped through the shadows with the dagger held above his head. In some dreams, the blade was coated in blood. In others, she could hear her mother's cries for help. Elizabeth bolted upwards, sweat hemming her hairline as she searched the still unfamiliar room for the light-haired stranger. When she couldn't sleep, she decided to walk, in hopes of clearing her mind. Most of the curtains were left open through the main foyer and down the halls, allowing the moonlight to paint the rooms in touches of silver and blue. She walked through the west and into the east wing, where against the pitch of shadows, a shimmer of orange under the east library door grabbed her attention.

The door was left ajar, just wide enough to fit her hand through. She moved forward, placing her hand against the wood before she quietly eased it back. As expected, the library was covered in shadows that were pushed back by the fire coming from the hearth. She craned her head around before pushing the door back just an inch further to get a better look.

Much to her surprise, inside stood a man, close to her age, pacing the room with an open book in his hand. He was dressed in street brown clothes, simple dark pants with a matching vest and the sleeves rolled up to the elbow on each arm. Without seeing his face, Elizabeth felt her pulse quicken. His back was lean but strong, pushing against the fabric as he hunched in his reading. Something primitive surged through her body. An instinct of danger.

He slowed his pace and eventually came to a stop, his lowered head ever so slowly arching upwards to glance over his shoulder at her. All she caught was a glimpse of his eye before the door slammed shut right in her face. She gasped and barely controlled the scream that rushed up from her lungs.

There was no way she was going to sleep tonight.

CHAPTER

SEVEN

AFTER HER SESSION with Harry, Elizabeth wandered back to the library to find a collection of books left unkempt and sprawled out across the desk and on the floor. Most of the books were classic literatures, fairy tales told to children and other mythical folklore. She dared a few minutes inside William's room to find nothing out of the ordinary. As she snooped through his wing, she came across a lone, back door at the end of the hallway. Inside, she was surprised to find a simple guest room with a bed untouched. The curtains were half drawn, allowing only a shaft of light into the room.

She walked over and yanked the curtains open. As the shadows were pushed back, she caught sight of a bag stashed underneath the desk. Inside the bag were more books. The books' contents sparked her interest. Inside one of the books, it spoke of mythical creatures known as Time Collectors. Page after page, there were stories of people's encounters with these supernatural beings and how they delivered death by temptation. The drawings were unpolished and simple, nothing that gave away much detail about what Time Collectors were or what they looked like. The one thing they all had in common was the shadow of death hovering above their head. They looked more like dark puppets with strings being pulled back and forth. She'd almost dismissed them as mere children's storybooks when an image of an all too familiar blade caused her to pause.

She brought the page up closer. It was undoubtedly the same knife she had seen on the night of her mother's death. The handle was sturdy and thick, the barrel seemingly empty except for a collection of cogs spiralled through the center like a twisted spine. With more questions burning inside of her, Elizabeth tore the page and folded it into a square, which she stuffed into her pocket.

ELIZABETH WANDERED BACK to her room, her fingers teasing the paper in her pocket. Her mind raced. The fabric of her reality pulled at the seams, opening new possibilities she hadn't considered before. Was it possible? The question grew fat on her tongue. She darted down the west wing hallway and opened the door into her bedroom. A voice stopped her from taking another step.

"It's rude to touch other people's things." She jumped and clenched her hands to her chest. A lone figure stood by her bedroom window, hands clasped behind his back while he stared out toward the garden. He cocked his head over his shoulder, bearing into her a set of deep, golden-brown eyes.

She whispered, "It's you."

As still as stone, the man merely stood there, eyes bearing into her face as Elizabeth slowly stepped up to him. He was taller than her by at least two feet, enough that his head tilted toward his chest to keep eye contact. His fierce eyes sparked in his concentration, looking beyond her into her most private thoughts.

"We haven't been introduced yet. My name is Elizabeth Blackmore." She extended her hand, which he didn't take.

"Klaus," he answered shortly. "But I am not here to talk. You have taken something of mine." He indicated toward Elizabeth's pockets. There was definitely some sort of presence in the room, stirring the air with static. Even without moving a muscle, Elizabeth felt herself being pulled into him.

"Klaus," she repeated his name. "If you're not busy this afternoon, I would love to sit down and chat with you over tea? I don't want us to get off on the wrong foot. Doctor Wicker has been keeping your presence here a secret...it makes a girl wonder." The muscles in his jaw tightened as he clenched to keep his mouth shut. Every moment sitting under his gaze felt exhausting; his mere presence sucked all the life out of the room. When he didn't speak, Elizabeth pulled the paper out from her pocket. She unfolded it to have one last look, reassuring herself it was the same blade from her memory. "You have so many books about this thing. What is it?"

"A tool," he answered.

Elizabeth twisted her lips. "What type of tool? It doesn't look much like the kitchen blades I've seen. Is it a decorative piece?"

"Nein," he answered again, just as blankly.

Elizabeth turned the paper in her hands, running a finger along the outline of the blade. "What are those books? Are they children's stories? It spoke about a creature they refer to as a Time Collector—"

"They are just stories." His voice carried a thick foreign accent that slurred his speech.

Elizabeth dared to take another step forward, closing the gap between them. A thousand things tore through her at once. The loudest thought left a sense of unease, replaying William's words of warning. There was something unnatural about Klaus, but she couldn't pinpoint what. It was in the way he slanted his chin and how his eyes tightened before he spoke. He watched with a chilling stillness. Carefully calculating.

She licked her lips. "Why are you so interested in something out of a story book?"

Klaus' eyes sharpened; perhaps she was walking into territory he didn't want to explore. "Because I hunt them."

Her heart squeezed in both excitement and dread. Was it possible that a Time Collector had killed her mother? The biggest question still burned on her tongue, *what are Time Collectors?* But she was unable to form the words. "So, they are real? Time Collectors exist?"

His chin dropped as a small smile pressed dimples into his cheeks. "Absolutely."

Overhead, the lights flickered, causing Elizabeth to jerk her head up. When she glanced back down, Klaus now held the piece of paper. She glanced at her hands, noticing they were empty.

"How did you-?"

"It was nice speaking to you, Miss Wicker." He moved toward the door before glancing briefly back at her. "But I must warn you; the next time you feel the urge to touch my things I won't be so kind." He stepped back into the hall and disappeared.

CHAPTER

EIGHT

IGNORING THE UNCERTAIN flutter of her heart, Elizabeth ran toward the east wing. She barged into the guest room but the bag was gone, leaving the rest of the room unscathed. There was nothing left behind, not even a fingerprint among the dust. She turned around before leaving, disappointed.

That night, Elizabeth had waited at the dining room table for William to come home. It was roughly eight o'clock in the evening, the second car gone once more and the streets eerily quiet. It was Harry who told her that William was in the east library, skipping dinner again. Determined, Elizabeth went to the east library before letting herself in.

"Miss Elizabeth?" William looked upwards. "Is something the matter?" He was back at his desk in the far corner, consumed with his books. A single lantern sat by his head.

She took a deep breath so her voice held some authority. "I want to know more about the man staying in this house."

"Harry?" he asked with uncertainty.

Elizabeth shook her head. "The other man. Klaus."

William stood up as if jabbed with a hot poker and slammed two hands against the desk. The pile of papers fell to the ground. "You went against my orders!" His voice strained in his anger. "You were not to approach him!"

"I know and I'm sorry for breaking my promise, but I need to know the truth. Who is he really?" Elizabeth's voice jumped with desperation despite her efforts to stay calm.

It felt too difficult to explain without sounding insane. She had never seen anyone like Klaus, so she couldn't pinpoint what it was exactly that made the hair on her arms stand up. He was different, but different in a way that tore her focus to shreds. It was the type of different that gnawed into her until her sanity snapped.

"Go pack your bags, you are leaving tonight. You can live with a friend of mine; there you can apprentice under her and become a fine seamstress!" He pushed back his chair and rounded the desk.

"I'm not leaving." Her voice rose. "Don't you want to know what really happened to my mother? I think Klaus has the answer."

"What are you talking about?"

"The night of her death, a man went into her room holding a weird looking blade. I recognized that same blade in one of Klaus' books."

William stopped moving immediately, and lifted a shaking hand to his mouth. "A blade?" Fear softened him. Elizabeth slowly edged closer.

"I didn't know what to think. I thought I was crazy."

"Did he see you? The man who went into your mother's room, did he see you?"

Elizabeth looked down to jog her memory. "I called out for him to stop, but he didn't react." In a different breath, she delicately whispered, "What are Time Collectors?"

William's face dropped two shades in color, making him even him paler. "Time Collectors? I've never heard of them."

"I believe a Time Collector killed my mother! I'm not going anywhere, something happened to my mother and I want to know the truth. Please?" Her shoulders dropped as she reached out to grab his sleeve. Desperation painted her in sweat. She dropped her hands before she could grab him, forcing herself to step back in an attempt to collect her composure. To show weakness was like to cut an artery, and she couldn't afford to bleed anymore.

Pained by his own thoughts, William turned back. "If the man went for Lady Ana then he may come back for you and moving towns won't stop him." He rushed to a shelf on the other side of the room before returning with a thick, poorly preserved textbook. "I'll tell you, but you must promise me, *promise me*, this information never leaves the room."

Elizabeth numbly nodded.

"Time Collectors come from mythical stories of an ancient curse placed upon the souls of humans, making them immortal and incredibly powerful." He planted the book down and flipped through the pages. Unlike Klaus' books, there weren't many pictures; the pages were mostly filled with lines of small print. "They are creatures capable of granting wishes to anyone who asks."

"Granting wishes? Are you being serious?" She scrunched her face up to stop from laughing. "So, they're like genies?"

"Not exactly. Genies are the retellings of Time Collectors where spirits live in lamps and grant limited wishes. Time Collectors aren't as glamorous or kind hearted. They are called Time Collectors for a reason; for every wish they grant, they create what they call a contract. In exchange for the wish, the person must pay with their time."

"Their time?"

"Their life expectancy. Every wish has a certain value. Big wishes can cost over thirty years, say for the wish of wealth or fame. You don't know how much it'll cost until after the contract is made." He turned the page where it opened on a similar image of the blade. He pointed at it. "They collect time by stabbing the person and withdrawing the soul through their blood. It doesn't leave any marks on the skin. Time Collectors are so scarce now; many believe they vanished centuries ago."

Elizabeth shook her head. "My mother never made a deal with a Time Collector. I mean, I don't think she did."

"No, you're right. Lady Ana never made the deal. It's actually the whole reason why I had to find Klaus. We need to hunt the Time Collector down and stop him."

"Why would you want to hunt down something that grants wishes? Do you want to kill them or make a contract with them?"

William reeled backwards as if Elizabeth had slapped him. "I will never make a contract with a Time Collector, not even in my darkest moments. It's completely unnatural and foolish to tamper with such dark magic. No one knows what happens to the souls touched by the Time Collectors. The old tales say they perish forever in a land of darkness. I needed Klaus here because normal Time Collectors take the time from the person agreeing to the contract, but there are other Time Collectors known as the corrupted. These Time Collectors grant the wish to one person, but take the time from another."

"So, someone else made a contract and took my mother's time for payment?"

"Exactly."

Her cheeks roasted. "That...that...but why her? Why target my mother?"

William shrugged, exhausted as though he had asked himself that question over a thousand times. "It could have been at random, an unfortunate draw for your mother. It also could have been targeted. I don't know."

Elizabeth wobbled against the desk. Someone had her mother murdered. Confirming what she already suspected didn't ease her. It tightened her rage. "Then what do they look like, the Time Collectors?"

"Unfortunately, that's the tricky part. They look like everyone else."

"Then how do you find them?"

"With a lot of difficulty. Klaus is the expert at this. He's a hunter, so his hunter genetics are wired differently to ours."

"Like telekinesis?"

"How did you know?"

"I witnessed it. He was able to slam a door from across the room. Seemed the only explanation."

William cleared his throat. "Yes, like telekinesis. I'm not sure if it's a new profession or an ongoing family legacy, as old as the myths themselves. He's also incredibly dangerous, like I've been warning you." Elizabeth nodded despite being overwhelmed with the tightness in her chest, remembering how Klaus loomed over her, completely freezing her up. "Time Collectors have a finely tuned survival instinct and a particular type of magic making it almost impossible to kill them."

"Then how do you plan on stopping it then?"

William stepped back and retrieved his suitcase from underneath the desk. "I've been working on a prototype for nearly eight years." The suitcase looked heavy as he placed it on the table. He unlocked the two locks on either side. As the top lifted, he revealed a secret compartment hidden in the cover of the case, where embedded in foam was a golden pistol. William carefully lifted the weapon upwards, which by the shine of its coat appeared to be made out of pure gold. "This pistol is the only thing that can kill a Time Collector. Well, we believe so in theory. We haven't practiced it yet."

"What makes you so sure if you haven't tested it?"

"We have collected the only type of mineral that can penetrate through their natural defense shields. It is a type of gold that isn't affected by their magic. Unfortunately, we only had enough to make one single bullet. The gun is made purposely to fire this bullet—can't have one without the other."

Elizabeth ran her fingers cautiously over the barrel of the gun. "Do you know who is using the corrupted Time Collector then?"

"I believe so, but Klaus informs me the Collector would have many contracts within the city, so we can't just focus on the one suspect. Just because I am telling you all this, doesn't mean I want you out there hunting down Time Collectors. If the Collector saw you, you're only safe here, under Klaus' trained eye." He packed the gun back into its suitcase and placed it carefully underneath the desk.

"Is Klaus even human?" Elizabeth whispered as though the walls could hear her.

William glanced down. "He is human enough."

CHAPTER

NINE

TIME COLLECTORS EXISTED. They were creatures capable of twisting fate, delivering incredible promises and taking time through the point of a blade. Elizabeth found herself infatuated with her father's books, reading as much as she could about these cursed immortals. Most of the stories were similar—people who wished for fame and fortune usually died young. Time Collectors hunted down their contracts mercilessly. It was this reason that Elizabeth guessed why Time Collectors were such hushed secrets; they killed off whomever they worked for. There was close to nothing written about the Time Collector hunters though.

That night she had trouble sleeping. She couldn't pinpoint the problem, maybe it was the cold; maybe it was Klaus and his mysterious persona and how William's forbidden rule made the temptation sweeter. Despite this puzzling thought, Elizabeth had found herself up and walking around the house in the early morning hours. She hadn't realized just how large the Wicker Estate was, consisting of an east and west wing, one armory, two libraries, a large oval pitch with a garden, ten bedrooms, two grand halls, a music room, eight bathrooms and counting. Heat pressed against the door into the east library. Elizabeth paused outside the entrance, her heart in her throat. She pushed against the door panel quietly. It swayed open.

She'd hoped for Klaus to be reading inside again, allowing her a second chance at some one-on-one time. But the room was empty aside from a pile of books scattered around the back desk. *Doctor Wicker must've forgotten to put out the fire.* She walked in and ran her hand along the mantel above the fireplace. The dying flame spat chewed up paper. The pleasant warmth hugged her from the chilly night. She took a book off the top of the pile and sat down in front of the hearth. The words blurred in her drowsiness. Her head dipped and jolted upwards, fighting off sleep. In the matter of only moments, from the time she closed her eyes and bolted up right again, Klaus had appeared, sitting in a chair opposite her.

She flinched and dropped her book. Klaus didn't look at her. Instead, his expression slackened in boredom. Nervous shyness backwashed over her initial excitement. The dread of sounding foolish rendered her momentarily speechless.

With a kind laugh, she feigned shock. "You startled me. You must really be a ghost. I didn't even hear you come in." Klaus sat in his chair, only shifting whenever the page needed to be turned.

"May I ask what has you so captivated?"

Again, he didn't answer.

A thought struck her. "Are you perhaps deaf, I wonder?"

The muscles in his neck tightened. He definitely heard that. Elizabeth brushed down her dress, smiling to herself. "Not deaf, just mute I see. That's quite alright. I enjoy speaking. Doctor Wicker told me briefly about your profession. About the Time Collectors." She scooted over so she was cross-legged and leaned against the stone of the fireplace.

Klaus stopped moving, implying he had also stopped reading. But his eyes didn't shift away from the book. He listened warily.

"He even went as far as calling you an expert. To my understanding, Time Collectors are not an easy creature to prey on. Can you assure me that killing these creatures is possible? Surely the least you can give me is a nod?"

Irritated, he sighed. "*Ja.*"

"It's a miracle! He talks." Elizabeth cheered in mocking enthusiasm. Klaus' glare hardened. "But alas, he does not speak English. I'm afraid I don't know what *ja* means."

His gaze shifted, "Ja means yes."

Shyness crept back into her voice, weakening her tone. "What's that accent? Are you from Germany?"

"Ja."

"How long have you been hunting Time Collectors?"

He turned the page, his eyes back onto the book. "A very long time."

"You can't be any older than twenty-two. Twenty-three max." She tilted her head to try to see his face, which he'd covered with his hand resting in his chin. "You don't talk much, do you?"

"You talk enough for the both of us. An unpleasant trait for someone of your intelligence."

Her smile dropped at his insult. "I'm trying to be polite, something you're clearly not capable of. I thought it'll be fun to know you."

"Fun?" He looked at her. "Why would you think it would be fun?"

"You hunt mythical creatures as a profession. How could that not be fun?"

Elizabeth must have struck a nerve as Klaus leaned back in his chair and snapped the book shut. His face, though it was always serious, seemed to tighten with annoyance.

"Ignorant," he growled before pushing back his chair. He tossed the book to the ground, causing the pile to topple over. "It is not fun. This is not a game."

"I didn't mean it like that," Elizabeth corrected. William was right; he really was dangerous. She could see it by how his eyes flashed in rage, and his hands automatically curled into fists. She felt sick with uncertainty. "Of course, I know this is serious, why else would I want to talk with you? I believe a Time Collector killed my mother."

"He did." Klaus turned and picked up his trench coat from across the back of the chair. He swung it around himself and slipped his arms into the sleeves. "Nikolas."

"W-what?" Elizabeth stuttered after him. "Is that his name? Nikolas?"

"Ja." He whispered before walking toward the door.

"Wait, Klaus?" He slowed enough to crane a look over his shoulder. "Don't tell Doctor Wicker I was here. Okay?" He nodded briefly—well, she hoped he had nodded—before making his exit.

CHAPTER
TEN

WILLIAM STARTED JOINING in with her morning studies. At the beginning, he merely observed, only staying for twenty minutes, but the next day he stayed for an hour. The following morning, he started to chip in with his opinion, making him an hour and a half late to work. He didn't seem to mind, extending his time at home a little bit longer every week. Elizabeth worked on economics. Biology. French. William was always quick to correct her, improving her grammar, her pronunciation, her problem solving. It kept her busy, but not busy enough to forget about Time Collectors, or Klaus. Knowledge built a foundation for her confidence, and soon even she was correcting William on certain topics.

Weeks later, she noticed Klaus' car parked outside. She pressed her nose against the window. A shiver ran through her, prickling under her skin. Her feelings toward Klaus had been clouded with fear and admiration. She brought a hand to her throat where her locket hung, picking away at her thoughts in an attempt at understanding them.

To ease her anxiety, Elizabeth took her violin and headed out toward the music room. She had a feeling where Klaus would be hiding, and though she still felt the itch of curiosity, she didn't want to approach him if it meant he was going to yell at her again. Instead, she played her violin. The crisp melody bounced about the entire room, completely removing her from reality. At times, she would hit an awkward note and she'd growl at herself, tweaking the strings.

"I must apologize!"

"Ah!" Elizabeth jumped in her surprise. She spun around at his familiar voice, surprised just how close Klaus got before announcing his entrance. He paused within a step from her. She clutched the violin to her chest. "Don't you ever knock?"

Klaus straightened his posture, cleared his throat and knocked twice on the table. Elizabeth did not find humor in his joke. "Right, my apologies, again," he said. "I realized I should not have been so hard on you last time. I did not mean to call you unintelligent. That was improper and incorrect of me." Elizabeth glanced around, unsure what to say. Klaus then indicated with a tilt of his chin. "You play beautifully, may I?"

"Apology accepted." She turned back around, her nerves frazzled. He did call her stupid last time, and it was an insult that bounced around her head a lot. Not having an education definitely lowered her self-esteem. Perhaps that's why he said it. He knew she was insecure, and was able to unease her with a comment she couldn't shake off.

Unfazed, Klaus stepped closer. "Handel, *Water Music*, one of my favorites."

Elizabeth clenched up as Klaus hoisted her violin into position under her chin. His fingers were long and slender; the perfect fingers for playing. He then reached over and curved his hand around her free wrist that held the bow, pulling her up toward the strings. Instinctively, she wrenched her hand down and stepped out of her chair.

"What are you doing?"

"I am helping."

"From memory, you wanted nothing to do with me."

Klaus perked an eyebrow. "You look like you could be fun too."

Unamused, Elizabeth squinted at him, prompting Klaus to sigh.

"I know I can be very stand offish. I was rude, inconsiderate and out of line. Please, Miss Wicker, accept my apology. I promise I will be more mindful of my actions in the future."

Elizabeth settled in her chair, hearing the sincerity in his voice. *In the future.* So he planned on interacting with her frequently. "I forgive you."

Klaus smiled. "Thank you. Please, allow me to show you how to play." He took her wrist once more, positioning the bow against the violin's strings.

"I know how to play."

"Then I'll teach you something new." The chill on the back of her neck pulled her entire body as tightly as the strings pulled along the board. He was inches from her, chin against her temple and his breath a dry warmth across her skin. He was far too close and intimate for her comfort. Elizabeth had had boys chase her before, but they always tried to win her favor by flashing cash or bragging about their latest gadgets. Klaus didn't play tricks or try to charm her with pretty objects. "Are you uncomfortable?" he asked.

She shook her head automatically, and then clenched her eyes shut embarrassed. He guided her arm gently. It was an eight-bar piece, which he got her to repeat, guiding her and quickening her tempo until he was able to drop his hand and step away. On her own, Elizabeth kept the tempo going, where Klaus stepped around to a nearby piano and joined in. She felt her heart melt at the shift of the tune. The sweet ring from the piano against her violin's fast chirp was harmonious. Time, which had felt too fast and broken, now slowed around her. Her world calmed beneath the melody.

"I used to play this piece a lot growing up," Klaus explained. His stare shifted beyond the walls and deep into his memory. Klaus abruptly stopped, causing Elizabeth to stumble out of rhythm. He whipped his head toward the door, alerted by a noise.

"What is it?" Elizabeth asked. Klaus immediately shot up and ran out.

TWO DAYS DRAGGED by since she last spoke to Klaus, but there wasn't a moment that passed when his face didn't cross her mind. Every corner she turned, every room she entered, her heart rate picked up, hoping she'd find him. Just as she let her guard down, Klaus appeared with a loud, triumphant cheer.

"There are only a few instances of true brilliance and Sir Wicker has been present for all of them." Elizabeth had been eating alone in the dining room and sat upwards in her chair. He was smiling, his upbeat mood capturing the room.

She smiled back. "Did Doctor Wicker tell you to say that to me?" she joked just as William stepped around the door, following Klaus in.

"Those are his words, not mine."

Elizabeth pursed her lips. She had hoped to hide any familiarity she had toward Klaus from him, in fear he'd send her packing to become a seamstress.

"And yes, I know about your little run-ins. Klaus confessed everything." He gave her a quick frown.

Elizabeth bowed her head, embarrassed. "I'm sorry."

"I didn't realize daughters tend to do the exact opposite of what their fathers say." His lecturing tone shattered with a quick, light laugh. "Guess you really are a Wicker."

Elizabeth perked back up. "I promise to behave better in the future." She then motioned at his formal attire, matching dark blue suit and vibrant gold tie. "What's the occasion?"

"Tonight is the Barricks' annual grand-ball. It had slipped my mind with everything happening, but as society dictates, we're required to go."

"We?" Elizabeth repeated.

"You are my daughter. You are expected to make an appearance to these types of gatherings. A life among the nobles can't be lived behind brick walls. With your transition into high society, it's very important to be seen at these events. With some luck, we may even find you a suitor."

Elizabeth's attention shot back to Klaus at the mention of her finding a suitor. Disappointedly, he didn't seem the least bit fazed.

"I don't know if that is a good idea. I don't know the first thing about these types of parties."

"Parties are networking opportunities. Standard pleasantries mixed with a degree of appropriate social etiquette should suffice." He leaned down to escort her out of her chair.

Reluctantly, Elizabeth pulled back. Appropriate social etiquette was not in the manual for servants at the academy. In the past week alone, she had already knocked the wine glass off the table five times. She couldn't imagine a ballroom packed with judgmental, wine sipping nobles watching her every trip and stumble.

"Will Klaus also be joining us?"

Klaus glanced at William before clearing his throat. "I have business elsewhere, Miss Wicker. Sir Wicker may have found a new lead on the whereabouts of Nikolas."

"How did you find a new lead?"

William fixed his collar. "A healthy heart doesn't just break overnight. There are signs of a Time Collector's influence. Sadly, the Robertson family had to pay the price. Two sons and the grandfather. Though, the grandfather may have been a coincidence. There's a pattern, families belonging to the mines seem to be struck down with a run of misfortune. Klaus is going to check it out. Usually, I would join him, but we have to keep up appearances."

"A new lead on my mother's murderer is far more important than some party," Elizabeth scoffed.

"Party or not, the Time Collector still wouldn't be something you'll worry yourself with," William countered. "Now, upstairs. I've set out an appropriate dress for you to wear with the matching Wicker cufflinks. You must wear the family crest on all formal occasions. You're nobility. It's time you start looking like it."

CHAPTER
ELEVEN

ELIZABETH DRESSED HERSELF in the gown William had prepared, but the sizing was all wrong. He overestimated her waist size and underestimated the space required for her breasts, which left her choking and slipping over the long trail. At least the gentle bronze was a flattering color against her pale complexion. She was also given an elegant gold and white mask that curved around her eyes in the shape of a flattened W. The mask covered up to her forehead, spiking behind into long, feather talons that folded against her pinned hair like a wing. From her gently curled hair down to her jewel covered chest, arms, wrists and leggings, Elizabeth felt like a completely different person. She twirled in front of the mirror, unable to recognize herself.

Her sense of wonder heightened after stepping into the ballroom to the Barricks. It was exactly how Elizabeth had imagined an evening with the noble families would unfold. Even the air felt stuffed with self-importance and expensive wine. Everyone paraded around in large eccentric masks, vaguely concealing their identity. All of the women had their hair curled and styled beneath large brimmed hats with matching necklaces, bracelets, and high heeled shoes all trimmed with expensive silk and silk cufflinks. As they walked, their large puffed dresses trailed behind them in rivers. The men were just as glamourous with top hats ornamented in copper frames and decorative charms. Elizabeth's neck craned back as she walked beneath the massive chandelier that rotated in a slow, steady rotation, its slim curved frame gently rocking the strings of pearls and diamonds dangling below it, making the room sparkle.

In the corner, a band of musicians played, bouncing along with trumpets, saxophones, and a piano. The room buzzed and twirled in its magic. Meeting the nobles as William Wicker's daughter and not a servant was hard to swallow; most of the families perked up their eyebrows unsure how to address her. Elizabeth felt just as awkward. She bowed like a servant. Walked like a servant. The only differences between her and the waitresses handing out finger food were their outfits.

"Miss Elizabeth, will you be okay if I step aside to speak with Sir Grove privately?" She had glued herself to William's arm since walking across the threshold, so she was reluctant to let him leave her behind. She nodded her head anyway, now alone and fully aware how alienated she looked from the rest of the crowd.

To avoid the horrors of small talk, Elizabeth pressed herself to the walls where she could gaze outside at the freckle of the city's lights. The golden city was a busy place, even this late into the night as the gentle roar of the overheard air balloons circled the skies. If she strained her eyes, she could see the tip of her old academy way off into the distance behind the walls separating the rich from everything else. Linking to her reminiscence, the touch of a familiar clammy hand grabbed her elbow.

"Someone needs to tell that doctor he can't put a saddle on a pig and call it a mare." She spun at Arthur's voice.

Her heart raced and she defensively crossed her arms. Nothing tore her down faster than Arthur's belittling stare and he had been tearing her down for years. Even dressed in such wealth did nothing for Elizabeth's self-esteem and with one look, she felt she was back in her old sweaty uniform. It was foolish to think wearing the Wicker crest would deter Arthur. But it *was* different. She wasn't a servant, not anymore. In all her years of running around corners to flee him, she finally didn't have to bite her tongue.

"Same old bark, I guess it's true what they say about old dogs and new tricks," she countered with raised eyebrows, mimicking his condescending tone. "I'm afraid the only one smelling of bacon is you, Beaumontt." She reached out and patted his round stomach. Arthur's golden suit did very little to slim his heavy frame. Not even the black pillow of frilly lace tucked under his chin could hide the chin rolls.

The veins in his neck jumped and for a split second Elizabeth couldn't believe what she'd said. She tensed, expecting his fist to come flying but instead of striking her, Arthur turned his head away in a strained, forced laugh.

"Common, tasteless girls like you don't last long in a lions' den. The fact you think you've escaped me tells me much about your lack of intelligence. You believe you're going to live a life of ease with that doctor. How pathetic." He ran his finger along the strap of her dress and followed the narrow bridge of her collarbone. "This world is mine. I am everything here. And there will be a day where I can finally shatter you into a thousand, tiny, broken little pieces. Not even the doctor can put that egg back together."

"Your fascination with me is the only thing that's pathetic." She snapped back. His eyes glistened with what she could only presume was sadistic joy, noting how his mere touch still made her body recoil.

"You never were a smart little piglet, now were you?"

"Smart enough to escape you."

"But you haven't, that's my point. If you want to survive this world, then you better pucker those lips up. As an apology, you will be present, for my amusement, at the Beaumontt mansion during the Red Moon Festival. I'm sure you know the house I'm referring to, you used to clean the toilets after all." He dug into his pocket to reveal a crisp, white envelope folded over with a red wax stamp sealing it close. Elizabeth eyed the invitation as though he had pulled out a knife. He couldn't be serious. Was he really inviting her to the Beaumontt estate? He must think she's as dumb as a potted plant to agree to that.

Elizabeth laughed, bewildered. "I would rather have my teeth pulled."

Over his shoulder, Arthur clicked his fingers, signalling to someone from across the hall. Darting through the crowds, a maid approached with a glass of wine. The moment she stepped out from between the guests, Elizabeth's world shattered. *Sara*. Sara's hand shook as she passed over the wine, her face carefully turned away as though trying to hide her fading black eye.

Elizabeth's look of horror must've pleased him, as Arthur took the glass and smashed it across Sara's face. Blood splattered across the white tiles as Sara did everything in her power not to scream. The surrounding nobles glanced away, their social protocols keeping them quiet. Elizabeth's body locked up. Specs of red splattered Elizabeth's dress and cheek. The swell of blood coloring Sara's face stunned her. Sara cowered away, protecting her face as Arthur dropped the remaining glass stem to the ground.

Elizabeth couldn't speak. She couldn't even blink. Her eyes swelled with angered tears, but her rage paralyzed her. Arthur smirked. "So clumsy. Not to worry, the servant will clean it up."

He looked at Sara, waiting for her to drop to her knees and sweep the remaining shards into her hands. Instead, Sara turned and ran back into the crowd. Elizabeth's stomach lurched her forward with a heavy dry retch. She wanted to chase her friend. She wanted to puke. She wanted to push Arthur out the window and slash that smile off his smug, rotten sadistic face. She wanted to cry, scream, and use her bare hands to hurt him. Instead, she simply stood there. Stunned.

"I'm sure we have an understanding." Arthur could see the hesitancy in her eyes. He winked and turned to leave. "Try and wear something not so embarrassing."

Her understanding of the world came into focus. Men like Arthur Beaumontt did not vanish. His cruelty had no limits, and even if it meant costing her life, she was going to stop him. Her mind clouded. Common sense hazed behind it. As Arthur turned away, Elizabeth picked up a shard of glass. She clutched the piece in her palm, adrenaline deadening her fingers that didn't feel the edges cut her.

She reared her arm upwards, her vision spy glassed onto the exposed flab on Arthur's turned neck when a hand grabbed her. Immediately, she tried to wretch her arm free and turned to a servant in a black fitted tuxedo. He glared harshly down at her and her body shrunk beneath his shadow. Even through her silk gloves, she could feel the crisp heat of his grip.

"Unhand me!" Elizabeth pulled away. He didn't shift despite her yanking, his expression unaltered until Lady Claudia approached.

"Miss Wicker? What's going on?"

Elizabeth twisted around, her humiliation overshadowed by rage. Lady Claudia's mask only covered a quarter of her face. The frame covered her left eye as the rest of the ornament curled upwards in mimic of a royal crown. Her face was perfection, from her apple green eyes, gentle blonde hair, and natural pouted lips down to her cream-colored skin.

Even scowling, she was beautiful. "Get out of our sight." She ordered and immediately the butler released Elizabeth's wrist. Before she could speak again, Elizabeth ran. Arthur was long gone, lost in the tightly packed suits. Elizabeth shoved her way toward the exit. She felt breathless. Her chest tightened, pain scratching at each sharp breath.

"Elizabeth?" A pair of arms grabbed her and pulled her into his chest. She almost collapsed out of exhaustion as William gently, and carefully, took her out from the crowd. "What happened? You've got blood on you! Are you hurt?"

Elizabeth shook her head, her thoughts spinning emotions too raw for her to grab. "Sara!" One of the maids, Arthur cut her face badly! Please, help her. Help her."

"Where did she go?"

Elizabeth pointed vaguely toward the way Sara had bolted. "That way."

William looked up, before nodding. "I'll look after her. I'll call the car around to take you home. I'll make sure your friend is okay." Elizabeth shook her head, unable to move. William forced her into a stand. "Go, this isn't a discussion."

He ran out toward the front and waved his car around. The driver stepped out, opening the door as Elizabeth disappeared into the backseat. She watched William race back into the mansion, rolling up his sleeves though preparing for surgery. She wanted to stay, she wanted to make sure Sara was fine, but the car pulled out of the driveway too.

Right then, watching the mansion shrink through the back window, Elizabeth promised to never be so helpless. Not ever again.

CHAPTER
TWELVE

ONCE SHE WAS home, Elizabeth paced the foyer in anxious strides. Hours ticked by, but sleep never crossed her mind. Flashes of red kept popping up, twisting her stomach in her disgusted rage. Over and over her hands would form fists but with nothing to punch. Heartburn fired up like a hot bullet. Worst of all was the guilt she couldn't swallow. *It was her fault Sara was targeted.*

The front door kicked open, startling Elizabeth. William's shadow stretched across the foyer tiles. Behind him, as the door came to a close, Elizabeth caught sound of distant sirens.

She rushed to him. "Is Sara okay?"

William smoothed his hands gently on Elizabeth's shoulders. "Your friend is alright. Nothing but some cuts and grazes."

Her chest deflated, greatly relieved. It was William's stiffened grip that gave away his anxiety. "What is it?"

"There's been another incident. With the Time Collector."

"Another one? What happened?"

William shook his head, running his dried muddy hands through his hair. Now that she looked closely, his entire suit was covered in dirt. "It wasn't his fault. There was nothing he could do."

He? Who is he? Elizabeth thought on it for a moment, before realising, "Are you referring to Klaus?"

The door swung open as Klaus charged in with his shoulders hunched. He walked past them, stormed up the stairs and barricaded himself in the east library.

William glanced after him. "I'm going to have a shower. You should rest. It's been a long night." William took to his room.

Instead of returning to her own chambers, Elizabeth followed Klaus to the library. Inside, the fire pit had cooled as she wrestled the door open, looking inwards to find it empty. Through the dead silence of the house, she heard something rattle and floorboards groan near the back of the room. The noise led her toward a lone door she hadn't noticed before near the back wall of the library.

She reached out to twist the handle, but paused at the sound of a loud thump. She hesitated, wondering if this was where Klaus hid during the day. Elizabeth ignored her better judgment and let herself in.

Aisles of books narrowed the space in front, forcing Elizabeth to turn sideways to walk through the room. The air was thick with dust, carrying with it a scent of damp wood. The banging of furniture against floorboards continued as Elizabeth quickened her steps, reaching the end of the aisle where it opened up to a dark attic. There were old, neglected couches, chairs, tables, books and frames stashed along the walls. Piles of boxes were stacked on top of each other high enough to almost touch the roof. Every time a loud bang sounded off, the stacks would rattle with the threat of tipping over.

"Klaus?" Elizabeth called out. The further she walked, the more she couldn't see beyond her shoes. Her arms panned out open in front of her, fingers spread trying to see with her hands. The outline of Klaus started to appear among the dense shadows. He was panting hard with two hands propped against a desk, his head bowed low.

Elizabeth's breath trembled. Along with the dark, the cold tightened ropes around her body, making her clumsy and stiff. In her blindness, she tripped over a box and fell into a bookcase, causing it to tip forward, spitting books from its shelves. Luckily, Klaus spun and caught the bookcase before it could fall.

"What are you doing?" he barked.

Elizabeth scrambled upwards. "Sorry, it's just so dark in here. Are you okay?"

There was a grunt as Klaus pushed the bookcase back into place. "You shouldn't have followed me here!"

"I want to know what happened."

"What do you think happened? I was too late! He got away." Klaus turned back toward the table and slumped over, resting on his palms.

Elizabeth paused briefly. "Did someone die tonight?" Klaus didn't speak, but he didn't need to. "You can't be so hard on yourself."

"Don't try to comfort me." Klaus jerked away from her. "This is my fault."

"How is it your fault?"

"I couldn't stop him." He exhaled in a low, angered sigh. "I was right there, and still..."

"The fastest way to destroy yourself is to take reasonability for somebody else's actions." Elizabeth stepped around the books and gently placed her hand against his shoulder. The warmth from his skin tingled her fingers.

Klaus turned his chin away. "You don't understand."

"I think I might, a lot more than you think. Before I arrived here, there was a man who was interested in buying me from the academy. I would've become his slave, a thing for him to torture. I was so scared of him that I jumped at the first chance I could to get away. And it is because of my small-minded cowardice that my best friend is now the one in his hands. Of Arthur Beaumontt. Because I wanted to save myself from his cruelty, I didn't think what that would mean for others."

"You were just a servant to be sold. You had no choice who bought you." Klaus tore away from her. Elizabeth took a step back.

"What have you got to be ashamed of? You hunt Time Collectors, the things that do these terrible things to people."

"Time Collectors are merely tools; they just obey. Nikolas is *my* problem. It's my one purpose in life. And I can't believe I've failed again." He pushed off the table. "You should go. Sir Wicker will not be happy knowing you are in here with me."

Angered, she wrenched her hands down to her side. "Stop it! Stop telling me what to do. I am so sick of being the helpless one here."

"If you want to be useful then stay out of my way." He turned to leave, but Elizabeth sidestepped to block him.

She pressed her finger to his chest. "Nikolas killed my mother. If you really are in charge of stopping him, then it is your fault she's dead." She swallowed to dislodge the tremble in her voice. "If you are this tormented by your guilt then I am the person you should be trying to appease. Only I can relieve you of that guilt."

Klaus jerked around at her comment. "What can I possible offer you that will grant your forgiveness?"

"Teach me how to fight."

The suggestion caught Klaus off guard, "What? Why?"

"For many reasons, but right now I need to stop Arthur."

Klaus straightened his posture. "You are willing to emotionally blackmail me to learn fighting technics?" She nodded. Klaus smiled. "You...continue to surprise me Miss Wicker."

In a fluid side step, he managed to get around her and walk toward the door. Elizabeth spun toward him. "So?"

"So what?"

"Will you teach me?"

Through the darkness, she heard him slow and stop. "See you tomorrow, Elizabeth."

CHAPTER

THIRTEEN

T HE NEWS FROM the previous night had already hit the radio podcasts. A mud avalanche had wiped out thirteen houses, completely crushing the families inside as they slept. It happened within moments. The sturdy boulders somehow shifted from their beds before ploughing down shacks, trees, roots and bricks onto the houses huddled below. It happened after midnight, roughly the same time they had left the party. The slopes were far on the other side of the city, far enough that she couldn't hear the devastation, aside from the ringing of sirens.

Elizabeth rolled over and touched her fingertips to her mouth. She was underestimating the power of Time Collectors. In a matter of seconds, he had killed over twenty people and made it look like an accident. A person capable of delivering such swift death to so many…was it brave or foolish to hunt them?

After her tutoring session, Elizabeth met up with Klaus within the hidden storage room at the back of the east library. Klaus appeared to be more relaxed since the previous night. His hair was swept back and his sleeves rolled to allow more movement. The curtains were pulled back, letting sunlight illuminate the whole room.

"First lesson in attacking is self-defense." Klaus loosened his collar and pulled at his tie so it hung lower down his chest. He stepped up to Elizabeth. "If you are ever grabbed by the wrist, you can rip free by pulling at the weakest point in the grip. The weakest point is where the tip of the thumb and fingers meet." He demonstrated by placing her hand to his wrist then pulling his hand out by forcing her thumb back. "Now you try."

He grabbed her wrist and immediately Elizabeth felt just how weak she was in comparison. She followed his instructions closely, but even so, she struggled to pull her wrist free. If Klaus was really attacking her, she would've been killed by now. She repeated the maneuver until she was confident enough to pull her wrist out of his grip. Her skin had been rubbed raw. They continued practising different defense stances, practising long into the afternoon. It had just ticked over to the afternoon when Elizabeth found herself unable to stay focused.

Her mind buzzed with questions. "How did you and my father meet?"

The sudden question caught Klaus off guard. He growled, disgruntled. "Concentrate!" Promptly, he stepped forward to grab her, initiating an attackers approach. Elizabeth sidestepped around him.

"I'm curious. You're not exactly an ordinary person and you don't seem the type to be out at fancy socials."

"Sir Wicker met me on one of his travels." Klaus turned to grab her shoulder. Elizabeth slapped his hand away, pretending to deliver an elbow to Klaus' nose. None of her hits made contact as she moved in slow, concentrated steps to ensure she got the technique correct.

"He had said he had gone looking for you specifically. Do a lot of people know you hunt Time Collectors?"

"Nein."

"Then what about your family? They must be concerned considering you're so far away from home?"

"Elizabeth, stop!"

"Have you actually met a nice Time Collector? How did you know they existed? Who taught you how to hunt? Is it a family tradition? Do you have siblings who also hunt?"

Klaus stepped around her, capturing Elizabeth by the wrist and pinning her arm so fast behind her back she yelped. She stumbled off balance, only being held up by Klaus' awkward hold.

"Concentrate. You are not concentrating!" he snarled as Elizabeth squirmed in his grip. He abruptly let her drop so she crashed onto her knees. He turned away, walking over to get his coat. "If you're not serious, then I am leaving."

Just as annoyed, Elizabeth rolled over and clambered to her feet. "Geez, Klaus, what's your problem? A simple, *I don't want to talk about it*, would suffice."

"You're obviously not ready for this. You're wasting my time."

"I am ready. I want to learn, Klaus. Just wait a moment, would you?" She reached out to grab him. Klaus knocked her hand away.

"Nein. No more. This was a bad idea."

Elizabeth crossed her arms arrogantly. "Fine, then I won't forgive you for my mother."

He frowned at her. "I won't allow you to manipulate me."

"I am desperate. Please? Klaus, please?" When he didn't respond, Elizabeth changed her tone back to yelling. "Regardless if you train me or not, I am going to take Arthur Beaumontt down. I won't let him hurt my friend anymore. I don't care if it ends up killing me, I will do what is right."

Klaus stopped, spun around, and flicked her forehead. Shocked, Elizabeth slapped her palm to her head. "What are you doing?"

"Even if it kills you? Do you have no love for those around you? Throwing away your life so easily? You do not respect anything. That is real selfishness."

"Selfish? How is that selfish?"

"You only think about yourself. You are so willing to hurt those around you through your carelessness, I thought you were better than that. Do you really think your mother would want this from you?"

"My mother is dead, so it doesn't matter now does it?" She snapped back.

Klaus twisted his lips to the side, disappointed. "Do not dismiss the dead so quickly. They still matter."

Elizabeth paused. She was surprised at her cruel comment, and lifted her fingers to her lips. "You...you are right. I am sorry, I don't want to be selfish. But, I can't let him continue hurting her. So will you please help me? Please?"

Klaus stepped closer. "Beating up a boy won't get your friend back. I know what kind of man you are dealing with. Ego is his biggest downfall. If you challenge him in front of his friends, he won't be able to back down. Make it a bet, winner gets the girl."

"And that'll work?"

"If you train well, ja. He will try to cheat, but we will ensure he loses. If he doesn't keep his promise, you can always send me in to... negotiate."

THE STRENUOUS EXERCISE on Elizabeth slowly took its toll on her heart. She had to take regular breaks, electing not to share with Klaus the truth about why she had to stop. She feared he'd react much like her father. It was enough William looked at her at though she was one sneeze away from shattering, she didn't need it from Klaus too. With his guidance, she trained harder than before, determined to never see that look of sympathy on Klaus' face. As they spent their evenings together, weeks into their routine, she noticed him change. It was subtle at first. A joke here. A relaxed smile there. It wasn't until she managed to trip him over, pinning him underneath his own weight that the change made sense. He was proud of her.

On their days off, they would play music together. She cherished these moments deeper than anything. Regardless if she had stumbled too many times and Klaus had lost his temper, they would always meet up to relax with music. Klaus found himself unable to step away from Elizabeth's company. He hadn't thought just how dangerous it was for him to get attached, for the both of them. On her time alone, Klaus would often find her in the music room, her stand propped up by the window and her silhouette bathed in gentle white light. He would stand by the doorframe and watch.

When she eventually spotted him, she would ease her violin down and wave him over to join her. Even at the piano, Klaus found his eyes turning away from the keys. When she played, it was as if she became a different person. Her elbows softened, her lips would gently part, and her nearly closed eyes fluttered in thought. There was something about the violin, when she played and turned her cheek against her shoulder, it was as though she was shielding away. It teased Klaus to look closer. Pay more attention to her than he already did. He had missed seeing this side of humanity. In moments like these, forever wasn't long enough.

CHAPTER

FOURTEEN

ARE YOU READY to tell me now?"

It had been weeks since they first started their training. They were back in the room behind the library, which had become their usual meeting place. Klaus was by the window, pulling back the curtains to let the little sunlight they had into the room. The heavy clouds outside thickened, creating an unbroken smear of gray across the sky. He wasn't surprised by her questions this time.

"Why is this so important? Can't you accept that your father and I are friends?" Klaus turned back to her and cocked an eyebrow, playfully grinning. Elizabeth shrugged.

"I don't know anything about you, aside from the fact you're German and you hunt Time Collectors. Oh, and you play the piano and violin wonderfully. Yet, you know everything about me. I don't think it's fair."

"I don't know everything about you," he corrected. "I don't know about your mother. I don't know about your siblings, or your life before you came here. So, technically, it is fair."

Elizabeth leaned back on her elbows. "You could always ask. I would answer you."

He sighed lightly. "Okay, what do you want to know?"

"Have you killed a Time Collector before?" She straightened up.

"Ja."

"Are you serious? What happened? How did you do it?"

Klaus grinned. "Nein. You've had your turn. Now, answer my question, the day of your bidding, if Sir Wicker had never come to get you, what would you have done?"

Her face tightened. "I...well..." The answer was hard to say aloud. Elizabeth glanced out the window, her mind returning to the moment Harold Beaumontt walked into her house. She remembered the poison vial. Holding her head under the water. How the shattered glass glistened across the bathroom floor. She knew her answer, but was too afraid to say it out loud.

"I apologize, that was rude of me to ask such a thing," Klaus interrupted her thoughts. "Sir Wicker would never have allowed you be sold to the Beaumontt's."

Elizabeth smiled weakly. "You and my father?"

Klaus straightened up his posture, his chin lifted up with admiration. "I respect your father, he is a great man with noble causes. I also trust him completely. I know your father will never make a deal with a Time Collector."

"How would you know something like that?"

"Because he was given the chance."

Her jaw dropped open. "My father had the chance to make a contract with a Time Collector?"

Klaus growled gently. "You're drooling."

"I mean, it's kind of just...and he said no?"

"If he couldn't resist temptation, even at the cost of his own life, then I would never have joined him," Klaus said casually before turning back toward the empty room.

"If you didn't have to pay time for your wishes that would be amazing. I know what I would wish for."

Mildly interested, Klaus asked, "Ja? What's that?"

"When I was younger I used to dream of owning this particular soft wood violin. I would walk past it every day to work." She said as she trailed her finger along the windowsill. A moment passed, darkening her thoughts. "But above all else, I would want my mother back. I would want her to be happy."

Klaus' voice dropped, "You wouldn't be able to afford such a wish."

"I said if we didn't have to pay for it." She rolled her eyes. "What would you wish for, Klaus?"

"Nothing," he answered automatically.

"Nothing? There's nothing you wished you had? Come on, humor me."

He sighed. "Liberty."

"Liberty?" She raised one eyebrow. "What do you mean?"

He pushed off the wall in a burst of energy. "Let's change the topic. When do you confront this boy?"

Elizabeth turned around also, her nerves bubbling at the reminder. "The Red Moon Festival. That's almost in a week's time."

"I don't trust him not to play dirty, so you will need something to protect yourself." Klaus reached over and pulled a suitcase out from underneath one of the tables. It was William's, the one that hid the pistol. Elizabeth licked her lips nervously.

"Won't he notice the pistol is missing?"

"You won't be bringing this one with you, of course. I'm just going to show you how to handle it." Klaus stepped around so he hovered behind Elizabeth before reaching down to cup her wrist. He placed the handle into her palm before securing her grip around it. Her heart accelerated at Klaus' closeness. Smiling, Klaus added, "Don't worry. It's empty."

He brought her arm upwards before placing her other hand on the bottom to secure her hold. She instinctively closed one eye and stuck her tongue out. Klaus went over the basic dynamics of the pistol. He explained the trigger, the barrel, the reload cylinder, and how to switch the safety lock off. He explained where to look when aiming and how to keep her balance with a wide stance, stopping the recoil from throwing her off. Elizabeth's mind wandered off, slipping between Klaus' cheek pressing against her own and listening to his instruction on line positioning. Every time he spoke, the purr of his voice sent tingles along the nape of her neck where she'd pulled her hair to the side to expose the skin.

"Good, you're a natural." He took the pistol off her and loaded it with metal bullets from the case. "Now, we will train with a loaded gun."

"Wait? Am I ready for this?"

Klaus chuckled. "As long as you don't shoot at me, you will be fine." As he finished loading the gun, the phone inside the library rang. He placed the gun on the table and went out to answer it. "*Guten tag*, Sir Wicker. How can I help you? Ja?" He nodded a few times at the receiver's muffled voice. Elizabeth watched his expression. Klaus put the phone back into its cradle before looking apologetically over at her.

"Let me guess, Doctor Wicker requires your assistance?" She glanced down. "And I am to remain locked up here like some fancy prisoner?"

Klaus' upper lip curled in a smile. "Actually, he requires your assistance. He wants to meet you for lunch."

"Pardon?" Elizabeth's cynical smirk dropped. "This is the first time he's invited me out for lunch. I–I better get changed!"

"I will escort you," Klaus offered.

"Thank you. I would like that." Elizabeth smiled as she turned on her heel and made a quick dash for the door.

CHAPTER
FIFTEEN

KLAUS ACCOMPANIED ELIZABETH down the leisurely walk to William's office. The gentle spit of rain became heavier as Klaus popped open the umbrella, offering his arm. Elizabeth hooked her arm with his. He squeezed her close to ensure none of the droplets would hit her head. It was quiet out. The crowds that usually littered the markets had scurried home, purses over their heads to protect their styled hair from uncurling. Out of the corner of her eye, Elizabeth caught sight of Sara shielding herself underneath a canopy. She stopped, and reeled backwards to get a better look. Sara must have seen Elizabeth at the same time, as she excitedly got onto her tiptoes and waved Elizabeth down.

"Oh my, that's Sara! Klaus, do you mind going ahead and letting my father know I'll be a few minutes late?" Elizabeth asked. Klaus hesitated for a brief moment, but slowly nodded before handing over the umbrella and continuing on without her. He stopped to check on her twice, as if in debate with himself, before stepping into the side street toward William's workplace. Elizabeth ran to Sara and greeted her with a firm hug.

"Sara, I've been so worried. Have you not received my letters?" Elizabeth stepped back and gently cupped Sara by the chin, lifting her face up. The cuts were gone, leaving soft, pink scars over her eyebrow, forehead, and left cheek where the glass had shattered. She eased Elizabeth's hands down, embarrassed by her slight disfigurement.

"I am okay, please don't worry. Sir Wicker is an excellent doctor. Arthur hasn't laid a hand on me since that night, and I've been taken into the direct care of Lady Claudia. Governor Beaumontt was so mad he banished Arthur from approaching me ever again. You must remember I cannot reply to your letters, Elli. Though, I do love reading about your adventures."

Elizabeth's heart sang. "Of course, I'm sorry. I am relieved you are out of Arthur's reach at least. I promised to storm the streets if he dared touch you again."

"Always so dramatic. But I must apologize for our last encounter, I didn't mean to ruin your special night. I wanted to say how absolutely breathtaking you looked in that gown. The collars look so elegant on you."

Elizabeth gingerly touched the collar, her smile weakening with shame. When she walked around in such clothes, standing next to Sara, who wore the common rags of a maid, she felt guilt expand inside her. "Please don't apologize, Sara. You know those parties mean nothing to me. Plus, these things are always itchy; it's really not as great as they pretend it to be."

Sara chuckled. "Do you mind walking with me? I have to get down the street, but I don't want to get Lady Claudia's coat wet." Sara motioned with a tilt to the golden coat folded over her arms.

"Of course." Elizabeth grinned as they descended down.

"I noticed you were walking with someone, are you sure he won't mind?"

"Not at all. I'm meeting up with Sir Wicker for lunch. He was escorting me."

"Is he a suitor perhaps?" Sara wiggled her brows in Klaus' direction.

"No, not a suitor, unfortunately. That is Klaus, Sir Wicker's apprentice. He's been staying at the Wicker mansion for a while. I'll introduce you next time. He is much dreamier up close."

"Klaus? What an exotic name. Must be a smart man to be wooing the rich doctor's daughter," Sara teased.

"Stop it!" Elizabeth blushed, playfully nudging Sara away. "I will be honest with you, I am fascinated with him, but he doesn't seem the type to concern himself with girls."

"Concern himself with girls? Oh, do you mean he rather the company of men?"

Elizabeth's cheeks burned. She hadn't thought of that possibility. He was always trailing around William's heels. Maybe there was something there she had overlooked with her own fantasying.

"Maid!" A voice barked. "We don't pay you to gossip out on the streets—" Elizabeth froze as Arthur Beaumontt walked out from the pub house opposite them. He stopped abruptly, and his smile curled. "Is that the Wicker whore I see? Look, boys, this is the maid I was telling you about. The ugly trout that thinks she's above us." Behind him followed three other men, all from noble families and all mimicking Arthur's curdled grin. They swayed as they walked, suggesting they'd been drinking. "Go back to the house, maid! You're not needed here," Arthur barked.

"What...b-but—" Sara glanced wearily at Elizabeth.

"I said, go back!" Spit sprayed as he shouted.

Elizabeth took Sara by the shoulder and ushered her along. "Just go, Sara, don't make him mad." She felt Sara pull against her. "Go, I'll be fine." She forced Sara to take the umbrella. "I'll see you later."

With a final push, Sara sprinted back to the house. Elizabeth turned back to Arthur, crossing her arms as the rain seeped through her clothes. She eyed all four of them, carefully aware how close they stood to her. "You really are a twisted creature, Beaumontt. Is hitting girls the only way for you to feel manly? Not surprised, there are a lot of rumors about your lack of manliness, after all." She prayed her voice didn't waver. The last thing she wanted was to present Arthur with a chance to dominate her. The rain had driven most of the residents inside, leaving the streets bare. Her jaw tightened, concerned.

He grinned. "I make bitches like her choke on my manliness if it serves me."

"Well, people do tend to choke on small things." She attempted to step around them only to have her path blocked. She took a quick step back, alarm bells flaring. "Even a pea-brained idiot like yourself wouldn't do anything in the middle of the streets. Like it or not, I'm a Wicker now. I'm nobility. You can't touch me!" The words felt hollow, untrue. She could see if in the exchange of their smirks even they didn't believe she had such a title.

"Oh, is that so? Well, I don't see any witnesses here. All I see is one skinny, stupid maid prancing around with a stolen last name. No one sees a noble woman when they hear the name Elizabeth Wicker, but a joke and the pathetic attempts of a lonely old man trying to buy himself a whore to dress up. Let me remind you of exactly what you are."

Arthur reached out to her, snatching Elizabeth's wrist and hauling her in. In one fluid motion, Elizabeth was able to twist her arm free, as practiced, before swinging her elbow into his nose. She felt her swing connect and the bone snap. Before she could run past, the wet weather made the bricks slippery. She skidded out and fell. Arthur cupped his bloodied nose, his eyes flaring with rage. She had given him enough incentive to attack. They created a wall of bodies around her.

"Get away from me!" Elizabeth screamed. They shoved her against the wall.

"Hold her down! Cover her mouth!"

Elizabeth struggled in their hands, using every muscle to thrash and tear away. Her throat was pinned beneath one of the boy's forearms, forcing her chin up. She clawed at his arm, desperately trying to inhale.

The other man grabbed her arms and held them above her head. He positioned his knee to part her legs.

The clouds above their heads clashed with thunder, covering their grunting as they feverishly tried to unbutton her blouse. Each breath became hoarse. Her chest convulsed as pain seized along her jaw, making it impossible to call for help. In a matter of seconds, Elizabeth felt her body painfully clench. Dizziness spun the world around her. Her left arm numbed. Her chest felt crushed beneath the weight of a concrete slab.

Everyone but Arthur let her go. Pins and needles pulled up her neck, spreading across her chest and shoulders. In her darkening vision, she spied two men sprinting down the alleyway toward them. One of them was Klaus. He moved so fast he was a mere blur. He tore Arthur back by the shoulder, slamming him onto the pavement. In the same movement, he caught one of the boy's lunges and snapped the man's wrist.

Shock coursed through the injured man, followed by painful howls. The three of them scrambled to get away from Klaus' reach. Elizabeth's body flashed between hot and cold. She slid to the ground. William rushed over and dropped to his knees, hoisting Elizabeth up.

"Elizabeth? Elizabeth!" Warm hands cupped her flushed cheeks. "Klaus, you have to help me! Do something!"

Pressure intensified against her temples. She lost consciousness and felt her body collapse into waiting arms. The unbearable pain abruptly broke into tingles. It soothed her, calming the shudders from her strained muscles. Darkness followed. In her subconscious, a rough current seemed to pull her under black water. She fell into the cold emptiness. Death. It felt like death, or the second before death could take her out of this world. Death would tear her soul from her body. Only death could stop her heart. All she could do was wait, so she waited.

CHAPTER

SIXTEEN

Tick. Tick. Tick. Tick. Tick. Tick.

COLORS SHARPENED. THE piercing bells of ticking cogs stirred her awake. Prickles ran up and down her body, sparking her into consciousness. When her eyes fluttered open, Elizabeth was back at home, sheets tucked up to her armpits and her hair damp from the rain. Immediately, she bolted upwards and clasped a hand to her heart. There was no pain, no tightness of struggle. *How is this possible?* The last thing she remembered was fear. A cold shower of fear pouring into her chest until the point of unconsciousness. Her body failed, rolling her eyes back into submission. Yet, here she was. There was no discomfort, no twitch or uneasy flutter. In the stillness, she inhaled a deep breath, closed her eyes and strained her ears. Undoubtedly, there it was, the ticking. It didn't pulse anymore; it just ticked. When she checked her chest for any surgical scars or bruises, there was nothing there.

Lightning and thunder tore through the skies, flooding the streets with dark water. Elizabeth trembled as she glanced at the door, unsure if she was dreaming. She noticed her necklace was missing. It must have fallen off during her struggle with Arthur. The memory left an awful taste in her mouth. Arthur Beaumontt. The monster. Perhaps her heart condition had saved her this time.

"Elizabeth?" She turned to see William standing beside her bed. His shoulders slouched in his relief. "You're awake."

"Sir Wicker? What happened?"

"You had a heart attack, but you're okay now." He sat down on the bed beside her. His face and tone hardened. "I will not let those thugs get away with what they did to you. Arthur Beaumontt will be brought to justice."

Tears threatened to spill. She felt incredibly embarrassed, but wasn't sure why. She didn't want to be seen like that. She didn't want her name associated with his, in any way, even as his victim. Elizabeth took a deep breath, swallowing down the fear. "I'm okay," she whispered. "You got there before anything could happen." She continued to rub her chest, unable to block out the sound of the foreign ticking.

William noticed her anxious rubbing and eased his hand onto her shoulder. "I'm sorry. I didn't mean to let that happen. At least now you're never going to have to worry about your heart condition again."

"I won't?"

"Not anymore. But, I'm afraid I can't stay here. I need you to continue my work. I will leave instructions to how to run the manor. Everything will be fine, this is just something I have to do." He promptly stood up and turned away as though pained by his own words.

Lost, Elizabeth reached out to grab him. "Wait? Pardon?"

"Harry is staying behind in my place and will help with anything you may need. I've also contacted my sister; Margaret, she lives on the other side of the country but she's aware of the situation."

"W-What situation?" Elizabeth managed to stutter out.

William swallowed fearfully, stopping by the doorframe as she kicked out the sheets. "I am so sorry, Elizabeth. I'm afraid I've done the unforgiveable."

"What are you talking about?"

"Your heart was in a more serious condition than I thought. You died because of my negligence."

Elizabeth hesitated from taking another step. "I died? That can't be possible…" Disbelief gripped her.

"It was the only way. I couldn't lose you." He lowered his head, ashamed. Outside the crashes of white lightning fired across the walls in a snapshot. "Your heart was too damaged. I had to replace it."

"You…you took out my heart?" Her hand shot to her chest. "But, there are no scars. No bruises…how is that possible?"

"With dark, unlawful magic, and a selfish man willing to pay the ultimate price."

Her world froze. It couldn't be. "You made a contract?"

Grief crossed his eyes as William gently cupped Elizabeth's cheeks and soothed his thumb across her skin. "I never got to say just how proud of you I am. I want you to wear our family name with pride and never let anyone make you think you're unworthy of the best."

She cupped her hand along his own, tears pressing to the surface. "You're my father. You have to stay here. You're all I have left. Whatever contract you made, we can fix it."

A soft gasp escaped his lips. He pulled her into his chest, cupping her neck and kissing the crown of her head. "That's the first time I've heard you call me that." A sharp ring from the phone down in the study caused William to drop his hands. "I have to answer that. I'll only be a moment." He stepped toward it but then stopped, remembering something. "Don't go near Klaus, Elizabeth." He returned and grabbed her shoulders to ensure she paid attention. "I've betrayed his trust. He is not a friend anymore. Promise me, if he returns for whatever reason, you will shoot him."

He pushed what seemed to be a long thimble into her palm before easing her fingers closed. It was chilled and cold to the touch. When she glanced down, the golden nugget was no larger than an ordinary bullet.

"What? Why?" The phone ring was a constant scream within the dark mansion.

William nervously checked over his shoulder then down at his pocket watch. "I really have to answer that. Please, wait here."

As he rushed off, Elizabeth was left speechless. She placed the bullet on the table next to her, unable to look at it. Her back hit the wall before she slid down in a state of exhaustion. How could it be possible? *I must be dreaming.* It was the only reasonable explanation. William would never make a contract. When did he have time to find a Time Collector? It had to be something else.

There was a loud bang of the front door being kicked open followed by the crash of thunder. Elizabeth sat up, alerted to the commotion, before creeping out into the hallway. Looking down from the stairwell, she could see into the empty main foyer entrance below. The flash of lightning reflected off a set of wet footprints left across the tiles.

Cautiously, Elizabeth went down to the ground level, peering down at the footprints then over at the front door swinging back and forth with the thrashing winds. Every now and again, a flash of lightning would snap, spraying the harsh white across the entrance. As she glanced over her shoulder, just as the lightning passed, she caught sight of Klaus' back walking down the hall toward William. She called out to him, but he slowed only enough to glare in her direction. Without a word, he stepped into the study. She could still hear William speaking obliviously on the phone and raced after them. She tried the door handle only to find it locked. She crouched by the study door so she could peek through the gap between the door and its frame.

"Was it worth it?" Klaus' voice cracked in his rage. She couldn't see Klaus, but she could see William as he bolted upright from behind his desk. He slammed the phone down, ending the conversation.

"You must understand."

"Nein." Klaus spoke near the door where Elizabeth crouched. She inhaled her breath, trying to be as silent as possible.

"Listen, I'm sorry, but I couldn't let her die. I couldn't."

"You promised me."

"I know, but she has to live. She has a right to live a long and healthy life. That's worth every sacrifice."

Annoyed, Klaus cut his hand through the air, gesturing back to the hallways. "You did not save her. It was all a waste. We were meant to stop Nikolas!"

"She has a new heart now. She can help you in my place."

"Nein." Klaus' voice dropped dangerously low.

"You know she is more than capable, even said so yourself."

"She will die too."

Stunned silence filled the room. William's pleading gesturing changed with his surprise. "That's not what we agreed on. I'm the one paying the time! Not her!"

"And after your death, your contract will no longer be valid." Klaus stepped up to her father, grabbing his shirt. "Once I take what you owe me, I will have to take away her new heart too."

As if a landmine exploded beneath her feet, Elizabeth's world shifted and broke beneath her. She couldn't feel her legs or her face from where she squashed it up against the wood panel. Above her shock, William's voice was a drifting echo.

"No! No there must be something else. Anything else!" William backed up into his desk. Klaus pulled a blade from his inner pocket. Her eyes widened at the familiar handle design and how close it mimicked that of a Collector's weapon.

"Klaus! Stop! Stop!" Elizabeth hammered against the door. William glanced over at her scream, his eyes lost in fear as Klaus delivered the knife into his chest.

A flash of golden light erupted from the puncture point. There was no blood. No tear in his shirt or skin. Just a gentle, wispy golden light. It was almost beautiful. The soft smoke burrowed into William's body before vacuuming out his soul into the empty handle of the blade. Klaus eased the blade out before carefully positioning William into his office chair. In seconds, William's body was emptied of color. In seconds, his eyes glazed and his muscles relaxed. In seconds, he was dead.

Klaus knelt down and cradled William's forehead against his own. A painful ache hit her chest. Another crash of white painted the halls. The air felt stale, heavy. White flickered. The door by her face was yanked open. Klaus appeared, spotlighted by white lightning. Elizabeth propelled backwards, scrambling to her feet.

"Get away from me!" She screamed and lurched into a sprint. Her long dress tripped her, throwing her into the walls. Klaus' presence sat on the back of her neck. His fingers curled out, ready to grab her. She grabbed a vase on the foyer table and hurled it at him. Klaus caught it and tossed it to the side.

Exhaustion felt like a death sentence. Her bare feet struggled to grip the wet tile floors. Just as she hit the staircase, Klaus caught her. He pulled her down so she lost her footing, her stomach hitting the edge of the steps before flipping her onto her back. She couldn't scream, she didn't have the breath. Her hands shot up to protect her face.

Before he could strike, Klaus spun and caught the lamp stand Harry tried to hit him with. Harry's feeble arms and aged body lost grip. Klaus tossed it aside and shoved him to the ground. He moved erratically, striking before seeing the threat.

Seeing her chance, Elizabeth scrambled back into a run. The hallways to the library seemed to extend longer than she remembered. She hit the library door, chancing a look over her shoulder to see Klaus catching up to her. He was incredibly fast, too fast to outrun. Elizabeth inhaled her scream, shoving her shoulder against the door and slamming it shut behind her. Darkness didn't slow her as she bolted forward, hands held out in front, fingers spread, frantically pulling herself along the book shelves as a guide. A burning headache pulsated through her head, the strain on her eyes ripping through her like fire.

Where's the gun? Where's the gun? Where's the gun? The library door was forced open behind her.

She didn't slow, even when exhaustion gripped her throat and squeezed the strength from her legs. Hands grabbed her. She screamed as she was spun around and shoved against the bookcase. Hot hands grabbed her throat, fingers along her jawline forcing her chin to the side. Elizabeth slapped Klaus hard across his face, but to no reaction. He reached into his trench coat and brought out the blade. Lightning flashed once more, bringing his face into light, allowing Elizabeth a second to look at him. Blood wept out of his nostrils, dragging bright red down his chin and neck. She managed to pry a book from behind her head and whacked him across the nose. His second hand instinctively caught the book and dropped his grip on her. Elizabeth slipped out of his arms. She spun around, snatched at the edge of the bookcase and brought it down on top of his head. All she could hear was a grunt as the bookcase crushed on top of him.

Sprinting onwards, she reached out and felt the doorknob leading into the second storage room. She ran in and slammed the door shut behind her. She turned sideways to move through the narrow aisles. Thankfully, the curtains were still pulled back, painting the room in the weak city light. The chaotic storm split the darkened skies into searing white veins and the howls of the wind masked her panicked breathing.

She fell into the table, fumbled for the gun before grabbing it, and turned back around with the pistol head up. Whiteness fluttered into the room, revealing Klaus two steps away. His shadow loomed over the top of her, his presence like a wolf cornering his prey. She didn't hear him come in. He was just *there*.

Despite the adrenaline coursing through her, sending her into a trembling mess, Elizabeth paused. Klaus' face was covered in blood. His nose bled like a broken faucet, pouring blood down his front and down his clothes. *So much red.* Thunder roared, jolting Elizabeth out of her trance and causing her finger to squeeze the trigger. It was impossible to miss. Klaus' torso was within range, the barrel inches from contact. Yet, as she clenched her grip, the gun replied with an empty *click-click.*

Click- click. Click-click. She had forgotten to take the safety switch off. Klaus whipped his hand out, slapping the gun from her grasp and sent it skipping across the room. Her spine hit the table as he climbed on top. Her leg shot out and pushed against his chest, stopping him from getting any closer. Klaus lifted the knife above his head.

"No! No! Don't! Don't, please!" Elizabeth held her hands out, her voice cracking. "I want to live."

"I'm sorry." She couldn't see his eyes beneath his ruffled hair. His arm stiffened, ready to strike down. "This has to be done."

Her attention shifted back onto the glimmer of silver from the knife, noting how Klaus' fingers flexed around the grip, his face lost behind the blood. He was not human; this was the face of a Time Collector.

Elizabeth's mind froze. In her last moments—even when facing Arthur, a life without her mother, a life of servitude—she had never really wanted to die. Klaus's distant words echoed back. *Throwing away your life so easily, you do not respect anything. That, is real selfishness.*

"I wish for more time!" She screamed without taking a breath. She didn't move. She couldn't. She couldn't even think. "I'll give you what you want. Liberty? I will give you liberty."

The world halted. The war of thunder behind them fell into silence. Klaus' face tightened, his eyebrows high and his eyes widened in disbelief. He struggled to speak, the words knotting on his throat. "Don't say that."

"Please?"

"Death is a better option." He seemed to beg. Time, the last few seconds she had of it, seemed to drag as Klaus' hand hovered, ready to deliver the blade into her heart.

He wore an expression of pure torment. The longer he lingered, fighting his body, the more the blood seemed to thicken from his nose. Then, he dropped his hand and rocked backward. Elizabeth pressed herself further away, finally letting her breath go.

He held the blade out, where in the handle the spiral of cogs started to spin. The color of ghostly white spiralled out in smoke and into the darkness. As the smoke escaped, it splintered into veins before soaking into Elizabeth's skin.

"I can give you three years," Klaus whispered, defeat ripping through his raspy voice. "And just like Sir Wicker, you will pay your price."

He then stood and left the room. All she could do was slump against the wall and cry.

CHAPTER
SEVENTEEN

WHEN THE STRENGTH returned to her legs and her body felt hollowed of tears, Elizabeth stood. She picked up the gun again before heading to her father's study room. When she reached the hallway leading into the study, the door was left ajar. Light spilled out into the corridor. Cautiously, she stepped closer and pushed it open. Inside, Harry attended to William, pressing his fingers against William's neck before dropping his chin. He started to cry, an awkward choking sob. Elizabeth stepped around the desk, her eyes trained on William and how his face had whitened, relaxed in his death. She reached over and swept his tussled hair away from his face. He was cold to touch, his body frozen as if he had been dead for hours.

She pulled her hand back. Rage replaced her fear. She could hear the pipes working through the wall from the upstairs taps. Her face curled into a snarl, her brows furrowed as she pushed off the table. She went back into her room and found the bullet that was capable of piercing a Time Collector's shields. She emptied the cylinder and placed the single bullet into place, turning it so it was next in line to be fired.

She stood outside the east side bathroom door, the hammer on the gun now cocked back. Steam and light spilled from underneath the doorway. She pushed the door open, welcoming the sound of the hissing taps. Inside, Klaus slouched over the sink with his back to her; his shirt removed so he stood only in pants and shoes. Dirtied water speckled the white tiles. He had his head bowed so his drenched, darkened hair fell over his face. Water rippled along his back where his shoulder muscles pinched. Elizabeth stepped behind him, her heart picking up pace. She hoisted the gun up.

Her hands shook, fearing she'd lose the courage to squeeze the trigger. Klaus slowly lifted his head. She caught sight of his blurred face in the mirror, before he turned to face her. She held the gun firmly, her hands still. He didn't look surprised at the confrontation. He didn't blink. Didn't falter. His eyes settled onto hers, and under his stare her body felt heavier. His natural intimidation was more than physical, drawing him up like a golden wall of broad shoulders and large hands. He was a Time Collector, a creature that wasn't human. His dagger had been dropped to the ground, the spiralling cogs motionless once more.

He reached out and grabbed the barrel of the gun, pulling it closer to his forehead. Elizabeth gasped at the gesture. Did he really think she wouldn't do it? Did he think she'd miss? That she'd choke? He inhaled deeply, preparing for the shot. Rage hit her again. But she didn't shoot. Something stilled her finger. Carefully Klaus eased the gun away, clicked open the cylinder and pulled the bullet out.

"This is not for me," he said before turning back to the mirror and placing the bullet on the edge of the basin.

Her breath trembled out. "How? How could—" She choked, unable to form the question. She stared at his calculating face, noticing how his expression didn't change with guilt or concern. "How could you do that to him? After everything he did for you. How?" When Klaus didn't reply, Elizabeth inhaled a loud, hoarse sob. "Don't you try and tell me you didn't have a choice. I know what you are. What you are capable of. You didn't have to kill him! You could've taken the time from someone else."

Klaus' muscles twitched, her words angering him. He spun around. "You want me to be corrupted? Like Nikolas? Do not make me the enemy here. Sir Wicker is the one that made the choice."

"He saved my life—"

"All wishes come at a cost. They cost time, and he spent everything he had to save you. But…" Klaus slowed.

"And so when you killed him, the wish was canceled. You had to take back the heart…" She whispered. "My heart."

Klaus didn't need to confirm. It was clear by the anger tightening his brows. "I still can't believe you're one of them," she growled. "After everything we went through. You tricked me into trusting you." The past few weeks flickered past her mind, discoloring with her new perception. Every smile. Every glance. Every touch. It was controlled, *manipulative.* Elizabeth's grip tightened on the handle, her rage curling her fingers. She felt so foolish, falling into his charming smile. How he must've mocked her behind closed doors. "Was none of it real?"

Klaus froze. *Was none of it real?* His mind spun, trying to decipher her obvious double meaning. But the question burned and caught him off guard, making his answer feel even more dangerous than the gun she pointed at him. It felt personal, something he didn't dare acknowledge.

"Sir Wicker knew what I was. I did not trick him."

"In the end, Klaus, you are the one who killed him. I hope you carry that guilt with you to your grave." Elizabeth walked over and snatched the bullet off the basin. "Get out, and if I ever see you again, I promise, I will kill you."

CHAPTER

EIGHTEEN

THE CORONER ARRIVED to collect her father's body. After examination, he declared natural causes had taken William's life. Elizabeth was orphaned again. The family she had built around her had shaped into armor. She allowed them in, she laughed with them, ate with them, talked about her dreams and futures with them. But now, that armor had splintered and brought down any sense of security, leaving her torn and painfully exposed. Her heart had broken once in the most excruciating way. She didn't think it was possible to survive another hit like that. But she did. Despite feeling hollow, she continued to stand, continued to eat and move. Beyond the surface of her polite, fake smiles she was no more than a body without a soul.

Days passed. Painfully, long, lonely days. Even when she sat in the center of everyone's attention it brought little to no comfort. The Beaumontt's organized a funeral for her father, which was to take place down at the Memorial Park near the Golden Oak Gardens. As promised, Klaus left the house that night. The thought of not seeing him again for three years should have left her feeling pleased, but instead heart break and guilt filled her. Ashamed by her feelings, Elizabeth did everything she could to shut them off.

She hadn't even thought about the Red Moon Festival until it popped up on her calendar. Despite their last interaction, Arthur would still expect her attendance. The foul taste was back in her throat, bringing with it memories of his hands roughly pulling at her clothes. As long as Sara remained with him, Elizabeth would never be out of his reach. She rested her hand against her heart. The gentle ticking didn't bother her so much. Maybe this was meant to be her life. One living on the edge of danger. A child born out of a love affair couldn't have asked for much more. Maybe, in the end, this was always meant to be her destiny.

BOUQUETS OF FLOWERS cluttered the front door the day of Williams' funeral. Lawyers had already been to see her earlier that morning, reading through her father's will and handing over what appeared to be the deed to the house and all of his worldly possessions. When she questioned it, they revealed the paperwork William had her sign when first coming to his house.

Material things weren't of interest anymore. Elizabeth distanced from things she thought she yearned for. At the end of her three-year count down, she would be a corpse with her heart torn out. She sat anchored to her bed, rubbing at her temples while trying to figure out what she meant to do with her life. If she was honest, taking the easy lifestyle felt unjustified, as though she had robbed it from someone else. But doing nothing would have been just as much as a death sentence as Klaus' return. A new thought ticked over. Did she even have to die? She glanced down at the bullet set inside William's old locked suitcase. If she shot Klaus and not Nikolas, would she still have to pay her fee? If Klaus disappeared, would it break the contract between them? Would her heart stop?

"Miss Wicker?" Harry's voice called from the hallway. "It's time."

Elizabeth nodded and stood.

The thoughts followed her as she went out, dressed in traditional black. A dark lace veil shielded her face. William's tombstone was impressive, a tall monument to his achievements and greatness. William Wicker truly had been a remarkable man and the loss of him hit her hard. Harry stood beside her, his old withered arm wrapped around her shoulders as they lowered William into the ground. His entire body shook as he cried. The Groves cried. The Wellingtons cried. Masses of mourners lined the streets. Except for Elizabeth. Her bloodshot eyes strained as she watched the brown coffin disappear. She would never be able to spend another morning with him, no more morning studies, debating over medication, learning about the affairs of the nobles. Every thought she had, she questioned the fairness of her life. Both parents were gone. Who did she have left?

She didn't linger after the funeral. She couldn't stand the smell of the earth anymore. She took a car home with Harry, but when arriving at the manor, found the front door dislodged off its frame. She stopped at the threshold whereas Harry stepped around her in speechlessness. The front foyer had been gutted. The missing heirlooms emptied the house of warmth. Family pictures, vases and decorative ornaments were stripped from the walls and benches. Curtains pulled from the railings, portraits dismantled in search for hidden safes, glasses shattered and thrown across the ground. She felt like someone had slapped her across the face. The shock was numbing.

Harry called the authorities immediately whereas Elizabeth went to her room to find all of her things had been riffled through. Unease twisted her stomach. Someone had pulled open her drawers and rampaged through her personal items. She reached underneath her bed where she had stashed her father's suitcase and felt the familiar touch of leather underneath. Relieved, she pulled the suitcase out but snapped her hands back. The locks had been left unclasped. She spun the suitcase around and opened the secret compartment. Somehow, they had found the hidden slot and had taken the pistol.

"Oh, no. No, no, no!" Elizabeth pulled at her hair. This was a planned hit, timing it well so everyone was out of the manor for William's funeral. Her mind immediately went to Klaus. He was the only one who knew of the gun. Only he knew of its importance. Her last threat to kill him echoed into the front of her mind. It made sense, except for the state of the manor. If it was Klaus, he didn't need to tear the house apart. *He knew exactly where it was…unless…* A glint of gold caught her attention. *They had left the bullet. So if not Klaus, then who?*

"I DON'T CARE about the jewelery. I just can't believe they took the gun!" Elizabeth growled over her meal. The bustle of foot traffic outside settled her agitation, reminding her more of home in the Pitts than the empty silence of William's mansion. Harry's house in Rosefire sat on the skirts of the Golden City, nestled along the large, domed walls and hidden within a lane of identical townhouses. Her living there was only temporary, but being outside the eyes of the Golden Gates turned out to be a small blessing. She hadn't realized how much it affected her, how every time she walked by the window in the mansion she felt the need to duck under. The wet weather was finally moving along as the day welcomed them with a cloudless sky. Elizabeth sighed loudly over her bowl of soup, stirring the spoon in her frustration.

"A young lady such as yourself shouldn't be this upset over a gun. It's not decent." Harry chuckled as he sat down to join her. "I'm thankful no one was hurt."

"We're away from the snobs of Divin Cadeau, decency doesn't matter anymore. It has already been a week since the break in. Does it normally take this long?"

"We have to trust the police officers to do their job. Even if they can't find them, there'll be another way to get your belongings back." Elizabeth didn't exactly share in Harry's trust in authorities, but her sulking wasn't helping the situation either. She glanced over at Harry's sister, Doris, napping on the recliner to ensure she wasn't eavesdropping.

"What do you think about all this Time Collector business, Harry?"

"I'm sure the opinion of an old goat like me isn't worth discussing."

"Of course your opinion matters. Matter of fact, you may be the only one I can talk to freely about such things."

Harry gently smiled. "I could never keep up with Sir Wicker's adventures. I'm afraid my attention never moved away from the dusting."

"Do you know why my father was interested in hunting the Time Collectors in the first place?"

"I'm afraid Sir Wicker never shared such views with me. For as long as I was employed with him, he always had an interest in them."

"And Klaus? How did they even meet?"

"To my knowledge, they had met each other years ago by accident. Sir Wicker hadn't thought twice about him until it became apparent a Time Collector was in the Golden City, a corrupted one. That's when Sir Wicker sought Klaus out. They trusted each other completely."

"You sound like you don't trust him?" Elizabeth nestled back into her chair.

"He's too cunning for a man like me. I could never understand what was going on in that boy's mind. A Time Collector hunting other Time Collectors—something smells fishy."

Elizabeth hummed her agreement. "Despite everything, they are fascinating people. If you had the choice, would you make a contract with a Time Collector?"

Harry snorted out a laugh. "I'm afraid, dear, I wouldn't have any time left to afford a tissue to blow my nose."

"Okay," Elizabeth chuckled softly, redirecting her question. "Say, in your younger years, if you came across a man who could grant you wishes, would you do it?"

Harry stared at her for a long, hard minute, the sketchy voices of the radio a gentle hum behind him. Doris turned her head down in her snores. "I would have, in a heartbeat."

"What would you have wished for?"

"To save my wife from her illness."

Elizabeth's smile dropped. Harry's eyes glanced down as he lifted his teacup to drink. There was a hint of sadness there, but was overshadowed by a warm smile. "I'm so sorry." Elizabeth reached out to touch his arm.

"No, it's quite okay. It happened a very long time ago." His hand trembled, accidentally tipping his tea over the table. Elizabeth bolted upwards and grabbed a napkin, patting the cloth dry. "I'm so clumsy. I'm so sorry, Miss Wicker. Please, let me clean it. You don—"

"You don't work for me, Harry. I'm more than capable of looking after myself and help mop up some spilt tea. Doctor Wicker had his rules and traditions. I understand that but," Elizabeth eased back down, touching the family crest on her collar necklace, "I was not brought up as a noble girl, and I sure as hell aren't going to be treated like one now."

"Does that mean you don't need me at the mansion?"

She briskly shook her head. "You're not losing your job, but we are going to start losing some of these traditions. For instance, I can cook and clean too. You don't have to escort me everywhere and you don't have to address me as Miss Wicker. Elizabeth is just fine. You can start taking days off too. You work way too hard."

Harry shook his head weakly. "I can't do that."

"That's an order." She grinned. "You shouldn't spend your life only thinking about the dusting." She gave him a playful nudge. "I want you to laugh more. I don't think I've ever seen a smile on your face."

Harry touched her hand kindly, his slack frown lifting at the corners. "As should you, Miss Wicker."

Elizabeth replied with a weak smile of her own, "I'll be a lot happier after tonight is over and done with."

"You don't have to go."

"Unfortunately, I do, but I'm going to be a lot more careful this time around." She lifted her leg to reveal the kitchen knife strapped in her thigh garter. Harry, embarrassed, looked away. "I won't be satisfied until I see pee running down his expensive trousers."

"Please don't do anything dangerous. Sir Wicker would haunt me beyond the grave."

Elizabeth laughed. "Sir Wicker had acted far more dangerously than I."

"Just promise me you'll be safe."

"I promise." She pushed back her chair. "I am of Wicker blood, but born in a Blackmore's life. I can definitely handle myself."

CHAPTER
NINETEEN

T HE CELEBRATIONS TO the Red Moon Festival started early, kicking off around six o'clock. As Elizabeth made her way toward the Beaumontt's, the calls of "Happy Red Moon!" scented the air with wine and smoke. She was still fresh from her mourning and thus, wasn't in the partying mood. When she finally arrived at the governor's house, Elizabeth stopped outside the gates to take a few deep breaths. The Beaumontt mansion was, as expected, an impressive palace with sand yellow brick gates guarding the four-story high structure.

She had been inside the manor once when she was a simple cleaning maid, before she was welcomed as a student at the academy. She was only nine years old at the time. It had been the first-time Arthur had seen her too. He had been cruel back then as well. He threw pencils at her, smeared dirt over the freshly washed floor and even tried to make her eat dog food. Blessings come in many shapes, sometimes in the moments of misfortunates. Elizabeth being fired that day for distracting the young master sent her to the academy, sent her to William Wicker. And to think the next time she was to enter the Beaumontt estate she would be a noble woman belonging to the Wicker household was almost laughable.

She was greeted by their older maid, who politely bowed and stepped to the side to let Elizabeth in. If she hadn't grown accustomed to William's exquisite lifestyle, she would've fallen over in absolute awe at the Beaumontt mansion. A chrome statue of Harold Beaumontt welcomed from the front foyer, standing straight with his arms posed at his hips and his expression lost behind the polished copper. Elizabeth had to take a few steps back, completely caught off guard by the giant monument. The statue's jaw unhinged in mimicked speech, but no words came out. *Funny, if it was Arthur, it would be twice the size.* Elizabeth thought. *And probably vomit insults.*

The maid left to fetch Arthur, leaving Elizabeth anxiously at the door. She wondered around the large foyer, stopping to admire the artworks and statues when something caught her eye. The door leading into a formal study was left ajar. Inside the office, a large mirror faced her on the opposite side of the wall, reflecting a distinguished glow of gold from an object sitting on the mantel piece. Harold Beaumontt paced inside, barking into the phone, but was too distracted to notice her head poking around the door frame.

But there it was. The golden pistol. It's curved handle, golden coat, and distinguished shape was a dead giveaway. Elizabeth paused, her eyebrows towed in confusion. The notion was almost ridiculous, but the harder she looked the more she was convinced.

"Miss Wicker?" A voice called for her. Elizabeth rushed back to her place by the front door, just in time to catch Lady Claudia peer from over the second-floor railing. She hadn't seen Lady Claudia since her father's funeral, and before, their only interaction was when her butler had grabbed Elizabeth's sleeve at the gala.

She awkwardly curtsied as she greeted the lady. "Lady Claudia. Happy Red Moon Day."

"To you as well, dear. I'm afraid Arthur has been called out on business so he won't be joining you tonight." Lady Claudia glided down the curved staircase, revealing the gorgeous full-length dress that popped with blood red and jewels. Elizabeth's chest deflated with relief.

"Another time then, my lady."

"How about I escort you instead?"

Anxiety jumped back up in her throat. Lady Claudia reached the bottom of the steps and reached out, gently taking Elizabeth's hand. The waft of rosemary perfume followed her gentle gesture. "It's such a wonderful night and I know you don't have anyone else beside that butler of yours to spend it with. Come with me. We'll go down together."

"I appreciate your kindness, but it's not necessary—"

"Nonsense, it'll be fun." She reached over and gently stroked the crest on Elizabeth's choker. "It looks so fitting on you, my dear, a true Wicker. We miss your father dearly."

"I miss him too. Thank you."

"Come, the night is still young and they'll be starting the fireworks soon."

Everything Elizabeth had ever heard about Lady Claudia was wrong. She hooked her arm through Elizabeth's as they walked down the streets and into the park where most of the celebration was happening. Down in central park, the festival was already in full swing. All the noblewomen wore their most glamourous frocks, with an arrangement of flowers teased through their hair and hats. The men armored up their sleeves and trousers in chrome casings. Each showing off their latest new gadgets. Above their heads, among the popping of the fireworks, chrome statues dressed as metal angels paraded around on stilts. They moved on springs, bouncing between each step as their large wings flapped. They tossed candy out to the gathering children.

Around the outskirts of the park, vendors set up their booths selling charms and trinkets, playing arcade games and apple bobbing, dancing to music and watching magicians entertaining for coin. Overhead blimps shaped like large beetles hovered just above-head height, their bellies casting rainbow lights over the stars and moon.

Locals clapped, danced and jumped about each other, linking arms and chasing the large beetle blimps with rackets as though to swap them down. Elizabeth rattled her head, thinking she was dreaming. In the Pitts, the Red Moon festival didn't mean much more than an extra glass of wine with dinner. The biggest difference may have been the drunks were drunk an hour earlier. It appeared not everyone was accustomed to Elizabeth's new status either. Most avoided eye contact, unsure how to greet her as she passed. Some of the more prestigious families were more forward in their unpleasantness.

"Did I do something wrong?" Elizabeth asked after she got the upturned nose from the Hemmingway's.

"Oh, don't worry about them. Some people just like to gossip." Lady Claudia smiled.

"About me?"

"Absolutely, your story is fascinating. It's as though it's written out of a children's storybook. Ordinary servant girl becomes one of the richest women overnight, all because her wealthy father dies mysteriously, leaving everything to you, his sole heir. Some are calling it a cover up."

Elizabeth stopped walking. "They think I murdered Doctor Wicker for his money?"

Lady Claudia slowed only enough to speak over her shoulder. "Many would, but as I said, darling, it's just rumors. There's no weight behind them, now is there? Come, have you met the Grovedales?" She pulled Elizabeth along before introducing her to the oldest noble couple of their district. She curtsied and greeted them kindly as they greeted her back. "They've been together for over sixty-two years, you know?" Lady Claudia informed as they started their leisurely walk again. "It's common for girls as young as seventeen to wed. I already assume your marital situation has been taken care of."

"My marital situation?" Elizabeth slowed.

"Yes. For a suitable husband, of course. Dear me, don't tell me your father didn't organize one for you?" Elizabeth shook her head. Lady Claudia's lips twitched as though trying to suppress a smile. "You're practically an old woman now. No one will want to marry you." The notion of marriage was a worry Elizabeth no longer had. Now, she had a count down. Three years. No one would want a wife for only three years. Lady Claudia continued, "I'm thinking of your well-being. You know I've always seen you as the daughter I never had."

Unable to stop herself, Elizabeth jerked her head back. *I'm the daughter she never had?* It was hard to believe Lady Claudia had ever thought of her as a human being let alone a daughter.

Lady Claudia stepped closer, unclipping her own bracelet and holding it against Elizabeth's wrist. "Oh, yes, doesn't the Beaumontt crest just glow against your skin?"

Elizabeth froze. There was no way Lady Claudia was hinting at her wanting to marry Elizabeth into the family, right? To only confirm her worst fears, Lady Claudia reached over and swept a loose strand of white hair behind Elizabeth's ear. "I've noticed you've taken quite a shining to my Arthur. Can't say that I am surprised, a girl with your ambitions would only have her eyes set on the best."

Without any self-control, Elizabeth flinched away from Lady Claudia's touch, repulsed by the notion of marrying Arthur Beaumontt. "I'm sorry, but you are mistaken. I don't have any affection toward Arthur Beaumontt."

Lady Claudia tensed for a moment, her internal glow darkening. "Pardon me?"

"I mean no disrespect. I don't feel like I'm ready for marriage," Elizabeth corrected herself.

Lady Claudia's lips distastefully curled. "I see. Well, only Timothy is groomed to follow in his father's footsteps and he is promised to an important businessman's daughter. Someone born of true nobility.

Unfortunately, Wicker blood is not enough to subdue that of a whore's." Her smile stretched, delighted by Elizabeth's verbal beating. "You have no one left who cares about you, child. I wouldn't start being too picky to those willing to burden themselves with your company."

Elizabeth grit her jaw. The name *whore* was thrown at her mother one too many times. Coming from Lady's Claudia's mouth, and spoken with such disgrace, was too much. "My mother was the greatest person I've ever known, far greater than any noble pure blood. She had strength, brilliance, courage, and decency, which I'm lacking to find with any *company* here."

The crack of fireworks sounded above them, lighting Lady Claudia's face in neon red. She stepped forward, closing the distance between them before grabbing Elizabeth's arm roughly enough her fingernails cut skin. She yanked her downward, pulling Elizabeth's off balance. "Tread lightly. I've had people disposed of for far less! Don't you know what happens to pretty little girls when they are left alone?"

"Is that a threat?" Elizabeth pulled against her grip.

"A warning. Despite many protests, in the eyes of the law you are now technically a Wicker. A flaw I intend to take full advantage of. Don't start believing this is anything more than a power play."

"A power play?" Elizabeth repeated.

Lady Claudia let her grip go and turned back toward the festivals. "A pawn, in my game of chess. And like them all, your only purpose is to guard the queen."

EVERYTHING ELIZABETH HAD ever heard about Lady Claudia was correct. Manipulative. Cruel. Cold. Lady Claudia may have plans for Elizabeth, but Elizabeth had her own plans with the Beaumontts. Plans that included breaking into a certain empty house to retrieve her stolen gun. With Lady Claudia's dismissal, Elizabeth made her way back toward the Beaumontt estate.

"Why did I wear such a ridiculous dress?" Elizabeth pulled at the length of her skirt, grumbling as it tripped her up.

She took the knife from her garter and sliced the dress up from her ankles to her thigh. She then tied her skirt into a giant knot behind her. She stripped out of her tight blazer, dressing down to a simple white blouse underneath. She then heaved herself up the wall of the stone gate and slipped over the top. Quietly, she snuck up to the house before pressing her body against the chilled brick building. Noise of the distant festivities helped mask the scrunch the dried leaves beneath her shoes. Sharing the shadows, she pressed against the walls before craning her neck to chance a look inside the windows. Inside, it was dark in its vacancy. She pushed her face against the window and cupped her hands over her eyes to block the moonlight out. Unfortunately, she couldn't see the pistol.

She ran her fingers along the windowsill's edge and pried her nails underneath the wood to hoist it up. It lifted slightly, enough to squeeze the tip of her finger underneath, but nothing more. There was a locked hitched on the other side. Elizabeth took the knife out and slipped it through the gap. Successfully, the pin lifted, unlocking the window and allowing her to heave the frame above her head. She couldn't reach the top panel, and without constant support, the window threatened to slam shut so she wedged her blade in the gap to act as a support beam. Hoisting herself up onto her stomach, she crawled through, easing her butt and legs onto the ground after her before rolling back onto her feet. The floorboards groaned beneath her weight. She halted. Glancing around, it was almost impossible to see anything beyond arm length. Slipping out of her shoes, she crept on, the creak now much softer.

Her eyes adjusted to the weak moonlight catching on the edge of objects, when a cough startled her. She swung around, accidentally knocking a vase from the table that shattered across the ground. A tall silhouette stood by the door. She couldn't see much, just a faint outline of his shoulders and head.

"Can I help you?" An accented voice asked.

"Oh, I was...I was just...I left my coat here. I didn't want to disturb—"

"A liar." The man cut across her stammering, "And a thief." He took a few steps closer. "I've always been weary of sneaky girls in bronze dresses."

Elizabeth cocked her head at the comment. *Bronze dresses?* The only time she ever wore a bronze dress was at the Gala. She strained her eyes to see the man through the dark, and was able to match his features to the butler that grabbed her wrist when she tried to slash Arthur. Outside of Lady Claudia's gaze he moved with more ease. "Looking for something?" He asked, twirling the golden pistol around his finger.

She swallowed hard. He was taunting her. "You call me the thief when you are currently holding my father's pistol?"

"You must be pretty confident that this is indeed yours to risk breaking into the Beaumontt's house to retrieve it."

"I am. Give it back to me."

"See, you're a liar."

"How am I lying?" She hissed.

"Because if you were the rightful owner then you wouldn't need to sneak in to steal it. Unless, of course, you weren't sure it was the same gun. Therefore, lying."

Elizabeth faltered. Behind his silhouette the foyer light flicked on. The man turned his head to catch the sound of footsteps approaching. The sight of his profile drew her out of the moment. It sparked a memory inside. His turned cheek, the shape of his nose, the way the light haloed his golden hair.

"Nikolas?" Harold Beaumontt's voice called from inside. "Are you talking to somebody?"

Elizabeth froze. The scene unfolded as though she still stood in her mother's hallway. The crackle of the glass breaking, the glint of silver from his knife. Nikolas, the corrupted Time Collector. The man who murdered her mother.

Nikolas' smile crept across his face. He cocked his head back toward Elizabeth. "I'm in the study with a guest."

"A guest? Who?" Before Nikolas could say anything more, Elizabeth spun back toward the window and bolted toward the front yard. "Who was that? Hey! Stop!" Harold caught just a glimpse of Elizabeth as she tumbled out the window.

She bolted across the yard, scaled the walls and cleared the property line before Harold could reach the front door. In her haste, she forgot her shoes, running barefooted out into the streets. Taking the first corner she came across, Elizabeth slipped into a dark alley and sheltered herself among the shadows. She paced back and forth unsure what to do, or what to think.

Her pulse raced. Nervously, she ran her hands over her face, clearing the sweat off. Her immediate thought was to find Klaus, but was reminded she had no idea how to even find him. *Harry can't help. Sara is under the Beaumontt's thumb. Mother is dead. William is dead.* She bit her thumbnail as she paced, when she turned into a man's chest, not noticing him approaching from the shadows. Large hands grabbed her face, silencing her shriek. He moved fast. Swiftly. Fireworks popped over head as he marched her back, shoving her up against the brick walls. Gold light crossed the sky. Nikolas held her firmly. His expression unfaltering.

"I can't let you leave so soon." She clawed at his fingers, trying to pry them off. Unlike before, his taunting wasn't playful. "Not without accepting my gift." From inside his jacket, Nikolas unsheathed the dagger and turned it toward her. Elizabeth's eyes widened. "Forgive me."

For the second time in her life, Elizabeth was pinned underneath the body of a Time Collector. For the second time in her life, she had to stare down the glint of silver and wait to die. She couldn't struggle. She couldn't speak. He had moved too fast, pinned her, muted her. Knowing her one defense were her words. A swift stab to her chest would only take a second to finish the job. Beyond his bold stare, she couldn't distinguish his face. He reared his arm back and swung.

She clenched her eyes closed but the blade never hit her chest. Nikolas hovered mid-strike, his hand trembling inches from contact. Blood seeped out of his left nostril. His eyes began to water, deepening into the color of red ink. Confused, he shoved himself away, dropping his grip. Her cheeks still throbbed where he had grabbed her. Now free, Elizabeth still couldn't find the command to scream. She simply pressed closer to the wall, wide-eyed and speechless. Nikolas didn't linger. Just as quickly as he appeared, he vanished.

It took her a few moments to comprehend what had happened. It was hard not to notice the similarities between Time Collector Klaus and Time Collector Nikolas. The touch of his hot-coal skin contradicted his chilling presence, and unlike Klaus' German tongue, Nikolas' Finnish accent didn't slur his words. All she could think of was getting back home. Her heart pooled to the bottom of her feet. She wasn't sure exactly how to feel. Being almost killed in an alleyway, with a chance of no one discovering her until the morning, definitely clarified her morality. Fearful of Nikolas' return, she went straight back to Harry's house in Rosefire.

CHAPTER
TWENTY

HARRY! HARRY, WAKE up!" Elizabeth jostled him awake.
Harry bolted up from his chair in front of the fire place, "What?
What's going on?"

"I know who the corrupted Collector is! How do I find Klaus?
How did William find him?" She gripped the chairs' arms, her body
towering over him in her urgency.

"What? Why?"

"I've found Nikolas."

"Nikolas?" Harry looked around her confused. "Who's Nikolas?"

"The corrupted Time Collector! He's the one we've been searching
for." An impatient bang sounded from the front door. Elizabeth shot
up straight as Harry shifted around in the chair. After a few seconds
of silence, the banging started again, just as determined and twice
as violent.

"Who on earth is that?" Harry rose from his chair, but Elizabeth
held him back. The person behind the door hit with such velocity the
entire house rattled.

"Wait…" Paranoia spiked. Carefully, Elizabeth approached the
front door and armed herself with an umbrella. The overhead light
swung on its cord. "Who is it? What do you want?"

The hammering stopped. Silence settled. There was no shadow

pressed against the glass windows. No shift under the door gap. Elizabeth's grip tightened on the umbrella handle, straining her ears for footsteps leading away. The knob twisted on its own and the distinct click of the lock flicking back pinged. A strong gust of wind kicked the door open the exact moment a figure crashed in from behind her. The man pushed Elizabeth to the side, running at the door and throwing his shoulder into it.

"Get away from the door," Klaus shouted.

He stabbed the door panel with the tip of the blade, creating a faint tissue shield that barred the door from being torn from its hinges. The hammering and banging didn't cease, yet the door didn't budge a centimeter more. Klaus took Elizabeth by the elbow and walked her back to where Harry sat.

"Klaus? How did you…? Why are you here?" She asked.

"I never exactly left," Klaus dropped his grip on her before walking over to the window to check the streets. "How did he find you?"

"How did he…wait a minute! You knew Nikolas was Lady Claudia's butler the whole time?"

"Of course I knew."

"Wait, but…why were you searching all over town looking for him?"

"Just shush, Elizabeth. Now is not the time."

"Not the time?" Elizabeth stumbled, overwhelmed. "You have to be the biggest con artist I have ever—"

"Don't be so dramatic! Both Sir Wicker and myself know who Nikolas is. I've already told you that. We need to find him, track him down."

"Bit of a dead giveaway considering it was Lady Claudia who Nikolas worked for." She scoffed.

Klaus weaved past her and crossed the room. He pulled back another curtain to see outside. "He has many contacts, not just her. In any case, that is why I am here in Divin Cadeau. Collectors, Nikolas in particular, like to keep a very low profile. He is usually very careful to stay out of sight. I once trailed one of his contacts for months and he still managed to avoid me. He's clever, he has to be."

"Clever? You're complimenting him now?" The banging continued, drawing Elizabeth's attention back around. "Is that him?"

"Nein. He wouldn't be that clumsy. He would send his gremlins. And before you ask the obvious, gremlins are shadow creatures Nikolas controls," Klaus murmured under his breath, frustrated. "But he won't be far. He's hunting you now, but we need him to come out of hiding."

"Hunting me?"

The relentless banging silenced. They both glanced over toward the front then back toward the window. Klaus held his hand up to shush her. He then reached behind him, speaking in a soft whisper, "Give me the gun."

Elizabeth shook her head. "I don't have it."

"What? Why not?"

"I er…"

"Never mind. I'll go get it. Wait here."

"Stop. You can't." He sighed and looked over at her impatiently. Elizabeth gulped. "Nikolas has it."

Klaus immediately straightened. He paused, looking at her, convinced he had misheard. "Nein. You must be joking—"

"He stole it when I wasn't home," she explained defensively.

Again, Klaus froze. Slowly, as he came to understand what she'd told him, his knuckles tightened. "You…gave him the gun?"

"He stole it."

"How could you be so careless?"

"I didn't do it on purpose! The very definition of stealing is to take without permission!"

Klaus shushed her again. He checked back over his shoulder toward the seemingly empty street. The strained quietness only emphasized the ticking of her mechanical heart. Shadows moved behind them, leaking out of the cracks in the walls. As the darkness approached, it thickened in texture, resembling sticky tar. In sluggish rolls, the lumpy blotch solidified and grew, forming arms, legs, a torso and a rounded head. It bubbled and popped, the noise turning Elizabeth around. Before she could scream or the creature could attack, Klaus' arm struck the creature through its skull with his knife. It squealed and dispersed back into smoke.

"Fine. We'll play it your way, Nikolas." Klaus wedged the dagger out and pulled Elizabeth to her feet.

"W-W-Wha—" Elizabeth splattered. Even Harry couldn't speak.

"I told you. Gremlins." Klaus dismissed her. "As long as you are here, they will not stop. Mr. Smith, I will be taking Elizabeth back to my place. You need not worry. These creatures are not here for you."

"W-What do they w-want with Miss Wicker?" Harry stuttered.

Klaus was careful not to reply. Perhaps saying, *to murder her*, would only further upset their situation. Instead, he took Elizabeth by the arm and pulled her toward the door. "I will be back to collect her things. Come, Elizabeth, you have to stay close."

Klaus lead the way out of Rosefire and back toward the poorer district. In his haste, Elizabeth struggled to keep up, her shoes skidding behind her as though she was being towed by a car. She had never seen Klaus act this way, as though he had heard a warrant for his own death. He eventually slowed when nearing a weed-infested dirt path and stopped outside an abandoned hut by a swamp. The cabin sat high on a hill top, casting a long view over the city and toward the Golden City.

"You live here?" Elizabeth stepped back as Klaus unlocked the front door. "Are you sure we're not safer back at Harry's?"

"Ja. Come."

"I'm just saying bacterial infection is the leading cause in most deaths."

Klaus grabbed her wrist and yanked her after him. "Come along, snob."

The entire shack shuddered on their entrance. Dampness softened the floorboards, making them creak and sink beneath their footsteps. Elizabeth held her hands close to her chest as she closed the door behind them. Rat droppings stained the furniture, creating perfect breeding grounds for clusters of fungus. Embarrassed, Klaus cleared his throat. "Well, there's not much a man can do on such short notice. You did kick me out first, remember?"

"Why did you bring me here?"

"Concealment spells marks the doors. Nikolas can't see you. Not even his gremlins can track you down. But I can't conceal any house. It has to be abandoned. Belonging to no one," Klaus answered with his back to her. He continued to rifle through his bag at the back of the room before pulling out his textbook. The whole dwelling was nothing more than a single room, with a bed in the corner, a one-man seat, table and chair, a basin with what appeared to be a broken sink, and a window. Elizabeth took the seat as Klaus placed the book in front of them. He pointed at the vague picture of a dark-colored creature, barely distinguishable, seemingly to climb out of darkness.

"These are the gremlins. Corruption magic."

Elizabeth inched the book closer to her to read the description. "Gremlins. Mindless creatures incapable of thought or will power. Gremlins are powerful dark magic, only accessible to tainted Time Collectors. Said to be the making of trapped, tainted souls, gremlins cannot be killed, but only temporarily delayed by sunlight. Only the Time Collector who conjured it can stop it." Elizabeth looked up at Klaus, alarmed. "Is it going to keep trying to kill me?"

"The question we should be asking is why is Nikolas chasing you? How did you get his attention?"

Elizabeth shook her head, trying to shake the fear out of her voice. "Oh, right, okay well I was at the Beaumontt's earlier where I happened to see William's gun. I thought I'll just return when everyone was out and steal it back. I almost had it too, but Nikolas caught me, but I swear, I didn't say anything about Time Collectors. I just ran. Then…" Elizabeth paused in her pacing, bringing her hand back to her forehead as a memory blazed. "He followed me. He pinned me against a wall. He tried to stab me, but he stopped. He got a bloody nose, just like, just like you did!"

Klaus' expression remained slack as he processed Elizabeth's words. "Ja. It's punishment."

"Punishment, for what?"

"When we fail to collect the time owing or when we refuse a contract, we are punished." He turned and slouched exhausted against the windowsill. "No doubt he now knows you're with a Collector. There goes my advantage. He'll be watching you too carefully."

"How would he know?"

Klaus sighed but didn't turn to speak to her. "Try and sleep. I promise, you are safe here."

Elizabeth cast a sideways glance at the bed. Adrenaline made sleeping an impossible task, and quite frankly it was the last thing on her mind. She tried again to get him to talk to her. "Why didn't he kill me when he had the chance?" Klaus didn't move. Elizabeth clasped her shaking hands and stepped forward. "Klaus? Please?"

"It's not why he didn't kill you, it's why he couldn't." He stepped away from the window and toward her. As he stared into her eyes his expression hardened, angered by his own thoughts. "And he couldn't because…you belong to me now."

SLEEP DID NOT come easy and it did not come fast. Elizabeth curled her knees to her chest and wedged her clenched fists under her armpits for warmth. The thin blanket Klaus provided did very little to shield her from the icy breath coming from the wind outside. Klaus didn't sleep, either. He had collected firewood and lit a small fire by the hearth, but it did nothing against the cold.

Hours rolled over as Elizabeth glanced out across the room from her bed, watching Klaus staring into the dying flames. Within her chest remained an insistent flutter she couldn't crush. A flutter of hope, or even worse, a flutter of joy at being in Klaus' company again. She turned over and buried her head into the blanket. She really must be a fool to think like that. By the time exhaustion outweighed the cold, the sky had already started to bleed red with sunrise. She got up, unable to stand another moment.

"Please tell me this isn't our permanent living condition. I couldn't sleep a wink at all."

"You can always add in a potted plant if that helps." Klaus suggested without glancing up.

"Not funny, Klaus."

Despite reading all night, Klaus' face didn't droop with drowsiness. He seemed unfazed by the cold, by lack of sleep or the uncomfortable smell seeping from the swamp. He eased back into his chair, turning his attention to Elizabeth. "The sun is up now. It's safer to walk around. I doubt Nikolas would send anymore gremlins your way. He must know you're with a Collector, or at least have contact with one. It may be enough to hold him back."

"Then we're safe to return to Rosefire? Or the Wicker mansion?"

"We? I'm invited back, am I?" Klaus asked sarcastically. Elizabeth rolled her eyes, causing Klaus to laugh. "Nein, our focus is on getting the gun back, that you so helpfully lost."

"It was stolen."

"In any case, it'll be for the best you avoid all Beaumontt's from now on, and stay away from places Nikolas can spy on you. I've kept my presence a secret from Nikolas so far, hopefully his attention on you hasn't jeopardized everything." Again, he looked at her bitterly.

"Where am I to live then?"

"I'll figure something out. There are a few things I need from the estate, but first I'll escort you back to Harry's so you can shower, perhaps change your clothes. Freshen up a bit."

Elizabeth cringed. "Subtlety is not your strong suit." Klaus grinned, and once he turned away Elizabeth sniffed her collar for an odor. "Maybe a shower won't be such a bad idea."

"Good thinking. Let's move."

CHAPTER
TWENTY-ONE

"OH, ELIZABETH THERE you are!" Harry was quick to greet the pair approaching his doorway. "Thank God you're okay. I've been sitting up sick with worry all night."

"I did say you were safe," Klaus stated.

"He means he was worried about me, Klaus. Not his own safety," Elizabeth corrected. "And thank you, Harry, but I am quite alright. May I please wash up? It's been a long night."

"Yes, yes of course, Miss Elizabeth. Come in." Harry sidestepped to allow her passage. Klaus didn't follow her in, but reached out to hold Harry back.

"Mr. Smith." He stepped closer and lowered his voice. "It is imperative that Elizabeth remain here until my return. I won't be long. I need to collect some of my belongings back at the Wicker estate."

Harry nodded. "I understand, but there is something I need to say first." Using his most dominating voice, Harry pulled Klaus closer by the collar. Klaus' eyebrow perked at the gesture. "After everything you've put this family through, for Sir Wicker, you must keep her safe. Promise me, you will keep her safe."

Klaus's expression tensed, alarmed. "Careful of what words you use around me."

Catching his meaning, Harry loosened his grip. "I will ensure

Elizabeth is reminded of that same danger."

Klaus gave Harry a brisk nod and glanced down the hallway to where the shower had turned on. He turned, and disappeared into the thick of the Rosefire crowd.

AFTER SHE SHOWERED and dressed, Elizabeth paced by the windows. She checked and rechecked the time, worried that Klaus was taking too long to return. She pulled the blinds back again to check the street just as a police officer approached the front. Before he could knock, the officer noticed her peeking and indicated her forward to chat. Elizabeth dropped the curtain and pulled the door open.

"Officer?" she greeted slowly.

"Morning, Miss Wicker. Sorry to disturb you, but I'm afraid you are needed down by the station." The chief officer motioned over his shoulder toward two others waiting beside a cop car. "We're here to escort you there."

Elizabeth clutched the door frame tighter. "Down by the station? What for?"

"We'll clarify everything on the way. Come along." With a brief nod from the chief, the two waiting officers stepped on either side of Elizabeth and took her arms, spinning her around.

"What? Why? What's going on?" She whipped her head between each guard as they walked her forward. She called over her shoulder to Harry, but was subdued and forced into the back of the van. Neither officer answered any of her questions as they drove toward the station.

Once there, she was dragged out, locked up behind bars, and left alone. Confused beyond measure, Elizabeth nervously paced her cell. She was quick to notice no other inmates shared her hallway, and no guards manned the door. After almost an hour of unanswered calls, her frustration peaked. She racked her brain thinking over the past twenty-four hours. All she could think of was Nikolas.

The answer came to her through a shrill laugh. "Suppose it was only a matter of time before you wound up behind bars. I suppose this does feel homelier to you." Elizabeth turned at Lady Claudia's voice. She approached her cell, smiling. Elizabeth unfurled her arms and held them strictly by her side.

"Lady Claudia? What are you doing here?"

"Surprised to see me? Why, I am the one who put you here, after all." Lady Claudia took her large, flamboyant hat off before primping her hair to ensure the bun held. Elizabeth craned her neck to see if Nikolas had followed her in. The fortune and luck that fell upon the Beaumontt's seemed to be endless, she wouldn't be surprised if it was thanks to the Time Collectors influence.

"You can't lock me up because I won't marry your son."

Lady Claudia glanced around, showing disgust at her surroundings. "There is something very important you must remember, Elizabeth. People in the Divin Cadeau have grown accustomed to a certain lifestyle. So when that lifestyle is threatened by rats they are all too happy to dispose of them in any way possible. Most rats like to think they are clever. But, lucky for us, I have a very, stupid rat." From beneath her folded arm, Lady Claudia revealed a soft yellow petticoat. "Look familiar?" Elizabeth's eyes widened at the sight of her coat. "I found this stashed outside my estate the same night a rat broke into my house. Now, I'm no lawyer, but I dare say this is incredibly incriminating evidence against you."

"I must have left it there from my earlier visit," Elizabeth said. "I was at your estate earlier, your maid invited me in. A witness."

"Witnesses are not your best line of defense. I have two of my own, ready to point you out in a line up." *Harold Beaumontt.* Elizabeth swallowed hard. *And Nikolas too, they both saw me.* "Can you imagine the scandal if I told everyone about this?"

"Like I care what they have to say."

"But your father would. In fact, he cared quite a lot about keeping the Wicker name honorable." Lady Claudia's smile grew. "How desperate are you to muddy up his name, and so soon after his death? How selfish can one silly, little girl be?"

Elizabeth slammed her mouth shut. Guilt quieted her. Despite her own opinion toward society's pressure, William Wicker was clear in his desires. She had embarrassed him. *Selfish?* Elizabeth thought over Lady Claudia's choice of words, thinking she meant her father again when it became terrifying clear it wasn't her only threat.

Sara stepped into the room with her head bowed. She dared a moment's glance at Elizabeth but didn't smile. Lady Claudia motioned Sara closer, and immediately Elizabeth understood the upcoming threat. Arthur had demonstrated the same callousness. It went beyond disgracing the Wicker name and taking away her freedom. It meant Sara had to suffer more black eyes. A bloody nose. A broken jaw. Elizabeth lowered her eyes, feeling trapped. She understood Lady Claudia's demands. The pawn to protect the queen.

Lady Claudia's smile grew. In their silent exchange, she read Elizabeth's submission. She shoved Elizabeth's petticoat back into Sara's hands. "The officers will be by soon to let you out. I suggest you get organized and meet at the house for the announcement tonight. If you try to run away, you know what I'll do."

ELIZABETH WAS STUCK behind a wall of misfortune. She had never had an easy life. She was accustomed to working until she was coated in sweat and her skin painted in bruises, but this type of struggling tore through her like hot knives. How often could the world crash around your feet, until you couldn't recognize the pieces anymore?

At a loss, she wandered back to the only place she felt safe, her old home in the Pitts. Being back inside her old house doubled the guilt, swelling her lungs and chest. Everything was exactly the same, untouched by time. The couch facing the fireplace was cold to touch. The kitchen, with its over-hanging pots on hooks remained hidden by shadows. The umbrella standing by the entrance now blanketed in months of dust. The only thing that was different was her old gutted bedroom. She dared not venture into her mother's room. Instead, she had found herself back in the lounge, legs curled up and her forehead pressed against her kneecaps. It must have been hours she sat like that, curled over in a mindless haze.

In her overwhelmed state of mind, she didn't hear Klaus break into the house. He had found out about her old address, and stormed over ready to reprimand her carelessness, but stopped when noticing her defeated posture. He didn't approach straight away. Emotions were never his strong suit. Ambitions, though, ambitions were easier to calculate. Often direct, selfish, controlling. Whereas emotions bubbled and swelled in the twists of turns of a hurricane. Just as powerful, and something he couldn't manipulate.

"What are you doing here?" He approached her carefully and knelt to her level. Despite his best attempt, his voice came across as rough. "What happened?"

She shook her head at him, unable to answer. He moved with an awkward coldness, hesitating to reach out and touch her. But as his hand brushed by her shoulder, Elizabeth immediately cringed away. "Please don't."

Klaus pulled his hand back. "You've been missing for hours. Tell me."

"Lady Claudia paid me a visit. She had me detained down at the police station. She blackmailed and threatened me into marrying her son, Arthur. If I don't marry him, she's going to kill Sara."

"The maid?"

"She's my best friend. Klaus, I don't know what to do!"

"Say yes."

Elizabeth glanced up. Surely, she had misheard him. "Say yes?"

Klaus' calculating face didn't change. "You can get the pistol back. I doubt Nikolas understands the gun's true power, so it'll be to our advantage to place you right under his nose—"

Anger hit her like a headache. "This isn't just about *getting* the pistol! If I marry Arthur Beaumontt, he's going to make my life a living hell! I can't say yes, but I can't let them hurt Sara either. I don't understand. Lady Claudia has a corrupted Time Collector. Why doesn't she wish for the things she wants? Why go through the hassle of threatening me?"

"Wishing for control over someone's willpower is very costly. Surely it would kill the wisher, ending the contract. Making the whole process null. She needs you to do it by your own actions."

"But why does she want me to marry into her family? What could she possibly be after?"

Klaus shrugged in mirrored confusion. "Whatever it is, it is something a Collector cannot grant her."

"I didn't think there was anything off limits."

"There are such things as too big of a wish. Nothing is simple, not when dealing with Time Collectors." He stood and extended his hand for her to take. "But sulking isn't going to help you."

Gingerly, she took his offer, allowing him to hoist her up. "What do you suggest?" The idea of marrying Arthur was sickening. Her skin crawled with the notion of Arthur's hands running over her.

"Go to them." Klaus said confidently. "And I'll ensure you and your friend are safe."

Wearily, Elizabeth glanced up. "How so?"

"Trust me."

CHAPTER

TWENTY-TWO

DREAD TASTED LIKE steel. Elizabeth felt like a lamb hanging on a hook, the perfect feast for the oncoming wolves. She arrived at the Beaumontt's despite every fiber of her being demanding she run away. She had to trust Klaus knew what he was doing, trust that he would come up with a solution to save both her and Sara. As she walked across the threshold into the Beaumontt's foyer, an uneasy flutter went off inside her stomach. The staff moved swiftly on her arrival, having been prepped to take Elizabeth to the guest quarters of the manor. Instructions were left on the dresser. Clothes to change into. Shoes to wear. The list even told her what shade of lipstick to put on.

What felt like the greatest insult of all were the two cuffs and one collar laid out on the dresser. It was of the Beaumontt drawn swords family crest. She was meant to wear them, a symbol of her becoming a Beaumontt, but Elizabeth couldn't bring herself to unclasp the choker. Her eyes searched the room. *They would be spying on me no doubt.* Lady Claudia didn't work this hard to trap Elizabeth and then risk her escaping last minute. Elizabeth ran her hands along the walls, searching behind shelves and frames for cameras. Behind one of the chairs she found something scratched into the woodwork. A peep hole. And another one by the dresser. One in the corner too. It was impossible to tell how many they had. Exactly how much they can see and hear.

"I can't believe you actually came here." A voice whispered with a timid knock on the door.

Elizabeth spun around and stood. "Sara?" Sara stepped inside and gently closed the bedroom door. She appeared unhurt, but the pink in her cheeks indicated she had been running. Elizabeth's eyes shot across the room. *Are they listening now?* The last thing she needed was Sara unravelling her plans.

"So it's true?" Sara spoke and tore Elizabeth's attention back down. "You intend to marry Arthur?"

"Yes," she answered.

"I don't understand."

"You don't need to understand."

"Why?"

"Sara, please—"

"It just doesn't make sense. You absolutely loathe him."

"I…it is complicated." Beneath Sara's disproving gaze Elizabeth's mask of confidence slipped off. She crossed her arms, feeling exposed. "Arthur isn't that bad after all."

"Isn't that bad? What have they done to you?"

"Nothing. I am being genuine." She couldn't say it was to protect Sara. Guilt was vicious, it would push Sara into doing something drastic to ease Elizabeth off her sacrifice. But it was also unnecessary. Klaus had a plan. Hopefully. "It makes sense, doesn't it? He is part of a wealthy, powerful family—"

"You've never cared for such things."

"I've matured. I understand now that it's best for my future."

"I know when you're lying, Elli." Sara stepped forward and brushed Elizabeth's arm.

Elizabeth stepped out of her reach. "Don't call me that. And it is not wise to act so familiar with me. Not here." *Not where Lady Claudia can hurt you.* She wanted to say the words, but couldn't. Her eyes shot straight toward the peep hole, hoping Sara would understand the hint. But instead, Sara took a step back.

"Earlier today, why were you imprisoned?"

"A silly misunderstanding."

"Lady Claudia bailed you out?"

"She is kind."

"No, she blackmails people. Threatens them."

Elizabeth smiled at Sara's quick understanding. "Politics, I believe. Nothing but standard upper-class hierarchy at play. Nothing I can't handle." She gave Sara a quick reassuring smile. As though relieved, Sara's chest deflated.

"You have a plan?"

"Always."

Somebody knocked and opened her door. "Miss Wicker?" A servant called. "You are required down by the ballroom."

Elizabeth nodded. "Thank you. I won't be a moment." He turned and left promptly. Sara casted a sorrowful look at the bracelets.

"You intend to wear them?"

"It only makes sense to wear armor when you go into war." Elizabeth smiled.

DESPITE THE CLOUD of warmth, sparkling wine and laughter, the celebration felt cold as Elizabeth approached the top of the ballroom stairs. She glanced out across the filling crowd, hoping to catch a glimpse of Klaus. Arthur stepped next to her from the other side of the railing. He was well groomed, stuffed inside a tuxedo with a gold handkerchief in his pocket square. There were brooches of golden watches and other badges pinned to his blazer, no doubt highlighting his wealth. He glanced at her anxiously. With all the commotion, she had forgotten about their last encounter, something he clearly had not. She wasn't sure if it was guilt or fear squeezing sweat from his brow. Elizabeth's fingers curled. There was no way she was going to marry this man.

"You don't look well. It's like you've seen a ghost," she taunted him.

The thick lump in his throat shifted as he gulped. "How are you even alive? I watched you die right in front of me."

"Remind me to thank you for that later."

"It wasn't my fault—"

"Announcing Sir Arthur Beaumontt and Lady Elizabeth Wicker." The booming announcer's voice tugged their attention back toward the party. Arthur reached his arm out as Elizabeth sourly placed her hand on his. Her grip hovered above his arm with her disgust to touch him. As they glided down the stairs, neither of them smiling, the crowd below applauded and cheered with raised wine glasses.

"Did you have a say in this?" Elizabeth hissed at him. "Can't have me as your servant, so you're taking me as a wife?"

"As if I would want to marry a rodent like you."

"Don't start pretending your vain insults aren't a cover for your infatuation with me," Elizabeth countered. "At least we're both equally disappointed in each other."

"What about you? Why are you agreeing to this?"

"Turns out, the only way to get a woman to marry you is through your mother."

Arthur turned away, greeting one of the Counts with a smile and a firm handshake. He played the role of happy fiancé well, even if two seconds ago he was unable to lift a smile. Elizabeth failed to mimic the fake delight. Purposefully, she would ease her hair to the side, bringing notice to her Wicker crest around her neck. Gentle gasps moved in waves around them. Elizabeth smiled, knowing Lady Claudia watched from the head table.

Arthur stepped closer. "Forget something?"

"What?"

"Your necklace?"

"What about it?"

Arthur sighed exasperated. "Embarrass us here and the consequences will be far more severe than a glassing." Elizabeth turned to face him, but before she could speak, Arthur walked away. He was right. She and Sara were both within the range of fire. The last thing she wanted was to paint targets on their backs.

An hour passed. Drinks continued to be refilled and guzzled. People danced. Congratulated them. Cheered. Ate food with their fingers. Elizabeth's wine had gone warm in her grip. She hadn't drank a drop. Arthur didn't approach her again for the rest of the night. She found him arguing with one of the maids off to the side of the ballroom. By the look of horror on his face, the maid must have broken something of his. He grabbed her arm and yanked her out into the hallway. Elizabeth took a nervous sip from her glass.

"Miss Wicker?'" A servant approached and handed her a note. "This came for you."

On the piece of paperwork was one word. *Garden.* "Who gave you this?"

"The guest only said you know who he is. But he did have a funny accent."

Klaus. "I do know him. Thank you." Elizabeth picked up the end of her dress and excused herself. Behind closed doors the noise from the party quietened into murmurs. The outside wind gently pulled on Elizabeth's hair, tickling her with a warm breeze. She glanced out and noticed she wasn't the only person taking refuge in the garden. Couples dotted the pathway, admiring the landscape and open starry night.

"Klaus?" She called in an urgent whisper. She stepped out from the overspilling party light and rounded the corner toward a gazebo.

"Klaus? I'm here." A calm quietness shifted over the garden. Elizabeth tucked her arms to her chest and leant across the gazebo railing as she waited. *Come on, Klaus. Where are you?*

"Oh, of course." She spun around at a voice. From the thick of the shadows, Nikolas approached with his hands clasped behind his back. Elizabeth's eyes widened. She clenched her jaw shut. "Yes, of course it is him. Poetry."

Oh no! Elizabeth's pulse raced. *Oh no! Oh no!*

Nikolas smiled, watching her face constrict with panic. "So, after all these decades he's managed to track me down." Elizabeth went to speak but couldn't think of anything to convince Nikolas he had misheard her. She had screwed up, badly.

"Are you going to run?" she asked, instead.

"I don't run. Only the guilty run."

"That's not what he says—"

"So fitting, he always did try to hide his weaknesses by pinning them on me. You two are made for each other." Nikolas stepped closer, coming within reaching distance. Elizabeth didn't move. She held her ground with her arms tightly crossed.

"How so?"

"I bet it would get lonely in that big house of yours. Makes sense he would bunker down with you. You must know all of his little secrets by now." He stepped closer.

"I know your secret too. I know what you are."

"And what is that?" He stared her down, challenging her courage.

"A murderer." Her breath shuddered, trying to repress the temptation to smack him across the face. Nikolas held her gaze with greedy delight, making it impossible for her to wrench free.

"That's not all of it. What else?" he pushed. Again, he stepped closer until his was close enough to breath down her neck.

"And a Time Collector. A corrupted one."

He paused briefly before a small smile crept across his face. His eyes sparked with understanding and opportunity. "Thank you."

"For what?"

He leaned down and whispered, "For being his downfall." Swiftly, Nikolas turned away. Elizabeth stepped forward to chase him, but he was quick to disappear into the darkness. She grabbed the railing for support, catching herself before her knees could give out.

For being his downfall. She pushed off the railing and rushed back into the ballroom. She needed to find Klaus. Warn him. Do something. Dozens of eyes followed her across the room. She couldn't take two steps without being stopped and congratulated.

"Your father would've been so happy."

"Thank you. Yes, thank you."

"Congratulations to the happy couple."

"Thank you."

"Are you thinking of a spring wedding?"

"I umm…I…" They spoke around her. She had to leave. She had to get out of there. A hand touched her back.

"Come with me." Her ears warmed at the brush of his thick accent. *Klaus.* He steered her through the crowd effortlessly, walking up the stairs. They slipped into a private room on the other side of the hallway. Inside, the working staff turned around, surprised at their entrance. Klaus shooed them out. Now alone, Elizabeth sat on the arm of a chair.

"Klaus, he knows…" she informed him breathlessly. "He knows you're onto him."

Klaus froze with his back to her by the door. His grip tensed, squeezing his fingers white. Carefully, he kept his voice low and calm. "How?" Elizabeth bit her lip. The guilt crossing her face was clear enough. Klaus pivoted toward her, wary to keep his expression emotionless. "What did he say?"

Thank you for being his downfall. "Only that he knows you're onto him." Elizabeth cleared her throat.

"Is that so…" His lean body went rigid, revealing a new level of alertness. "I have to go."

"Wait? What? Go where?"

Klaus didn't respond straight away. Instead, he looked around the room, perhaps searching for escape routes, perhaps calculating the possibility of Nikolas' hidden attack. "I told you, he's going to run."

"But…" Elizabeth stumbled forward. "What about me?"

"What about you?"

"The plan, Klaus! Your plan to keep Sara safe. Me safe."

"It doesn't matter now."

She choked on her breath. "Doesn't matter?" His choice of words tore through her. Inhuman. She forgot about his nature and her error was about to cost her everything. "Klaus, this is my life. You're a Time Collector. This is what you do. You make the impossible happen."

Klaus' expression tightened. "I cannot do anything to help you. I can only grant wishes with contracts, and Elizabeth you are living on borrowed time."

"You're throwing out excuses! You can still help me if you wanted to."

"I have my priorities!" As soon as he spoke, Klaus clenched his jaw and jerked his head down. "That's not what I meant."

Behind them, three quick knocks tapped against the door. "Miss Wicker? Are you in there? Is everything alright?"

Elizabeth inhaled a shaky breath. "Just a moment. I-I'm fine." She then directed her tone at Klaus in a harsher whisper, "How much time will it cost?"

"You cannot afford it," he replied bluntly.

"No not for my freedom, for Sara's? How much time?"

Klaus' eyebrow perked. "All of it. But—"

"Okay. Then take it."

"Nein, wait a moment—"

"Stop!" Sara's voice called forward. Crouched at the back of the room, she stepped out and placed the utensils she had been cleaning onto the table. "You're marrying Arthur…to protect me?"

The banging from the door continued with less patience, the doorknob now rattling. "Lady Wicker?"

"Sara, you were listening?" Elizabeth held her hand to her mouth as Sara made her way over. Klaus' stare hardened to the point of glaring, yet Sara didn't shift her attention away from him.

"You can help me escape?" she asked.

Tension ran up Klaus' neck. "Yes."

"How?"

"No!" Elizabeth urged over the top of him. "Sara, I will get you out of here."

"Elizabeth, you can't do this for me. You can't marry Arthur. If this man can help me, then I will take it." She turned back to Klaus with a begging voice. "I will do anything to get away from them."

"Sara, you don't know what you're getting yourself into—"

"I…I…" The words jumbled up on Klaus' tongue. Pressure swelled, spiralling in his vision. Every new thought dismantled instantly. After all, his was a creature controlled by a code. "This does not concern you anymore, Elizabeth." With his telekinetic abilities, Klaus unlocked the door and shoved Elizabeth out into the arms of the servant outside. She had only ever witnessed his power once, when he had slammed the east library door in her face from across the room. Elizabeth jumped up and threw herself against the door, both fists hammering.

Klaus returned to Sara, the darkness in the room thickening. Her trembling body fell back away from him.

"What? H-How did you do that?" she stuttered, gesturing back to the door. Klaus straightened his posture, his face void of emotion.

"It doesn't matter. What matters is I can get you out of here."

Her back hit the table, cowering from Klaus' advancement. Ever so delicately, he reached across her and picked up an apple from the fruit bowl. He offered it out. "How badly do you want to leave?" She glanced at the apple, then back at Klaus. She couldn't answer. Fear squeezed her voice box close. Klaus continued, "Do you want freedom?"

"Y-yes," she stuttered.

"I can give you what you want, but, I need something in return."

"Like what?"

"Your time."

"How much of my time?"

"Now, that depends on what you wish for." He pierced the core of the apple with the blade, pumping the fruit with magic through the tip. "Make your wish, then bite this."

ELIZABETH'S HAMMERING DIDN'T cease. Timothy, the Beaumontt's oldest son, weaved around the crowd toward her. The male servant glanced around in panic, unsure how to control Elizabeth's erratic behavior.

"What's all this fuss about?" Timothy held Elizabeth's arm back from swinging. Immediately, her attention moved onto the red, flaky rash covering half his face. Looking past his black gums and thinning hair, Timothy could've passed as an exact copy of Arthur. The moment he grabbed her a loud thump came from inside the room. Following it was a distinct crash before the ping of the latch unlocking.

They all rushed in and stopped at the sight of a collapsed body. Sara's eyes remained open, unblinking, and her body limp in her death. Color that shouldn't have been washed away until hours after her passing had already drained out of her. Timothy knelt beside her and checked her pulse. The drop of his head confirmed Elizabeth's worst fears. Cradled in Sara's loose clutch, was a large apple with a bite-sized piece missing.

Disbelief silenced her. Elizabeth didn't move. Didn't speak. She grabbed her heart, feeling it break. Shock gripped her throat, silencing the scream climbing up from the broken parts of her soul. Dead. Sara was dead. It spiralled her vision inward, blurring out the details of the room.

"Someone has poisoned the food." Timothy's voice sounded distant. People moved around her. She felt someone grab her shoulders and steer her out into the hallway. But it didn't make sense. *Dead? Sara couldn't be dead!*

Her legs wobbled as she turned and walked away. Noise rose from the party down the stairs. Laughter. Music. The clink of wine glasses. A pool of golden warmth sat at the bottom of the twenty-step decline. The marble steps were steep, creating a waterfall of white. Elizabeth approached the stairs and numbly gripped the railing. With the slightest tilt, she fell.

CHAPTER
TWENTY-THREE

WHITE FLUTTERED ABOVE. Pain spurred, originating from her ribs and forehead. Among the clicking of an overhead fan, the sound of distant coughs echoed down the hallway. Elizabeth's eyes opened further. White roof. Blue curtain, pulled closed around her. A figure in a dark suit stepped up to her side. Most of the details were still blurred, but she was sure in his hands was a folder of papers. His expression remained hidden behind the haze, but he moved quickly, as though flustered. Elizabeth touched around herself and picked the familiar sensation of cotton beneath her fingers. A bed, more accurately, a hospital bed. The man walked over, checked her temperature and spoke. She couldn't understand anything and eventually he called out to someone down the hall.

Elizabeth tilted her head backward in an attempt to clear her eyes, but a wave of pain pulsated from the back of her skull. She slammed her eyes closed to stop the room from spinning.

"She's awake. You can come in now."

"Thank you, Doctor." Harry's withered voice entered the room. His hands gently touched her own, and relieved, Elizabeth opened her eyes again. "Thank the heavens you're all right."

"Harry?" Her raspy voice broke. "What happened?"

"You fell down a flight of stairs. You'll be sore, but thank the heavens, it's nothing beyond bruising and maybe a concussion. I don't know what I would've done if I had lost you as well."

"I did?" Elizabeth raked her memory for the moment she fell.

"I packed you a change of clothes for when you woke up." Harry turned around and fetched out an overnight bag. He carefully passed it over.

"Thank you. What time is it?"

"Late, but the doctor was kind enough to let me stay. You'll have to stay here overnight for observation, but you can come home tomorrow."

A sharp knock on the door turned them around. Lady Claudia walked in, her mood anything less than relieved or worried. "Good, you're awake."

Harry turned around and stood. "Lady Beaumontt?"

"I would like to have a word with my future daughter-in-law in private."

"Daughter-in-law?" He glanced down at Elizabeth.

Lady Claudia's voice spat with venom, "Yes, and while you're here, your services with the Wicker household will no longer be required. You can leave now." Elizabeth struggled to sit up to defy Claudia's authority, but Harry held his hand out to stop her. He puffed his chest out and left. Lady Claudia's attention shifted back onto Elizabeth. "If I had known you wanted to kill yourself, I would've helped."

"Get away from me."

"Once you've married Arthur, you can throw yourself down staircases all week long for all I care."

"Somebody just died—"

"A maid has died. No one of any importance," she scoffed. Elizabeth sucked her breath in, her body physically shaking with rage.

"Lady Beaumontt? May I please have a word?" The doctor called by the door, signalling her over. Lady Claudia joined him out in the hallway and continued to speak privately. Elizabeth's hand unfurled from around the sheets. What was she going to do? The memory of falling down the stairs was washed with springs of pain and dizziness. The only reminder of the evening was the sharp jabs every time she took a breath.

"Many people brag about making an entrance," a voice spoke, stepping out from behind the drawn curtain. "I see you're more of an exit type of drama queen."

Elizabeth jolted and grabbed at her chest. "Klaus!"

"Glad to see you're finally awake. Are you aware that you snore?" Elizabeth glared him down, unable to form the right string of insults to properly translate how furious she was with him. Klaus perked an eyebrow, genuinely confused. "You're angry?"

"What do you think?"

"It's hard to tell anymore, you don't seem to have a whole range of facial expressions." Her glared hardened. Klaus awkwardly laughed. "I'm sorry, I'm trying to lighten the mood."

"Is Sara really dead?"

"Well, this is an awkward topic."

"How could you?"

"Shss!" Klaus rounded her bedside, "Keep your voice down. I don't want them knowing I'm here."

She jerked away. "Why *are* you here?" His eyes flicked up, holding hers. His expression said it all. What she first thought was a look of concern tightened in disappointment. Disapproval. Elizabeth shuffled back. "You think I did this on purpose?"

"You tell me," Klaus said. Elizabeth clenched her jaw, refusing to speak. Impatiently, Klaus glanced over his shoulder. "Fine, you don't have to trust me, but at least listen. We are not safe here. Look around you. Think of where you are and who has looked at you. What do you think is about to happen?"

"What are you talking about?"

"Possible cracked ribs, internal bleeding, spinal injury...where do you think they will look?"

Realization dawned on her. "Oh my God! Of course."

"And there's only one explanation."

"A miracle."

Klaus reached over and helped ease her out of bed. "More like wishful thinking. They will ask questions, questions you cannot reveal to them. Your only option is to leave this place."

"Leave forever?"

Klaus didn't answer, but promptly placed his finger to his lips as they neared the door before gently easing the door back. Elizabeth slowly edged her head out. The tight bark of Lady Claudia's voice carried down the hallway.

"Yes, Doctor, what is so important now?"

Doctor Boreman flipped through the pages on his clipboard, his motorized goggles churning to adjust his lenses. "As Miss Wicker's closest family, I wanted to check in with a few details that I don't understand."

"What makes you think I know anything?"

"Well, there's something strange I've noticed. Doctor Wicker, did he ever perform any surgeries on her?"

"How would I know that?" she asked, irritated.

"There's something very strange about her—" He turned to reveal his diagnosis, but Lady Claudia pushed the clipboard away.

"As long as she's still breathing, I don't care." She turned to leave but the doctor sidestepped to block her.

"That's the thing. Transplants aren't an uncommon practice, even with alternative organics or mechanics it's still possible, but this, this is a nothing short of a phenomenon. Impossible even. I need to know some more information about her condition."

Lady Claudia lowered her voice, "Condition, what condition?"

"She doesn't have a heart." Elizabeth's fingers clenched into the woodwork. Lady Claudia slowed before twisting back around. "We've done some tests. She still has a pulse, but the presence of an actual heartbeat isn't there. When placing her down on the ultrasound, the shape wasn't natural. It almost sounds like…well, it's just so unbelievable. Inhuman."

Lady Claudia licked her lips. "Like what?"

"Well, an ordinary clock. A pocket watch or a locket." Doctor Boreman's voice felt distant against the ringing in Elizabeth's ears. Klaus started moving. He indicated with a sharp jerk of his head for Elizabeth to follow.

"Incredible, but I agree doctor…" Lady Claudia turned her hardening gaze back down the hall toward Elizabeth's room, watching the door swing shut. "Not humanly possible."

CHAPTER TWENTY-FOUR

NIGHT CRAWLED OVERHEAD. The streets emptied, drawing attention to the rowdy bars and drunken partying. Among the spurs of the nightlife, loud pops cackled. Movement of red and orange surfaced above the gates, spitting out ambers. Pillows of smoke caressed the sky. Not an hour after finding out the Wicker's secret, did the Wicker estate go up in flames.

Lady Claudia stepped out of the carriage on the opposite side of town, beneath the clear and smoke-free breeze. She held her arm across her chest, hugging the warmth and keeping her fur pelt scarf from dropping. Nikolas waited for her by the pond. He pushed off from the tree he rested against, his face doused in soft moonlight.

"You work fast," she praised him from afar. As they met, he cupped her cheeks and tilted her head, drawing her lips to his. "Not now." Lady Claudia tilted her head to the side, pushing Nikolas away. "I have another request. There's a Time Collector here, I want you to find whoever it is, and bring them to me."

Nikolas' smile weakened. He had been dreading this moment. Especially as he already knew who the other Collector was. Subtly, he tried to dodge the request. "I cannot track Time Collectors."

"But you can track people though. Elizabeth Wicker happens to have a clock instead of a human heart, and there's only one creature capable of doing something like that."

"What makes you so sure the Collector is still around?"

Her tone sharpened. "Just bring me the Wicker girl. Once we have her, we can extort the information I need."

"And why do you need another Collector?"

She sighed, looking away. "Don't ask me such questions."

"There is nothing another Time Collector can do that I can't." Nikolas defended himself.

She stepped closer. "Then do as I say and capture Elizabeth Wicker. Nikolas, darling, don't be so selfish." She ran her finger along his chin. "I thought you wanted to make me happy."

"Of course I do."

"And what makes me happy is to find this other Collector."

Nikolas raised his brow. "You want to make me jealous?"

"You know I don't care for such games. If you really are the man you say you are, the man I love, then you will do this. For me."

Nikolas gripped her face between his palms, "I'll throw myself off the edge of the earth if you want me to," he assured her, coating his words in thick Finnish allure, "*Kuolema ei voi pysäyttää minua.*" (*Death cannot stop me.*)

A shiver tore through her. She reached up, her nails clipping his neck where she grabbed his collar and pulled him close. She kissed him, tasting the burn of his passion, his arrogance, his yearning and desperation to please her. She shoved him back.

"Don't disappoint me." She turned and made her way back to the car.

Nikolas chased after her with his eyes. "As you wish."

ELIZABETH WATCHED FROM on top of a hill as the flames destroyed her home. It took moments for everything to collapsed. The walls buckled, the roof snapped and fell, even the cars exploded, shaking the entire street. Everything she ever owned, her family pictures, her violin, her clothes and sanctuary, were destroyed in two blinks.

Instinctively, she looked toward the Pitts then toward the stretch of dotted lights where Harry's house stood. Klaus shook his head, watching Elizabeth from behind. "You can't."

"Harry could be in danger."

"He will be if you go to him."

Elizabeth backed away from the cabin window. "Where am I to go?" Klaus couldn't answer. The chilled breeze froze her tears against her face, causing her skin to tighten and itch. She hugged her arms into her chest, grateful to Harry for the change of clothes. "Why is she doing this?"

"She is trying to smoke you out. Make you desperate." He turned away, his fingers poised in thought beneath his chin. A flurry of different scenarios came to mind, all of them leading down one road. No matter which way he turned, Klaus found himself cornered. And it wasn't like the old days. Disappearing wasn't an option. There was a loose thread out there for Nikolas to grab. To unravel and follow. "Right now, the only safe spot for you is here."

"But I can't stay here forever," Elizabeth pointed out. Klaus nodded. He understood that. Uneasily, he checked his pocket watch before approaching the door. "Klaus? Where are you going?"

"I need to be alone."

"Why?"

"To think." Klaus left Elizabeth in the shack and promptly made his way back into town. Sunlight crawled up. It being the only indication that time had passed. In his haze, Klaus couldn't focus on the world around him. In return, it seemed the world never noticed him either. He was lost in a crowd instantly. No one ever looked at him, never spoke to him or touched him, but wove around him as though he was a lamp post in the middle of the footpath.

It was true. Elizabeth could not hide forever, which meant he couldn't hide. He stepped into the queue for a train ticket, his mind already racing, trying to find the perfect place to relocate. Where could he go that Nikolas wouldn't be able to follow? His options were narrowing. All this careful planning, stalking Nikolas for decades, working with William to create the ultimate weapon and he was to be undone because of one girl.

It was the crackle of bones that turned him around. Klaus glanced over his shoulder, tracing the sound of Nikolas' gremlins. They scurried over a pile of luggage, sniffing Elizabeth's scent out. *He is watching the train station. No doubt watching the airships, watching the roads.* Klaus stepped out of line. He hitched the collar of his trench coat up and made his way to the exit. Darkness thickened around him and the sound of popping steered Klaus left. He redirected his path toward the side exit only to come across an inflammation of shadows covering the entrance. Windows blocked. Doors, guarded. He slowed. *No of course…not watching for Elizabeth. Watching for me.*

He took a shaky breath and turned back around. He approached one of the small shops set up inside the station. The café remained at a constant pace, feeding the quick traveller with coffee and cake. Klaus pulled a chair up and sat down at a table. He need only wait moments before Nikolas approached.

Sunlight from the overhead sky roof cast a sheet of white across them. Nikolas pulled a chair out to sit opposite, carefully aware of Klaus's poised hands. At first, neither of them spoke. The air around them became overstuffed with strained silence. Klaus didn't move. His hands remained clasped, mindfully aware to keep his demeanor vague. Beneath the surface, his pulse raced.

Nikolas' focus narrowed, reading into Klaus' stony expression. "How long?"

"Months now. You were very slow."

Nikolas smirked as he reached over and poured them both a glass of water. "Something we have in common." He eased the glass closer to Klaus, but neither of them took a sip. The bustle of London moved around them, bringing contrast to their stalemate stand-off.

"You surprised to see me?"

"Hardly. I knew it was only a matter of time."

Klaus nodded. Without looking away, he searched the station for exits, weapons, places to hide. "Interesting choice of retirement."

"I can say the same for you."

"She is only a contract," Klaus said

Nikolas grinned. As he spoke, his fingers tapped the table top. "I know what she is. What did you have to do?"

"For what?" The conversation felt strained between them. Each question, loaded. Each moment of silence, deafening. Klaus slowly came to understand Nikolas' meaning. He reached over and took a long gulp of water. His face tensed painfully. "A deal."

"And she's prepared to burn?"

Klaus shuffled back, uncomfortable at the question.

Nikolas tilted his head at the change in Klaus' posture. Slumped. Worried. There was something there in the grip of his fingers, something he was trying desperately to shield away. "Amazing."

"What?" Klaus defensively jerked upward.

"One bump and look how fast you fall." Nikolas stood and buttoned up his blazer.

"So...not now?" Klaus asked, watching Nikolas leave.

"That's entirely up to you." He turned to walk away, but stopped and spoke over his shoulder. His voice softened. "Word of advice, little brother...keep falling."

CHAPTER
TWENTY-FIVE

EVEN IF KLAUS had rushed back, he wouldn't have been able to stop them.

Nikolas did in fact have eyes everywhere, and now that he was aware his brother was in the city, it was just a matter of placing them in the right spot. Since discovering Elizabeth's connection, he ensured to keep her always within reach. Klaus' natural repellent would bar his sight of her, making her location flicker and disappear. But the moment he stepped away, it took Nikolas moments to send men down to their secret little shack. Magic may shield Nikolas' entry, but he had other methods of kidnapping someone.

Under his order the two hired men dragged Elizabeth out from the hut. They temporarily drugged her, knocking her unconscious and returning her to the Beaumontt estate. Nikolas waited inside, watching from out of sight as they dragged Elizabeth in and left her to sleep on the guest's bed. Minutes after her, Lady Claudia stepped up to the doorway. Despite giving her what she'd asked for, she wasn't pleased. She was already planning ahead, calculating what must be done. She spoke to Nikolas without facing him. "To go ahead, how much will it cost?"

"A lot."

"Will it last?"

"Only moments."

"But will it *last?*"

Nikolas glanced at Elizabeth's drugged out state. Her eyes began to flutter. "Yes, long enough."

Lady Claudia turned and disappeared down the hallway. As Elizabeth slept, Nikolas peered out through the bedroom window to the courtyard out front. Nothing stirred among the morning shadows. His gremlins bubbled and popped, confirming the silence. *No Klaus.* He lifted his chin higher, boasting his pride. *He hasn't chased her.*

Nikolas promptly took his leave out into the hallway. As he stepped out, Timothy made his appearance from around the corner. As it has been for the past twenty-six years, Timothy trembled in Nikolas' presence. It being one too many times Nikolas has had to track him down after the bidding of Lady Claudia's requests. Each visit deepened the scars on his flesh, blackened his gums and thickened the rash. He was the only Beaumontt who understood what Nikolas was, and who understandably shrank into the shadows under Nikolas' presence. But in this instance, Timothy stepped closer.

"She plans on doing it to her, doesn't she?" He asked. "To Miss Wicker?"

As with all the other Beaumontt's, Nikolas barely acknowledged him. His interaction dwindled down to brief visits and though he only ever stood at Lady Claudia's elbow, he never saw himself as an equal to her husband. He was more than that, more than contracts and vows. The connection between them was spiritual, something no manmade ceremony could mimic. It went into their souls, becoming a part of their bodies and thoughts. Nikolas turned to leave, speaking briefly over his shoulder, "I don't need to know her intentions."

"Then you truly are a fool," Timothy shouted. "You must be, if you love her as much as you say you do." Nikolas slowed and Timothy took the chance to confront him. "I saw her body, that young maid's. A corpse only a Collector could leave behind. But, that wasn't your work. I know it wasn't, because otherwise you would've paid me a little visit."

Nikolas turned sharply. "What are you implying?"

"I know you couldn't be the only one of your kind out there. Is that why she is so interested in Miss Wicker? Why she is so desperate to marry her into the family?"

"I don't know."

"Yes you do. You can see the symptoms clearer than I can. She won't have much time left, not at this rate. Neither of us do."

A ping of alarm unsettled him. Nikolas brushed the worry aside. "You can't save her. Miss Wicker won't be able to leave this premise. I will ensure all the exits are bolted."

"I'm not talking about Miss Wicker." Again, another spur of worry. "Will you not listen to reason?" Timothy pushed.

"When I hear it, yes. But for you, Timothy Beaumontt, any remarks made about your mother has been tainted by your unfortunate history—"

"Unfortunate history?" Timothy scoffed. "She has destroyed my life. She has taken everything from me. That woman is no mother but a selfish mon—"

Nikolas spun and grabbed Timothy by the throat. Effortlessly he picked him up. "Speak ill of her again and I will ensure your tongue rots off."

He dropped him. Timothy stepped back, feeling the truth in Nikolas' threat. "Will they come for her? The other Collector? Will they come?"

The question poked at the unsettled parts of Nikolas' mind, trying to revive the flames. He didn't know. He hoped, no prayed, that Klaus' fear for him would deter him away from the manor. But, as long as Elizabeth sat in Lady Claudia's grip, so would Klaus. He had to get rid of her before that could happen. He didn't respond. He merely turned and walked away.

KLAUS STEPPED UP to the gate of the Beaumontt mansion. Immediately, he felt the tension of Nikolas' gremlins scurry back inside. His presence was the tripping wire, ready to set the bomb off. Yet still, he couldn't bring himself to cross the threshold. His mind burned with thought. If he ran, Elizabeth could be killed. If he stayed, Nikolas would get him. The smell of magic curled under his nose. He could smell it on the windows, on the door handles, even on the walls. It masked Elizabeth's faded scent, making it impossible to trace her. But Nikolas was panicked, his work sloppy. In his rush, he hadn't properly concealed Lady Claudia's scent. But how could he, when everything she touched reeked of the taint?

Klaus stepped inside. The shadows cut long bars across the room, cramping the foyer. He moved, following the scent toward her chambers. Inside, Lady Claudia sat opposite a young maid who carefully applied lipstick along her lower lip. The girl's hand shook despite her best efforts to steady herself. The clicking of the closing bedroom door caused them both to jolt. The young maid immediately jumped up. Lady Claudia swivelled in her seat at Klaus's entrance. He stopped at the threshold, both hands held behind his military straight back. Immediately he read the missing clues on Lady Claudia's face. A soul full of rotten taint, but without a blemish on her. Not even wishes could conceal such dark magic, which left only one possible answer. *A sacrifice.*

Klaus stepped forward. "Looking for me?"

The shocked look on Lady Claudia's face shifted with realization. "Leave us." She ordered the girl, who bolted out of the room. Lady Claudia turned so she could face the mirror, speaking to Klaus' reflection. "I can only assume a man capable of breaking into my chambers under Nikolas' detection is that of a Collector. Let's introduce ourselves properly, I don't want there to be any bad blood between us. I'm Lady Claudia, wife to Governor Harold Beaumontt. What shall I call you?"

"My name does not matter."

"German? How exotic. Can't say I've ever touched German soil before." Klaus didn't respond to her flirtations. Unfazed, Lady Claudia swiftly stood and turned to face him. "How are you enjoying London? We always do get such beautiful white snow."

"I don't care for snow."

"Don't you?" She teased the question and glanced at the clock in her room. She smiled. "Ten minutes isn't a very long time for someone who doesn't care." His back stiffened as Lady Claudia ran her eyes up and down his body. She sighed and glanced away, mocking him. "I guess Germany is a cold enough place."

"What do you want?"

"Your company."

"Why?"

"Don't worry." She laughed, "I don't intend to harm you."

"But you intend to harm someone?"

"If you came running all the way over here to play the hero I'm afraid you're out of luck. I suggest wearing a suit next time, it is a more appropriate attire."

"For what?"

"A wedding, of course."

Klaus cocked his head to the right. "On a strict deadline, are we?"

"With the bride-to-be throwing herself down stairs, no one is surprised."

Klaus cleared his throat. "Perhaps that's a big enough hint that the bride-to-be does not wish to marry."

"Wishes are to be left between you and me."

Her comment made him pause. "You were the one searching me

out?" *And not Nikolas?*

Lady Claudia looked away, knowing the next question Klaus was about to ask, and knowing she could not say her reason aloud. She said instead, "Elizabeth must wear white today so I do not have to wear black. That is reason enough to do what has to be done." His understanding clicked. A deadline, but not for who he first thought. Lady Claudia continued, "Collector, I wish you will not leave this room for the next hour. I am going to need you very soon."

Impulses fired up Klaus' spine and into the back of his eyes. Promptly he unsheathed the blade and drove it into Claudia's lower rib. She didn't flinch as the snap of gold escaped into the churning barren. With it, Klaus sensed the walls, windows and door shimmer with an invisible blockage. He withdrew the blade, his eyes locked on Lady Claudia as she turned and left, leaving Klaus trapped behind.

The possibility of Nikolas' demise struck a chord with him. *The enemy of my enemy is my friend. Is that not how the saying goes?* All thoughts of Elizabeth dispersed into smoke. He understood what intentions Lady Claudia had. He should be relieved, pleased even. Half an hour passed with no signs of Nikolas or Lady Claudia. Nikolas would know he was there without a doubt, but why hasn't he come to kick him out?

Klaus continued to pace. As fate had it, it indeed would be Klaus' hand that destroyed Nikolas and at the request of his love no less. A truly tragic way to go. The more he thought about it, the lighter his steps became. Nikolas was going to die and in the most awful way. Time weaving was a cruel act, the biggest betrayal in all sense of the word. Not that Klaus could do much about Lady Claudia's plans. He was, after all, a creature put on earth to obey. This was one request he didn't mind helping. That was, of course, until another Beaumontt knocked on the door.

Klaus turned at the entrance of Timothy, who stepped around the door as though he was walking into the den of a monster.

"The maid told me you were here. My mother has been expecting you." Timothy gently closed the door behind him. Klaus turned to face him, returning to his cold, expressionless demeanor. "I know what you are. You don't need to hide from me."

"Obviously." The taint from Nikolas' influence covered Timothy down to the needles of his veins, discoloring his body in a reddish rash. *This is her sacrifice.*

"The ceremony will be over soon. We won't have much time."

"What do you want?"

"I want you to release me."

Klaus' eyebrow perked. "Why?"

"Look at me."

Klaus exhaled loudly. Perhaps fate had not delivered him his one desire, but teased him long enough to wrench the opportunity away. He paced again, letting his thoughts turn into speech. "I'm beginning to understand. One son to carry the taint, and I'm aware you have a brother, Arthur, who no doubt will be killed in a bid to time weave Nikolas. Lady Claudia walks free and is allowed to live a full life untainted. You and your brother won't be so lucky. Looks like Elizabeth will be a widow faster than she could have hoped."

"This is not a joke."

"I am not laughing." Klaus stopped. "I still want to know why. It has to be more than just bitterness. Brotherly love perhaps?"

Timothy stepped forward. "Justice, for what she did to Rose."

"Rose?"

"Rose Bell was the sweetest person I had ever known. Intelligent. Kind. Beautiful. But because she belonged to a common household my mother did not approve of us. I had to be with someone within the city walls, someone of the same status as myself. I told my mother of my intentions to marry Rose, and so she sent her pet Nikolas to disfigure her. He ended up controlling her family dog to attack her that same evening. When I finally reached her in the hospital it looked like she had been mauled by wolves." Klaus could hear the strain in Timothy's voice, the catch in his speech revealing this was a traumatic memory, but one he had replayed enough times not to break at its mention. "She thought herself too hideous for me. Called herself a beast and threw herself off the rooftop. If only she had lived long enough to see me, to see the real beast, she may have decided to stay. Every night I wish I had jumped after her. But, of course, I couldn't."

"Because Nikolas wouldn't let you die, not if your death would take Lady Claudia down with you." Klaus slowed in his understanding, but it was still not enough to change his mind. Lady Claudia's plan meant killing Nikolas, a common desire he had with the cruel woman. "If her freedom means Nikolas' end, then that is a deal I am willing to make."

"But that is not the deal I am asking of you."

Klaus turned away, feigning disappointment. "Even so you cannot afford the time to kill her. I suggest you try good old fashion poisoning. With Nikolas gone, she should be easy to take down."

"Alas you misunderstand, Collector." Timothy said. "It is not her death I wish for."

CHAPTER
TWENTY-SIX

NIKOLAS STOOD AT Lady Claudia's side, feeling the emotional narrow space between them widen in his uncertainty. He watched her turned head, familiarizing himself with the curve of her neck as one would watch a loved one before death. Lady Claudia sat with Arthur and the minister talking about weddings, but Nikolas couldn't hear a word. A familiar pain spread across his chest. A pain he'd felt when watching her marry Harold. A pain he felt listening to her vows. The same pain he felt while watching her love another man so openly, while he was always pushed away.

He never complained. It was his own fault he loved a mortal woman. That's what they do: they marry, they move on, they vanish. Despite watching many of his past loves crumble under the hand of time, Lady Claudia felt as immortal as him. A perfect partner, to allow himself to fall into the grace of human love. But of course, she was still a mere human. Of course, she couldn't live forever. It was a thought he had barred himself from, and one Klaus always managed to resurface. The gremlins manning Elizabeth's room perked up with chatter the moment she woke. Nikolas gently touched Lady Claudia's shoulder, alerting her to Elizabeth's state, before leaving the room.

ELIZABETH SPRUNG UP. Her mind spun, hazy behind the drug as she swung her arm out to fend off attackers that were no longer there. The last thing she remembered were two men storming the hut. The weakened door was kicked down easily. They grabbed her and smothered her screams with a chloroform soaked cloth. It took her a few minutes to eventually pass out. Fear spiked the moment she woke. She swung out. She squealed and propelled backwards as though frightened awake by a nightmare. She glanced around the room, delirious in her panic. At first, she couldn't recognize where she was, but the presence of Nikolas helped piece everything together. He stood by her bedside, as if waiting for her to wake. Without a word, his presence filled the room like thick smoke. She automatically held her breath.

"Miss Wicker?" Beneath his shadow, Elizabeth felt herself shrink. It felt so surreal, so unnatural, being so close to him. He was the corrupted Time Collector. The bad guy. The villain. He was the man who killed hundreds of people. He was the same man who drove a knife into her mother's chest and inhaled her soul. Yet, every time Elizabeth felt anger swell and her eyes turn sharply to him, she would hesitate. His face was calm, soft even and warm. His eyes did not sting with malice as Lady Claudia's did. She could even feel an essence of loving warmth radiate off his skin, like he was truly happy and had no ill thoughts.

"What am I doing here?"

"You're home."

"Home? This is a cage." Elizabeth climbed out of bed. She wobbled, but refused to grab the furniture to brace herself. "You kidnapped me?"

"I like to call it an invitation one can't refuse."

"Where's Klaus?"

Nikolas' frown tightened with his annoyance. "He left town. I ensured it."

He could see the flutter of her fear and disbelief. "He wouldn't."

"Klaus is wise enough to know when he is threatened, and I do not threaten people lightly." As he spoke, he took a step forward, drawing back his coat and revealing his Collector's blade.

"What are you going to do with me?"

Nikolas motioned his head sideways to a simple white dress hanging off the door hook. Elizabeth tensed at the sight of it. "Now?'

"They're waiting for you."

"And what if I refuse?"

"That's why I'm here." Nikolas turned his head down, smiling. "I can be very persuasive."

Elizabeth licked her lips nervously. He may as well point a gun to her head. "What does Lady Claudia want out of this marriage?"

"Right now, your obedience. Come, it's time." Elizabeth left the room with Nikolas at her side, having refused to wear the wedding gown Lady Claudia had set aside. As they walked, Elizabeth searched the halls for Klaus, while trying to think of her own way to escape the Beaumontt's clutches. "There's no point in dragging your feet," Nikolas said. "You should be happy. Marrying into a prestigious family like the Beaumontt's is every girl's dream."

She glanced at him, "You do not know of my dreams. This is a death sentence."

"You will not be harmed."

"I am not scared of the Beaumontt's. Same as I am not scared of you!" Elizabeth snapped. "There is nothing left for them to harm me with. It is not fear that slows my steps."

Nikolas weakly smiled. Her fighting spirit glowed within her, tightening her fists and pulling her shoulders back. The confidence of a strong woman was what pulled Nikolas into Lady Claudia's hands. An equal companion to spar with. A love that pushed him to become better. "I'm sorry that you've been dragged into all of this. It's not my intention to keep you trapped here. Perhaps, one day, you will not think so poorly of me," he said as they slowed outside a room.

Elizabeth gawked at his apology, unable to see the genuine expression and mistook it for mockery. "You say one thing, but do another, your actions hollow your words."

Nikolas stepped closer and cupped her chin while he placed his other palm flat against Elizabeth's forehead, sending a sharp zap into her head. Internal strings pulled at the pressure points at her temples, sending a hot spike to the back of her eyes and throat.

"What—" She touched her forehead, checking for blood.

"Lady Claudia is a cautious woman. Whenever the minister looks at you or is within earshot of you, your body will freeze. You won't be able to talk to him or make any indication of your discomfort. The only words allowed out of your mouth is *I do*."

Elizabeth's terror pulled on her face. She grabbed his hand reaching for the door knob. "Please, don't do this."

Nikolas hesitated briefly before opening the doors to Lady Claudia, Arthur, and the minister waiting inside. He sidestepped for Elizabeth to enter. Magical strings in Elizabeth's head pulled on her back muscles, tightening her posture till the point she was standing rigidly upright.

Lady Claudia stood on her entrance. "Wonderful, we are all here."

Like a plank of wood snapping, Elizabeth's back bolted upright at Minister Geoffrey's approach. The minister looked at Elizabeth. "It's lovely to see you, Miss Wicker. We can start this wondrous ceremony now."

Her body had completely frozen. Like a hiccup, the words, "I do," jumped out of her mouth before she could stop herself.

As Minister Geoffrey turned to get his bible, Lady Claudia lowered her mouth to Elizabeth's ear. "Just so you know what's at stake here, if you do anything other than stand there and say the words, Nikolas will destroy that little academy of yours. Let's not forgot about your half-brother and sister. Their deaths will be slow and very, very painful. Do you understand me?"

Elizabeth understood completely. She lowered her head and whispered, "I do."

NIKOLAS STOOD IN a separate room on the other side of the hallway from the ceremony. In front of him, three young girls sat around a table, eating their meals. They faced away from him, their heads bowed over their feast. They chatted, laughing with one another, completely unfazed by Nikolas' presence. Promptly, he walked across the dining area and stabbed one of the girls in the spine. The attack was silent and undetected. Her eating slowed. Her appetite vanished. She leaned over her plate moments from vomiting. It took thirty seconds for her head to drop into her dish. The girl next to her glanced over, alarmed. She shook her shoulder, only to have Nikolas stab her in the back as well. She turned, prompting the third maid to stop eating and notice the knife. She shrieked and kicked back from the table,

As did the first maid, it only took the second girl moments to be drained of her remaining life. She managed to stand before collapsing into death. The power to control others was a steep price, eating into their time rapidly. The third made a run for the other side of the room, but Nikolas moved incredibly fast. He delivered the killing blow to her stomach and watched as she slid down the wall. Her last few moments left him feeling chilled. Three young lives lost to control Elizabeth for twenty minutes. It was hard to justify his behavior, but like he did after all of Lady Claudia's selfish demands, he merely turned away.

THE CEREMONY DIDN'T last long. That was exactly how Lady Claudia had planned it. When it came to answering the minister's final question, Elizabeth glanced once more at Lady Claudia, then back at the door, praying Klaus wasn't too far off. By the time the words "I do" slid out of her mouth, the thought of Klaus saving her had completely diminished. She stood as an erect pillar opposite Arthur as Minister Geoffrey pronounced them husband and wife. Along with the rings exchanged, there was the swapping of the chokers. Almost giddy with joy, Lady Claudia stepped up behind Elizabeth and unclasped her choker from around her neck. Unable to move, Elizabeth couldn't catch the Wicker choker as it dropped to the ground by her feet. The new choker was fitted around her neck, scratching her skin. Arthur stepped in closer and kissed Elizabeth's pressed lips.

"Congratulations, Mr. Arthur and Mrs. Elizabeth Beaumontt!" Minister Geoffrey cheered as Lady Claudia's sharp claps sounded off through the quiet room. As the words from the minister hit the ceiling, Elizabeth felt her frozen body unlock. She turned away, so furious she was afraid she was going to spit fire.

"Thank you Minister Geoffrey for your service. Please, come by tomorrow morning so we can celebrate properly with the whole family." Lady Claudia led the Minister to the door before ushering him out.

The word *husband* churned Elizabeth's stomach. When Nikolas reappeared in the room, Lady Claudia made deliberate attempts at avoiding his touch. Pain tightened his face. He could see his own damned fate in Elizabeth's expression. She turned away near the brink of tears, yet Nikolas did not have the luxury to display his agony. The longer he watched Lady Claudia, the more of Timothy's warning echoed in his mind. He had watched her enough times to read her body language accurately. Nervous. Rattled. Hopeful. Panicked.

Lady Claudia took Arthur by the arm. "Now, for your wedding present. Come with me." She walked forward before Nikolas could reach out to stop her. This was it. It was time.

CHAPTER

TWENTY-SEVEN

THE AIR STANK of magic. Three lives were lost in the span of twenty minutes. They sizzled out like a flame against a storm, leaving behind wisps of smoke that scented the air. Klaus' attention moved into the hallway, pinpointing the void where there was once life. *Nikolas.* The entire house flooded with their off-scent, but Klaus' attention focused back on Lady Claudia's return.

The moment she stepped inside the room, he felt the blockages collapsed around him. Now free, Klaus could easily escape into the hallway, but when noticing Arthur walked in behind her, he looked down to the new wedding ring on his finger. Klaus' mind momentarily went to Elizabeth. He imagined she'd hoped he would swoop in to stop the ceremony. One big romantic gesture, the passionate shout of "I object" as he ran down the aisle. But of course, Klaus was barred to Lady Claudia's chambers until her return. Even if he wasn't, gate crashing the wedding where Nikolas would be waiting was not on the top of his list. She would be disappointed in him, but perhaps it was a good thing Elizabeth learned to be disappointed.

Lady Claudia walked with a skip in her step. Everything was going to plan. Everything she wanted, no, *needed*, was falling into place nicely around her. He had half the mind to warn her of Timothy's intentions.

Arthur stopped at the entrance, confused at Klaus's company. "What? Who are you?"

Lady Claudia stepped around them both and fetched her dagger, hidden in her drawers. Klaus' eyes trailed her, ignoring Arthur as he stepped closer. "Wait, I know you! You're that doctor's apprentice! You punched me in the face. What the hell are you doing in my mother's room?"

"I was invited." Klaus smirked. "Can't time weave someone without me."

"Time weave?" Arthur turned to his mother. "What is he talking about?"

Lady Claudia held the knife behind her back as she carefully approached. "Don't worry. He won't be here for very long." She stepped around Arthur and dragged her hand along his back. There was no hesitation in her movements. No moment of guilt.

Klaus almost applauded her indifference. "For a cold-hearted person, even this seems cruel. You should at least warn him. He is so convinced of your love I'm sure he'll want to hear your final goodbyes."

Lady Claudia smiled. "I have nothing left to say." Standing behind Arthur, she reared her arm back. "I have to worry about myself first."

Klaus' eyes sparkled. His heart rate accelerated, waiting for her arm to swing down. A noise shifted in the corner. He didn't need to look to see who it was. Even so, he was surprised when Nikolas didn't try to stop her. The moment it took for Lady Claudia's arm to swing down slowed. It would take half that time to push her off balance. Just one blink to a gremlin would send Lady Claudia to her knees. He could stop her, if he wanted to, but he didn't move.

Nikolas stood there, watching, and the gesture completely stunned Klaus. Strong devotion, even in the face of betrayal, still controlled him. The act was laughable. Disappointment surged through Klaus. The little respect he had for his brother shattered into pieces. *Such a fool.*

Lady Claudia drove the blade down into Arthur's spine, only to have the dagger shatter on impact. Klaus slowly closed his eyes. His heart raced uncomfortably, pumping erratic impulses into his body.

"What?" She dropped the handle to the ground. "What's going on?"

From behind her closest door, Timothy stepped forward. Lady Claudia and Arthur both turned toward him. Timothy's expression tightened with his misery, a mixture of disappointment and relief washed over him. "I can't let you."

"Timothy?"

"Timothy? What are you doing here? What's going on?" Arthur stepped back, unaware his life had just been saved.

"I won't let you continue anymore. This is my final wish."

Lady Claudia choked. Realization dawned on her and panicked, she stepped back. "What did you wish for?"

"The only thing that'll stop you."

Both Klaus and Nikolas moved at the exact same moment. In the blur of the commotion, Lady Claudia didn't have time to react. Arthur was thrown to the ground by the clash and scrambled back. Klaus rushed in and grabbed Lady Claudia by the throat. At the same time, Nikolas grabbed his wrist to stop him. But Klaus' fingers clenched, instantly destroying Lady Claudia's voice box. Nikolas was quick to throw him off, slapping Klaus' hand away with such force Klaus stumbled back for balance.

Nikolas blocked Klaus' advancement, but the damage had already been done. "No! Klaus!" Nikolas pleaded. In his most sincere, vulnerable voice, Nikolas held his shaking hand out, begging. "Don't do this."

Klaus stepped backward, the dagger already in his hand. Tears clouded Nikolas' vision. There was nothing he could do to stop it. All he had was to plead, to beg Klaus not to destroy his one chance of happiness. He allowed himself to break down in front of his brother.

He allowed himself to shake, to tremble in fear, to show Klaus just how real his emotions were. Lady Claudia dropped to the ground as she clawed at her own throat, trying desperately to scream. No noise came out, not even a squeak.

Klaus shook his head. "I always said that love will destroy you. Here's my proof."

In the next fluid twist, Klaus drove his blade into Timothy's chest. The sharp white snapped as specs of gold escaped Timothy's body, draining him until all color had been vacuumed out. As he died, Lady Claudia crumbled beneath the taint. She didn't react when her skin began to blister and burn. Her hair fell out in clumps of gray, her face hollowed as deep, veiny cracks formed around her mouth. She shrivelled into herself, her wrists curling in, her knees turned to her chest, resembling a burnt prawn than a human being. The room fell into a hushed silence. Nikolas watched Lady Claudia drop, watched her disintegrate and shrink. He fell to his knees beside her body, unmoving, as she eventually rolled over and went still. Arthur didn't move either. Right before his eyes, his mother and brother died at the hands of Klaus. Shock silenced him.

Klaus stepped back. Released from his contract, his body cooled as the magic left him. As his mind cleared, he came to understand the damage he had done. The pain that must be overwhelming Nikolas, turning him quiet and rigid. Heartbreak wounded him. It tore into his muscles, taking his breath, dissolving his mind into sharp sparks of pain. He couldn't breathe beyond a tremoring gasp. The world as he saw it darkened, breaking his willpower as though it broke his bones. Darkness gathered behind Nikolas' back, creating a long black veil. The shadows shifted as they climbed out of the walls and up from the floorboards. Klaus looked down at the gremlins teaming together.

"What are you doing?"

Each rage-filled pant exhausted more darkness around Nikolas, the thick smoke spiralling into dozens of spawning gremlins. His voice shook from the deepest part of his throat, wrenching up his agony. "If your intention was to break me, then consider me broken. But know this, Klaus, with every breath, every passing moment, I promise I will return the favor. I will do more than just shatter you, I promise to set your whole world on fire."

Klaus' eyes widened, watching the shadows creep up and drench the walls and ceiling like shimmering moss. The house began to shake, the overhead light bulbs flickered and exploded in concession pops. Rage enveloped the room, pushing Klaus out into the hallway where he sidestepped the crumpling debris from the ceiling and walls. He started to run, keeping one step ahead of the moving tidal wave of darkness. Elizabeth's scent remained masked from him, but the death of the three girls led him down the halls with the ease of following fire. Nikolas was going to tear the house down. Klaus had to be quicker.

ELIZABETH JERKED AROUND at the creak of the timbers snapping. The chandelier above her head bounced as though dropped and caught again. She stood up from the couch she sulked on, watching the shadows seep out of the furniture and the corners of the rooms. The floor beneath her shook with the ferocity of an earthquake. She grabbed the couch to steady herself.

"Elizabeth?" A distant voice called. Elizabeth turned toward it. "Elizabeth?"

"Klaus?" She ran out into the hallway and turned toward his voice. Klaus ran into view, propelling himself off the walls and lurched toward her. He didn't slow on his approach, but instead pulled Elizabeth along into his sprint. She spun around and was dragged behind him, Klaus too rough with his panic.

"Klaus!? What?!"

"Just run!"

The floor beneath them cracked, splintering the wood panels as the ground shuddered in stress. Elizabeth squealed as large junks of debris dropped off the roof, missing her head by inches. Klaus kept his pace, spotting a window. He didn't slow to think what would happen to Elizabeth if they were to jump through. The second-story drop was high enough to break bone, but not kill her. *Hopefully*. He held his arm up to shield his eyes from the incoming impact.

Elizabeth didn't have time to brace herself. Klaus leapt forward, shoulder first into the window, smashing the glass. He pulled Elizabeth into him tightly, wrapping his arm around her shoulders and shielding her face against his chest. She felt weightless as they took to the air. Her legs tensed up, propelling her along the wind. As they dropped, instinct overtook Klaus' body. As a nerve twitched, he shoved Elizabeth away. The sudden gesture forced Elizabeth to crash land into the bushes below, drawing long, razor cuts up her arms and gashed her cheeks. A sharp pain shot from her shoulder where she landed on it. She grabbed her arm, fearful the bone had popped out of its socket. Though the muscles felt swollen with bruises, she hadn't broken anything. Klaus landed flawlessly right next to her.

"Sorry." he reached over and hoisted her up. "Collector survival." Without wasting another moment, the two of them scrambled out of the way as the Beaumontt mansion crumbled into ruins.

IN LADY CLAUDIA'S chambers, Nikolas exhausted smoke like a chimney of ash and despair. Arthur craned his head up, watching as the walls buckled into splinters. He then looked down at his mother, who was almost unrecognizable, and his brother's dead body. Both were lifeless and still.

"W-what did you do?" he shouted, unable to speak without choking on the dust. Nikolas turned his head upwards, his blood red eyes weeping beneath his matted hair. "Move it, Nikolas! I need to get out of here!" Nikolas didn't move. He barely budged from his slouched position over Lady Claudia's body, his watery eyes strained with pain.

Arthur ran for the door, but it vanished beneath the carnage. The only exit was blocked and the roof above him struggled to hold. He looked around, realization of his doom sinking in. "Nikolas! D-do something! Get me out of here!" Nikolas clenched his jaw. Blood trickled from his nose. "I said get me out!" Arthur screamed. A nerve snapped, spinning Nikolas around as he leapt up and snatched Arthur around the throat, effortlessly hoisting him up. Arthur gurgled.

"You could have saved her," Nikolas whispered. He took the blade from his belt, driving the point into Arthur's chest. Arthur gasped as Nikolas threw him through the roof and out into the garden bed. He landed on his shoulder, snapping the joints. Pain drove him howling into the dirt. Behind him the house collapsed, swallowing Nikolas and the remaining Beaumontt's underneath a cloud of dust and rubble.

CHAPTER
TWENTY-EIGHT

*A*S THE DUST settled and ambulances surrounded the Beaumontt mansion, Elizabeth and Klaus hurried back to the refuge of Harry's place in Rosefire. Elizabeth tended to her wounds with a dampened cloth. The bruising in her shoulder stiffened her movements. Despite the terror, the pain, and her legal marriage to Arthur Beaumontt, she still sighed in relief, finally feeling safe from Lady Claudia. Klaus did not mirror her feelings. He checked and rechecked outside the windows.

Harry placed a warm cup of tea by Elizabeth before sitting next to her, helping cover some of the larger gashes with bandages. He unclasped the Beaumontt choker and replaced it back with one of the Wicker crests from the mansion. She touched the collar fondly.

Vehicles raced past by the dozens, followed by crowds of people coming out of their houses to watch the spectacle unfold. Large horns blasted the news on top of cars, calling it the *Beaumontt Reckoning*. Elizabeth gave her account to the police, but refused to speak to the crowd of reporters trying to profit from her story.

Klaus' pacing was a constant click. He pinched his chin; his eyes focused downward. Elizabeth and Harry exchanged brief glances before Harry took his leave, taking with him the bowl of water.

"Klaus, are you okay?" Elizabeth asked. He glanced briefly at her, implying he had heard her, but didn't want to answer. Elizabeth tried again. "What happened back at the Beaumontt's?"

"A mistake," he growled before correcting himself. "No, more like a wasted opportunity."

"I don't understand."

"Of course you don't."

Elizabeth cringed at Klaus' snappy comment. "Then explain."

Klaus swung around, irritated, "That bastard Timothy destroyed everything. Everything! I had Nikolas in my grip, she was going to time weave him!"

"Time weave? What's that?"

"Pretty much the only way for someone to completely destroy a Time Collector. The sacrifice of blood and magic."

"Klaus, you're not making any sense. Please, calm down."

Klaus slowed and took a big breath before taking a seat opposite her. He leaned forward so his elbows balanced on his knees, his face tight in his seriousness. "There are consequences to everything we do. Corrupted Time Collectors leave a rot in the people who contract with them. This rot builds with every wish, it disfigures their body, mind, and soul into a grotesque state. In the case of Lady Claudia, she had offered up Timothy as the bodement of her punishment. This is called the sacrifice, and can only be passed on to the wisher's offspring. Timothy was to take the physical damage of her wishes, but she still carried the taint in her mind and soul. Of course, when Timothy died, the taint had nowhere to go but back onto Lady Claudia. She didn't have much time left before the taint was going to destroy her anyway. That's why she needed me. She had hoped to shove that taint back onto Nikolas instead, destroying him so she could live."

Elizabeth sat up higher in her seat. "Timothy died?"

"He had wished for me to take his mother's voice and the time owed to me would kill him. He took her only chance of saving herself by removing her voice. She couldn't speak to Nikolas. Even with her voice back, the taint was so deep it had completely incapacitated her."

"Oh my God! Is she dead too?"

Klaus smirked. "Nein, but she may as well be. In his overwhelmed state Nikolas decided to tear the house down. He's always been like that. Overdramatic and irrational." Elizabeth cringed at Klaus' heartless dismissal. Klaus caught the look and straightened up in his chair. "What? Do you consider me cruel?"

"I didn't say anything," Elizabeth said.

"You don't need to speak. I can read it on your face."

"It's…just heartbreaking."

"Why are you sympathizing with him?" Klaus grew defensive, hardening his voice. "Even after he tried to kill you?"

"He didn't try to kill me."

"So pulling the house down while you're still inside isn't considered attempted murder?"

"Klaus." Elizabeth put the damp sponge back on the table, feeling Klaus' frustration at her grow. "Why are you so mad? Is this still not a victory?"

"No, this is the exact opposite. This is a loss. Before, when Nikolas had Lady Claudia, he had a weakness. A thing to which he was leashed, but now he is free and incredibly angry at me. And it's thanks to you that he now has a real chance of destroying me once and for all."

"Thanks to me?"

"Yes, you, and your *mortal* life. The big difference between Nikolas and myself is that Lady Claudia was his source of power to gravitate toward but you are just a hooked hand I cannot rid myself of. He wanted his flaw, I do not." His words hurt her as though he had reached over and slapped her. Elizabeth promptly stood and Klaus followed.

"No, wait, I'm sorry. I'm sorry, I didn't mean that." He reached out and grabbed her arm. He stepped in close to whisper, but his nerves rattled his voice, revealing his panic. "I am in trouble, Elizabeth."

Elizabeth looked down at his frightened grip. "What aren't you telling me?"

"Time Collectors cannot track each other and that is how I've been avoiding Nikolas for all these years, but now that you and I are linked together, he will always find me. My only chance to kill him first is with the gun."

"Can't you time weave him?"

"Time weaving is only achievable through mortals. I cannot do it on my own."

"I'm a mortal."

Klaus rolled his eyes and stepped away. "It's not that simple. I need that gun, Elizabeth. If not to stop Nikolas, then what is your purpose? What is your point in being here? He killed your mother, Elizabeth. Don't you wonder why her? Was it on purpose? Was it an accident? Doesn't she deserve justice?"

The memory had been buried down deep that remembering it unearthed pain. Remorse swelled up from the back of her throat. "Is revenge my purpose in life?"

"Not revenge," Klaus corrected. "Justice. Truth."

"Miss Elizabeth?" Harry's voice called as he stepped back into the room. "There was a letter that came for Sir Wicker, it was marked as important." He shuffled forward, extending out a letter. Elizabeth flipped the note over but she couldn't recognize the sender's name.

"Thank you, Harry." She flipped the note over before tearing the edge open. "Lady Rose? I've never heard of her before." She read over the short message.

William,

My, how you turn my hair gray! I have tried calling you many times to no avail. You seemed quite distressed on the phone before we lost connection, and I am surprised after six years of silence to hear from you so suddenly. I worry you are in some kind of trouble (again) despite my many, many lectures. I hope you are alright.

I have managed to get word out to others travelling in your direction, they should be calling on you in the next few weeks. I am aware they have arranged accommodation at The Rap Rips down by the docks, please call on them and ease a sister's worrying. Despite my verbal misgivings, my dear Catherine has insisted on joining them. You must take responsibility and look after her. I hope to hear from you soon.

Sincerely,
Margaret.

Elizabeth tucked the letter into her pocket. Margaret, William's sister, was the last person William spoke to before he died. He had warned her about Klaus, but Elizabeth couldn't be sure exactly how much Margaret Rose knew before the phone call was cut off.

"Is everything okay, Miss Wicker? You've gone pale."

Elizabeth jerked at Harry's voice. Even Klaus seemed to be paying her too much attention, having now stopped his pacing and angled his body toward her. Elizabeth nodded.

"Yes, it was a letter from William's sister, Lady Margaret Rose."

Klaus turned away, losing interest. Harry said quietly, "That is surprising. I am aware Lady Rose and Sir Wicker weren't on speaking terms."

"He had tried reaching out to her before…" Elizabeth cleared her throat, not needing to remind everyone what happened to William Wicker. "She doesn't know."

Harry slowly nodded. "Despite not having much family left, Sir Wicker and Lady Rose weren't very close. A long history of family turmoil, I believe. I had thought that was the reason why Lady Rose wasn't present at his funeral. It wasn't my place to request her attendance." He turned toward the phone. "I will make the call. She has a right to know."

Elizabeth settled into her chair. She elected not to tell Klaus about Lady Rose's contacts by the docks, especially if they were sent to them to deal with him.

ELIZABETH STOOD AT the threshold of the Raps Rips motel the following day, staring up at the large twin doors leading into the low star establishment. The noise from the docks pressed up to her ears, surrounding her with the grunt of working fishermen and the crashing of waves. The letter did not reveal a lot of information about the contacts Lady Rose had sent, nothing beside a woman's name: Catherine.

Elizabeth walked inside the motel foyer of the Raps Rips and into the heavy fog of second hand smoke. One man stood behind the front desk in what appeared to be a throne made of newspaper stacks. Keys, pens, and business cards scattered across the front counter. Behind his head was a switch board with fifteen different light bulbs aligned in columns of five. One of the lights turned orange, following by a quick three ring whistle.

Elizabeth cleared her throat. "Excuse me? I am looking for a guest."

"Name?"

"Miss Catherine Rose."

Without taking his eyes off the newspaper, he reached across and picked up a clipboard as though to read it before tossing it back onto the table. "Nope."

"You didn't even check." Above their heads, footsteps paced the room upstairs. Muffled voices rose into an argument, before the distinct thump of a falling body shook the roof. The orange light promptly changed to red. Without peering away from his comic, the man picked up a phone and said, "Clean up, room 22B," before hanging up again. The light changed green.

"Your room will be ready shortly."

"I don't want a room. I'm looking for a guest staying here."

"If you don't want a room, then get out."

"I just need your assistance."

"No room, no service."

Elizabeth pushed away from the counter. "Incompetent." She made her way back outside. She had only gotten a few steps away when a voice called her back.

"You must be her."

Elizabeth turned as a man around her age approached, his hands tucked into his pockets and ice blue eyes peered beneath shaggy brown hair. Over the top of his vest and tie were sleeves of knives, bullets, and holstered twin pistols. Immediately, Elizabeth felt wary.

"You're looking for Catherine, yes? We've been waiting for you." She carefully nodded. "Who are you?"

"Hudson, an acquaintance of Lady Rose. Are you here alone?" His eyes shifted out across the busy street. Elizabeth nodded again. "If you would like to follow me, I can take you to her."

"Take me where, exactly?"

Hudson indicated over his shoulder. "She's visiting family."

THE CHAOS OF the docks brought stark contrast to the somber emptiness of the Memorial Park. Grave stones peppered the lush fields, breaking up the sea of green much like frothy waves hitting the shore. Hudson led Elizabeth toward the graveyard before indicating for her to wait. In front of her father's grave stood a lone woman.

Hudson touched her back. She turned and wiped her tears away. He whispered to her, immediately swinging her around to face Elizabeth.

The family similarity was striking. Elizabeth didn't share many traits with her half brother and sister, but the Wicker gene proved strong in her and Catherine. Despite Elizabeth carrying the white hair and blue eyes, and Catherine inheriting long, twisted dark brunette curls matching with green eyes, they could almost be mistaken for twins.

At her approach, Catherine's demeanor changed. She straightened her back, forcibly concealing her vulnerable side. She reached out and gently touched Elizabeth's white locks, smiling fondly at a memory they didn't share. "Miss Elizabeth Wicker, it's a pleasure to finally meet you."

Elizabeth smiled back. "You too, Miss Rose."

"Catherine Rose-Wicker but please just call me Catherine. My mother informed me yesterday to my Uncle's passing. It breaks my heart I couldn't be here to say goodbye. It's not until they're taken away that you realize the importance of family."

"I couldn't agree more."

"Uncle William did speak fondly of you. I'm sorry we have to meet under such awful circumstances."

"He spoke to you of me?" Elizabeth stepped back. It was a strange thought, in her household the topic of William being her biological father was strictly taboo.

"On the rare occasions that we did chat, yes. Couldn't believe you were legitimate, but now that I've seen you with my own eyes, all of my doubts have been put at ease."

"Are you okay?" Elizabeth asked.

"Family burials are old scars reopening. It is always hard, but does not cut so deeply anymore. Wicker blood carries short lives, weak hearts. Uncle William carried the disease, as did his father and grandmother. It was a truth he accepted many years ago, one we've all grown familiar with." Something shifted behind Elizabeth's back, catching Catherine's attention. Catherine glanced at Hudson who nodded, acknowledging her concern. "I see you've gotten my mother's letter, so you must be aware of why we are here. How much did Uncle William share with you, exactly?"

"What do you mean?"

"In regards to his problems."

Elizabeth stilled. *Is she talking about the Collectors?* "Enough to understand the dangers they impose."

"I see. Are those dangers still present?" Elizabeth wasn't sure which one she was talking about, Klaus or Nikolas, and her hesitancy to reply was mistaken for fear. "You can trust us, it's what we do. We destroy the supernatural. Witches and Bactes mostly."

"Bactes?"

"Short for Bacterial Infested Creatures. They are monsters who enjoy spreading disease wherever they nest. Nasty things, have caused thirteen plagues so fair."

"And you hunt them?"

Hudson stepped closer. "Yes, tracking down Bactes and witches are easy enough but Collectors, Collectors are nearly impossible to find. That is, of course, unless they are silly enough to show themselves. Speaking of which." He swivelled and fired one of his guns over Elizabeth's head, causing Elizabeth's shoulders to snap up to her ears in shock. She spun around to see his target just as Klaus stepped out from behind a nearby tree. The bullet skimmed the bark, missing Klaus by a hair. "Are you enjoying the show, Time Collector?"

Klaus' attention didn't shift from Hudson's face or the gun. He barely flinched. Elizabeth looked between them, startled at Klaus' presence and scared Hudson would try to shoot him again. She reached out and gently tried to lower Hudson's aim. "Please don't."

"Which one are you?" Hudson demanded without dropping his arm.

"Dietrich, Klaus Dietrich." Klaus stepped closer. "I am, *was*, Sir Wicker's apprentice."

"And Collector Nikolas Vorx?" Catherine asked. "Where is he?"

"I don't know."

"You know of Nikolas?" Elizabeth turned back around. "How?"

"All Guardians know of Nikolas Vorx. He's an infamous legend."

"More like an infamous idiot," Klaus muttered under his breath.

"Guardians?" Elizabeth questioned.

"It's what we are called, this entire organization we are a part of. Uncle William and I shared a common interest in hunting down the supernatural. He had special interests in Collectors though, and was understandably interested in learning how we managed to trap them."

"Trap them?" Klaus repeated, his voice sceptical. "That's not possible."

Catherine's grin spread up to her eyes. "We've got our secrets, as I'm sure you have yours."

"So you hunt all kinds of Collectors? Not just the corrupted?" Elizabeth asked, breaking up the stare down between Hudson and Klaus.

"Collectors are an unnatural balance to our world. They are beings without a soul, just weapons of mass destruction. They are incredibly dangerous tools and are threats we cannot ignore."

The muscle in Klaus' jaw clenched. "Sounds like the humans are the ones you should be hunting."

"An army of humans can't do nearly as much damage as a single Collector."

"History begs to differ."

Catherine smiled at Klaus' comment, before reaching over and lowering Hudson's gun. He obeyed without hesitation. "I believe we are about to make history ourselves."

"Am I to be exterminated?" said Klaus.

"Not at all. In fact, I was hoping for a truce. With your help, Klaus, we can finally stop Time Collector Nikolas Vorx. There are three other members in our group. I would like you to meet them."

"As thrilling as that sounds, it isn't exactly wise to invite a Time Collector to a Guardian's party."

"You will not be known as a Time Collector to them. Only Hudson and myself know of your true nature. Come by the Raps Rips tomorrow, I'll get the rest of the group caught up." As Catherine and Hudson turned to leave, she turned back, giving Klaus one last look. "I'll be interested in seeing exactly what you can do, Time Collector."

CHAPTER
TWENTY-NINE

KLAUS DRUMMED HIS fingers across the table top. Elizabeth sat beside him, her hands squeezed between her knees. "Are you sure about this?" she asked him again.

Klaus didn't look away from the elevator door. His fingers continued to tap. "Right now, it's me versus Nikolas. Having experienced Guardians on my side could do me some good." Catherine's words bounced inside his head since yesterday. *He had special interests in Collectors though, and was understandably interested in learning how we managed to trap them.* Klaus shifted in his seat. *Trap them. But how?*

Since the destruction of the Beaumontt estate, Nikolas hadn't made another peep. His silence fueled Klaus' unease. He needed to figure out a way to attack and kill Nikolas first.

"Does Nikolas have any other contacts other than Lady Claudia?" Elizabeth asked, reading Klaus' body language.

"I'm not sure." He answered bluntly, his focus not moving from the door. Wide entrance. Fast escape, if he needed one. He kept his attention carefully on all possible routes, watching the overhead vents for snipers. Listening carefully to every whispered conversation passing them by.

"You and Nikolas," Elizabeth started but hesitated when Klaus' jawline tightened, "what happened between you two that could cause such hatred?" Klaus' focus didn't shift. He stopped tapping the table. "I didn't realize Nikolas had such a reputation. Catherine spoke as if he is a prize to be won." Elizabeth continued speaking, causing Klaus to sigh with frustration.

"Apparently so."

"Do you think they can stop him?"

As soon as he looked away, Catherine approached from the elevator lift. She walked alone, her attire entirely different from the long blue dress she wore yesterday. She walked in large boots and wore tight pants where hidden in her interior jacket, she revealed two pistols. "Morning. How good is your aim?"

Elizabeth stood uncomfortably. "Not great."

Klaus stood as well, his expression clearly annoyed. "What are we doing here?"

"Proving to the others you're worth bringing with us. Especially Dennis, he seemed the most upset about your involvement. Said he didn't have time to babysit snobby rich girls and her father's pet."

"Snobby rich girl?" Elizabeth scoffed at the remark.

"Pet?" Klaus repeated as well, just as offended.

"There's a Bufo Bact close by, or commonly known as the toad, and we've been hired to exterminate her. She's a type of fungus, gotten herself the nickname Mural and has taken up residence over by the mines. She has been contaminating the water, making a lot of people sick."

"Wait a moment, are you talking about killing someone?" Elizabeth asked.

"Not *someone*, something." Catherine corrected then turned back to Klaus. "Should be easy for a creature like yourself."

Klaus snorted. "Obviously."

"But you want me there too?" Elizabeth asked, feeling slowly pressed out of the conversation.

"Of course." Catherine said. "To my understanding, you've stood your ground against Nikolas, so a Bufo Bact will be easy."

"Where have you heard that?"

"Uncle William of course. He didn't go into much details, only that you and a Collector named Klaus were involved. He wanted us to look out for you."

Elizabeth was surprised by the comment. "To me, he had made it very clear I wasn't to be involved with Time Collectors."

"And yet, here you are."

THEY HAD TRAVELLED down the town's borderline, sticking close to the forest hemming the edges. The residential areas were less congested and the roads were paved with hard, yellow sand. The buildings appeared older, or perhaps it was the natural decay of nature taking back the land. Most of poorer families lived in this district that clung to the boarders of the mines. Elizabeth glanced upward at the rocky walls facing the residents. The site of the avalanche was still uncleared, but had police tape sealing off the entrance to the crumbled houses. Bouquets of flowers remained against the boulders in remembrance of the families lost. There was an old paper mill with holes poked throughout the bricks and crows nests taking up residence. On the other side of the paper mill, Hudson waited with two other men and one female, all of whom appeared ready for combat.

Catherine approached the group. "Elizabeth, Klaus, I'd like to introduce you to Benjamin Kyneton, Dennis Moore and Leah French."

Dennis Moore made his disapproval known. He stepped forward before either Klaus or Elizabeth could get a word out and balanced his shotgun over his shoulder.

"Did you snatch this one out of a crib?" His attention focused on Elizabeth, who was clearly the youngest person among the group. His trained eyes moved to her grip on the gun, immediately recognizing her uncertain tremor. "She looks way too inexperienced."

Elizabeth looked to Klaus for help, but it was Hudson who stepped in. "We already spoke about this."

"Yes, and I said we don't accept charity cases. We're here to solve a Time Collector problem, not babysit some wannabe adventurers."

"They are not inexperienced wannabes—" Catherine argued, but Dennis cut her off with a mocking laugh.

"Oh, yes of course not. They've had dealings with Nikolas Vorx, isn't that right?" He laughed. Dennis used his larger frame to size himself up against Klaus. Not surprised, Klaus's expression didn't shift, giving nothing away except for unending boredom. "And this one, the doctor's apprentice, right? What could you do against Nikolas Vorx? Check him for measles?"

Klaus didn't speak, instead stared Dennis down, challenging his courage. The blonde female, Leah, stepped forward to brush Dennis aside. Her blue eyes sparkled as she looked at Elizabeth. "Nothing wrong with expanding our group, Dennis. Welcome, Elizabeth Wicker. I'm Leah French. I heard you were inside the Beaumontt estate when it collapsed." Elizabeth nodded. "Was Nikolas Vorx truly the reason it went down?"

Again, Elizabeth nodded and Dennis scoffed loudly. "Don't believe them, Leah. It's all rubbish."

"How did you get out?" Leah asked, intrigued.

"I, err...leapt through the second story window." Elizabeth was surprised to hear her voice shake. "Nearly broke my arm." She glanced at Klaus as he shifted and cleared his throat.

"Fascinating." Leah beamed.

"Ludicrous," Dennis argued.

The remaining man of the group sighed from the back, clearly annoyed by the whole conversation. "Enough. Isn't this the point of bringing them here? Let them prove they can handle the life of a hunter. Send them into the Bufo Bact."

"Benjamin is right," Catherine agreed. "If they can do this, then they are welcomed. Now, no more arguments. Into your positions, everyone."

Hudson took to the neighboring tower. He had his goggles back on, adjusting the lens so he could use them as binoculars. Dennis and Benjamin kept close to the front door as back up. Leah and Catherine took their position to the back of the property in case the Bact tried to escape through the windows.

Catherine pulled Elizabeth and Klaus aside. "First thing first, with bufo toads is to watch out for their acidic spit. She will go for your eyes, so you must wear these." She passed over goggles. "The best way to beat her is with heat. First, throw in these two canisters. It erupts with steam that will overheat the room. She'll go for the windows. That's where Leah and I will have her blocked off. It's your job to incapacitate her. Try and steer her away from the walls. If she gets to the rafters, you're going to have a problem. We call it raining acid, if you know what I mean."

Elizabeth laughed nervously. "This sounds like fun."

Klaus motioned to his hand-held pistol. "I don't need a gun to protect myself."

"A Collector won't, but a human does." Catherine pointed out. "Be careful in there. She may only be a class five Bact, but that doesn't mean she's not feisty."

"Class five?"

Catherine clicked the barrel of her gun back into place. "Low rank. Don't worry, you'll be fine. Just remember what I told you." She retreated to her post by the side of the house.

Both Klaus and Elizabeth fit on their goggles and adjusted the straps so the band didn't droop. The front door was jammed against the frame and Klaus barged his shoulder through to force it open. Dust thickened around the beams, shifting into the air at Klaus' intrusion. Around them, dimness settled in the corners, covering the corpses of headless rats left behind. Rotten wood planks boarded the windows, allowing splinters of light to squeeze through the slits. Cautiously, Elizabeth eased in first. Klaus followed. His gun remained clipped in his hip holster.

As instructed, they rolled the two smoking canisters in, filling the room with steam. Through the mist, an old woman scampered to the back of the room, shielding herself behind a woolen shawl. Elizabeth lifted her gun. The woman cocked her head sharply left and right, her nostrils flaring, but appeared unthreatened by the heat.

"Mural?" Elizabeth called out. The figure cowered behind her hands, crouching into a ball to appear as small as possible. Her inexperience with Bactes made her hesitate. *Exactly what were these things capable of? Can they speak? Do they have thoughts? Could they be reasoned with?* The weight of a gun felt unnatural to her. Elizabeth lowered her aim. "Excuse me, are you Mural?"

As she glanced at Klaus, the creature lunged forward and slapped the pistol away, throwing Elizabeth to the ground. The creature's scaly grip grabbed her wrist, pinning her hand and the gun to the floor. Her smile reached from ear to ear, curling the creature's mouth into a stretched, long slit. Its eyes budged white, revealing her blindness. Her senses must've come from her large nostrils and bulb ears. The Bact unhinged its jaw and spat a projectile clot of tar, the shot only missing thanks to Klaus' swift upwards kick, knocking the Bact's chin to the side and hitting the back wall. The Bact leapt off Elizabeth, and on all fours, fled down a trapdoor beneath the floorboards. Klaus helped Elizabeth stand.

"Are you okay?"

Elizabeth's clock heart raced. She grabbed at her chest, feeling herself wobble. The smell from the acidic spit drenched the room in fumes. When she glanced at it, the black goo melted through the bricks. "Yeah, I'm fine." They both glanced at the trapdoor. "At least we have the right person. For an old woman, she sure moves quickly."

"It's an illusion." Klaus corrected. "She'll be twice as strong as you, and three times as fast."

"Why didn't you shoot her?" Elizabeth asked.

"She was too close. I didn't want any backlash."

"Worried about ruining your outfit, huh?"

Klaus turned, speaking in an equally snarky tone. "Getting hit by the hot tar will be the equivalent of having boiling water poured over you. But sure, I didn't want my outfit to be ruined."

HUDSON OBSERVED THE brief exchange, but wasn't alarmed. It appeared normal. The Bufo Bact defended itself with tar and a sense of disoriented blindness. The Bact was fast, but clumsy. It was difficult to keep track as most of the windows were boarded up, giving him a limited view. The Bact disappeared from sight after Klaus kicked her head, throwing her aim off. He was fast, obviously a trained fighter with quick reflexes. Elizabeth, on the other hand, would probably kill herself tripping over her own laces.

Unfazed, Hudson kept his attention on Klaus and Elizabeth. It wasn't until they disappeared from the room that he felt his pulse accelerate. He sent out a distress flare to warn the others. Catherine pressed against the window and tried peeking through one of the holes. Darkness made it impossible to see, so she signalled to Benjamin and Dennis to move. Both boys rushed into the dwelling with their guns held high. On his shoulder pad, Benjamin turned on his torch to illuminate the empty area. It took them ten minutes to finally notice the trapdoor.

Benjamin turned around as Catherine and Leah stepped inside with their weapons drawn. "I think they went down here."

"Christ!" Catherine dropped to her knees by the trapdoor and lowered her head down the long descent. "It's pitch black down there. Elizabeth? Klaus? Can you hear me?" she called with no response. "Leah, go and get Hudson. Benjamin and Dennis follow me."

Beneath the floorboards, Elizabeth and Klaus stepped onto the soft bed of earth at the bottom of the stairs. The steps down were steep and uneven and dipped with their weight as they passed. At the bottom of the staircase was a thin tunnel. Klaus ducked his head to pass underneath the low ceiling. They both turned on their shoulder lights to see better into the pit, revealing the tunnel stretching further than the light could touch. There were no doors on either side of the burrow, giving them a direct pathway down. Off in the distance, they could hear the scurrying footsteps of the Bact racing away.

Elizabeth and Klaus tracked the Bact to the end of the route that opened up into a high ceiling cave. Pockets of light broke through the ceiling and a thick smell of swamp water, suggesting they had ventured outside the resident district and further into the woods. There were ledges chipped into the walls ascending to the top of the cave, creating steps. It was difficult to judge, but it appeared the top opened up into the gutted body of a tree trunk.

"Well, now we know how she got into the building." Klaus touched the wet rock when a noise chirped beside them, turning them around. The sounds the creature made were inhuman, drawing influence from birds.

From a nook in the structure, a long, thin woman stepped forward. Her legs wobbled, the large knobs of her knees knocking together with each step, unbalancing her as she walked. Long black hair concealed her narrow face, stopping at her starved bony hips. "Five hundred moons pass but no time has changed my enemy. Collector, the bones of temptation. Lost steps lead you down wrong paths."

Klaus stepped back from the wall. Elizabeth held her gun up, but felt no safety behind the weapon. Klaus cocked his head. "Who are you?"

"A footprint self in soil gone unnoticed by eyes lost to wonder."

"Give me a name!" he demanded, losing patience.

"Nature names not but through devilish tongue I carry Si."

"Si?" Klaus clarified. "What are you doing here?"

Every bend in the creature's posture bowed her out of shape, shrinking her naturally long physique as though crippled by arthritis. "Klaus?" Elizabeth whispered, "What going on?"

"Just look and listen, Elizabeth. We have an elder Bact in our presence."

Elizabeth glanced at the haunting woman, uneasy with her presence. The creature's bones crackled as she moved forward, unfazed by Elizabeth's weapon. "Through warmth fire, through water flood, wind break trees by armies. Built by peddles mountains do not bow. Does not man grow thumbs to climb?"

"What on earth is she on about?"

Klaus grinned, slowly understanding the creature's mutterings. "She's talking about evolution. An evolution of the Bactes to take down the humans."

The creature chirped gleefully, "Flowers root from weeds, matter not. In blood carry our promise, the death of all. Droplets to form oceans, oceans to take lands."

His back straightened at her threat when a voice called through the tunnels. "Klaus? Elizabeth? Are you there?"

Elizabeth turned toward Catherine's voice, dropping her attention long enough for the Bufo Bact to jump her. Mural snared Elizabeth by her hair and leapt onto her back, throwing Elizabeth down on her knees. Flashlights flooded into the cave as the rest of the group caught up, their heavy panting covered by the scrambling of the fight. Elizabeth screamed, tearing Klaus' focus away from Si. Si leapt to him and sank her teeth into the exposed skin on his neck. The bite was fast, brutal, clearing a junk of muscle off into her mouth. Klaus propelled himself around, ripping her off of him. He held her throat in his grip, his Collector's blade ready in his other hand, but ended up dropping his hold on her to stop Mural from biting him. A gunshot went off, the noise amplified inside the pipe. Klaus flinched as the bullet shot past him and clipped Si out of her mid-air jump. She hit the wall and scurried out of range. Blood ran the length of his collar, the stinging, exposed nerve throbbed with the rush of adrenaline.

Effortlessly, he snapped Mural's neck and dropped her. His hand found the wound on his neck, feeling the missing skin and tissue already start to heal. His bloodied fingers trembled as he held them to his face. Si feverishly climbed up the wall toward the opening. Elizabeth followed her with her gun but the creature had vanished.

"Klaus! Elizabeth!" Catherine ran at them. Elizabeth's entire body trembled, coating her in cold sweat as Catherine forcibly peeled the gun out of Elizabeth's shaky grip. "It's okay, it's okay you're safe now."

"That was an elder Bact." Benjamin spoke in disbelief between puffs. "What on earth was it doing in a place like this?"

Dennis walked over to Mural's body before nudging her with his shoe. Her neck had been twisted so far around it had tore her neck muscles into shreds. "How did you do this?" He looked up at Klaus. "What type of doctor are you?"

Klaus couldn't hear Dennis. His attention stuck on his wound. Carefully, Klaus felt around the bite mark, but the sensitive tingling vanished under his touch. Hudson caught up with Leah and crouched down to study the Bact's corpse. "She definitely is dead." He glanced around the walls where claw marks scaled the rocks. "Scratch marks? These aren't from the bufo."

"No, these marks belong to an Elder Bact," Benjamin informed. "Amazingly, Klaus and Elizabeth managed to fend her off on their own. If I didn't see it for myself, I wouldn't have believed it."

"I knew I liked your company." Leah grinned, stepping around them. "How about that, Dennis? Can't say they're incompetent now."

Elizabeth glanced at Dennis. His red hair remained flattened by sweat, and despite Leah's teasing, he didn't look at all pleased with Klaus' work. He glanced at Mural once more and then turned to leave. Behind him, Catherine proceeded to take photos.

"I'm sure we can all agree they are capable. You did exactly what we were contracted to do. One dead bufo means a massive payday for us."

CHAPTER

THIRTY

ELEBRATIONS BACK AT the Raps Rips were lost on Elizabeth and Klaus. Both were too shaken from the previous events. Elizabeth sat down on one of the lounge chairs, her body angled to watch her cousin through the mirror over the mantel piece. The others huddled around a table drinking, leaving mountains of empty glasses scattered over the counter. Every shift in the shadow turned her around, her mind playing tricks. She reached over and took a shot of hard alcohol, trying to calm down.

"Are you alright?" Catherine approached and took the seat opposite her. "You seem shaken up."

Elizabeth smiled weakly. "Sorry, I think the realization is finally sinking in."

"What realization?"

"About how weak I am."

Catherine shrugged thoughtfully. "Nothing a bit of training can't fix."

"Not just muscle weakness. I couldn't even stand on my own two feet against a Bufo Bact. I choked up. How am I going to survive against a Time Collector such as Nikolas?"

"You've already survived him once before," Catherine reassured her. "Bactes are different. They're unpredictable, feral almost. You weren't prepared."

Elizabeth sighed. "Why do you do this type of thing? It can't be for the money."

Catherine twisted her lips thoughtfully. "True, I don't need the money."

"Is it the thrill then?"

She shrugged. "Partly. Plus, I get to carry around some neat weapons and beat up boys who look at me weirdly."

Elizabeth laughed. "I don't know if I should admire you or send you off to the psych ward."

Catherine smiled and looked down. "My reason for hunting Bactes isn't as glamorous as revenge or as selfless as hero work, but it's slowly becoming a part of my identity. My mother was upset when I told her of my intentions. She, of course, blamed my uncle's influence. She wanted me to be some sort of elegant lady who attended charities balls and tea parties, but that isn't who I am. I love the thrill of the chase, the heart pumping danger. Speaking of which," Catherine shifted around to search the room. "Where is that mysterious companion of yours anyway?"

"You mean Klaus?" Elizabeth asked, looking around. "I haven't seen him since our return."

"Is he alright?"

Elizabeth cocked her head at the question. "I would think so, why?"

"He doesn't care to celebrate victories?"

Elizabeth brushed it off. "More like he doesn't care much for the company of others. He works better alone."

Unbeknownst to Elizabeth, Klaus' isolation only deepened his troubles. He caught his reflection in the window of a parked car, his fingers searching the smooth of his neck for the pain from a wound now healed. The attack from the Bact wasn't what scared him, but her passing words. A war not only against humans, but against Collectors as well. The fact she jumped and bit him came as a massive surprise, especially as Bactes do not tend to attack Collectors. They shared a similar DNA, one forged through magic and missing human emotions.

Beneath his feet, darkness flickered. Klaus noticed the shift out of the corner of his eye, and in a sudden lunge, he drove his Collector's blade into the road. A tiny whistle erupted from the crack in the bricks. The gremlin deflated as fast as a punctured balloon. A sharp zap shot upwards through the blade and into his hand. Klaus flinched and inspected the skin between his thumb and index finger. Black ink bled like a bruise, forming the shape of a tattooed compass. He closed his fist tightly. This was as much of a threat as it was a reminder. Elizabeth was always within Nikolas' reach. Gremlins were his shadowy hands, the eyes of ghosts haunting him.

He made his way back into the tavern and found Elizabeth conversing with Catherine on the lounge seats. Both women sat up on his entrance, but his eyes fell automatically to Elizabeth. It wasn't until he had slowed down and properly looked that he noticed just how much the confrontation shook her. How much all of this had shaken her. Whereas he hid behind his blade and natural abilities, she faced the same threats completely unarmed. In the face of fear, her courage rang as loud as a gunshot.

"Klaus, what is it?" Elizabeth sat up straighter, "What's wrong?"

His voice lowered. "I know where to find him."

"WHAT MAKES YOU think you know where Nikolas is?" Benjamin asked across the breakfast table.

Klaus ate only small portions, enough to sustain himself for the day. Klaus was careful to bandage his new tattooed hand with a handkerchief, explaining it away as a mere injury.

"The Elder Bact told me through a series of riddles. He is to be at Westicher Palace." He glanced sideways at Elizabeth's confused expression, but he'd guessed she was confused throughout the entirety of Si's speech and therefore wouldn't call him out on his lies.

"And you're certain?" Dennis asked, sceptical.

"It took me a while to figure it out but ja, I am positive."

Leah pursed her lips. "Since when did Bactes and Time Collectors work together?"

"There have always been a great divide between the creatures touched by magic and those without. It's not that big of a surprise a Bact would work with a Collector."

"It's a bit like a dog teaming up with a wolf, but I get your point. They do belong to the same pack in many ways."

Klaus' face tightened distastefully at the comment, an expression Elizabeth caught. It was hard to remember sometimes that Klaus' human exterior might only be that: an exterior. Exactly how human he was on the inside was still to be figured out.

"The fastest way to Westicher is by train. The fog over there is too much for airship." Catherine stated.

"And we know this isn't a trap, how?" Dennis pointed out.

Klaus smirked. "If you are worried about one's safety, I suggest picking up a different profession. I for one, don't want to miss this opportunity."

Dennis clenched his jaw. Catherine sighed. "Nikolas is no ordinary Collector. We'll just have to be extra careful."

AS THEY WAITED in line to purchase train tickets, Elizabeth stepped out of earshot to speak privately to Klaus. "What are you planning?"

"What?" He turned to her.

"Going to Westicher? That creature, Si, did not mention Westicher at all."

Klaus coyly smiled. "No, but a gremlin did."

"What?" Elizabeth's voice lowered fearfully. "Nikolas is here?"

"No, but his spies are never far. He has his little pets tracking you, waiting for the moment I step away to home in on your location. He left me this." Klaus peeled the handkerchief back and showed Elizabeth the tattoo compass on his hand. "A meeting point."

"For what?"

"I imagine to kill me."

"That's usually the type of thing you try to avoid. And you still plan on going?"

"He has already shown he's capable of tracking me down, so I can't run from him forever. I figure my best chance is to bring a team of Guardians to back me up."

"Then why doesn't he attack you now?"

"One of Nikolas' last threats to me was setting my world on fire. Who knows, maybe he plans on blowing up Westicher Palace with me still in it."

"Sounds dramatic." Elizabeth tried to laugh, but her voice quivered with uncertainty. Klaus noticed the hesitation, same as he had noticed her fear yesterday at the bar.

"Are you alright?"

"Yes of course."

"No." Klaus growled, "Don't just say that to sound tough. Are you alright?"

Elizabeth glanced up at him, but before she could speak Catherine approached with tickets in hand. "Everything is ready, let's go."

SUNLIGHT BATHED OVER the chrome cabin. Tracks cut along the border of fields and ploughed across the open grounds. Leah and Benjamin sat against the window, immersed with their card game. Benjamin pulled nervously at his collar as the game advanced in Leah's favor. Elizabeth sat beside them inside the narrow carriage. In the hallway, directly outside the sliding door, she watched Catherine and Klaus talk. They both had their backs to Elizabeth, their expression shielded by the privacy of the conversation. Every now and again, Catherine would reach out and stroke his arm, but Klaus never slackened his military straight back. Elizabeth's world turned hazy as the banter between Leah and Benjamin dropped to white noise. She could feel her fingers tighten.

"You'll get used to it," Leah chuckled, drawing Elizabeth's attention away from her cousin.

"I'm sorry?"

Leah motioned with her chin at Catherine. "Guarding your man?"

"I'm what?" She flustered, embarrassed. "No! What?"

"Don't worry, Catherine isn't the one with a reputation for partner stealing. It was Hudson who stole her from her fiancé, amazing what high cheek bones and a taste of adventure can do to a woman's heart."

Elizabeth glanced at Klaus again. He was in an elite class of his own. Every look, every tilt of his chin or twist of muscle was elegant and smooth like a wave. He never lost composure. Even when he blinked, it looked like he controlled every eyelash. How could there ever be anything between them? He referred to her as a hooked hand, a flaw he didn't want. He was a Time Collector, an immortal being capable of granting wishes. Even if he wasn't all of those things, he just didn't seem to be interested in her as a person. At every major corner, they clashed, leaving Elizabeth to play catch up behind him. He walked as though he was above them all, and in many cases, he was. *Of course there was nothing between them. Of course.*

"There's no relationship between myself and Klaus, so…I'm not worried." She laughed, weakly. "He was my father's apprentice, that's all."

"I doubt it's as simple as that. A doctor's apprentice searching for corrupted Time Collectors? It doesn't add up."

Elizabeth shrugged. "Why does anyone hunt down the supernatural? A doctor by trade means he's invested in helping others. To stop monsters is another way to save lives."

"No doctor can snap a Bact's neck the way he did," Benjamin pointed out.

"I'm sure you can," Leah teased, giving Benjamin a quick nudge.

"Yes, but I've trained my whole life to be able to do things like that. Doubt he'll find the time, not with being a doctor and everything."

"Oh?" Elizabeth perked up in her seat. "I didn't peg you as a fighter."

"Everyone underestimates me because I'm so short." Benjamin went on smiling. "Makes victory all the sweeter when I punch them out."

"Great things come in small packages as they say." Leah grabbed his arm.

"How did you two meet?"

"Way back before we joined this group. Benjamin Kyneton, the great Two Punch Titan, could take on any opponent across the country. But of course, he is no match for me," Leah answered.

"You're a fighter too, Leah?"

"A dancer."

Elizabeth looked at her confused. "I'm sorry?"

Leah laughed. "Everyone looks at me like that when I tell them. I don't need to hit you to take you down. I've been dancing ever since I was a little girl and I've managed to turn it into my own fighting style. Not even Benjamin's lightning reflexes would be able to catch me."

Benjamin smiled. "Hudson is a crack shot, best I've ever seen. Catherine has her throwing knives and of course, Dennis is as brilliant as he is brutish. A real natural at hunting. What about you? Perhaps you're a trained assassin? Secret spy? Or are you more of a behind the scenes master? Poison specialist? Explosive? Mechanics engineer? A genius for traps?"

Elizabeth's smile dropped. She hadn't realized just how out of place she was among these people. The thought pained her, when matter of fact, she had been feeling inadequate for a very long time. "A lucky shot," Klaus answered for her, smiling.

"Yeah, lucky not to shoot myself," she mumbled, before laughing off her own comment.

"Sorry to interrupt." Klaus motioned over his shoulder. "Your cousin wishes to have a word with you."

"Oh, yes of course."

Elizabeth joined Catherine out in the hallway, "Come, I want to show you something." They went down toward the women's quarters near the end of the carriage. Catherine sat down and patted the mattress next to her for Elizabeth to sit. She then reached underneath the bed and fished out a velvet pouch. Inside she revealed a plain white cloth wrapped around the shape of a spike. Catherine unwrapped the linen to reveal the weapon. Under closer inspection, Elizabeth realized it was made from old bone that had been chipped away to form a shiv.

"Is that bone?"

"It's from an ancient Collector," Catherine confirmed as she held it up. "The only thing that is capable of stunning and paralyzing other Time Collectors. This is a family heirloom, belonging to Dennis' family—Lord and Lady Moore. The Moores are part of the three noble families who founded the Guardians centuries ago. Time Collectors can't even touch this thing without falling under its toxicity. With other pieces of the Collector's skeleton they had chiseled it down into dust to fill bombs and bullets. This stuff is noxious to them, slows down their reaction speed, their thought processing, sometimes even knocks them out cold. Once they are poisoned, we stab them in the heart with this. It turns them into stone, as a survival technique to protect them from further damage or death."

"Are they still alive after they have been turned to stone?"

"We're not sure if there is brain activity or any consciousness."

"How long are they frozen for?"

"The last Collector to be stabbed was nearly two hundred years ago, and he is still frozen to this day. The Moores have him locked up in their underground prison under their house. That's the the thing with Collectors, despite all their power and strength, they are still creatures who live by a very strict code. They seek the desperate, trying to bargain their life source. They can't help themselves."

Elizabeth slumped further into her seat. "And this is how you plan on trapping Nikolas?"

"We used to think this was the only way to stop them, until Klaus informed me about the gun he and Uncle William were making. Made from Chrétien's gold, the one known substance capable of neutralizing magic."

"Klaus told you about the gun?"

"He did, thinks we can use it to our advantage against Nikolas. I first thought it was suspicious that a Collector help create a weapon capable of killing himself, but I figured better the devil you know than the devil you don't. At least he has one hand controlling the wheel."

"You do not see Klaus as a creature to slay?"

Catherine sighed and looked down thoughtfully. "Though the others would disagree, I do not see Collectors as monsters. I do not blame the gun, but the shooter. That being said, I'd rather live in a world where guns do not exist."

KLAUS FOUND COMFORT alone, sitting within the public lounge carriage by a window. Calming music played above, accompanied by the gentle chatter of couples and families sitting down for lunch. A voice would cut across the music, explaining the significance of the Carolina Rose fields they passed outside. Klaus didn't look away from the passing of pink, not acknowledging Dennis approaching and sitting down opposite him.

"I'm not much for plants," Dennis commented lightly. "Can't

say we have the time for that sort of thing." Klaus didn't respond. Dennis slumped comfortably into the chair, drawing a small blade from his pocket. He proceeded to cut up an apple. "So, you're a doctor's apprentice, right? Travelled from Germany to work under the guidance of the great and renowned Doctor Wicker?"

Klaus glanced at him. "You're interested in my life story?"

"Only in those I don't trust." Dennis smiled. Klaus took a deep breath, trying not to engage. Dennis continued. "When one hears doctor they must think large lab coats and scary disease. It's a noble profession, one taking on to save people's lives except, you're the type who snaps Bact's necks and chases Time Collectors."

"I'm complicated." Klaus smirked.

"Probably easily bored, too." Dennis jabbed back and popped another piece of apple into his mouth. "My family has been hunting these things for generations. Time Collectors, Bactes, wild witches, you name it, we kill it. I still remember the first time I ran my blade into a Bact's belly. She squealed like a farm pig."

"You take pleasure in killing," Klaus noted, plainly.

"So do you. I can see it in your eyes, the way you snapped that Bact's neck. Can't be playing doctor forever, no, you need to get your hands dirty. Don't worry, I agree with you. These parasites on humanity, they give off a certain, err, well, a certain *scent*. I've learnt to pick a Bact out of a crowd of hundreds. Witches too, but Collectors are trickier. They blend in with everyone else. Evolution designed them to become invisible. But there's a trick to catching them out. It's just six simple words and they can't help themselves. 'I want to make a contract'."

The moment the words slipped free, Klaus' entire body clenched up. Pressure intensified, speeding up his heart. His tongue swelled fat, the sudden rise in his temperature dampening his hairline with sweat. Dennis glanced down and ran his blade along the apple core, prying himself another slice.

"With that alone, they are in my control. These suppose godlike immortals of mass destruction and chaos, are in fact, no different than a puppet with a hand up their arse. The others are ignorant. They believe Collectors are these superior beings to cower from."

Klaus couldn't concentrate, he could barely breathe as if his internal nervous system was being set on fire, filling up his lungs with smoke. Klaus subtly gulped and turned his gaze away. "Hmm."

"That's what they are, isn't it? Dogs obeying their masters! They are humanity's slaves. Mindless 'yes' men."

"I can see the humor in their irony. Creatures given unequal power but with no willpower to control it. I'm not surprised you mock them." His body language shifted, turning his attention unnervingly onto Dennis' face. "And yet, it is mortal men who sell their souls for momentary gain. Humanity is as much enslaved to their desires as Collectors are to their codes. One by choice, the other by nature."

"Guess you have a point. Like men trailing behind pretty girls, you and Miss Wicker are fine examples."

"What are you implying?"

Dennis smiled. "I'm not implying anything. You just don't seem too fond of people."

"I wouldn't take offense, I'm not fond of anything. I would complain about heaven if I ever saw it."

"Excuse me, Klaus?" Klaus turned at Elizabeth's approached. She paused beside him, leaving him question just how much of the conversation she had heard. "Am I interrupting?"

"Nein, I believe Mr. Moore was just leaving."

Dennis stood. "It's no problem, we weren't speaking of anything important." He gave her a brisk nod. Klaus watched him go, unable to drop the frustrated snarl off his face.

"Is something wrong?" Elizabeth asked as she took Dennis' seat.

"I hate banter. Especially with idiots." Elizabeth sucked her breath in, hesitant to speak. "What is it that you need?" Klaus asked, releasing a pent-up sigh.

Embarrassed, Elizabeth stood. "No, nothing but further banter I'm afraid."

"Wait, please sit." Klaus reached out. "Don't place yourself at their level. You may be the only person here I can tolerate."

"Comforting. I wanted to talk to you about my conversation with Catherine. You told her about the gun?"

"Ja, and in return, she told me about the old Collector bone shiv. It is…unique."

"I wasn't sure if it worried you, but she does not see you as a threat."

"That doesn't worry me."

"But something does?"

Klaus didn't move. He could hear the sympathy in Elizabeth's voice, but didn't know how he was meant to react to it. He gulped uncomfortably. Elizabeth could see more than she gave on. He was letting his mask slip, and that was dangerous.

Instead, Klaus changed the topic. "Will you stay with them?"

"With who?"

"Catherine Rose-Wicker. Once we have stopped Nikolas, will you stay with them?"

She looked away in thought. "I haven't exactly thought that far ahead."

"They are your family, the only ones you have left," he added as if the words had a bitter taste.

Elizabeth bit into her smile. "Why do I get the impression you don't want me to?"

"You know too much," he chuckled.

"I doubt they would want my company. After all, it is yours they need."

Klaus shifted, angered. "Looks like we are both guilty."

"Of what?"

"Of not giving you enough appreciation and respect." He reached forward, resting his elbows on his knees. "In the face of danger, I do not protect people. I'm sure you're seen enough evidence to agree. They do not need a selfish man, but a selfless woman. You carry far more value in just your presence than I do in the entirety of my being."

"Klaus..." Elizabeth whispered.

The curl of her voice, the way her eyes softened with emotion, touched by what he now understood must've sounded like a declaration of his feelings, melted her in front of him. Klaus could taste the words on his tongue, unbearably sweet and unfamiliar. *Word of advice, little brother...keep falling.* Nikolas' echoing words pulled his smile away. Reality snapped him back like an unforgiving force. "Don't misunderstand. I compliment birds for singing, this doesn't mean anything."

Elizabeth smirked. "You never compliment anything."

His heart started to beat a little faster. "And you know me well."

Elizabeth crossed her arms, forcing authority into her voice. "What about you? What will you do after we catch Nikolas?"

"I will mourn him."

"And then what will you do?"

"Then, I will just continue to exist."

CHAPTER

THIRTY-ONE

SUNSET DREW CLOSER, and with it Westicher's fog thickened over the horizon. Dinner gathered everyone into the lounge area. The hours rolled over, and soon the lounge emptied, leaving Catherine and her group as the only occupants. Klaus and Elizabeth joined the others around the table. Conversation shifted between politics, the destruction of the Beaumontt's manor, hunting Bactes, and the limits of magic. Except for Dennis and Elizabeth who sat secluded on the other side of the table. They spoke in whispers. Laughter. Giggles hidden behind cupped palms. Dennis was quick to refill their glasses of wine.

"Have you been back to Germany since you started your apprenticeship with Doctor Wicker?" Leah asked Klaus casually.

"Nein."

"Don't you miss your family?"

"Nein." Klaus picked up his wine glass and tentatively took a sip. Leah's voice sounded distant as he strained to catch the conversation between Elizabeth and Dennis. He cleared his throat to get rid of a tickle.

"I've never been to Germany before. What is it like?" Benjamin asked.

Klaus barely glanced over at him. "It's quiet."

"I've heard there's a bit of unrest there."

"Oh, yes there was news about the movement of the rebels," Leah added.

"Has your family been affected? I had assumed that's why you travelled to London to work."

"Nein."

"I had a friend travel to Turkey to cover the crisis over there. Terrible circumstances for the locals, but a great job opportunity for a journalist."

Their voices sounded muffled. Unable to resist, Klaus shifted his attention back to Elizabeth. Something wasn't right, but he couldn't pinpoint *what*. His earlier confrontation with Dennis played in the back of his mind. *Can't be playing doctor forever, no, you need to get your hands dirty.* An unfamiliar unease tightened his stomach. Being a Time Collector meant many things. Danger. Temptation. Destruction. A life of being chased and used. He lived at the calling of others' desires, often forgetting about his own. Elizabeth glanced up, as if she felt Klaus' eyes on her face. *You carry far more value in just your presence than I do in the entirety of my being.*

"I don't know about you, but this wine isn't sitting right with me." Catherine's voice broke through Klaus' concentration. He abruptly turned his attention away from Elizabeth.

Hudson leaned over the counter to address the whole table. "We will be arriving at Westicher within the hour. The reservation I booked is at the Und Hänsel Gretel hotel a street away from the Palace. Will be a good stake-out."

"Security is going to be tight. We won't be able to bring in our equipment," Catherine pointed out.

Dennis leaned back on his chair. "I know what we can do. We should summon the stone protector." A moment of silence filled the room.

"Don't be absurd!" Catherine said, dismissing the notion.

"A little overdramatic, don't you think?" Hudson added.

"Many thought it was only a fable." Leah said.

"And Collectors are only fables too, Leah?" Dennis countered. "We have the capabilities of summoning it, and this is Nikolas Vorx, a Collector who has haunted us through generations of Guardian protection. If we have a chance to stop him, then we shouldn't take it lightly."

Hudson shook his head. "So your solution is to release a lion and hope it goes back into its den?"

"Lions can be controlled."

"By larger men with whips, not mortals."

"Who's the stone protector?" Elizabeth asked.

"Mortalem." Dennis answered, "The gargoyle."

Mortalem. Hearing the name made Klaus rise from his chair in a sudden rage. "Are you insane?"

"What's the problem?" Dennis laughed, pleased by Klaus' outburst. "She's no threat to us."

"Who's Mortalem?" Elizabeth asked.

"Mortalem is a gargoyle, an ultimate weapon against all those of supernatural blood. It was concealed within the spirit world by the greater supernatural gods," Catherine explained. "There are stories of people summoning it in great peril. A creature so powerful its skin can burn Bactes to the bone."

Klaus' voice lifted with uncharacteristic panic. "That is no lion but a dragon you tamper with."

"Dragons to some, a knight to others," Dennis said.

"This argument is pointless," Benjamin said. "Mortalem is in the spirit world now, a place we cannot fetch it. For that, you'll need someone with magic. A powerful witch, probably. Not that you'll be able to find one willing to help."

Dennis crossed his arms smugly. "We don't need a witch when we have a Time Collector." Klaus froze. His mask, that mask of calm control, fell.

"You can't be talking about Nikolas," Benjamin scoffed.

Dennis looked toward Klaus, as if making a final confirmation. "No, as a matter of fact, I'm not. How does the wine suit you, Collector?"

Klaus' eyes trailed down, linking the bubble of unease in his stomach to his clouded drink. *Poisoned, but with what?*

"Dennis, are you out of your mind?" Catherine scolded. "Klaus is a friend of my uncle's!"

"Not a friend. A fraud." From beneath the table, Dennis revealed the bone shiv and a pistol. Seeing it, Elizabeth stood up, but Klaus didn't move. He instead prepared himself by straightening his posture, knowing where this conversation was going. His identity as a Time Collector has been found out before, and usually it cost the other person their life. Temptation was too sweet, too great, to allow a creature such as him to walk away. They were often greedy. Short-sighted, they were not aware of the true costs behind their conversation. But this time, it seemed his life was under threat.

"Collector, I wish you would finish your wine!"

His skeleton feeling as heavy as concrete, he picked up his drink unwillingly. His control and dignity felt ripped out of his grasp. Stunned, the group watched as he finished the wine. A fever spiked across his forehead.

"Enough! Klaus, don't play along with his games." Elizabeth said, trying to discredit Dennis, but the look on the others' faces proved it wasn't working. Leah's eyes darted back and forth. Benjamin's fists tensed, as if to challenge Klaus. Catherine and Hudson shared quick glances, but they too knew enough about the situation to stay quiet. The secret was out. Klaus' identity was confirmed the moment the last droplet hit his tongue.

Dennis lifted the pistol, but Catherine stepped forward. "Dennis, don't," she said softly, trying to calm the intensity of the room. "He's willing to help us."

"You knew?" Benjamin gasped. "You knew, and you still brought him here? You let him stay with us?"

"He's not going to hurt you!" Elizabeth said.

"No he won't." Dennis stood and aimed the gun. "I won't give him the chance."

Klaus stared down the barrel of the pistol, feeling the poison twist at his insides. He felt weak and gripped the table for balance. The poison swirled his vision, blurring the details of the room. Tingles climbed up his neck, deadening his senses. Sound faded into murmurs as smells dulled. Even his thoughts disintegrated, darkness pillowing into the corner of his eyes. Unconsciousness would come soon.

Klaus moved the same moment Elizabeth did. He turned for the corridor as she stepped across, using her body as a shield. Dennis fired. The gunshot sounded off across the room, hitting the wall with a crackling echo. Klaus swung around and hit Elizabeth across the chest, throwing her to the side. The bullet skewered his bicep. The wound sharply stung and hotness spread into his shoulder and neck. The pain circled around the puncture point as it travelled with his blood through the rest of his body. The sickness unbalanced him. There was no doubt in his mind that they had filled the bullets with poison. His eyes clouded. The train rocked them sideways, but to him it felt as though the world was about to tip off its axis.

Alarms rang inside his mind, making him charge forward. He cleared the table in one leap and speared Dennis' neck with his Collector's blade. The force shoved Dennis over. His back hit the windows beneath him. The glass splintered. Time zapped out of his body. Dennis tried to shoot again, but Klaus smacked the gun from his grip. Instead, Dennis reached for the bone shiv, only to drop it as

Klaus grabbed him by the throat. He was fast. *Brutal.* He squeezed with all intentions of killing him. He *wanted* to kill him. It was going to be easy.

Benjamin tried to separate them and Klaus spun around with his elbow bent. He struck hard, harder than he intended, his body still hot with rage and panic. He heard bone snap, felt the brunt force of his swing drive into Benjamin's temple. Klaus felt the warmth pulsed within Benjamin's chest, circling his head momentarily, and then blinked out. With his eyes still open, Benjamin's body fell.

Before anyone could register what had happened, Catherine leapt onto Klaus and drove the bone shiv deep into his shoulder. Pain exploded. She had stabbed him with such force the blade snapped inside his muscle. Klaus flung himself through the train window, the momentum catching Catherine and bringing her with him. They dropped down a five-meter slope of trees, tumbling head over heels'. Before Leah could scream, they vanished.

DEATH WAS NEVER easy to accept. Even in a profession such as hunting, where death was witnessed and killing was practiced daily, it still could shake a person to their core. An emergency crew waited at the train station to save Benjamin's life, but he was gone the moment Klaus' elbow connected with his head. Leah broke. Her screams howled down the corridors. There was nothing anyone could do. Elizabeth saw herself in Leah's devastation. Heard herself in her shrill cries, as well as in the silence of her disbelief and agony. The police questioned them about Benjamin's death, and blamed Klaus for the murder. Crowds formed around the train carriage as Benjamin's body was carried out.

Elizabeth gripped her arms. She sat quietly on a public bench feeling the suffocation of loneliness creep back. Klaus and Catherine were gone. Dennis didn't speak. Leah wailed. Hudson perched on top of their suitcases in the middle of the crowded platform. The overhead clocks hit their chimes, signalling midday. Elizabeth fell into a still silence, guilt burrowed deep into her mind. She didn't know what to say to the others. Not like they would listen to her anyway. Eyes from the crowd glazed over her. Amongst the swirl of the busy platform, a face popped out. Eyes of familiar blue, smooth brown hair braided down the side. The pinch of a smile, pulling on her left cheek, just like Elizabeth's. Elizabeth bolted upwards. She couldn't believe her eyes. "Mother?"

Ana Blackmore stood meters away, her attention on the crowd. She turned around, searching the faces before walking away. Impossible. Ana Blackmore was dead. Yet, Elizabeth was certain she saw her mother's face. Elizabeth fought against the natural current of the crowd, unable to find her voice to shout out. Ana's head bobbed into the swell of the people.

"Wait...wai—" Elizabeth sprinted as she saw Ana duck behind a pillar. Hope fluttered. Disbelief. Need. Possible scenarios rushed to the front of her mind, trying to explain how Ana could possibly be there. She caught up with the woman and grabbed her shoulder, spinning her around. Under closer inspection, Elizabeth noticed the inconsistencies. Ana's body walked as though slanted, tipping her slightly right. Her skin was cold, sticky, and her eyes dulled as though they were painted on. Elizabeth retracted her hand. This thing wasn't Ana. It wasn't even human.

"Hello, Elizabeth." A chilled voice ran up her neck. The Ana clone crumpled into shards, dissolving back into shadows and the bendable forms of Nikolas' gremlins.

Elizabeth stumbled back, feeling her heartbreak all over again. "How dare you!" she choked, nearing tears. Nikolas stepped closer.

"Where is Klaus?"

Elizabeth shook her head, trying desperately to stop the whimper in her voice. "You're a monster."

"Fear is good, but there's no point in fearing monsters, Elizabeth. It's not going to help you."

"What do you want?"

"Fear is a powerful motivator. Desperation, even more so. I know he's capable of it, I just need to play this game carefully. Delicate hands to hit those pressure points." Nikolas held his fingertips to her forehead, seeping shadows through her skin and into her mind. He caught only fractions, burns of images, sharp colors, shrilling echoes, and disrupted white noise. Among the fray of distorted memories, he witnessed Klaus fling himself through the train window taking with him an unknown woman.

Pain threw Nikolas' head back and his connection on Elizabeth dropped. She dipped unconsciously into Nikolas' arms and he carefully laid her down by the pillar. As he crouched, droplets of blood spotted the floor. He dabbed his nose clean, the weight of magic burning dark blotches over his vision. He wobbled, having to grab the floor to stop from toppling over. *Can't keep doing that.* The gremlins bickered, biting bruises on his neck, arms, and knees, but Nikolas paid them no attention. Only minor details remained. A bullet wound, cut through Klaus' bicep. A white dagger, too small to see clearly, snapped in half. A swell of panic. Five different people. *No wait, only four. One is dead now.* Bruises lined the dead man's temple, matching the shape of Klaus' elbow. Nikolas cast a long sideways look. The gunshot on Klaus' body reminded Nikolas of his own old scars. *There's only one thing capable of inflicting that type of injury and I assume they are here for me.*

Careful not to overextend his capabilities, Nikolas sent the gremlins toward the travelling group. At the forefront of his mind, he watched through the gremlin's foggy eyes as they scurried around their feet, collecting swabs of smells. *Wine. Detergent. Perfume. Sweat. Tobacco. Leather. Gold. Gun powder.* They climbed the woman first, then the two men. Among them were two unaccounted aromas. One belonged to the dead man, the other to the woman thrown from the train. The gremlins rushed into the docked train, searching the carriages for the spot where the man had died. They caught one of the scents, eliminating the last remaining smell as the woman's. He concentrated on it, expanded it, and like trained sniffer dogs the gremlins singled out the trail. *Follow it.* The shadows lurched forward, seeping through the slits of the metal panels and galloped down the tracks. The scent thickened into a smoke trail, homing in on the woman's location, until it disappeared. The smell dulled and the gremlins slingshot back to him.

Nikolas grinned. *Klaus is still with her, for now. Guess I'm going to have to find him the old-fashioned way.* His attention shifted back to the group. Pieces of Elizabeth's memories blurred together, but it was clear enough the blue-eyed male had the closest connection to the missing woman. Her scent was all over him.

Similar to how he baited Elizabeth, Nikolas conjured the gremlins and spindled them into a distorted copy of Elizabeth's form. The copy was flawed, awkward, but from far away the shadow could convince him it was really Elizabeth. The creature waved the man over. Nikolas smirked, "Thank god for human error."

CHAPTER
THIRTY-TWO

WILL IT WORK? This little plan of yours?" Nikolas took a deep breath. Grief pulled at him, slouching his back and numbing all his emotions except for rage. The desire to inflict torment on Klaus drove his every move, controlled his every thought. The woman beside him reached out, coaxing Nikolas' attention back. "Nikolas?"

"With her, I believe so." He didn't look away from Elizabeth, unconscious on the thin mattress. She would be the perfect thorn to plant into Klaus' side. Nikolas took a long drink from the bottle of wine he carried.

The woman sighed. "I may not know Klaus as well as you, but I know what he isn't capable of."

"You didn't see it, Juliet," Nikolas whispered. "He is so afraid, so desperate."

"And how will that make him fall in love?"

"Fear controls Klaus. It's what allows him to live unattached from others. I want to heighten that fear, make him desperate enough that his need to protect Elizabeth blurs his judgment. Dress him up as a hero, and Klaus may just believe he is one."

"How endearing." Juliet smiled.

"He needs a heart first for me to break it." Noises carried down the tunnel. Nikolas turned toward it. "Time to play. The other one is for you."

"Not exactly my type," Juliet pouted. "Can't we swap?"

"After we're done. Best you go and check on our friend."

With a nod, Juliet walked into the tunnel. Nikolas lingered, watching for signs of Elizabeth stirring out of sleep.

Elizabeth awoke on a mattress. She sat upright, alarmed, and turned around, trying to make sense of the strong murky smell, the stone archway above her head, and the echoing drip of a leaking pipe. Dark, wet bricks stretched into the narrow tunnel. Around her, shadows danced against the flicker of a steady bonfire flame. Stripped mattresses lined the walls, sheets of old blankets left in bundles, dirty dishes, trolleys full of clothes, and cardboard boxes scattered the space. A network of homeless lived here, but how *she* ended up here remained unknown.

Elizabeth slowly stood. On the table beside the bonfire, a glint of silver caught her attention. A Collector's blade. Realization dawned on her. *Nikolas. He must have taken me here.* She searched the dim lit room for him, remaining wary of the dark corners. Nothing but silence, yet he was known for his quiet presence. *He will be here, watching from somewhere.* Elizabeth approached the table and hovered over the weapon. *He left it behind?*

The patterns of the twisted cogs were structured differently from Klaus'. It was long and slightly crooked like a deer's antler.

"I wouldn't touch that if I was you."

She flinched at hearing Nikolas' warning. Elizabeth watched him carefully cross the room. Darkness collected beneath his eyes, shallowing his face whereas the orange flames haloed around him, warming the yellow in his hair. He reached over and picked up his blade, examining it fondly. She searched his face, growing madder at the curl of his smile. Nikolas had taken so much from her. He was nothing more than a ruthless romantic, listening to the commands of his tyrant lover. "You have questions?"

"Just one."

Nikolas smirked. "Let me guess, why did I kidnap you? Come on, Elizabeth, you're smarter than that."

"That wasn't my question."

"What then?"

Elizabeth stepped forward, lifting her chin. She had been sitting on this thought for so long it felt raw to say it aloud, but seeing her mother again, allowed her to speak through the pain. "Why did you pick her?"

"Who?" Nikolas took another mouthful of wine.

Her jaw clenched angrily. "My mother. Tell me, why her?"

Nikolas didn't speak. Elizabeth couldn't read his blank expression. His eyes remained vacant and blurred from the alcohol. Her anger deepened, dropping her voice into a whisper. "It's the least you can do for me…"

"And why should I do anything for you?" His demeanor changed, hardening with his rage.

"You *destroyed* my life."

"Then I guess we're even."

"I didn't harm Claudia."

His face tightened at her name. "No, but Klaus did." He turned away to face the fire. "I'm not blind to her betrayal. I'm sure Klaus called me foolish. He is a man without feeling. An animal, focused only on surviving."

"I don't believe that."

Nikolas smiled. "No, all seasons change, don't they? This is a game, Elizabeth, a slow trick of the mind. Klaus will learn there are things far deadlier than me."

"Like what?" she asked.

Nikolas smirked. "With any luck, human error."

A loud groan carried down from the end of the tunnel. Elizabeth turned toward it as Nikolas took another long gulp of wine, emptying the bottle before throwing it into the fire. "He's awake."

"Who? Who is that?"

"I believe you know him." Nikolas sidestepped to allow Elizabeth passage. "A friend to keep you company."

Elizabeth walked past him warily and followed the tunnel down toward a separate room. Inside, Hudson sat on a wooden chair with both wrists and ankles tied up. Beside him waited a young woman leisurely reading a book. Hudson looked up at Elizabeth's entrance. "Elizabeth?"

"Hudson?" She hovered by the door, confusion holding her back. "What are you doing here?" Her attention shifted to the other woman. Her beautiful brown skin did little to hide the cosmos of freckles stretching across her cheekbones and onto the tip of her nose. Her brown eyes sparkled as she stood, subtly brushing loose black curls behind her ear.

She smiled warmly in greeting. "Good evening."

"Who are you?" Elizabeth asked.

"An accomplice," Nikolas answered as he entered behind them. Elizabeth stepped back until she reached Hudson's side. Nikolas continued, "Unlike Klaus, I do not buck against the company of others."

Hudson straightened up in his chair, focused on Nikolas' face. "Is it… I know you! I know what you are!"

"Yes, I'm sure you have my picture hanging on the walls at those little meetings of yours." He laughed, smugly. "Don't take offense if I don't return the interest, I don't bother to learn the names of dead men."

"We kill creatures like you."

"History begs to differ." Nikolas cocked an eyebrow. "Funny, you try to threaten me but welcome Klaus into your pack."

"Klaus isn't corrupted," Elizabeth said.

Nikolas sighed and rolled his eyes. "The word *corrupted* is thrown around so easily nowadays, but do you know what it means?" At their silence, he continued, mockingly. "So typical of humans. You act without thinking and hate without understanding. Corruption only means I do not live by the code. I can deny contracts at my whim and those I do accept, I get to keep the time for myself."

"What do you mean you keep the time? To do what with?"

"To live longer, and of course, the added extras. Interesting aren't they?" Nikolas answered by pointing to the gremlins. "The power of a mortal's life. Pure energy manifested into the shadows. Things for me to control. Unlike Klaus, we are not controlled by words."

"We?" Elizabeth whispered, looking toward the woman. "You're a corrupted Collector too?"

The woman's smile widened. "My name is Juliet, and I am so much more than that. I also enjoy moon gazing, if you're interested?"

"Why bring us both here?" Elizabeth demanded.

"Oh, I think you know why."

Hudson bucked against his restraints. "You can go to hell."

"I can see why he likes him." Juliet beamed. "Fiery."

"I'm afraid not this time, Juliet." Nikolas corrected, much to Juliet's disappointment.

She looked away. "How boring."

"Is this part of your game, Nikolas?" Elizabeth interjected, "Baiting Klaus?"

"More like saving him from a lesser evil. As your time cannot be touched, Elizabeth, I'm going to have your companion here offer it up for me instead. Don't worry, it won't cost much." He gave Juliet a brisk nod. She stepped up to Hudson and placed her thumb to his forehead. As she prepared, Nikolas turned away, directing his attention mostly to Elizabeth. "We all have our special talents, Elizabeth. I have my gremlins, a network of shadows I can manipulate at will. Juliet's is a bit more focused."

Her thumbnail cut into Hudson's forehead, drawing a line of red across his skin. Above their heads, the lights flickered. Darkness thickened, seeping out from Juliet's shadow and upward into her fingertips. Hudson started to convulse. He screamed, violently shaking in terror.

"What are you doing?" Elizabeth panicked.

"Only nightmares," Nikolas said, dismissively. "Tricks."

Hudson continued to shout, his face blooming red with stress. Juliet's body tipped slightly forward with exhaustion, but she was careful to keep her thumbnail embedded in his skin.

His screams were too real, too raw for Elizabeth to handle. "Stop it, please! Take the time from me!"

Nikolas ignored her.

Through his grunts of pain, Hudson shouted, "Please, I'll do whatever you want! Find Catherine, save her!" Juliet stumbled off of him, immediately losing her grip. She collapsed to her knees against the wall. Nikolas drew the time from Hudson's unconscious body before tending to Juliet. Elizabeth ran to him and checked his pulse. It raced erratically.

"Hudson? Hudson, are you alright? Hudson?"

"He's fine. A dead contract will break the wish after all," Nikolas said. Pulses of magic filled his veins, expanding within his lungs with every breath. The gremlins bubbled up with excitement, the tiny, black rodents already chasing down Catherine's undisturbed scent. Even within Klaus' presence, the wish wouldn't be disrupted. "Juliet will ensure he is looked after. You and I have a family matters to attend to." He helped Juliet sit up on the chair and dropped his voice to a whisper. "Keep him here." She nodded as she dabbed her bloody nose clean.

"And what about those other Guardians you spoke of?"

"You know what to do. Leave Mr. Hudson until last."

CHAPTER
THIRTY-THREE

P INS AND NEEDLES worked into his shoulder. Klaus howled.
His voice cracked under the strain. Fire ran up his arm. He
shook feverishly, sweat dampening his collar and forehead. Veins
pressed to the surface, exaggerated by the intensity of the damage. He
didn't know how long it lasted as time suspended around him. Over
the pain, tingles shifted like forming ice, expanding over the wound
and crystalizing his arm into rock. His body cooled but still trembled
with the aftershock.

Once the pain was gone, he collapsed into the dirt. The entirety
of his right arm was tucked against his body like a broken wing. His
fingers were frozen in a clenched fist, immortalizing his struggle. It
took him a few moments to catch his breath before gingerly sitting up.
A few meters away, he could hear the struggling gasps of Catherine.
She was twisted around a tree, her shoulder popped up against her
ear, wrist broken, legs turned out in the wrong direction and her ribs
shattered. Blood ran from her nostril, mixing in with her tears and
sweat.

"Help me – help me – help me." Her voice barely lifted, but he
could hear the fluid in her lungs as she spoke. "P-Please."

Klaus' eyes narrowed with rage. "I should leave you."

"Please—"

It wasn't a full wish, but it was enough to tickle his Collector's code. The genuine desire was there, and fearing the punishment, Klaus hobbled over to her. He rubbed his hands together to draw in spiritual energy before carefully distributing it along her broken body. Catherine relaxed beneath the healing, her eyes fluttering blissfully once free from the pain. She sighed with relief. "Thank you. Thank you."

He pricked her with his blade before collapsing back into the dirt. The wish had weakened him, draining his mind of thought. For the next few moments, they both didn't speak and recovered silently amongst the dirt. The overhead sky was covered by thick tree branches, fanned out across the entire mountain. Klaus ran his free hand over the stone cast.

"What have you done to me?"

Catherine eased up and glanced at him. "We can fix it."

"How?"

She changed the topic. "We need to get out of here. Will it cost me much time to teleport back?"

"No more wishes. I need to recover first," Klaus said breathlessly.

Catherine whispered, "I'm sorry about stabbing you. They weren't going to stop."

"Then perhaps you should have stabbed them."

She glanced away guiltily. "You rest. We weren't far from Westicher. Shouldn't be too difficult to walk there."

Klaus watched her stand unsteadily and scan the area for the dropped dagger. He growled and looked away. Hours passed until Klaus had the energy to stand without support. The poison dripped out of him like sweat. He felt around the puncture wound and was able to detect the splintered end of the bone shard lodged in his arm. Thanks to the hard stone, it was impossible for him to dig it out.

"Can you walk?" Catherine asked.

"Ja."

She walked over to carry Klaus over her shoulders, but he shrugged her off. "Nein. I'm fine."

Hours passed. The sun rose, heating up the air around them. Catherine stumbled to a stop, propping her arms against the tree trunk in an attempt to stay upright.

"I can't take another step. I need some water," Catherine whimpered, her tongue roughened from dehydration. "Please, Klaus, I don't care how much it'll cost. I want a drink."

Klaus sat down on a fallen log and wiped the sweat off his brow. "Don't be so quick to throw your time away." He unwound the handkerchief and examined the tattoo again. The coordinates remained the same. Elizabeth would be at Westicher, and no doubt Nikolas would be watching. He'd see her among the others, the Guardians, and know of Klaus' plan.

The bullet wound ached as he absentmindedly touched his stone arm. It was then he noticed tracks in the soil. Footprints. Lots of footprints. He pointed it out to Catherine. "Someone lives around here, we're close."

They struggled up the hill and eventually came across a field of *Vitis vinifera*. "Hallelujah!" Catherine rushed toward the entrance of the winery. Crowds lined the fields, following tour guides explaining about the different type of wines and the process in making them. Klaus's stone arm remained covered by his large coat, the only visible part being his clenched hand that he kept close to his heart.

"I've left a message for the others at the *Und Hänsel Gretel* letting them know I'm okay." Catherine informed as she and Klaus waited inside the winery around a table. "There will be a car arriving to take us the rest of the way."

"No mention of me?" Klaus asked.

"Thought better not. I'll just tell them you deserted me after the commotion."

"Good choice. But what of Elizabeth?"

"I'm sure she's fine."

"She will be worried," he insisted. "She does that, she worries."

"Not unlike yourself." Catherine bit her lower lip to hide her smile. She poured them both a glass of wine, offering one out to Klaus. "The car won't be here for a while though. We could use this time to get to know each other. How did you and Elizabeth meet?"

Klaus accepted the drink cautiously. "Not poisoned, is it?"

"No, I promise."

He was still reluctant to drink. "Her father and I knew each other. I met Elizabeth when she moved into the mansion after her mother passed away. I helped her train for a short while. She was rather pathetic at combat; can't shoot straight to save herself," he chuckled.

"She matters to you though, doesn't she?"

Her words tied up his tongue. Every time he thought of Elizabeth, a hopeful tightness gripped him. Klaus glanced away, uncomfortably. "Don't they serve anything stronger than wine?"

"How does it work exactly?" she asked instead.

"What do you mean?"

"The rules with Collectors. I've never had any personal experience with them. I mean with, well, your kind before."

"I don't understand what you're asking me."

"You must have rules, right? Boundaries to what people can and cannot wish for? Or is anything possible?"

"Well." Klaus cleared his throat. "We cannot be ordered to kill or track other Collectors."

"Why?"

"We have a natural repellent, helps Collectors hide from threats. We also have a powerful instinct to survive, able to react to dangers faster than any known creature on earth. Our indestructibility was a parting gift from our master Chronos. We work for him, he provides us with the code and the blade, and in return, we split the collected time for him. Half to us, half to him. Keeps him immortal."

"Chronos? What is a Chronos?"

"The original Time Collector."

Catherine shifted back. "Where is this Chronos then?"

"I have no idea," he admitted. "I'm not even convinced he is a real person, but a presence, like a thought or a dream."

"Are there any other restrictions to wishes then?"

"Nein, technically, you can have any wish, as long as you can afford it. You can wish to kill a man, but it may cost you thirty years. You can wish to fly to the moon, but it'll cost you over a hundred. Anything is possible, if you have the time. Most people barely live to fifty, so such wishes cannot be achieved. Wishes cannot be pulled out of nowhere. It must come from something. Like alchemy, exchanging items of equal value, but when a person dies, the contract is void. The wisher must be careful in their desires, for it could be taken away from them after death. That's not to say a broken contract would bring a dead person back to life, but it could mean taking away certain things." He thought on it for a moment. "Like wealth or a working heart."

"Is it even worth wishing from a Time Collector then if you end up losing what you want?"

"Your lives are so short. Why not make the best of whatever time you have left? Either way, you will die. Why not die happy? If you're smart about it, even with an invalid contract, your wish could remain."

She nodded her head slowly. "Wish for something that if it's taken away, doesn't mean you lose its benefits."

"Exactly."

"Do you have to use the sentence, I wish, though?"

Klaus chuckled. "No, there's no exact phrase that has to be pronounced. It's an understanding between both parties. Like out in the forest, you didn't exactly wish to be healed, but I understood your desire enough to act on it. If it's genuine, then it can be made real."

Catherine smiled. "Thank you again for that. So where do you come from? You're not just born as a Time Collector?"

Klaus again calmly nodded. "Ja. All Collectors had normal mortal lives once. Even though we are Time Collectors, we are still living, breathing beings. We still need to eat and drink, like normal mortals. If we stop collecting, we'll run out of time and die a normal death."

"So you're not immortal?"

"Technically, no." Klaus went to lift his glass, but his grip trembled.

Catherine leaned closer. "Listen, let me fix it for you. It is my fault after all. And partly yours."

Klaus perked his eyebrow. "How do you intend to fix…" But he didn't need to finish the question to understand what she meant. Gratitude fluttered within him. "Are you sure?"

"It won't cost me much, right?"

"Not a lot, but make sure you are specific. Every detail counts. There's a shard stuck in there, but I can't get to it because of this irritating coating. Hopefully, if I remove it, the wound will heal itself."

Catherine thought on it for a moment, and then cleared her throat. "Okay. Okay, I'm ready. Klaus, I wish your right arm wasn't covered in stone."

The wish ran up into his spine, tingling his fingers. Klaus secretly revealed the Collector's blade from his inner jacket and immediately Catherine flinched. "Please be careful."

"You won't feel a thing." He turned her hand over and gently pricked the end of her finger. The stone coating on Klaus' arm rippled back into soft, human skin. He could feel tingling under his arm as warmth extended from his shoulder down to his fingertips. He wasted no time. The moment his skin was breakable, Klaus drove his blade into his shoulder and pried the remained bone shard out. The broken shiv fell to the ground soundlessly.

Relief washed over him. "*Danke*. Thank you."

Catherine smiled, picking up the shard and pocketing it. "My pleasure."

Klaus flexed his right hand, uncurling his fingers. A small smile crept across his face, softening his eyes. As he celebrated silently, his arm trembled. Pins and needles orbited the stab wound, and shifted back down his arm. Klaus kicked back from his chair. "What?" He couldn't do anything other than watch his skin discolor back into gray rock, and painfully his fingers curled again into a fist. "*Nein! Es hat nicht funktioniert!* (*No! It didn't work.*)"

"Klaus, I…I don—!" Catherine stammered.

The bone shard was out. He was positive of that, but traces of it lingered. He grabbed his arm, picturing a life with a limb frozen to his chest. Panic flared once he noticed the pain travelling further into his back, tightening his muscles. *It's going to spread?*

"We can still fix this. Lady and Lord Moore can—"

Fear pushed him away. He turned from Catherine, his mind in shambles as he tried to find the door. He didn't know where he was going. He didn't know what he was going to do.

"Wait! Where are you going?" Catherine stood, but Klaus disappeared from her sight.

CHAPTER

THIRTY-FOUR

ARKNESS COVERED THE ground beneath her feet and left tingles over her skin. With Nikolas's grip on her, Elizabeth felt the world around her shift into a foreign cosmos. Colors flickered, breaking through the dimensions of space and time, and stepping out of the dark void onto the outskirts of a winery. Elizabeth's eyes squinted against the setting sun. Nature chirped around her, bringing contrasting warmth from the chilly underground tunnel they stood in just moments ago. Hudson's wish carried them to Catherine, leaving them on the skirts of a winery. Elizabeth felt awe of a Collector's abilities and came to better understand Klaus' fear of Nikolas. A man who can teleport and control shadows at his own whim. Klaus, of course, had his own set of abilities, but nothing of this grandeur.

The gremlins scrambled back into Nikolas' shadow. The woman, Catherine, was inside, but Klaus was nowhere to be seen. Gremlins scoured every inch of the property, expanding as far as Nikolas could reach before sling-shotting back into his pocket.

"Not here?" Nikolas growled. His attention moved to the estate. "She'll know."

"What? Who?" Elizabeth turned just as Nikolas disappeared from sight. *She? As in Catherine?* Realization struck and she rushed inside after him. Yet, Nikolas was too quick.

He approached Catherine silently where she sat alone beside the back window, gazing out across the fields. From behind her, he gently reached out and touched the back of her head, trying to dig into her memories as he had done with Elizabeth. But before he could pull up any images, something hard knocked him back. Pain popped to the front of his eyes, and around him the gremlins bubbled. Immediately, blood started to weep out of his nostrils. *I'm too weak.* The only reason why Collectors were able to do what they do was thanks to the transformation of a soul. It became energy, matter to construct and deconstruct at the users' desire. With Nikolas, the only time he took was his own.

Catherine heard his yelp of pain and turned around. Like Hudson, she recognized Nikolas' face and immediately reached for the bone dagger in her pocket. She swung, but Nikolas caught her wrist. Catherine kicked out of his grip. She was fast, able to weasel out of his reach before he could secure a grip on her. She used the furniture to barricade his approach, tipping the table over and smashing the glasses in the commotion. But she couldn't run from his gremlins. Both her ankles were lassoed to the ground, held there by sticky black matter. Catherine tripped and fell, landing on her back.

"What on earth?!" She swung downwards, slicing through the gremlins. They squealed and tunnelled back into Nikolas. Nikolas' attention went straight to the dagger and his eyes enlarged with need.

Elizabeth ran inside and heard the banging of furniture at the back of the room. Most of the winery had emptied, leaving only the staff behind who also moved in to check out the noise. There, she saw Nikolas towering over Catherine. "You…how did you get that?" He pointed to the shiv while drawing out his own Collector's blade.

Elizabeth's mind spun. She charged and tried to hit Nikolas over the head with a wine bottle, but he turned and caught it. The Collector code gave them incredible reflexes, and this was a fight Elizabeth wasn't going to win. Which meant Catherine was at the mercy of a man she knew was capable of murder.

"Nikolas! Don't!" Elizabeth started to beg. Nikolas turned his back on her. The remaining staff ran away in panic at seeing him reveal his weapon. The gremlins bit Catherine's hand, pinning her wrist to the floor. For the second time, Elizabeth was going to have to watch someone die. Her father first, and then Benjamin. She had already lost too many family members to the Collectors. Her mother and Sara both. She felt as helpless as she did at William's gates, begging him to help her. Elizabeth closed her eyes, her voice scratching as she spoke. "Oh, God please just stop him!"

As the words left her mouth, her mind immediately went to her old house in the Pitts. She remembered the slanted tilts it was built on, the warm hearth that nested their fires. Nikolas froze and Elizabeth opened her eyes in time to see the horror cross his face. He looked at her from over his shoulder, and without breaking eye contact, the roof folded away into gray smoke. Magic pulled the earth sideways, the ground beneath their feet sunk as the room blurred in a spinning motion. Catherine disappeared. The winery disappeared. It felt as though they stood still and the rest of the world spun backwards. All that remained clear was Nikolas. His large bewildered eyes, his face tightened. Then everything stopped. Fishy smells hit her. Noises of busy traffic. She stumbled forward, dizzy in her disorientation and caught herself on the wall. She was back home, clinging to the grime sleeked walls in the Pitts. Familiarity stung with its own type of pain. She staggered backward, her head tilted up at the crooked buildings above. *What? What happened?* People wove around her as she walked out into the middle of the streets, looking for Nikolas.

"Isn't that her?" Elizabeth turned at the sound of whispers. People slowed to gawk, some being as bold as to point straight at her. "Why is she here? Isn't she in recovery?"

"Nikolas?" Elizabeth hissed as she ducked down an alleyway. When she glanced up, she was faced with a wall covered completely in posters of Arthur's face. Among the clutter of his self-made shrine, there were also declaration of civil-war, of a terrorist organization to defeat and a call to rise against the traitors. *It was no tragedy. It was murder.*

What on earth is happening? Elizabeth stumbled back and turned around. Protesters lined the streets. Flyers turned the roads into a sea of dirty crumpled sheets. Elizabeth darted around the crowds to a newsstand selling the local paper. All over the press there were talks of scandals, devastation, panic, and unrest. It had been four days since the destruction of the Beaumontt manor. Four days since Harold, Lady Claudia, and Timothy Beaumontt had died. Within those four days, Arthur had scrambled to secure power of the country. To secure his family name. Secret meetings were made. Mysterious fires set over parliaments. Men of opposing politics were killed. Families threatened and fled. Rumors about Jeremy Beaumontt's return from war flooded the headlines side by side with details of Arthur's and Elizabeth's secret wedding. *Elizabeth Beaumontt, the new Lady of the house.*

Elizabeth flicked through the paper to find two pages focused on just her. *…And where oh where is our new fair lady? Only daughter and heir to late Doctor William Wicker, the white hair beauty hasn't been seen since the attack at the Beaumontt estate. Claims of woman hysteria and exhaustion has ailed our mysterious Cinderella where she recovers in the privacy of the new Beaumontt estate. Sir Arthur Beaumontt's quick thinking and bravery was what saved our damsel in distress from meeting the same fate that took our Governor, Lady Claudia and her eldest son, Timothy's, life. It is still unknown when we will get to see the new happy couple amongst the turmoil of a country's grief.*

Elizabeth stumbled back. *Oh no. Oh God, please no.* Arthur Beaumontt had survived. She had thought Arthur had perished in the Beaumontt tragedy, but alas there he was, as terrifying as a nightmare.

And she was married to him. Elizabeth pocketed the newspaper.

"Oi! Are you going to pay for that?" The store clerk stepped out from behind the counter. Elizabeth fled into the dense channels, travelling deeper into the cesspool that was the Pitts. She knew every crack and nook of the backstreets, hiding in places where no one looked and waited for night. Sunlight lowered, drawing out the yellow glow from the lamps lining the roadways. Darkness helped hide her most of the way into Rosefire and up to Harry Smith's front door.

She knocked urgently. "Mr. Smith? Mr. Smith, are you home?"

Movement shuffled behind the door panel. Moments later, an anxious Harry answered, first peeking through the gap in the curtain before swinging the door wide open. "Miss Wicker?"

"I'm so sorry." Elizabeth whispered. "I didn't know where else to go."

CATHERINE SCRAMBLED BACK up. It didn't make sense. Her brain couldn't work out the science behind the trick, trying to understand how Elizabeth and Nikolas could disappear within inches of her. All that was left were the throbbing points where Nikolas had grabbed her wrist. People helped her stand and started gossiping about witches. Catherine walked out of the winery, calling for Klaus.

Klaus slowed from pacing the dirt track. The air around him chilled, filling up with the coppery scent of Nikolas' dark magic. *No! Impossible!* Klaus glanced toward the vineyard for signs of his prowling gremlins. *Nikolas is here? How did he find me?* In the next moment, a strong metallic taste climbed up his throat and red hives covered his left hand. *What? What is this?*

"Klaus? Klaus! Klaus, where are you?"

Klaus turned at Catherine's desperate calling. He rushed back to her to find her panicked and sweaty. Catherine's cheeks flushed red. "Where on earth were you?"

"I'm here now, what is it?"

"Nikolas was here! He has Elizabeth!"

Klaus' heart dropped to the bottom of his chest. Really, he shouldn't be surprised that Nikolas went to Elizabeth the moment Klaus was gone. Of course he would, but still, the confirmation only further set in Klaus' fear. The hives on his hand and the taste in his mouth made sense. *The taint. She's made a wish.* Klaus swallowed, trying to keep his composure. "What happened?"

"He attacked me, tried to take the bone shiv. Elizabeth was with him, and then they vanished. Teleported away."

"Where?"

"I don't know."

"Then what good are you?" Klaus snapped.

Catherine placed her hands on her hips, equally as irritated. "A lot more useful than someone storming off and sulking like some child."

"I wasn't sulking," he growled and shook his head impatiently. "What were her exact words?"

"Something like, *oh God please just stop him.*"

Well, that didn't help at all. "She must've been thinking of something, something she wanted bad enough that Nikolas would feel compelled to grant." Klaus mumbled under his breath and started to pace again. *They vanished, teleported, meaning Elizabeth was thinking of a certain place when she said those words. If Nikolas really was attacking Catherine, she would be scared. Panicked. Where would her mind go if she were frightened?* The thoughts clicked. "I think I know where she is."

"Let me come too. I can help."

"Clearly you can't." Klaus cleared his throat to correct himself, remembering Elizabeth's scolding. "Sorry, yes, maybe you can help. Find out what you can to unfreeze my arm. I will go get her."

"But where is she? Where did they go?"

Klaus sighed uneasily. "Home."

CHAPTER

THIRTY-FIVE

T HANK YOU SO much for allowing me to stay here, Harry."
Elizabeth sat down and wrapped herself up in a blanket to fight
off the cold. She dared not go near the windows or the front
door in fear of being spotted again. She picked up her tea cup and
took a long drink, trying to settle her nerves.

"Is everything alright? I thought you were travelling with Sir
Dietrich and Lady Rose-Wicker across country." Harry set up his tea
next to his arm chair. "I worry about you being here, there is a lot of
unrest regarding the Beaumontt's and politics."

"I can see." Elizabeth reached over and picked up the paper. Her
name was plastered on every second page. "Look at this. He parades
my name around like some sort of trophy. I don't intend to give Arthur
the chance to drag me back into his clutches."

Harry reached over and gently touched her shaking hand. "Where
is Sir Dietrich?" he asked. "Shouldn't he be looking after you?"

"I'm afraid we've been separated."

"You can always try and contact your aunt, Lady Rose-Wicker?"

Elizabeth chewed on her nail. "But I'm a stranger. Why would
she want to help me?"

"You are family."

"I'm the estranged love-child of a brother she didn't like very much.

I cannot burden her with my problems." As she flipped through the papers, she noticed one of the pages had been torn out, leaving only the shredded spine behind.

"Well, you are more than welcome to stay with me, but I worry you'll be discovered here. Arthur Beaumontt has a lot of men working for him."

"But I also can't hide forever."

Harry thought on it for a moment. "I think I may be able to help. I have friends outside of the country who can help you out."

"I could not ask—"

"I insist." Harry walked over to his phone book and started thumbing through the pages.

She spent most of the night listening over Harry's conversations. Each phone call ended the same. Sorry, but we can't help. Sorry, but we don't have the space. Sorry, we don't have the money.

"I have my inheritance. I can compensate them for their help," Elizabeth offered.

Harry smiled. "We can pay you for your troubles…. You will help? Oh, thank you, bless you sir. I will call you back to discuss details." Harry set the phone down, his exhausted voice gone dry. "Your father's check book should be in here." Harry motioned to a large box set aside with William Wicker's belongings. They were mostly things from his clinic, as most of his other possessions went up in flames at the Wicker estate. They searched through the box when Elizabeth noticed a crumpled piece of paper hastily shoved behind the tea set they were using. She picked it up and unfurled it as Harry continued talking. "Mr. Brighton lives at least four hours east of here. His lovely wife has recently started a book club and I'm sure she will enjoy your company—"

"Harry?" Elizabeth whispered as her eyes trailed down the page. "Is this true?"

Harry glanced over and slowly lowered the folders back to the desk. The missing page went into details of a scandal of a love-child. The kiss and tell of a woman who birthed a Beaumontt son. Arthur's son. Though blurred, there was a picture attached to the block of writing. A woman's face with too much familiarity.

"Miss Wicker." Harry started with genuine concern. "Please, pay no mind to gossip. Arthur Beaumontt is not a man of proper morals."

"A love-child." Elizabeth whispered. "Just like me."

Harry closed his mouth. "I did not mean to imply that."

"But is it true?" Her chest squeezed. Tears surfaced, threatening to spill. Harry shuffled forward, pained and confused by Elizabeth's emotional reaction.

"I'm so sorry, Miss Wicker. I tried to hide it, but I didn't know you were coming here. I'm sorry this news has hurt you."

Elizabeth shook her head. "You misunderstand Harry. I believe I know this woman."

NIKOLAS WATCHED HIS large hands shake. The loss of freewill resurfaced old memories, pulling him back into wars he never wanted to fight, to assassinations, to cheats, to liars and the cruelty of man's greed. His hands felt warm, uncomfortable, and sticky. *It doesn't make sense.* The Collector's code flared within his body, overwhelming him. It had been so long since he had felt overpowered by it and the aftershock numbed him. She had only whispered, yet her voice rang as clear as bells.

He couldn't follow her. The moment they both stepped out of the shadow plane, Nikolas disappeared. He fled into the bulk of the crowd, becoming lost among the criss-crossing paths of the locals. He collected the time owed to him, but paid no attention to whom he stabbed in the busy market street. It didn't matter. His plan had taken a step backward, separating him from Klaus and tearing his brother out of his reach. Due to Elizabeth's influence.

Nikolas felt out of place amongst a city he once called home. Before he had noticed it, night had crawled overhead. The streets emptied. Nikolas glanced up at the large golden gates wrapped around Divin Cadeau. His mind traced back to the first time he set eyes on it. *On her.* The sparkle of green in her eyes. Her light blue dress against her figure. She had been mean to him the first time they met. She mocked him for picking the wrong apple from a large batch.

"Rotten," she had lectured, biting back a smile. "It wouldn't last the day." Nikolas smiled over the memory. The bond was a delicate instrument. No thicker than a piece of string, but with the strength of unbendable steel. It could come in an instant. In the lock of eyes, the glimpse of a smile. It was spontaneous. Addictive. A drug to both build him up and tear him down. Lady Claudia did not perish at the Beaumontt reckoning, but knowing she was still unreachable was just as much as a death sentence.

Nikolas' attention fell upon the left-over flyers littering the streets. The flutter of white the only movement in the quiet night. *Arthur Beaumontt fights for the truth. Betrayal within high-society. Seeking justice for the murder of Governor Beaumontt. The exciting announcement of the new Lady Elizabeth Beaumont.* Opportunity sparked. *Of course. The whispers of Elizabeth's return. A new villain to defeat.*

There were only a few places for Elizabeth to hide. The shack was one of them. Nikolas sent him gremlins to the tiny hut to find it cold and deserted. He redirected himself, knowing she'd also visited the Raps Rips in the docks recently. But again, there was no sign of her. Nikolas pondered on the thought, before remembering she once took refuge in a place in Rosefire. He sent his gremlins across and immediately picked up her scent pacing the front door.

Nikolas smiled and teleported through the shadows to the manor. A new plan formed. Another hook to reel Klaus to him, and invite the heart-pumping danger into their game. *Can't hide forever, Elizabeth Beaumontt. I'm sure your husband is worried.*

DARKNESS PUSHED AGAINST his eyes. The last thing Klaus could remember, before the swell of black swallowed him whole, was nauseating pain. His shoulder ached. His arm felt compressed, tethered to his side. The poison was spreading faster than he could walk. Klaus caught a ride with a travelling group of soldiers heading back to the small army town of Landmark. On arrival, he made his way to the train station eager to catch the last train back to Divin Cadeau.

A young man stood on the empty platform beside him. His face was concealed behind a hat and the collars of his coat turned up, covering his cheeks and mouth. Klaus barely glanced at him, but took note of the stuffed bag he held with his left hand. He didn't place it on the floor, but held it, despite knowing the train was still fifteen minutes away from docking.

Klaus' eyebrow perked. The man felt Klaus' attention and glanced over, only to give him a brief smile and nod. "Evening." Klaus didn't respond, his mind too preoccupied with staying conscious. Darkness circled in. The pain doubled. "Are you alright?" the man asked.

"Ja," Klaus said.

The man nodded and looked straight again. "War wound?"

"What?"

"Your shoulder."

Klaus glanced over as the man pointed to his injured arm. "The way you're carrying it, looks like you've broken it. Whoever set it for you has done it all wrong. The arm should be set naturally along your waist line, holding it up can cause blood flow problems."

"And you're a doctor, are you?" Klaus mumbled.

"I was a medic," he confirmed. "Volunteer for the war."

Klaus looked him over once more, noting the strict military stance and the badge of service he tried concealing in his breast pocket. "You're also a soldier."

"I'm sorry?"

Klaus motioned to his pocket. "That's a badge of service, is it not?"

"Can't a man be both?" He cleared his throat. "Are you sure you're alright? You don't look so well."

Klaus' vision blurred. He swayed, barely able to balance himself. Sweat coated his entire body, the temperature beneath his skin skyrocketing. He tipped forward onto the tracks. He didn't feel any pain when he landed, only the heavy thump of hitting the ground. The man scrambled across and leapt down onto the tracks after him.

"Sir? Sir!" He turned Klaus over onto his back and checked for gashes, broken bones and a heartbeat. As he pulled Klaus' collar aside to check his pulse, he noticed the discoloration of his skin. He peeled the shirt back further, following the black veins to the puncture point in his shoulder. His arm wasn't set in a sling, but had crystalized against his body.

"What on earth?" He glanced around before hoisting Klaus up. "Don't worry, I can help."

KLAUS WOKE TO a fever burning across his forehead, dampening him in old sweat. A light moved across his eyes, crossing from left to right, back to left again.

"Sir? Can you hear me?" The man's voice echoed above. Klaus's sore eyes fluttered.

"Ja."

"What's your name? Sir, can you tell me your name?" Klaus clenched his eyes closed in pain, unable to respond. The man continued. "My name is Sam. Can you please tell me your name?"

Klaus' thoughts swirled around his head. *Name. Name.* Everything moved in a hazy facade. He felt numb, light, ghostly. His body tingled, slowing waking from sleep. "Klaus," he answered, his voice dry and raspy. He felt so far away from his own body, as though he floated above himself.

"Thank you, Klaus, now can you tell me what's happened to you?"

"I've been stabbed."

"With what?"

"Poison."

There was a moment of pause. "Like…magic?"

The mention of magic tickled his ears. Instinct was to deny anything to do with magic, to distance himself from the word supernatural, but the agony in Klaus' body blocked out the voice of sensibility. He was almost pleading. "Ja. Magic."

Klaus' eyes fluttered closed and Sam ducked around him, dampening a cloth and lying it across his forehead. The chilled temperature helped ease the pressure off Klaus' headache, and he sighed with relief. The young doctor's jacket remained bundled into a ball, holding Klaus' neck up as his long body took up the entire of the bench, leaving Sam no choice but to crouch over him.

"Can you tell me anything else? What type of magic? What did this to you?" Klaus didn't respond as sleep took him. Sam stepped back and wiped his hands down his mouth, tasting his stress. He paced the aisle of the empty church, trying to think. His hands felt clammy, and he nervously listened over his shoulder for sirens. His thoughts were blurred from the spirits he drank earlier, trying to calm himself down. He had said he would never return there, but still his mind went immediately back to the barracks, to the clinic. But he couldn't go back, not that they would welcomed him anyway. *Abigail.* Sam remembered. *Yes, of course, Abigail.*

"Okay, okay, please, just stay here, I will be back shortly with help."

Sam ran out into the dead of the night. He avoided the main streets, dodging the street lights and weaving between the trees when cars passed by. Beside the police station, Sam reached the public phone and dialled Abigail's number. A sleepy voice answered it after five rings.

"You really must want to be turned into a toad for calling me at this godforsaken hour! What do you want?"

Sam softly smiled, feeling joy at hearing his friend's quick temper. "And here I thought witches knew everything."

A moment of silence passed before the female voice spoke again. "This can't be you, can it?"

"I'm afraid so."

"Why are you still here? Oh no, are you in trouble?"

"Not me, but I do need your help. Can you come by the Blacklock community church? Bring your witchy spells and potions."

"Sam? What—"

"Please, Abigail. I have a bad feeling about this."

"Okay, I'll be there in twenty minutes. Just, be safe."

"Thank you, thank you so much."

Sam returned and paced the church aisles again, wringing his hands, watching the sky through the colored stained glass, praying for sunrise to stay away. Klaus didn't move beyond the occasional breath. Twenty minutes passed and Sam couldn't take his eyes off the mysterious man. Between the sweat that glistened his hairline down to the unusual cracked skin coating his arm, he had found himself immensely fascinated.

There was a knock on the door, followed by a voice. "Sam?"

"Yeah, I'm in here." Sam met up with Abigail at the front entrance. She carried with her a large backpack of supplies, just as instructed. Abigail's taller figure loomed her over Sam's shoulder. She wasn't exactly above average, it was more Sam was short, his height stunted thanks to a childhood illness. She stepped around him into the church, while rubbing one hand up her arm for warmth. The full length of her vibrant red hair was messily braided down her back. The smoky smell of incense followed her in. Even if she hadn't burnt any for days, the aroma seemed to be part of her DNA.

"What is so important?" She glanced around before spotting Klaus. She approached cautiously and knelt beside him. "Who is this man?"

Sam knelt next to her. "Honestly, I just met him, didn't speak more than two words to me before he collapsed at the train station. Check this," he peeled Klaus' collar back, revealing the infection, "have you seen anything like this before in your voodoo spells?"

"Watch that tongue of yours," Abigail lectured. "it is not voodoo, my craft is from the ancestral Celts, but no, I have never seen anything like this before."

"What about the others from your cult? I mean clan. I mean... group?"

Abigail gave him a disapproving look before removing Klaus' trench coat, vest, tie, and all the undershirts so he was stretched out on the bench in just his pants and boots. She gently touched his shoulder where the grayish taint covered his entire arm and half of his torso. "There is strong power here, dark and forbidden magic. I'm...I'm not even sure if he could be human."

"How could he not be human?"

Abigail tilted her head left and right, looking at Klaus at different angles. Her attention landed on the Collector's blade hitched to his belt. The object sparked with familiarity and warning. Sam also noticed the weapon and reached out to touch it.

"Incredible, I never seen this type of blade before."

The moment he reached for it, Abigail caught his wrist and held him back. "Don't touch that."

"What? Why?"

Thoughts churned and spun. Memories from Ma's teachings rushed to the front of her mind, and one word felt to stick to the image. A dark thought, covered in unlawful magic she was wary to touch. She retracted her hands. "He needs some serious help. We need to take him out to the coven. Ma will know." Sam looked away uneasily and Abigail scolded his hesitation. "You once chose to love rather than to kill. Are you still that great man?"

"I think you mean dead man."

"An honorable man."

"Honorable? Ha! Depends who you ask." Sam smiled uneasily.

"Sam Blackmore...do you believe in fate?" She reached out and touched his check tenderly. Sam took a steady breath, and gently nodded. "Then I believe you are fated to save this man."

CHAPTER
THIRTY-SIX

ANY NEWS FROM Catherine?" Elizabeth asked as she set the newspaper down. Talk of the mystery woman had left the headlines weeks ago at what Elizabeth suspected was the stern request of Arthur Beaumontt.

"Nothing, I'm afraid." Harry approached with a fresh cup of tea to replace her cold untouched one. He then handed over a note. "But this letter came addressed to a E. Blackmore. Perhaps it's for you?"

Elizabeth took the ash covered letter eagerly. The writing was feminine, giving Elizabeth even more hope. With Harry reading over her shoulder, Elizabeth tore into the note.

Elizabeth.

Dare I believe it really is you? The papers speak the truth? I have birthed the son of a Beaumontt. I hope you are not mad with me, it was not my choice. I was just a servant in the Beaumontt kitchen, and there's little I could do against his advances. If it really is you, please meet me by the Burning Man tonight at sundown. Come alone, for I fear for my life. I hope it's not too forward for me to ask, but please bring money to help feed me and my starving son. We are homeless and penniless. I fear we won't last the winter without help. I need you, little sister. Please help me.

Love,
Penelope Blackmore.

Elizabeth slumped back into her chair, her fingers clenched tight on the note. "It's true."

"Miss Wicker?"

She almost couldn't say the words. "The mystery woman in the papers. Her name is Penelope Blackmore, my sister."

Harry frowned, "What do you intend to do?"

"I will help her, of course." Elizabeth stood and started rampaging through William Wicker's belongings. "Arthur has left her with a son to feed all by herself. I have money I can give her. Things she can sell, whatever was left from the Wicker fire she can have."

"Miss Wicker." Harry looked after her concerned. "You must think of your future, too."

She slowed at the thought of her own impending fate. Her ticking heart was a constant reminder of her time slipping away. "My future is now, Harry." She turned to face him, faking a smile. "Does Doris have a wig I can borrow?"

DORIS' SEMI-BALDING HEAD allowed Elizabeth the chance to step out into public. She fitted the short, brown bob over her head, ensuring every strand of white hair was carefully tucked out of sight. Her large lumpy coat and dirty pants disguised her, allowing her to slip underneath the radar of police officers and officials alike. Not even Arthur would glance her way.

There was, however, one man who didn't let her go from his sight. Nikolas perked up from his seat the moment Elizabeth stepped out of the house. Her disguise was good, hunching her over like an old lady, but the gremlins' couldn't be fooled. He followed her calmly, biting into an apple as he waited across the street from the bank she visited.

"Where are you Klaus?" he grumbled and glanced into the crowds. The silence from his brother was disturbing, making Nikolas think his threats on Elizabeth were too light. Klaus wasn't taking this seriously. *Maybe she really wasn't his type, he did like brunettes after all.* He thought back to the Beaumontt mansion. To Klaus' face and the terror that twisted him. He started to doubt his assumptions when Elizabeth stepped out of the bank with cash in hand. *Enough of this waiting.* Nikolas cut across her the moment she was alone.

"That's a good look for you," he joked, startling Elizabeth into spinning around. "Going shopping?"

"Nikolas?"

"Surprised?"

"Not a nice surprise. I haven't seen you for weeks, I had hoped you had left."

"And miss the chance to see you play Old Mrs. Scrooge?"

"Why are you still here? What happened before?" Her voice dropped with her seriousness, indicating back to the moment they teleported back into the Pitts.

Nikolas answered half-honestly, "You wished."

"And you listened?"

He did, even though he didn't want to. He was nervous that the code would overpower him again, that there was something in Elizabeth's choice of words that could undermine his control. Perhaps it was his rage, making him lose his grip over the code. Nikolas sighed and glanced away. "Klaus wasn't there. Didn't see a purpose in staying."

"Well, he's not here either." She pointed out with more disappointment in her tone than she intended to convey. *She cares for him. Too bad it isn't mutual.*

Nikolas shrugged. "Not yet. But he will come, the knight will always come to save the damsel in distress."

"I'm no damsel." Elizabeth turned to leave. Nikolas blocked her path. She crossed her arms. "Is there nothing I can say to make you leave? Or do I have to do something more extreme? Like setting you on fire?"

Nikolas snorted. "How ambitious of you. You may actually find my company interesting."

"I highly doubt that."

"Do you know why Lady Claudia was so keen to marry you into the Beaumontt family? Why she had me scavenge through Doctor Wicker's estate?"

"Why she targeted my mother?" She asked instead. Nikolas perked his eyebrow and Elizabeth grumbled under her breath. "Okay...then tell me? Why?"

"A riddle."

"What riddle?"

Nikolas craned his head back, "An ancient script that was written about your family, the Wicker bloodline. Sun and Moon. Ying and Yang. Life and Death. Through Wicker name can stars be dulled. Through Wicker name can time be stopped, love uncapped and death reversed. Through Wicker name the game's blade turned back. Broken circles, union through rings, draw on Wicker name."

"What does that even mean?"

"As I said, it's a riddle. Unions through rings, is pretty obvious. Marriage. Stars be dulled, time be stopped, love uncapped and death reversed sounds like magic not even Collectors can achieve without great sacrifice. And a weapon, the game's blade, seems to be the key to it all."

"So, you broke into my house looking for a weapon?"

"And I found something." Nikolas indicated to the golden pistol he carried next to his Collector's blade.

A lump wedged in her throat. "That's nothing but an old family heirloom. It's useless."

"Sure. That explains why you wanted it back so badly."

"It has sentimental value."

Nikolas looked down at it fondly. "It sure does. The Wicker myth is as old as witches and Collectors," he said. "All we know for sure is that you need a Wicker to unlock it. Ever notice no Wickers ever got married? None that carry your special gene, that is." He reached out to touch her white hair.

She swatted his hand away. "I won't be married for long. Once Klaus and I defeat you—"

"Klaus and you?" Nikolas repeated, holding back a laugh. "I think you're a bit deluded. What are you expecting at the end of all this? A happily ever after? A sweet taboo romance turned wild with desire? Klaus has no interest in romantic things. He'll sooner rip your heart out than give you his." Nikolas touched his lips, feigning shock. "Oops! He's already done that, hasn't he?"

"I had a heart attack. He saved my life."

"He killed your father."

Elizabeth bit her lip. "And you killed my mother."

"He also killed your friend."

"This isn't a competition."

"If it was, he'd be winning." Elizabeth chewed on her lower lip, stopping herself from revealing how upset the conversation made her. Nikolas cleared his throat. "Why him then? I don't understand, he has caused you so much pain? Why him?" Nikolas had seen the beginnings of romance more often than he had felt it. The senseless loyalty, the ability to overlook the other's flaws, the helpless hope and faith.

Elizabeth inhaled a shaky breath. "I don't know what you mean."

"Yes, you do. That's the thing with Klaus. It is not love that will drive him back to you, it's an obligation."

Elizabeth went to argue, but couldn't. The thought hit her hard.

It was true. Klaus only cared about stopping Nikolas. He had already proven this when he was willing to marry her off to Arthur Beaumontt if it meant a chance to ambush him. *Had I really made this up in my head?* Her girlish crush had blinded her. Every bone in her body felt heavy with doubt.

She swallowed back her remorse. If Klaus had feelings for her or not wasn't relevant. "It is not love that I seek from him."

"Then what?"

"A promise." Sirens turned her head around. Over her shoulder, she noticed the setting sun. "You've wasted enough of my time. I have somewhere to be."

"Yes of course." Nikolas stepped back. "I'll see you soon, I'm sure."

THE BURNING MAN was the main power plant sitting further out on the south side of town. Its primary use was to pump burning coal into large industrial buildings and aircrafts. It had achieved its nickname due to its human profile, and how at night, the internal fire made the six-story man appeared to be boiling from the inside. Despite being operational around the clock, during the night shifts the staff dropped down to a skeleton crew with little security. The Burning Man was not an unknown place for Elizabeth. In fact, when she used to struggle to sleep, she would sneak off to the Burning Man and curl up under the floorboards. Beneath the structure, the dirt was soft and warm. If it weren't for the bugs, she may have stayed there every night. And, of course, the soot she dragged home with her. It was probably the combination of everything: the muffled footsteps, routine churning of gears, the warmth and solitude that helped her remain at ease. It was like listening to a giant robot's internal system. The heartbeat of a sleeping god.

The heat radiating from the chrome building breathed out of the windows in bouts of steam, keeping the entire area a constant soggy, lukewarm temperature. She crept along the outer walls when a startling noise came from inside. The sound of a baby's cry.

Elizabeth slipped through the side door and down the steps, leading her down a narrow staircase which opened to a large furnace. Inside, Elizabeth's eyes fell upon Penelope. Her face carried the same youthful pout in her cheeks, inherited through Ana, but her large brown eyes aged with crowfeet pinched at each corner. When she squinted, the lines became more prominent. Her bulb nose had grown larger to match her growing face and her brown hair was wedded with soot and sweat.

For a moment, Elizabeth's world of aristocrats and Time Collectors dwindled down into the size of the furnace. Both girls stared at each other in a moment of silence before Elizabeth rushed forward and pulled her sister into a hug. Her arms trembled, her mind pulled between delight and devastation. "I have dreamt of this day for so long."

"It's nice to see you too, little sister." Penelope tensed beneath Elizabeth's arms. "You've become quite the celebrity." She wiggled out of Elizabeth's embrace and held her hand up to admire the pearl of her white skin. Blemishes marked her body from years of study at the academy. Penelope smiled at the scars. "Not as pretty as they say."

Elizabeth eased her hand back. "Your son? Can I see him?"

Penelope motioned sideways to the makeshift cradle on the counter top. Elizabeth edged closer and peered into the basket. The child slept peacefully, his cheeks roasted pink from the breath of hot air from the furnace. She gently touched her lips, feeling the pride of becoming an aunt, at seeing part of herself in his blotchy, chubby face. "He is so beautiful. What is his name?"

"Aaron." Penelope smiled. "A strong name, for a strong leader. Did you bring the money?"

Elizabeth nodded and dabbed her eyes clear of tears. "Yes, but they only allowed me to withdraw so much in one go."

"How much?"

Elizabeth revealed the cash. Penelope's eyes widened at the sight of it, but she didn't extend her hand to take it. "I haven't seen that much money in my whole life. You poor, pampered little princess."

Elizabeth flinched, "You are mad at me? I came here to help you."

"Help me? No, you're here because you found out I had a Beaumontt son. You're here to threaten me, aren't you? Are you going to tell me to back away from your husband?" Elizabeth took a step backwards. A deep seeded hatred curled Penelope's lips. "How you mock me. Dressed in rags, pretending to be one of us. You're a beloved Wicker, not a low-life Blackmore."

"I am a Blackmore!" Elizabeth defended. "Well, I'm both."

"No. You're a precious, spoilt, shitty little nobleman's daughter," she snapped. "Our whorish mother only took you to high-society. Her favorite daughter. She left Sam and I in the hands of a drunken man with large debts."

"High-society? Penelope, my life is not as glamourous as you think! Mother loved you, but father was the one who kicked us out," Elizabeth countered. "Life was hard on us and she did not want you to suffer like we were. Father had money to feed you at least, but we starved out there on our own. We went cold on most nights and I had to steal all my clothes off the clotheslines from the neighboring kids just to have something to wear. I spent most of my life training at the Academy of underprivileged ladies where I was going to be sold into servitude."

"That!" Penelope lashed out and slapped the cash from Elizabeth's hand. The seal broke, bursting the notes out across the room. "Is that not Wicker money?"

Elizabeth's heart hammered. Penelope's rage stemmed from her sense of abandonment. She was a terrified young mother worried about her baby. Elizabeth gulped, and carefully held her hand out. "I want to help you."

"Help me?" Penelope scoffed. She turned and picked up her screaming child, who was startled awake by their yelling. "You really think I'm stupid? I know what you're trying to do. You're trying to chase me out of town by bribing me. I want more than money. I want to be the governor's wife. I want power. I want a mansion and servants. You're only helping me so I'll leave and you can have all the Beaumontt riches for yourself. That isn't fair, you already got the Wicker fortune. Why do you deserve to have the Beaumontt fortune too?"

"I...I don't—" Elizabeth stuttered, but stalled at the sound of footsteps approaching behind her. A man stepped into the light of the furnace. He didn't speak, but smiled eagerly down at Elizabeth as though she bled diamonds. He didn't need to say anything. His intentions were as clear as the knife he carried. Elizabeth trembled. She glanced back at Penelope, pleading. "Don't do this."

"Arthur will never recognize me as his wife with you around. I've already given him a son, he'll come begging for me once he sees his trophy-wife is tarnished."

"Wait, Penelope, please let us talk." Elizabeth took another frightful step back. The room felt smaller. "I don't want to be his wife. I didn't ask for this."

"Yet you take it still? You're given everything, aren't you?" Penelope screamed. "You don't know what it's like to fend for yourself. Our mother chose you over both Sam and I. Father sold me so he could drink. I sold myself just to eat. And when I had to lock my door every night to keep out the drunks, you were running around with that doctor, dressing up like you're better than us." Her voice cracked as she shouted. She saw in Penelope just rage and abandonment. It thickened the redness in her cheeks. She licked her lips and turned away. "I promised you money. Take the cash, but make sure she's dead before you leave."

She turned and abruptly left. Elizabeth leaned forward to speak but the shock clamped her voice box closed. He moved in, fast and feral, like a dog diving on a tender piece of meat. She didn't have time to react, her training with Klaus blocked behind her shock and she buckled instantly when a knife plunged deep into her side. Pain ripped underneath her skin. Choking her, taking out one knee as she hit the ground. She couldn't scream, her breath caught as the knife struck her a further three times into her back, torso and chest. The wounds opened in slashes. Warm red blood wept out. Her entire body tensed and crumpled. She hit the ground. He started scooping up all the money, ultimately forgetting about Elizabeth bleeding out on the ground.

Her mind darkened, unable to see the world around her. Her death was definite. Her wounds were far too deep for Elizabeth to drag herself to the streets. Her cheek faced the door, her body motionless, crippled by pain. Above her head, his silhouette remained behind to watch her die. How she cursed him. How she wanted to scream, but no sounds came out. The figure dropped to their knees and cupped her cheeks, bringing her face to their lap. Warm hands. Familiar hands.

In a slurred voice, he pleaded. "Elizabeth, let me help you."

Her eyes widened, forming the connections. Details sharpened into the warmth of his eyes, his soft mouth, and the curve of his dimpled smile. *Klaus? But…how?* The impossibility of it was astounding, but there he was, holding her up. From the pit of her stomach, she managed to whisper in her last weakened breath, "Save me."

CHAPTER
THIRTY-SEVEN

ENJAMIN KYNETON. BRAVE *fighter, caring and loving fiancé, treasured son and brother.*

Catherine squeezed her eyes shut. Her tears had gone dry, but her cheeks still glistened with their leftover streaks. The funeral was hard, it chiselled down their brave faces into twisted expressions of loss and grief. Benjamin was kind, his love for Leah was pure, and his kindness had no equal, yet it was him who was killed. Leah's eyes darkened as they lowered Benjamin's coffin into the ground. Part of her was buried with him. A large part of her died the moment he did.

Catherine didn't know the true risks of the Collector's company. She allowed him in, covered up his identity and because of her, Benjamin was dead and Hudson has gone missing. Their group, as with their world, splintered and fell apart. Weeks passed in silence. Catherine found her way back home, but found no comfort with her family. Her heart pulled her back out into the world, to help rebuild the broken pieces she helped shatter.

"No matter what happens Catherine, you're one of us." Dennis had confided in her. It was late the night when he came to collect her. Storms passed overhead, shaking the house. "Let's do what Guardians do best."

He motioned over his shoulder to their hunting suits. Catherine approached and lifted the scattered suit up. She proceeded to attach the different parts to her body. Over her right shoulder, she clipped on a massive steel shoulder cap, reinforced with weights down her bicep where attached to the elbow bend was an automatic machine gun with a hand grip. Woven across her back was a slash of throwing knives attached to the smooth chrome chest guard. Perhaps the most impressive was the jet engine back pack curved along her back.

Leah waited for them outside of a large Bact nest. Sleepless nights darkened the circles beneath her eyes, shallowing in her cheeks. She welcomed Catherine with a nod. The forgiveness wasn't there, not entirely, but it'd be a long time before Leah could feel anything beyond betrayal. Bactes scurried out as Dennis, Leah and Catherine stormed inside, their weapons blasting. All of the Bactes were lower classes, nothing above a three in the chain. Dennis gunned them down, torching their nests and shoving them out into the streets. Catherine picked them off as they tried to run, landing her knives into the bend of their knees and shoulders. Leah's suit was small to match her fluid movement, the spiked chains woven around her arm garnet clinked and crunched as she lashed them out like extendable whips.

Even under torture, none of the Bactes spoke. "Where are the Elders?" Dennis demanded, working into the fifth hour of holding a chicken box Bact to his torture chair. She gargled and spat at his feet. He turned up the pressure, locking the creature's shrivelled arm behind her back. She yelped, letting out a loud slurping cry. "Noisy water. Noisy water."

Dennis let go and took the information to the others. "Noisy water. What do you think that means?"

"Water parks? Water mills?" Catherine started listing off.

"No…" Leah said. "Something abandoned. More like the old industrial water pumps."

"Of course," Dennis agreed. "Vacant. Easy to infest. Human

contact close by, but not close enough to stumble upon them. It's the perfect nest."

Leah corrected, "It's the perfect killing ground."

TURNING UP TO the old industrial estates, the three of them stepped out of the car and made their way down the heat cracked roads. The buildings were blackened by overrunning decay and crumbled into stripped skeletons. They kicked in the warehouse doors and marched into the heart of the empty warehouse. Signs of Bactes infestations was strong in the leftover rot dripping off the walls.

It didn't take long until their intrusion caught the attention of the Elder Bact. There were three of them present, one they recognized back at the paper mill as the Elder Bact with Mural. Si staggered forward as the other two Elder Bactes circled the group. Catherine unhitched her knives, readying them. Leah's grip tightened on her weapon. Blisters lined her palms.

"Show yourself!" Dennis roared into the darkness. He shot a blast of flames forward, lighting up the dark warehouse. Ten pair of eyes scurried back from the waft of heat, terrified. Si did not falter in her approach.

"Tongue of death. Devil none. Devil!" she hissed at Dennis. "Blood fed weeds. Noise carries, sisters in soil. Break you, break you!"

Leah stepped up beside Dennis. "Shut it. We need to kill the Collectors, and you are going to help us."

Si chuckled in quick, short chirps. "Snow bites. Snow cuts. Weave your path back, only destruction at the touch of blade tips."

"Enough of your riddles, creature. You are going to summon the gargoyle for us." Dennis spoke again. "If you don't, we will continue to burn all your nests, killing every cockroach we trap inside."

Si screeched. Panicked noises drummed up behind her.

"We've already hunted down fifteen nests in the past few weeks."

Leah announced. "We will kill them all. Us, and every remaining Guardian."

"Harm be done to those monsters reek." Si gurgled in her sudden laughter. "Mortalem?"

Catherine shifted uncomfortably whereas Leah stepped forward, determined. "Summon it. Summon it, and we promise not to harm anymore Bactes. We hunt Collectors now."

Si thought on it, listening to the chirps and hisses from the Bactes prowling behind her, before slicing a long gash through the center of her palm. She waved Leah closer. Leah cautiously approached, but as she did, Si shoved her weeping wound onto Leah's mouth. Leah leapt back and swung her weapon around. She spat the putrid blood out as it sizzled against her tongue and lips.

"Wear your words," Si jabbed, before cracking her neck back and releasing an unnatural croak from the base of her throat. The air thickened. A foreign, shifting smoke rose beneath the concrete with a faint whistle. It slithered into Leah's mouth, nose, and covered eyes. Leah dropped her weapon. Dennis rushed to her as she fell to her knees.

"What have you done?"

"Chaos," Si pointed out. "Stone to flesh." The other two elder Bactes leapt forward onto Catherine's turned back, pinning her down. She hit the floor with a heavy thump, hearing her metal suit crack under their weight. In the next moment, Si sliced her own throat and slowly sank into death.

JULIET STEPPED BACK from peeking into the Guardian's parked car, her gaze turning toward the empty warehouse. The stench of Bact deaths followed the group in thick fumes, making it easier for her to track them. They were determined. Ruthless, but she had to remain patient. Wait for them to slow down, to sleep, and separate. To exhaust themselves, or hopefully, clash with a Bact nest they couldn't take down.

Juliet waited outside the warehouse, but the smell of burning caught her attention. It wasn't burning as in flames. It was the melting of spirit. The breaking of cosmic chains. Alarm bells went off inside her head and Juliet pushed off from the car. *It can't be.* She sprinted into the warehouse to find herself standing in the middle of a barbaric ritual. Bactes circled the Guardians. One girl was pinned beneath two Elders. The single male was stunned. An Elder Bact's body wept with blood pooling out of her throat, self-inflicted. The remaining female's spirit had been vacuumed out, and replaced with the growing stench of destruction.

"No!" Juliet ran in and speared Leah in the heart. The remaining Bactes bolted into the shadows, scrambling off Catherine and fleeing the warehouse into the streets outside. Dennis turned his weapon on Juliet.

"You can't stop us, Collector!" But her attention didn't shift off Leah.

Juliet's face paled. White sparks flared out of her Collector's blade, electricity splintering through the glass handle, crackling from the intense pressure. She was too late. It had been summoned. She only managed to whisper, "You've trapped the devil here," before an enormous bang exploded across the room. A surge of raw heat penetrated Juliet's body, firing up her spine and bursting through the top of her skull. Almost immediately, Juliet was thrown backwards and slammed into the back wall. She dropped as her entire body hardened into crystalized rock.

Leah tipped over onto her back as though she was too sleepy to remain upright.

"Leah? Leah?" Catherine rushed to her and dropped to her knees. Leah remained unresponsive with Juliet's Collector dagger protruding out of her chest cavity. Catherine touched her neck and felt a faint pulse. She didn't dare touch the handle. "She's alive, just unconscious. Oh my God, oh my God what have we done?"

Dennis paced behind her, panicked and breathless. "I don't know."

"We have to help her."

"How? How do we help her? Who could possibly know about all this stuff?"

"Don't your parents know? Surely, Lady and Lord Moore—"

"My parents? They're halfway in the grave themselves, they can barely remember to put on pants let alone deal with…whatever this is." Dennis waved toward Leah.

"Dennis, we need serious help. We need to undo the spell. Mortalem is trapped inside of her, I…I don't even know if Leah can survive something that like. We need a witch. A really, really powerful witch!"

"Have you ever heard of any witch being able to cast Mortalem out? Only a God could help us."

Catherine sat back onto her heels. "Or something close to a God." Dennis turned back to her, slowly understanding. Catherine said. "What we need is a wish."

CHAPTER
THIRTY-EIGHT

SAM WATCHED THE mob form in front of two men in the middle of the busy market street. He stood on the sideline, hidden beneath his hat, turned up collar, and a basket of fruit tucked under his arm. The mob booed the two locked up men and threw rotten tomatoes at them, chanting derogatory comments at their bowed heads. The ground was soon covered in the smashed food, bleeding red over the roads.

"Sam?" Abigail hailed him over, tearing his concentration away. "More political riots? What on earth is happening over in Divin Cadeau?"

"I don't think this is a political fight. Not this time."

Together they returned to the massive clock tower where they had been living for the past few weeks. The twenty-story climb killed his calves, making excursions into town a gruelling exercise. The older witch, Ma lived secluded behind the face of the giant clock, turning the cogs, bells, and beams into clotheslines and racks for her many trinkets. Wind chimes tickled at every turn of the hour, shifting at the sudden drop of the hour hand. Rugs covered most of the wooden floorboards, turning the dusty attic into a warm, colorful home. Abigail's coven of witches Abigail were made up majority of the homeless, refusing to partake in currency, society, or any mundane human lifestyle. It made sense that most of the coven elected to live inside caves beyond the reach of man. Ma, on the other hand, felt that living in the face of the largest clock tower gave her a better view, therefore understanding and predication, over the entire world.

Sam kicked his shoes off at the entrance, now only noticing the red stain over his heels. *Damn. These were my favorite pair too.*

"Doesn't that boy ever stop talking?" Ma impatiently shushed Sam without looking up from her books. The gray in her long hair was covered in oil, changing the colors into blues and greens. The multiple layers she wore fattened out her tiny frame, convincing Sam she was larger and stronger than she appeared.

"I haven't said a word." Sam glanced at Abigail, confused. "Plus, I've been out getting supplies for the past two hours, you couldn't possible have heard me speak."

"I could hear you thinking the whole way there and back," Ma snapped. She picked up a cooper cup and started grinding the red powder into paste. "It's very annoying."

"Now I know where you get your charm," Sam grumbled at Abigail.

"Better her yelling at you than yelling at me." Abigail knelt beside Klaus' sleeping body stretched out across layers of blankets, the rock casting now spread across the majority of his torso, climbing up his neck and across his heart.

"Out of the way, Billy." Ma shoved past Sam again.

"It's Sam," he quietly corrected. "You should know that by now. We've met at least a hundred times before."

Ma slowed. "Didn't I shoot you?"

"No, Ma. Not him." Abigail said.

"You shot someone?" Sam said, terrified and amused.

Ma turned and pulled on Abigail's elbow for her to follow her out onto the balcony. "The nightingales are ready tonight. With the full moon, we can remove whatever has ailed this man."

"Yes, Ma."

"You must ensure the soil has been sweetened."

"I said yes, Ma, I'm not a child."

Sam settled down next to Klaus and continued to dab the sweat off his forehead. Sunlight caressed Klaus' cheekbone and set shadows across his turned head. If it wasn't for his thick brows furrowed inwards, he would've looked rather peaceful. He eyed his mouth and traced the taunt muscle down Klaus' neck and onto his open shirt. He was a man built for battle. The vacant scent of gunpowder filled Sam's nose, bringing him back to the grunt of war, his skin glistened with sweat and where the earth rattled beneath his feet, pumping his heart with adrenaline. He imagined Klaus would do quite well at war, huddled with him in the trenches. Sam's attention shifted behind him as another argument broke out between Abigail and Ma, who were so identical in personality they could've been fighting with a mirror.

"Women," he said, careful to keep his voice down. "I wonder if you ever had trouble with women." Sam checked his left hand, noting the lack of a ring. "Not married. A bachelor, just like me. Can't be much older than I am. Are you also fleeing the chains of marriage, I wonder? Is that what cursed you? A scorned woman? There's still unrest in the outside world, mostly political problems revolving around the Beaumontt's. I don't tend to follow the qualms of the powerhouses. My voice alone can't rise against religion and moral decency, so I stay where I can make a difference. War can be brutal, but it's a place I can be …well, me. I almost envy you. No one there to pressure you. No hearts to be broken. The only thing you have to worry about is surviving."

"Don't tell me you're starting up again with your running monologues!" Abigail teased from behind him. "We won't need this potion with you chatting into his ear constantly. Surely, he'll wake up just to slap you quiet."

Sam laughed. "Well, I may as well enjoy it before he starts yelling at me, too." Behind him, he heard Ma's disgruntled mumblings. Sam bit back his smile. He glanced at Klaus, eager to see this mysterious man awaken.

A WARM PRESENCE ran up and down through the darkness of his mind. It was bodiless, weightless, just a break of light through the shadows. *No one there to pressure you. No hearts to be broken.* The voice left quakes behind it and Klaus clung to it like a life raft against the storm. His only path back was through the echoing voice, this faceless stranger who carried far more importance than he perhaps understood.

The only thing you have to worry about is surviving. Klaus took a long breath, trying to tighten his invisible grip on the invisible presence. In the long moments of its absence, the silence felt fatal. The voice spoke to him for weeks, but it felt like a lifetime of memorising the tickle of its tone. His name, Sam, became a root to return to. Elizabeth's face appeared in flashes, but the more time passed, the less Klaus was able to see the details of her. Blue eyes, faded. White hair, blurred. Her voice deepened into the man's voice above him. As she disappeared, Sam's presence grew stronger. *Well, I may as well enjoy it before he starts yelling at me too.*

Silence returned. Klaus' grip fumbled, trying to hang onto an echo rolling further out of reach. Hours passed, but it felt like years trapped within his own crumbling conscience. Silence suffocated the air, until he heard the voice again. Klaus leapt for it, grabbing the edges desperately.

For the last time it's not Billy, it's Sam. Klaus mentally closed his eyes, trying to picture a life where he had to cling to this man's voice forever. It was madness and left him vulnerable, weak, yet despite his pain, his instinct couldn't allow Klaus a moment of surrender. *Over here? Yes, okay, no need to shout I'll move it.* A moment of not looking for the voice was an eternity in death. *Careful, you're going to set the whole place on fire.*

Do you need me for anything?

Don't leave. Klaus tried to beg. Please don't leave.

I won't.

Klaus' mind buzzed, momentarily hopeful he had somehow communicated with Sam, thinking he had broken through to the other side. Behind the darkness, flashes of pain appeared. He felt tiny prickles along his arms. He was thinking, understanding, feeling again. He sensed a dangerous manifestation move over him. The smell of burnt hair and aromatic smoke lingered from a lifetime of practising witchcraft. A witch?

"Time Collector," a withered old voice accused. It smacked Klaus out of his daydreaming. It was real. Firm, loud, not an echo of a distant dream. It also wasn't Sam's voice. Someone else's. Klaus strained to open his eyes. Danger pricked at the back of his neck. "Nothing but evil follows your poisoned promises."

"Wait, stop!" Sam's voice rang clear. Klaus's attention jumped to where it oriented from. His eyes fluttered madly, trying desperately to open. "What are you doing?"

Klaus' energy returned in pulses of heat. His eyes slowly opened and pain rippled into the back of his head. Darkness, but with flickers of orange. Warm light. A moon's caress. Among the blurs only Sam's face was clear. He had caught the swing of the witch's attack, stopping her from piercing Klaus's heart.

The old woman lashed out, grabbing Sam by the chin and pressing her thumb against the inside of his mouth. He coughed and choked on the sudden intrusion, easily shoving her hand off, but not before feeling the coarse patch of her thumb run along his lower lip, collecting a smear of his salvia. She then pressed her thumb onto Klaus' wound.

"Eww! Oh, dear god!" Sam spat and rubbed his mouth.

"Ma? What are you doing?" A second witch, a younger one, ran back into the room and restrained the other woman's hand.

"Did you just stick your dirty thumb in my mouth?" Sam shouted.

Klaus' eyes fully opened and he sprung upwards, scaring everyone around him. Immediately, he grabbed for his arm and flexed his fingers. *The stone cast is gone. Did she get the poison out of me?*

"He almost gave me a heart attack!" Abigail gasped.

Klaus searched the room. Smoke hazed around him, coming from the dozens of candles carefully placed across the floor. With the return of his consciousness, his fear returned. How close had he came to disappearing? How close had he almost been trapped in hell, living behind a wall separating the dead from the living? Klaus touched his quivering lips. *Elizabeth. I have to get back to Elizabeth.* Sam's voice bounced around his head, remembering the stories of the Beaumontt's turmoil.

"Hello? Sir?" Klaus turned at Sam's touch. His swelling panic calmed and Klaus took a deep breath, letting his head hang in between his knees. "You're okay, now, you're okay."

"Where am I?"

"We're at the Bell Front Towers. You collapsed a few weeks ago and we carried you here. Abigail, can you get him some water please?" Sam asked. The younger witch fetched Klaus some water and carefully passed it over.

"How are you feeling?" she asked.

Klaus took the drink and downed it in one gulp. "Grateful." He glanced down, noticing his shirt and jackets had been removed, leaving him bare-chested. "Err...my clothes?"

"Right, sorry." Sam fumbled as he passed over Klaus' shirt. Klaus quickly dressed.

"Thank you, Sam."

"You remember my name?" Klaus caught the lift in Sam's voice, recognizing the surprise. During his time trapped behind stone walls, he'd developed a deep understanding of Sam. He could figure him out with one sentence. Flattered.

"Of course," Klaus smiled. "You wouldn't stop pestering me while I slept."

Sam warmly laughed. "Do you know what happened to you? How you got that wound?"

"I'm just not very popular."

"Well, you're safe now. We didn't think you were going to make it. You must have a guardian angel looking over you."

Klaus smirked as Abigail chipped in. "Not a guardian angel exactly, though she has been called far worse, haven't you, Ma?" She turned smiling toward Ma, only to be met with panic. Ma shook her head, almost unable to speak. Her terror carried over to Klaus who promptly stood.

"What? What is it?" He looked back down at himself, expecting to find an extra limb where there shouldn't be one.

Ma shook her head and stepped backward. "I didn't…the creature pulled my hand." She then turned to Abigail, the conversation private. "This isn't our battle, child, let Billy accept his fate."

"Ma?"

"What?" Sam looked between them anxiously. "My what?"

"The transferring of fates," Ma pointed from Klaus to Sam. "The ultimate sacrifice."

Klaus scrambled back the moment Sam's body started crystalizing. Gray stone started to form on his shoulder, mimicking the wound Klaus carried, and then spread across his torso, down his waist and to his crouched legs. Abigail grabbed Sam's shoulders as though she could physically stop the stone skin from spreading. Sam didn't have time to react. He looked down at his hands then up at Abigail, his stunned expression immortalized behind the cracked, gray rock climbing up his neck and over the rest of his head. In moments, before Klaus could speak, Sam had completely frozen.

"Sam!? Sam!" Abigail screamed before turning to Ma. "What did you do? Ma! Undo it!"

But Ma's attention remained on Klaus. He glanced back at her, feeling the reasonability fall on him. "You cruel creature." She snarled. Klaus looked down at Sam, then back to Ma. "You really will do anything to survive." Her words stung him with the truth. Klaus hadn't intended it, but his desire to escape his fate behind the rock had transferred onto Sam, whose desire to save Klaus was at equal measure. A reversal wish.

Klaus denied any wrongdoing. "It was through your hands, witch, not mine." Yet, Klaus could feel the magic through his veins, the pulses of heat, the power only Collectors can conjure up through wish fulfillment.

"No witch can do this." Ma gestured to Sam's body.

His fingers twitched to reach for his blade, the final confirmation it was indeed Klaus' doing that Sam was trapped behind rock. He fought against the temptation, but knew it was a battle he was going to lose. Blood trickled down his nose, the rebellion already kicking in, demanding he collect the time owed. He pulled out his blade and carefully cut Sam's shoulder. "I didn't mean to."

"I don't care if you are a Time Collector, you can still help him!" Abigail pleaded. "That's what you do, isn't it? You make the impossible, possible. Take back your curse."

"I don't know how," he honestly admitted.

Ma stepped further away until she was pressed against the back wall of the tower. "Leave, Collector. There is no time left here for you to scavenge."

Abigail looked between them, confused. "No, he has to fix this."

Ma shook her head, feeling defeated. "A witch's soul cannot be harvested. Our time is not ours to give, therefore it is barred from the Collector's hands. I'm afraid we have been taken advantage of here. The Collector will not help us."

"I never intended—" Klaus rose into a shout but bit his tongue from saying more. There was no convincing them, and he couldn't be placed back behind the disease of the bone's poison. Not again, not after feeling the depth of its madness. "This was never my intention," he finished in a softer voice. Klaus turned to leave, hiking his coat collar up as he did. "Please...forgive me."

FOR HOURS, KLAUS was stuck in a trance. He didn't stop to drink or eat. He didn't stop to think. Every time Sam's face popped into his mind Klaus forcibly clouded the memory. He was thankful he didn't get to hear the panic in Sam's voice, but he heard it play in his head as though Sam had actually screamed for help. *Was he now trapped in the darkness like I was?* The whistle of the train docking shook Klaus out of his daze. He glanced out at the familiar buildings, looking toward the large gates surrounding Divin Cadeau.

Weeks, he had said. Weeks. Elizabeth's presence was lost to him. That's to say, if she still was even in Divin Cadeau at all. He checked her old house in the Pitts first, then over to the hidden cabin by the swamp. She didn't have any friends aside from Sara, leading Klaus to the only person left Elizabeth could turn to. Klaus approached Harry Smith's house in Rosefire to find the residence surrounded by police. Harry stood out the front amongst the officers in a heated argument.

"I've told you, I have no seen Lady Elizabeth Beaumontt at all. How many times do I have to repeat myself? It is only myself and my sister living here, as it has been for the past five years."

"Sir, there was a report just an hour earlier today of money being withdrawn from the Wicker account, aside from Lady Beaumontt, you are the only other person in possession of Doctor Wicker's check books. Do you care to explain?"

Harry shrugged. "I've never touched the Wicker money. Never."

"Looks like we have to leave it up to our investigation team to find out the truth."

Klaus stepped back behind the neighboring building. *She isn't here either.* The very fact the police were scavenging Harry's place in search for her also indicated Arthur Beaumontt didn't know where she was. But, he was keen on finding her and Klaus was more than happy to use that to his advantage.

CHAPTER
THIRTY-NINE

I T WAS THE simplest of things to set off the trigger. This time, it
was an ordinary apple. The fruit tumbled off a cart and stopped at
Nikolas' feet, its soft skin bruised. *Ripe green. The color of her eyes.*
Memories flashed past, stabbing him with longing. Nikolas caught
himself on the wall, bracing against the cold reminder of her absence.
It's amazing how I still have a heart to break. When he loved, it took
everything out of him: his awareness, his common sense, his control.
Being in the presence of Lady Claudia felt as if he was lost among
smoke—he couldn't think or breathe without her. Every gasp of air
was for her. Every step he took was for her. To remove his love was
to remove his reason to live.

The true pain of a man self-destructing. Nikolas' fists clenched. *Klaus
never felt this. Not yet, but he will.*

The gremlins bubbled. Excited chatter. Panic. Nikolas shooed them
away, but they returned in packs. Something was wrong. *Elizabeth.*
Nikolas pushed off the wall and stepped out of the shadows outside
of the Burning Man. Tunnelling smoke saturated the air, darkening
the skies in a never-lifting storm. The eternal night, as it was called.
The only warmth he felt was made by fire, and when it rained, the
puddles turned black with ash and soot.

He found her easily. She was inside the lower furnace room at the bottom of the staircase, lying on her back with patches of blood soaking through her clothes. Her eyes were distant, unable to focus and each breath came in short and sharp. He knelt beside her, and felt nothing but distant disappointment. *How sad. He doesn't even love you yet.*

There was a strange beauty behind her death. The stunning red bled into her bulky clothes, pooling around her waist and staining her chilled pale skin. The thorn to Klaus' side. Nikolas' hidden weapon. He stood to leave, allowing her the chance to fade in peace, but then stopped.

Her lips opened in soft pulls, mimicking that of speech.

He inched closer, bringing her cheeks into the warmth of his palms. "Elizabeth, let me help you."

As soon as he spoke, Elizabeth's gaze snapped toward him, her blue eyes dilating. Her expression wasn't something Nikolas had seen before. It felt as if she finally saw him and his soul beyond the corruption. Her deep longing plucked his breath from his lungs. No one had ever looked at him in such a way, not since Lady Claudia. Even so, back then Lady Claudia had studied him as if he was some rare bird to capture. Elizabeth's eyes begged silently, wanting him, *needing* him. For the first time in a very long time, Nikolas' mind froze. He couldn't breathe. Her stare paralyzed him.

"Save me."

Nikolas' world crumpled. At her command, Nikolas felt his joints unfreeze and the clouds in his mind disperse. He gasped. The smoke in his lungs cleared. Devoted obedience crippled him. God, damn it, he wanted to obey.

He tilted her chin up and gently touched his lips to hers. She drooped in his arms. With each breath, he filled her lungs with bursts of magic-coated oxygen. The magic stopped her body's decline and sped up the healing process. The wounds healed themselves inhumanly fast and the blood she lost was recovered. Nikolas pulled away. Her eyes fluttered open. Still dazed, she searched around before landing on Nikolas' face.

"Klaus," she mumbled. "Thank you."

Exhaustion took her away and she slumped in Nikolas' arms. Nikolas slowly closed his eyes, his grip on her trembling. *Yes...amazing.*

NIKOLAS TURNED AWAY, panicked and breathless. She had called *him* Klaus, thought he was *Klaus*; only looked at him in that way because she *saw* Klaus. The mistaken identity wrenched at his heart, making it ache as if she'd crushed it in her hands. Heartbreak was not a foreign pain, one he quite often mistaken for love while within Lady Claudia's presence.

Lady Claudia's final days were left in the hands of Heart's Hospital. A white room. No flowers. No pictures. She was alone, attached to a machine, her brain activity deadly quiet. Her heart pumped for a body hollowed of spirit. In many ways, Nikolas saw himself in her. Now, more than ever.

He had his Collector's blade out of its unsheathed the moment he stepped foot into the room, but as soon as he saw Claudia, his mind slowed. His strength evaporated out of him until his knees weakened and he hit the ground. Carefully, he reached out to her, gently cupping her flaking, chalky wrists. She stared out into the room, her eyes milky and unfocused. If she could see him or hear him, it didn't matter now.

Nikolas could only whisper. "I always thought I would die by my own hands and yet here I bleed from a fatal pinprick. If we are both dead, then you must be in heaven, for I walk alone here in hell. *Jos haluatte sen, minä hajoaa.* (If you wish it, I will fall apart.) *Jos haluatte sitä, me elää ikuisesti.* (If you wish it, we will live forever.)"

Nikolas drove the blade into Lady Claudia's chest, vacuuming up the last strands of time she had. In the softest breath, she gasped.

Colors snapped and dulled. He eased the blade out and gently brushed her eyelids close. He didn't shed a tear for her, not a single one, despite how vicious the pain tore through him. The machines let out a long, flat line beep. It continued to ring in his ears as he walked away.

He shivered. The disconnection spread like electricity. The strings broke, separating the magical bond between Nikolas and Lady Claudia. Heartbreak tore through him viciously, wishing he could sever himself from his heart as he could with magic. Eventually, the cold chilled his blood. The ropes binding him to her snapped, and soon, the love that warmed him died.

THIS PLACE WAS meant for them. An empty ballroom framed by mirrors on one side, glass windows on the other. Cracks in the roof scattered sunlight across the hall. Vines climbed the corners, turning stone pillars into trees. A private garden: the harsh white of marble warmed by dirty, earthy tones. This was their secret spot. The center of his life.

Nikolas gutted the ballroom when Lady Claudia first fell to the taint. The torn curtains bunched together on the floor. The smashed mirror left in pieces at the feet of its frame. The red lounge they shared had been destroyed. He promised the next time he returned it would be to set it on fire, but instead he brought *her*. What remained was a single chair for him to sit and a makeshift bed for her to rest, positioned carefully away from the windows. Soft blankets. Large pillows. Fresh clothes. A tea tray with a boiled kettle was placed within reach from her bed with a lemon wedge tucked beside the cup. He watched her sleep silently from across the room. The taint colored her white skin with rashes, climbing up her wrist into the bend of her elbow. He took a pained breath. He must be a monster, for everything he touched started to rot.

Elizabeth woke. Birds chirped overhead. Soft white surrounded her. She touched the sheets beneath her body. Soft, silky, not the bed at Harry's and not the hard floor of the furnace room. All she could remember was pain. It momentarily dazed her, tilting her off center as she grabbed desperately at her waist. The pain spiked where she moved. She shuddered and collapsed.

"What happened?" she asked.

"You were attacked."

Elizabeth glanced sideways at Nikolas, poised on a faded blue, cushioned chair. Dirt marred his usual clean suit, scuffing his knees and elbows. "Stabbed, three times," he said.

She gently touched her side. "Penelope..."

"Yes, sibling rivalry. I can relate."

"Where is she?"

"Gone." Nikolas shrugged and looked away. "It doesn't matter now."

"I need to talk to he-arh!" She tried to sit up, but buckled beneath the pain. She flopped back into the soft mold of the bed sheets.

"There is no magic left, you must allow your body to recover naturally."

"Wait...you healed me?"

"Yes. If I remember correctly, your exact words were *save me!*" he mocked.

She looked down, trying to scavenge the memory within the fog. No, it couldn't be. It was Klaus; she was sure of it. Her neck still itched where his warm hands had cupped underneath her head, how his golden eyes had softened and his voice tilted as he spoke. *Wait... his voice.* The more she thought about it, the clearer the memory took shape. The lump in her throat didn't shift as she recalled hearing him whisper, *let me help you.* It was missing Klaus' German accent. Elizabeth slowly closed her eyes. It was only an illusion, and disappointment weakened her voice. "I want to see Mr. Harry Smith."

"No, I think what you want to say is thank you."

"Why did you bring me here? Shouldn't I be in a hospital?"

"This is your hospital. You'll recover here, out of the eyes of the public. Can't have Arthur Beaumontt finding you."

"Didn't know you cared."

"This isn't caring, this is…convenience."

"For how long?"

"For as long as it takes."

"Why?"

"Well, no point throwing a hook out there if I don't have any bait."

"No, I mean why? Why are you doing all of this for me?"

Nikolas glanced at her. The truth was too dangerous. He could be shattered and rebuilt by her words. With just her smile, his world could cease to exist. But unlike with Lady Claudia where he welcomed the warmth, the building heat made him uncomfortable. Nikolas took a deep breath. "Because…you asked me to."

"And you do as I say now?"

"Only if it suits me."

Elizabeth's voice waivered. "But…my time cannot be touched so…" He followed her eyes down her arm where the rash had spread. She touched it gingerly, understanding the weight it carried. "Did someone die to save my life?"

"No. I promise, no one died." Nikolas stood and shoved his hands into his pant pockets. "Rest. I'll be back with proper food. You must be hungry." He turned away.

"Nikolas, wait…"

He slowed at the door.

"Thank you."

HE HEARD CONCERN in her voice, not anger. The way she gently touched the blemishes on her skin, the marks of his corruption, seemed grateful, not upset. Nikolas ran his fingers along the walls of the ballroom. The wallpaper peeled off and hung like stripes of skin, yet he still considered it beautiful. Lady Claudia hated it. Rotten, she'd called it.

"I would really rather it if I went to a proper doctor." Elizabeth's voice brought his attention back into the room. Nikolas dropped his hand as he walked closer.

"Why, are you embarrassed in front of me?"

"It's not decent."

"No one is here to judge."

Elizabeth winced as she struggled onto her side. Her fingers shook as she tried to lift her top to check the bandages. Nikolas knelt beside her and she retracted her hands, covering her stomach. "Excuse me!"

"Oh please, who do you think bandaged you up in the first place? Plus, I have no interest in your complete lack of curves."

Her glare hardened. "And you called yourself a gentleman."

Nikolas smirked and proceeded to carefully change over her bandages and help wash the wounds. Elizabeth looked away to hide her embarrassment. "You must be bored, sitting around here all day watching me sleep."

"I don't sit around here all day," he said.

"Oh? Where do you go?"

"Nowhere of importance. Why? Are you telling me you're bored?"

"I wouldn't mind company."

Nikolas smiled at the comment. She proceeded to pout. "You could at least give me a book to read?" she asked.

"Your wounds are healing quite nicely, I say you won't be stuck here for too much longer." Carefully, Nikolas secured the bandages and proceeded to clear Elizabeth's breakfast from the floor. "I'm sure we'll have you back into hiding in Rosefire in no time."

"Rosefire? You've been watching me?"

"Of course, how else do you think I know how you like your tea?"

Elizabeth scoffed. "What an immoral thing to do."

"Considering I steal time for a living, this isn't exactly my darkest hour."

She snickered and then winced at the sharp jabs to her stomach. "I honestly don't know what you are. Sometimes I feel like I'm your hostage, sometimes I feel like I'm some trophy, and sometimes..." Nikolas glanced over at her hesitation. She sighed, followed by a shrug. "Sometimes I find it hard to hate you."

He smiled warmly. "I must be doing something right, then."

"Or I'm doing something wrong."

His smile dropped. He knew in every relationship, be it in the making of an enemy, a friend, or a lover, there was a defining moment. His and Elizabeth's moment presented itself in the silence of a room. They both sat on the unanswered question on how they fit into each other's world. The enemy. The bait. Friend. Nikolas cleared his throat. "I am truly sorry you know," he whispered, "about your mother."

Elizabeth's grip tightened on her blanket. It took her a few moments to speak, and when she did, rage-filled tears hazed over her eyesight. "Tell me...why?"

Why her? Why did she do it? Nikolas didn't ask such questions when Lady Claudia pointed him Ana's way. It didn't matter. How ignorant he was to think it didn't matter. Of course, it did. It mattered a lot, but it was too late now.

"Because...she asked me to." His intention was not to shift the blame. It was the truth, after all. She wanted him to, and so, he obeyed. Elizabeth looked at him furiously.

"That's not good enough."

"I am sorry." He didn't know what else to say. What he could say. "I didn't mean to harm—"

"Stop it!" she snapped. "Just stop! Stop talking. Stop looking at me. Stop being nice." She winced and grabbed her stomach. Nikolas didn't move to help her, but dropped his head with guilt. Elizabeth continued through a whisper. "Stop trying to trick me."

"It's not a trick."

"Yes, it is."

Nikolas sighed softly. "I don't blame you for feeling this way. But that's what we are, Elizabeth. Klaus too, we are beings controlled by desires. We are controlled by words—"

Grief trembled her voice. "But you could have said no. Is that not what corrupted Collectors are capable of? You could have said no."

Her words tore through him like bullets. He could have said no. But he didn't. He didn't want to. "Yes..." He took a shaky breath. "I guess...I could have."

A STORM PASSED over. Rain pelted down, darkening the sky and filling the garden with muddy water. Nikolas did what he could to stay out of Elizabeth's sight. He brought her books to read—classics, his favorites—but he no longer sat down with her for meals. He did everything she asked, even fetching her a violin after hearing how she missed listening to the instrument.

"You're bribing me now?"

"And failing, apparently." Nikolas smiled. Elizabeth rolled her eyes and looked away. He stepped closer. "Let me guess, stop being nice to you?"

"I know you don't find it difficult."

"It's not exactly in my nature." He grinned.

Elizabeth reluctantly picked up the violin and looked over it. "You didn't kill anyone to get this, did you?"

"I do know how to steal, you know."

"Yes, I'm aware." She smiled as she ran her fingers across the strings. A simple smile, yet it was genuine, sincere.

"Well, it's there if you want it." He left her alone to play. The bond was vicious. It was irrational, illogical, and without mercy. Considering Collectors work for masters by nature, to appease that instinct as a corrupted Collector meant seeking acceptance and worth from others. Lady Claudia rules were always strict, everything she did was controlled. But not with Elizabeth. With her, there were no boundaries. It was just the passing of time. Simple, unforced, as natural as breathing.

The sharp reminder that she wasn't his came in the headlines of the newspaper. Nikolas went into town for supplies where he heard about the death of Arthur Beaumontt. A mysterious disease had taken him. Nikolas recognized the symptoms immediately. Fossilized. Swollen glands. Black veins. A Time Collector.

He shoved the paper back on the rack. *Klaus came back for her.* His plan could work, *would* work. But, his priorities weren't clear anymore. He hesitated. *Stop it Nikolas. None of this is real. Just a crack in the mirror. It isn't real.*

Nikolas returned to Elizabeth plucking the strings of her violin absentmindedly. He recognized the chords from his childhood. Klaus' chords. When they were young, Klaus used to practice the melody constantly on the piano. Nikolas hated it. Hearing it again caused him to slam the door on his entrance.

Elizabeth lowered the violin. "Is everything alright?"

"Yes," he answered sharply, and dumped the shopping beside the door.

Elizabeth flinched. "Are you sure you're okay?"

"I'm fine."

"You don't seem fine." Nikolas slumped into his chair with an irritated sigh. Elizabeth glanced back down, her expression pained.

"What? What's with that look?" he asked.

"I'm just thinking…why didn't he come?"

Nikolas immediately knew who she was talking about, but he

cleared his throat as though it meant nothing. "I think you know why."

She gently nodded. "I'm afraid I do."

No, you don't. His heart fluttered as he cleared his throat again. *He did come. He's here. He came for you.* He couldn't shake the panic from his voice. "You still haven't answered me from before."

"About what?"

"Why him?"

Elizabeth took a moment before answering with the exact words Nikolas didn't want to hear. "I think you know why."

He nodded. "I'm afraid I do." His eyes trailed around the ballroom, picking out the flaws. Broken. Rotten. Falling apart. Dark thoughts clouded his mind. Being back here was poisonous. White rose, the smell of her perfume. Hot tea with a wedge of lemon. When she slept, she kicked the covers off to the left. These were things Nikolas shouldn't know about her. The curve of her smile.

On a scrap piece of paper, Nikolas wrote the words: '*R. Incognito Promenade.*' He folded the paper into his pocket. "But none of it is real, is it? It's time to move forward."

Elizabeth gently touched her violin. "Yeah, it's just a trick."

CHAPTER

FORTY

ARTHUR BEAUMONTT SAT alone. His hand gripped his cup. Scattered among his cold food were bits and pieces of old diaries, literature, plans, and newspapers. The only light within the dim room came from the flickers of a dying flame. Insomnia made him pale, leaving his eyes red and itchy and his mind burning for answers. His brother, Jeremy, limped across the room and sat on the other side of the table. He clasped his hands together beneath his chin, revealing scars that marred the length of his arms.

"So, what? Another night of silence?"

"If you don't like it, then leave," Arthur snarled. "I never invited you in the first place."

Jeremy shuffled back into his seat with an exasperated sigh. "We have our real enemies outside that very door. You can't let this obsession with mythical creatures distract you from the real battle."

"You saw her for yourself." Arthur motioned outward. "Tell me, what could make her transform into such a hideous creature?"

Jeremy bit his tongue. "I don't know, but we need to concentrate on the things we do know."

"And I know what I saw."

"You haven't seen anything. Nothing beyond these walls. I've seen the true face of battle."

Arthur jumped and smacked his food clear off the table. "Stop with your lectures. You choose to go to war."

"And it has turned me into a rational man. I have half the mind to enlist you, myself." Jeremy ran his hands over his short hair. "This isn't a game anymore, Arthur. You think the council are going to listen to you? You have to present yourself as a logical adult, not some traumatized child chasing after demons. And what of your wife?"

"What about her?"

"Where is she? People are talking."

"Let them gossip about stupid women. I'm focused on what's actually important."

"Don't say it—" Jeremy groaned.

"Time Collectors."

Jeremy slammed his hands down. "That is enough. Tomorrow morning, I will attend the meetings alone. You will remain here where no one can listen to your psychotic ramblings. That's an order."

"I don't take orders from you," Arthur said.

The shrill ring of an incoming phone call sounded before a maid rushed into the dining room. "Sir, it's Heart's hospital. It has to do with your mother." Arthur didn't budge. Jeremy stood to leave.

"I'll be right there." Jeremy nodded toward her before turning back to Arthur. "Listen to my wisdom, Arthur. Leave it be." He then left for the hallway, leaving Arthur alone once more.

Arthur slumped back into his chair and ran his hands through his oily, black curls. Every time he closed his eyes, there *it* was. The memory. The moment his mother disintegrated into the burnt body of a shrivelled prawn. The moment the foreign doctor stabbed Timothy in the back. The shadows crept like living creatures, tearing down brick and wood around him. Arthur shook. He started to doubt his own mind, the evidence of his eyes. *Crazy. I'm not crazy.*

Pressed against the wall of the room, Klaus inspected the new hives on his arm. The steel taste had remained in his mouth for days. The evidence that Nikolas still had Elizabeth was as clear as from the red spots spreading across his body. He clenched his fist. *What are you wishing for, Elizabeth?*

Klaus stepped up behind Arthur and held the Collector's blade to his neck. Arthur's back tightened, fighting the instinct to spin around. His breath caught in his throat.

"Don't try to call for help," Klaus whispered. "If you do, I will kill you."

Panic flooded Arthur's body. He slowly straightened up. "So, I take it you're not an assassin. Who sent you?"

"No one sent me." Carefully, Klaus stepped around into view without lowering his blade.

Arthur's eyes bulged, tracking Klaus as he sat down beside him. Hints of fear and joy crossed his expression, a confirmation of sanity, while still understanding the danger.

"We are going to have a little chat, you and I," Klaus said.

"What do you want?" Sweat lined Arthur's forehead. Klaus stabbed the Collector's blade into the table between them, a constant reminder of danger and insurance of Arthur's cooperation. Arthur eyed the weapon fearfully.

"Elizabeth Wicker…when was the last time you saw her?"

Arthur looked back confused. "Why? Why does she matter?"

"Just answer the question."

"I haven't seen her since the day you attacked us." Arthur's expression shifted as new memories resurfaced. "You rescued her at the markets, you came for her at my wedding too, and now…why are you so interested in my wife?"

Wife. The word strained from Arthur's lips. Arthur wielded it as though the word could wound Klaus. *Wife.* Is that what people are thinking now, that Klaus was interested in Elizabeth romantically?

Klaus snarled, "What about Nikolas?"

"Is he one, too? Whatever you are?" Klaus glanced at his blade and Arthur's eyes followed. He swallowed uneasily. "I don't know where he is."

"Do you want to find out?"

"How?"

"All you have to do is ask."

Arthur broke out into laughter and wiped his pale lips with shaky hands. "They said I was crazy, you know. Everyone thinks I'm crazy."

"Well, you're not."

"No, no, because you're going to convince them."

"That's not why I'm here."

Arthur clasped his hands together. "You will help me. You must. I don't know what you are or what you are capable of, but I do know you're not human."

"I don't care about any of that."

Arthur shook his head. Strings of salvia wedded his mouth as he spoke. "You must. You will. Just—just let Jeremy meet you."

Klaus hardened his stubborn expression. He went to stand, which prompted Arthur to panic and leap across the table. "You can't leave!" he said. At first, Klaus thought he was lunging to attack him, but noticed too late Arthur's attention shift to the blade.

"Nein! Halt!" As soon as Arthur's fingers curled around the blade, a sharp spark flew up into the air. Arthur's body seized up. He tipped backwards onto his back as stiff as a plank of wood. Black veins pressed to the surface as the glands around his throat swelled. Decay reeked from his pores. Klaus ripped the knife out of the table and pocketed it. Voices approached from the hallway and Klaus fled the room before Arthur's body was discovered.

Klaus slipped back into the busy streets, his mind rattled. Elizabeth Wicker could be anywhere, and Arthur was his key to tracking her down. Klaus did consider Harry Smith to make the contract, but unfortunately, the old man couldn't afford the wish. *Only months left, he'll live till Christmas at best.* His older sister Doris was no better. Unsure whereas to go, Klaus worked his way back to Harry Smith's house in Rosefire, but stumbled to a stop across the road. Elizabeth Wicker sat on the front steps wrapped in a blanket. She cradled a cup of tea in her hands and was reading over a note, her expression shielded by the wisps of her white hair. Doubt overshadowed his sense of relief. *She's here?* It felt too neat, too convenient that Elizabeth appeared within his reach. Nikolas was always two steps ahead, leaving Klaus to play catch up.

She perked up as he approached cautiously. "Elizabeth…"

"Klaus? You're here. I mean of course, I can see you but…" A soft pink touched her cheeks. "I'm glad to see you. It's been…well, I'm just glad to see you."

Klaus lingered back. He scanned the shadows warily. "Are…are you alright?"

"I'm fine. Was at the police station helping clear Harry's name over a mix up but…" She slowly stood, noticing the shift in Klaus' focus move along the shadows. Looking, no doubt, for Nikolas. She frowned softly. "He isn't here."

"Hmm?"

"Nikolas. He's gone. He left Harry a note." Klaus stepped closer and took the offered letter. On the front was the name of an old, deteriorating ballroom called the 'R. Incognito Promenade.' It was an ordinary place abandoned by the squabbles of a divorcing couple. On the back of the note was written, 'She is safe. Please come,' with a more personal message beneath: 'Elizabeth. I'm sorry.' Klaus squinted at the writing. Elizabeth sighed. "I must admit I was very surprised to see Mr. Smith come by to collect me. He said the note was left on his kitchen table. It scared the living daylights out of his sister. But, you know gremlins, they can get into anything."

"Hmm…" Klaus read the passage a couple more times, but still couldn't figure out Nikolas' plan. "*I'm sorry?*" he questioned. "Sorry for what?"

Elizabeth shook her head. "It doesn't matter anymore." A smile pulled on her lips despite her many attempts of trying to hide it. She stepped closer and touched his arm. "I was worried about you."

Klaus handed her back the note. "Your cousin Catherine was kind enough to pierce my shoulder with the bone shard. It almost killed me. I was incapacitated for weeks."

"Oh! I didn't know, but you're—"

"Fine? Yes, well a couple of witches helped. Took the poison out of my body and transferred it into the body of a young soldier, instead. Catherine did say the Moore family were the original creators of the weapon. They should know how to fix him."

"Soldier? What soldier? Is he okay?"

"He has been frozen back at the Bell Front Towers. The witches are friends of his, they are looking after him."

Elizabeth nodded. "Catherine did call the house asking about you."

"She's not planning on stabbing me again, is she?" Klaus asked.

"No, but she did seem rather panicked. She said they needed your help."

"They?"

"The Guardians."

"Inviting me over for round two?" Klaus snorted and turned away. "They really think I'm going to allow them the chance?"

Elizabeth gulped uneasily. "Klaus, listen, they summoned Mortalem."

Klaus' spine stiffened. His heart pulsed loudly against his ear. *They had done it? Summoned the gargoyle? But how?* He stepped back and gripped his hair, fighting the urge to fall into his panic.

"I don't know much detail, but it's trapped inside of Leah French."
Elizabeth watched him pace anxiously.

"Are you positive?"

"That's what they said. They have her over in Gothsworth with
Lady Rose."

Klaus stepped back, his mind racing as fast as his heart. First
Nikolas, then the bone shard poison and now Mortalem. Klaus turned
away and started making his way toward the station. Elizabeth put
her cup down and chased after him. "Klaus? So, you do intend to go?"

"Of course, I'm going," he snapped over his shoulder. "And once
I throw that creature back into the spirit world, I'm going to beat
them all into a pulp."

DECAY FORKED AROUND the bricks of the Bell Front towers,
sinking potholes along the roads and paths of the surrounding streets.
The stench of witches was always easy to find. The birthplace of witches
stemmed from disease, more importantly, the crossover of Bact and
human through long transitions. All witches are born human, and
so share human qualities such as their appearance, logical thinking,
problem solving, and emotions, but through ritual and many years
of ingesting Bact blood they mutate with abilities to connect with
cosmic energy, mainly belonging to nature. The more they practiced,
the heavier the toll took on their human form, deforming them and
taking away their humanity. Many of the older witches ceased looking
and acting like humans at all, making it possible to extend their life
beyond the normal capacity. It also made it impossible for Collectors
to take time from them. The lack of a human soul—the only energy
Collectors were interested in.

Their human side limited their reach with the magical arts, but
gave them powerful insight to the secrets of the world. A witch could
read the lines of war through the broken stem of a flower. They could

smell death in a breeze. Nikolas hoped they understood the powerful bond which enslaved him to Elizabeth. Many witches lived outside of society, taking to caves and the woods, except for one. Nikolas approached the Bell Front Towers and stopped outside of the witch's hideout. He could smell her power all over the walls, cementing her presence in the very cogs of the clock tower.

An invisible blockage barged the entrance to the attic, blocking him from entering. Spells marked the doorway, freshly chiselled into the woodwork. *A protection spell? Nice try.* His gremlins sank into the frame and dissolved the wood until the marks warped. Nikolas stepped through.

His attention immediately went to the frozen body of a young soldier draped in a quilt. His horrified expression didn't match the warm setting of the witch's den. Gremlins bubbled around him. *This is Klaus' work.*

The floorboard creaked behind him. He spun in time to catch the wild swing of a young witch trying to stab him with a wooden spike. He grabbed her wrist and kicked out her legs easily, sending her into the ground. "Hello witch." He looked over her, determining her age. She was too human, the smell of her witchcraft dulled with her inexperience. Not powerful enough, and not the scent he was chasing. *An apprentice, of course.* "Where's the other one?"

A distinct smell filled the room seconds before a thick fog completely doused the room, blinding Nikolas' sight behind a haze of white. He recognized the scent and blindingly pulled the young witch to his chest where he held the Collector's knife to her throat. "Drop it!" he shouted. "Drop the spell, now!"

Seconds later, the smoke dispersed and the older witch stepped out from hiding. Nikolas didn't lower his blade as gremlins bubbled and popped in their excitement.

"Careful, Collector." The older witch, Ma, slowly stepped around him. "I can throw you out the window with one look."

"You can try, but I'll be taking this girl with me," Nikolas said. The witch eased her hands up, showing her sign of cooperation. In his grip, Abigail's body shook. "Obviously, you understand what I am and what I am capable of." Nikolas said.

Ma nodded slowly.

Nikolas continued, "Collector bonds, what do you know of them?"

"We do not help your kind."

"Oh, really? Something tells me you do." Nikolas indicated to the soldier's body. "A Time Collector's handiwork, is it not? Does the name Klaus ring any bells? I'm only going to ask you once more before I plunge this knife into this girl's throat and add her to your statue collection."

"Bonds are obedience spells, linking Collectors to their masters."

"How do I break the bond?"

"I cannot help."

"Am I not clear about your cooperation?" He pressed the tip into Abigail's neck, lightly cutting her. Abigail tensed and craned her head away. From the puncture point crystals started to form.

"Ma!?"

"What I mean is there's no spell I can offer," Ma said. "The only creature powerful enough is no friend to Collectors."

"Tell me!"

Ma took a steady breath, calming her tone. "The gargoyle Mortalem, of course."

Mortalem? Nikolas bared his teeth. "You speak of the destroyer of the supernatural?"

"It has been summoned by a black stone Bact."

"It's here?"

"Trapped. Inside the body of a Guardian. Look for the old water plants surrounded by the dead nests of Bactes."

"How do you know all of this?"

Ma motioned to the row of decaying plants along the balcony. "It's written in the decay. Mortalem has crossed over. The Bactes grow in power. A Collector lies trapped."

"Guardians, huh? I know exactly whom you speak of." Nikolas dropped Abigail and shoved her away. Abigail pulled a knife from her ankle boot and swung around only to cut empty air.

CHAPTER
FORTY-ONE

K LAUS AND ELIZABETH boarded the large airship to make the long trip across country to Gothsworth. The airship glided across the skies. The large balloon housed rows of seats, cafes, an indoor garden, and open balconies for people to look over the railings. Clouds settled overhead, casting a long, gray blanket across the horizon. Klaus' eyes trailed down his arm, his fingers lightly touching the taint of Nikolas' corruption.

"What did you wish for?" he asked.

Elizabeth turned away from the window at his question. She glanced down at his arm and reached across to soothe the rash. "You have it too?"

"When it comes to magical wounds, we are connected." Klaus pulled his sleeve down. "What did you wish for?"

"I'm not entirely sure," she answered honestly. She wasn't sure what she'd asked of Nikolas, or what exactly he'd done for her. He saved her life. That was one thing she knew for sure, but felt reluctant to tell Klaus about the betrayal of her sister and the comfort from Nikolas. It all felt private. Something to be hidden.

Klaus gently nodded and then turned away, showing disinterest in further conversation. He proceeded to act cold toward her for the rest of the trip, pretending to be interested in the inflight newspaper to avoid her questions. And as they walked, he intentionally walked too fast, making it difficult for Elizabeth to keep up. Every time she checked to see if everything was okay, he'd feign ignorance and brush it aside. He couldn't explain exactly why he acted this way. It wasn't his disinterest in her company, despite his body language saying that it was. Whenever they were alone together, he couldn't help but feel overwhelmed by her. As soon as they sat in the car Lady Rose sent to collect them at the port, he understood the feeling. Vulnerability.

Gothsworth consisted of large columns of houses stacked on top of each other like shelves and domed around a grand cathedral in the center. Bridges connected the segregated community in criss-crossing channels, while automatic trolleys moved up and down each column in massive, cage elevators. The entire complex resembled a beehive, a city squashed into four quarter circles. The entire community had been jammed packed so tightly together that the only space remaining was on top of their neighbors' roof. As earthquakes were the deathly fear of the city, they installed massive steam powered pegs that gripped the earth and stabilized the entire foundation.

Elizabeth craned her head back as the high-rise towers disappeared into the low hanging clouds. Even with the giant pegs, the buildings would wobble and shift. Lady Rose lived at the top of the tower, which must have been seen as a luxury. The driver escorted Klaus and Elizabeth to one of the pulleys and it clicked and clanked its way up the structure, passing by other houses so close Elizabeth could see through their front windows. She gripped the handle bar as the open cage swayed with the wind.

The trolley came to a shaky stop outside the top house, opening up to the rock garden and outwards to a massive earth colored two-story manor. At the front door, they were greeted by an elegant woman waiting for them.

A tight French braid kept her brown hair away from her face.

"My word," she gasped, "I don't believe it." Lady Rose leant closer to Elizabeth before grasping her hands. "You must be Miss Elizabeth. You're a spitting image of William."

"Lady Rose, thank you your hospitality." Elizabeth curtsied.

Lady Rose touched the end of Elizabeth's hair fondly, as if cherishing a memory. "Such beautiful manners, I wish such grace would rub off on my own daughter. You must call me Aunt Rose, I insist. You are family, it is only proper. My brother always did speak so fondly of you. I admit, we didn't always see eye to eye, but I miss him like he was part of my own soul. I'm so happy to see a piece of him remains within you." She looked over at Klaus and tightened her voice. Her kindness dropped just as fast as her smile. "You must be the Collector."

Klaus noted the unwelcomed greeting and cleared his throat. "Klaus Dietrich. I understand if you feel uncomfortable around me."

"Uncomfortable is an understatement."

"Elizabeth? Klaus?" Catherine's voice carried from the back of the hall. She rushed over to greet them. "I'm glad to see you are alright, thank you for coming."

"Tsk, Catherine you must welcome your guests like a proper young noble woman," Lady Rose corrected her, and then turned to Elizabeth with an exhausted smile. "Fifteen years of schooling and she still can't get it right."

Catherine rolled her eyes and curtsied. "We don't have time for pleasantries, mother."

"Without social etiquette, we may as well grunt around like animals."

Elizabeth curtsied back warmly. "I'm glad to see you're okay, as well."

Catherine's attention moved to Klaus's arm, and her eyebrow pinched in confusion at his perfect health. Klaus spoke before she could ask any questions. "Where is she?"

Catherine indicated over her shoulder. "This way."

Upstairs in one of the guest rooms, Leah French slept plugged to a heart monitor. She might've looked peaceful if it wasn't for the blade protruding out of her ribcage. Dennis sat by her bedside. He stood up but didn't hide his displeasure at Elizabeth's and Klaus' return.

"Creature," he greeted Klaus coldly, before looking at Elizabeth. "And the traitor."

"Dennis!" Catherine scolded, when Klaus stormed across the room and punched Dennis with such strength he fell off balance. Dennis' head bounced off the wall before he slumped to the ground unconscious. Catherine and Elizabeth leapt forward to pull Klaus back. Klaus shook their hands off him.

Catherine checked Dennis' pulse. "Elizabeth, do you mind fetching me some wet towels please?"

Elizabeth glanced between them and left. Klaus paced around Leah, clearly irritated. Undetected to the common ear was a low pitch ring originating from the blade. He recognized the weapon. It belonged to an old Collector friend, Juliet Christ. The fact it had parted from her was not a good sign.

"I think you've quite injured him." Catherine heaved Dennis up and placed him on a chair. His head rolled downward, revealing the faint bruises starting to swell over his temple.

Klaus scoffed, uncaring. "How could I? There cannot be anything in there to worry about injuring." He then leaned closer to inspect the heavy cracks throughout the blade's glass handle. "What happened?"

Catherine stepped beside him. "An elder Bact did this. The same one you encountered at the paper mill. She slit her own throat to summon Mortalem, but a Collector jumped in and pierced Leah with her blade before the ritual was complete. The Collector turned to stone, just like what happened with your arm, but this time she was completely crystallised from head to toe." Catherine's eyes moved back to Klaus' arm. "How did you fix your arm?"

"A witch," he said, dismissively. "Back to the point, are you telling me the Bactes helped you summon it?"

"They weren't really given a choice."

Klaus growled and turned away. "Such brainless creatures."

"Can you help?" Catherine followed after him. "I know we have acted out of hurt and pain, and I see now that summoning Mortalem was a terrible, idiotic mistake but—"

Klaus spun back. "A mistake? That's putting it lightly. What do you expect me to do? No wish can rip Mortalem out of your friend's body."

"If not you, then what creature *can* help us?"

Klaus snarled, his voice full of mocking spite. "Oh, I'm sure if you were clever enough to draw Mortalem out then you'll have a plan to put it back inside. Didn't you once say it was like a lion in a cage?"

Catherine asked, flustered. "And the blade?"

"Only the Collector who owns it can remove it and she's been turned to stone. My, what a conundrum you've created here."

Catherine grabbed his arm. "Enough of your mocking. I understand the situation. If you cannot help us with this, then perhaps you can help me with something else." She chewed on her lip, her nervousness showing. "There are two reasons I called you here."

Klaus straightened his posture. "A wish?"

She nodded. "I cannot bear to think he is…" She stopped herself before she could utter the word. "Please, I need you to find him as fast as you can and bring Hudson back to me."

THE WRETCHED SMELL could have knocked him over. Nikolas stepped out of the shadows at the curb of the water plantation and immediately covered his nose with his sleeve. The witch spoke the truth. There was a trail of Bact's exterminations leading up to a large nest outside of Lovibond. The gremlins dispersed over the empty lot, each propelling toward a different area of the massive planation. It didn't take long before a small number of gremlins reported back with news of a corpse.

Nikolas traced the gremlins inside the infested warehouse where the touches of Bactes saturated the entire building. It was hard to ignore the witch's words. The Bactes' stench reflected their power and the touch of their decay reached beyond normal perimeters. Inside, he came across the rotten corpse of the elder Bact, a long, deep gash sliced across its neck. A week old, if he had to guess.

Yet, it was not the corpse that attracted his interest, but that of Juliet's collapsed body not far from the creature. Nikolas knelt beside her and touched her freezing cheek. Her cocooned body was trapped beneath cold stone, her mouth open and her hair clumped together and fanned out behind her head. She had landed and frozen simultaneously. He lifted her trench coat to where her belt was, revealing the empty sheath for her Collector's blade.

Gently, Nikolas cupped his palm over Juliet's forehead. She wasn't dead. He could feel the warmth of her thoughts against his hand, but she wasn't consciously thinking either, more like she was dreaming. He mastered up enough strength to dig into her mind, drawing up her last moments.

The Guardians. A ritual. Panic. A blonde female slumped against the ground. A nest of twenty Bactes watched behind the darkness. Catherine, she was there too, pinned beneath the bodies of two elder Bactes. Her armor uniform was crushed. The smell of Bact blood assaulted their nostrils. The whistling of Mortalem's presence. Darkness swelled. He caught a glimpse of orange eyes. Juliet speared her blade into the woman's chest. White fire burnt over her view. Everything snapped shut.

Pain threw his head back, causing him to drop the memory. The last few images continued to burn across his mind. His knees buckled.

Blood trickled down his nose and he wiped it off. *Mortalem*. Gremlins scurried and buzzed. He threw them forward, anxiously.

"Find Catherine."

They bolted, catching her scent before hitting a blockage. *Klaus's natural repellent. He is with them.* "Find the blonde woman."

The gremlins scurried ahead before rebounding off again. Something inside his head pinged, catching Elizabeth's scent as though she were a vacuum pulling him toward her. It dragged his gremlins across the city and into Gothsworth. She was in the bathroom rinsing towels hurriedly under a tap. She turned and rushed down a hallway. The gremlins followed her into a bedroom where the blonde-haired woman rested.

"Catherine? Klaus?" Elizabeth called into the bedroom. Juliet's missing blade stuck out of the woman's chest cavity. Elizabeth stepped around the bed cautiously before tending to the unconscious redhead slumped across a chair. The gremlins scurried back into Nikolas' shadow. He knew where they were.

CHAPTER
FORTY-TWO

HUDSON COLLAPSED BACK onto the mattress. His mind spun, dark shadows pressing into the peripherals of his vision, distorting the walls around him. Images clashed. Old touches of familiar faces. He had been asleep for so long. His last memory blurred behind the haze of her spell.

He remembered it, vaguely. The image of Elizabeth on the platform, pacing to and fro as though in distress. The moment he approached, a pain knocked him out and he awoke inside a cold, brick room. His wrists bound behind his back, ankles tied to the legs of the chair. Moisture dampened the walls, leaving puddles beneath the leaking pipes. He groaned and jerked against the chains, the noise no doubt alerting his kidnappers.

He didn't expect to see Elizabeth there, and she seemed just as confused to see him. Behind her approached the corrupted Time Collector, Nikolas, and Hudson's back tensed with apprehension. Nikolas' face remained untouched by time, keeping him as young as the day Dennis' grandfather tried shooting him down seventy years ago. The Collector, Juliet, then cut him with her fingernail and a deep darkness pulled him down. The nightmares tore into him. He couldn't wake. He couldn't escape. He knew he must be dreaming. There were monsters he had never seen before. Creatures as large as houses. Swords for legs, eight eyes, and black, scaled bodies. He was weightless, his hands numbed to the touch of the world built around him, but nevertheless the fear was real. He was trapped inside his own mind and became convinced. He would never see Catherine again. And slowly, bit by bit, the dream world became the only world he understood. Fear eroded his identity away, eroded his name, his memories of his friends and family. He crumbled beneath the terror until the spell broke.

A white fire tore up the front of his mind, throwing him back and jolting him awake. He scrambled up, dazed, but his head still pulsated with the remains of his torment. Hudson glanced around the dark cell to find himself curled up on a mattress. Old wounds marred his wrists and ankles, signs of being restrained.

"You're finally awake?" A voice called across to him. Hudson turned toward two men huddled around a bonfire, their hands held up against the breath of the flame. Layers of dirty, ripped clothes covered them. "That was quite some dream you had there. What type of drug could induce that?"

"That's no drug, Fred, that's witchcraft, I tell ya." The second man nudged him, his front missing teeth creating a whistle when he spoke. "You've been here for weeks, boy. Tossing 'n turning, rambling 'bout monsters and death. Weren't sure you were gonna wake."

Hudson tried to stand, but he stumbled. His body felt weak, starved of nourishment. "Where am I?"

"The slums, lad." The younger of the two homeless men walked to him. He knelt beside him and pushed over some canned food. "Hungry?"

"Starved." Hudson took the beans and shoveled the food in. His stomach twisted painfully. The spell had kept him alive against starvation and dehydration. Now it was broken, he felt every painful cry of his body.

"What's your name, son?"

"I…I don't know."

"Only witchcraft could do this to a man," the toothless man suggested again. "Mark my words. Witchcraft."

"I can tell by your clothes you're not one of us," Fred went on. "What brought you here?"

"I can't remember," Hudson admitted. He rolled over onto his back, the heaviness from the induced coma keeping him anchored to the floor. "I can't remember anything."

"It messed you up good. I'm Fred Cooper, and this is Earl Wells. You can stay here with us as long as you need, Grumbles." He clapped Hudson on the shoulder and stood.

"Grumbles?"

"It's what we called you. You grumble in your sleep."

Hudson relaxed into the mattress. Grumbles, a name he could use. "Thank you."

Beyond the spurs of his nightmares, he couldn't remember anything. Every night when he slept, small sections of his past resurfaced. The smell of gunpowder. A woman's smile. Brown hair, long and curled down her side. Words started to reappear, attaching names to faces. Small details sharpened. Bits and pieces returned in disjointed sequences, like his name, *Hudson*. The memories recoiled painfully like a snapping band. Among his flashbacks there were scenes he couldn't understand. A different time. A different place where he was called by a different name. He couldn't help but feel trapped when he slept, as though his skin had hardened into clay.

He lived among the underground network of homeless, rebuilding his forgotten past when a hand came down on top of his shoulder, waking Hudson up. He turned around to a stranger's face leaning over him.

"Hudson?" the man asked, his voice slurred with a German accent.

Hudson's tired eyes widened. "You know me?"

Confusion crossed the man's face. He reached forward and touched the mark on Hudson's forehead. "Looks like I found you just in time. What do you remember?"

"Who are you?"

"Your guardian angel. Now, what do you remember?"

Hudson struggled up onto his elbow. His sluggish words jumbled together in his exhaustion. "How do you know me?"

"Does the name Juliet Christ ring any bells?"

"Yes."

He sighed. "You've been poisoned. Listen, my name is Klaus and I am a friend of yours. Plainly speaking. You've been caught up in one of Juliet's spells, I'm afraid. Come, I'm required to bring you home."

"Home?"

Klaus nodded and helped heave Hudson up. His month-long stay in the slums had thickened his beard and teased the brown curls into knotted tangles. His skin glistened with the mixed smells of sweat and sewer. "First a shower, then back to Gothsworth. I dare say you'll need to see a doctor too. Lady Catherine is waiting for you."

REALIZATION DAWNED ON Klaus with a single look. It wasn't the look of shock at seeing Hudson's deterioration after weeks of silence—his face narrowed, his arms thinned, and his skin paled by illness. It was the lack of recognition. The cold welcome of a stranger. Lady Rose, Catherine, Dennis and Elizabeth all met up with Klaus and Hudson on their arrival to Gothsworth hospital. Doctors admitted him straight away, and fed fluid into his body through a tube into his veins.

"I've contacted his family. They are on their way." Lady Rose settled down in a chair beside his bed.

Reaching over him, Catherine gently cupped his slack hand. "Hudson? Can you hear me?" She gently ran her thumb over the new scar on his forehead. His eyebrows pinched, pained by the touch.

"It's a miracle he's even alive, look at the poor boy," Lady Rose said.

Dennis glanced out into the hallway toward Klaus and then back at Catherine. She looked away from him guiltily. "Yes, a miracle." Elizabeth caught the brief exchange, and tenderly smiled to herself.

Klaus ensured to stay out of the room, but he remained close enough to overhear the conversation. He sat on one of the benches along the hallway, his hands poised nervously beneath his chin. Catherine appeared from the doorway and joined him.

"He'll be alright now," Klaus said without looking up. "I found him out in the slums. A bit malnourished and dehydrated, but nothing fatal."

"Thank you, Klaus," she whispered. "I know you risk a lot being here with us, but I really am grateful for your help."

Klaus weakly smiled. Behind them, Hudson stirred awake and the room soon filled with excited chatter. Catherine turned to walk back in, but Klaus snatched her hand to prevent her from leaving. "Just a moment…" he started, but the words swelled on his tongue. Catherine looked down at his hand and back at him. He released her. "No, nothing, sorry."

Chatter turned Catherine around and she joined the others inside Hudson's room. Hudson's blue eyes fluttered open. He glanced around, his expression confused and slightly alarmed.

"Welcome back, Hudson." Dennis smiled and clapped him on the shoulder.

Hudson gently smiled back. "Where am I?"

"Gothsworth hospital," Dennis explained. Hudson glanced at Catherine and fell into a hysterical panic.

"No! No! Don't you come any closer!" Hastily, he grabbed the vase of flowers set up on the bedside table, and tried to hit her with it. His reaction startled everyone. Dennis grabbed his wrist to subdue him.

"Hudson? What's the matter with you?"

Hudson's eyes didn't leave Catherine's face. "Get away from me. Get away," he screamed, fear cracking his voice. Catherine stumbled back. Frantically, he tried to unhook the tubes to his arms, but the nurses managed to repress him.

"You should leave," the nurse said and pushed everyone out into the hallway. As soon as Catherine was gone, Hudson collapsed back against the mattress.

"What happened?" Catherine demanded. Klaus looked down as she stormed closer to grab his attention. "Why did he react like that?"

"Juliet Christ..." he whispered. "That mark on Hudson's forehead is the scar she leaves with her victims."

"What? What victims?" Lady Rose gasped. Dennis stepped around Klaus, his face reddening with rage. His fists bunched, and Elizabeth felt a surge of panic for Klaus' safety.

"A Time Collector's influence, I'm afraid," Klaus explained. "She's a mind breaker. She destroys memories and replaces them with new ones. Often terrifying memories of familiar faces."

Catherine stumbled back into a chair. "Can we fix him?"

"Not through magical means."

"But can he be fixed?"

Klaus slowly glanced up. "I don't know."

"A Collector did this?" Lady Rose walked angrily forward. "Heartless creatures like yourself?" The word *heartless* stabbed at Klaus. "William warned me of you. Said you weren't to be trusted."

Klaus glanced up as though he had just been slapped. Even though Klaus couldn't control his Collector side, he had thought at least with William, he had been seen as a companion. Someone to trust.

"That's what they do. They only care about themselves," Dennis added. Catherine buried her head in her hands. Lady Rose crossed her arms, matching the aggression from Dennis. All the while Klaus sat back. His eyes cast down as though accustomed to the hate.

"Wait a moment." Elizabeth stepped between them.

Lady Rose cut across her. "I said it once, I'll say it again, I will not allow any more of my family be harmed by abominations—"

"Aunt Rose, please."

"It's not in good society to be running around with such a dishonorable man—"

"Enough, Aunt Rose." Elizabeth stepped between Lady Rose and Klaus protectively. Everyone went quiet. "The last scared words from my father won't change all the wonderful things he said about Klaus, and it won't change my mind either. He's here, isn't he?" She turned and looked at Dennis. "Even after everything you've put him through, he still came to your aid when you asked him. How is that anything less than admirable? You're happy to use his powers and capabilities when it suits you, but you can't blame him when things go wrong. You can't condemn him for being what he is. He is a Collector yes, but he is also kind, brave, selfless, sometimes arrogant and rude, but that's okay. He's human, too."

Human. Klaus' back tightened. *She thinks I'm human, too.*

Lady Rose tenderly lowered her arms. "Miss Elizabeth, you speak wisdom beyond your years. I apologize, Sir Dietrich. I may have my objections to your kind, but clearly you're one of the good people. William did speak kindly of you. Even before his death, he never blamed you. It was wrong of me to judge you so harshly."

Catherine rose from her seat and gently touched Klaus' arm. "You did bring Hudson back, and I can't thank you enough that. In any way I can help you, please just ask."

Dennis scoffed, "If you see fit to stand around and hug each other then so be it. Know my alliances is always on the human side, no matter what." He stormed down the hallway and out of the hospital.

Klaus looked from Lady Rose to Catherine and back to Elizabeth again. A sweet pain hit him. He looked down at his trembling hands. He hadn't realized how badly he needed to hear those words from her. And the realization of it scared the wits out of him.

THEY MADE IT back to the mansion in silence. Relief lifted up his shoulders as he walked, but Klaus' hands still trembled. They reached the front manor, and Lady Rose and Catherine walked on ahead as Klaus pulled Elizabeth back. He lingered by the doorway, waiting for the others to step out of earshot. Her last words ran back and forth across his mind, leaving echoes in their wake. The more he thought about it the deeper the prints sank into his memory, making him agitated.

"What's the matter?" Elizabeth asked, reading into his stern expression.

"What you said before..." he started in a whisper. "None of it is true, is it?"

"Why? Did I insult you with my praise?" she tried to joke.

Klaus shook his head. "But they are right."

"Right about what?"

"About me." Klaus turned and gestured outward. "Every bad thing that has happened to you is because of me. It is because you keep the company of Time Collectors."

Elizabeth's smile dropped. "Since when has that bothered you?"

"I am not kind. I am not generous or selfless. You use those words to try and make me out to be something I am not."

Elizabeth scoffed and turned away. "How fast you are to turn every conversation into a duel. Why not just tell me the truth? Clearly, it is my company you hate."

Hate? Klaus cringed at the word. "This is not hate. I am trying to protect you."

"Protect me? Or protect yourself?"

He stepped back at her sharp, direct hit. What terrified him was how much she saw into him and how much others saw too. "How can you not understand?" He turned, frustrated.

"How could I understand when you don't tell me anything?"

"Look at me. Just look." He grabbed her hand and pressed her fingers to his neck. His heart raced against the tip of her fingers. Her cheeks warmed, startled by the gesture. "A creature as cold-blooded as I should not feel this."

"Well, clearly you are no cold-blooded creature."

Klaus' head bowed. He gently let her hand slip through his grasp. "To be loved by a Collector is to be loved by death. It's a curse, a burden. Who could possibly want that?"

"Is that how you truly feel?" She took a quivering breath. "And yet…isn't love the unconditional acceptance of an imperfect person? Klaus, you save my life…and I owe you my heart." She eased her fingers against his cheek, turning his face toward her own. But, again, he dropped his gaze. Beneath the cusp of his golden-brown eyes, Elizabeth could see the walls he'd built between them. The fear of vulnerability. The fear of pain, heartbreak.

"You don't owe it to me. I took it, and gave you a pocket watch instead."

"Lady Rose!? Lady Rose!?" A house maid called out as she dashed down the hallway. "It's Lady French, she is missing!"

Klaus and Elizabeth exchanged panicked looks before racing to the guest's chambers. Inside Leah's room, behind the flutter of white curtains, a window panel had been smashed and the silk sheets kicked back, revealing an empty, warm bed.

DUSK WAS UPON him. As Nikolas turned the switch and killed the engine he slumped in the driver's seat. His fingers tapped the steering wheel in an anxious beat. After a few breaths, he kicked open the car door and stepped out. The wind kicked up the dust, spinning the dirt into a miniature cone of leaves and twigs. He walked to the trunk of the car and heaved the body out.

Working in the sunset's red light, Nikolas understood he didn't have much time left. He sat her upright on the edge of a well before taking the bag off her head.

Leah remained in what appeared to be in a sleeping state, her chin pressed to her chest and her hair tumbled down her face. Nikolas wiped his mouth, swallowing his anxiety before he knelt beside her. Carefully, he reached out and tugged on the handle of Juliet's Collector blade extending out of her chest.

At the sudden jerk, Leah's eyes snapped open revealing a deep, cloudy orange gaze. Beneath her heated stare, he shivered. It was a strange sensation he hadn't felt in years.

"Mortalem," he whispered her name, but the wind caught it and dragged it out across the dunes.

Her expression remained dull, void of any emotion or thought. She merely nodded, acknowledging him. "Collector Nikolas Vorx. I wasn't expecting you." Leah's voice had been ripped apart, no longer belonging to the female host. Accent curled her words and broke up her speech. To hear it speak pushed Nikolas back. "You're nervous?" she noted.

"I'm sure you understand why."

"I do, but you must agree I cannot remain in this vessel. It won't be able to hold me, and if it breaks while I'm still inside—"

Nikolas wrapped his arms around himself. "You want out? Okay, what's in it for me?"

Leah perked her eyebrow, her facial expressions seemingly the only muscles in her body capable of moving. Everything from the neck down remained rigid in attention. "What do you want?"

He thought on it. "I want to break a bond."

"Destroy the contract at the blood source."

He shook his head. "I can't kill her. Her time can't be touched. You can fix this, can't you? I want this bond broken and I want a lost love to be returned to me. For that, I promise, I will give you your freedom."

Leah seemed to consider it for a moment, "The one you love is long gone, Nikolas. Not even my reach can bring her back. She belongs to Chronos now, down in the darkness with the other tainted. But you must have a heart as rotten as death to pursue her."

His face tightened. "Why would you say that?"

"You seek love in the darkest of places. Your devotion to a woman set to betray you is amusing. Your new bond to the mortal girl, Elizabeth, was no accident. You chose her specifically because you know deep down she'll never love you back."

"You make it sound like I enjoy being trampled on."

"It's your fate," she replied coolly.

"What if I don't want it to be my fate anymore? What if I don't want to be haunted and condemned to a life of rejection?"

"Elizabeth will be your greatest downfall. You chose her knowing she is the only one who can destroy you. The power you need can only be achieved by Chronos himself."

Nikolas threw his hands up. "Perfect, Chronos, eh? The God of Time is the only thing in the entire spiritual universe that can help me?"

"Not entirely. You carry the power to change everything right there, in your pocket."

"What? My blade?" Nikolas reached into his pocket where his knuckles knocked against the pistol.

Leah's lips twitched. "That gun."

"This piece of rubbish?" He gestured to it.

"That weapon has been carefully crafted with ancient scripts embedded in the barrel. With it and the matching bullet, you can not only defeat Chronos but you can also inherit his God-like powers. You would be able to do anything, even retrieve Claudia from the dark."

"If that's true, where's the matching bullet?"

"With another Collector. I cannot tell you where."

"Fine! Say I find this Collector and take the bullet. How do you suppose I summon Chronos?"

"If I tell you, do you promise to set me free?"

Nikolas nodded. "I swear on my life and code."

"Very well, Chronos can only be summoned at the death of a Time Weaver."

"What?" Nikolas stood back, feeling cheated. "But, Time Weavers have been extinct for decades! I personally made sure to kill every single one of them myself."

"Not all of them." Leah smiled, amused by Nikolas' confusion, "Sun and Moon. Ying and Yang. Life and Death." Nikolas froze. *It couldn't be.* "You've been travelling with her all along."

He almost couldn't say her name. "Elizabeth Wicker?" The words echoed in his head like sirens. Elizabeth's smile lingered, the brush of her hand, her upset glare as she scolded him. The bond clenched his heart, making the idea so repulsive he gagged. He couldn't. Not to her.

"You're crazy." His anger churned as he stood and faced Leah straight on. He lifted his knee up to his chest. "I will never set you free," he said, and struck, piercing the blade further into Leah's heart as she was kicked from the ledge. Her body fell into the dark abyss of the well behind. Nikolas pulled the concrete slab across the top, sealing her tomb.

He slumped back against the well. Eternity seemed to move in seconds. Everything he desired—freedom from his curse, the return of his lost love and the power of a God—was offered to him at the exchange of Elizabeth Wicker's life, the last remaining Time Weaver. The thought of her death pained him, devastated him. But the thought of losing Claudia all over again hit harder. Sun and Moon. It was time to decide.

To be continued...

ACKNOWLEDGMENTS

Thank you:

Writing a book is never easy and takes an amazing team to help bring everything together. Such a team can be found at Ragnarok Publications who have been some of the hardest working people I have ever had the pleasure to meet and work with. Time Weaver would not be the book you see today without the amazing work from the editors, cover designers, publishers, publicists and fellow authors at Ragnarok. The team have been a continual source of inspiration, and I hope to continue working with them with future releases. A big thanks to Tim Marquitz and Joe Martin, for they have been the champions of the Ragnarok name and I owe them all so much. Thank you for believing in me.

Special thanks to my parents, David and Jacqui Burns, for being my very first fans. They are, and always have been, my greatest supporters and have given me everything I could ever need to take this journey into the publishing world. Every success I have in life is thanks to them. And thanks to my brother and sister, Jason and Melissa Burns, and all my family who have sent hours and nights up with me, for your continual enthusiasm and endless support. I know I can always rely on you and you have never let me down.

Thank you to my kind friends who became the voices of encouragement when I lose my own. Jessie Gawne-Buckland, Jessica Lam, Danielle Martinson, Vanessa Murray, Tom Stefancic, Kerri Kemp and of course, to my partner James Teh. I know I can tackle every obstacle in life because I have you all by my side. Thank you for the gift of strength and courage to continue on.

Thank you to my amazing street team, Maree's Madness, for making me smile, giving me hope and showing me such amazing kindness throughout the years. You helped better my life in so many ways, and I am eternally grateful for your confidence and support.

Thank you to the writing community who have walk with me every step of the way, Jo-Anne Mcleary, Leah Watterson, Christine Maree, Heather Savage, Rachael Grace Micallef, Marley Galea (and family), Chris Clark, Nick Stewart, Ellen Naismith, Bree Walsh, Alain Goodman, Kimberley Clark, Laura Hunter, Danica Silva-Peck (and family), Kathryn McDonald, Nathalie Salvato, Lauren Bearzatto, Mandy Lou Holt, Brittany Hayes, Glenn Clark, Gavin McNab, Maise Louise, Rhonda Helton, Jessie Potts, Belinda Crawford, Catherine Davenport, Lauren McKeller, Carmen Jenner, Amber Garcia, Tina Gephart, Caroline Angel, Becky Johnson and so, so many others. It is thanks to all of these people and others that the writing community has become an amazing family, full of comfort, support, understanding and encouragement. I can't express how grateful I am to be able to call you all friends. Thank you.

ABOUT THE AUTHOR

Born in Melbourne Australia, Jacinta Maree considers herself a chocoholic with an obsession with dragons, video gaming and Japan. She writes a variety of genres including YA paranormal, steampunk, horror, new adult, dystopian and fantasy.

Winner of 2014 Horror of the Year, she is the author of the My Demonic Ghost YA trilogy, and is currently working on The Immortal Gene series starting with book #1, *Soulless*, which won AusRom Today's 2015 Reader's Choice Award for "Cover of the Year."

Jacinta writes to bring enjoyment to others while fulfilling her own need to explore the weird and the impossible.